TRIBULATIONS

BOOK TWO IN THE HAPPENSTANCE SERIES

PHIL SHEEHAN

WILDBLUE
PRESS

WildBluePress.com

TRIBULATIONS published by:
WILDBLUE PRESS
P.O. Box 102440
Denver, Colorado 80250

Publisher Disclaimer: Any opinions, statements of fact or fiction, descriptions, dialogue, and citations found in this book were provided by the author, and are solely those of the author. The publisher makes no claim as to their veracity or accuracy, and assumes no liability for the content.

WILDBLUE PRESS is registered at the U.S. Patent and Trademark Offices.

ISBN 978-1-952225-74-1 Trade Paperback

ISBN 978-1-952225-73-4 eBook

Cover design © 2021 WildBlue Press. All rights reserved.

Interior Formatting by Elijah Toten
www.totencreative.com

Book Cover Design by VilaDesign

TRIBULATIONS

ACKNOWLEDGEMENTS

For all the reviewer comments I received on my first novel, "Happenstance," I would like to offer a sincere "Thank you." I appreciate your input, both positive and constructive, as a means to further hone my novels.

I would like to express thanks to Micah Dudley and J.D. (Goodreads) for being the first to identify the military rank errors I made in "Happenstance" when I incorrectly used military titles for Blake's SEAL team that were from their original military branches; my apologies to the military community. Had my USMC dad still been with us, I am confident he would have kept me clean. So, with that acknowledgement, I am happy to announce the new go-forward titles for Blake's team:

U.S. Army Maj. Blake Thompson (O-4) changed services to the Navy SEALs and should have properly been called a lieutenant commander. Assuming one promotion before leaving the SEALs for the U.S. Space Force, he is now a full commander (O-5). I will use that title going forward as the U.S. Space Force has been launched, but official titles have not yet been established at the time of this writing. If the Space Force follows Navy tradition, the rank of commander will still be correct. If not, perhaps Blake will have another future title and/or rank change!

USMC Cpl. Diego Velasquez (E-4) has transitioned to the Navy SEALs and has been promoted to SEAL petty officer first class (E-6).

Air Force First Lt. Sean O'Rourke (O-2) has been transitioned to the Navy SEALs and has been promoted to SEAL lieutenant (O-3).

Specialists Harry Lundrum, Patty Myers and Li Zheng are retitled as SEAL warrant officers, Harry as a W-5, Patty and Li as W-3s, but all three will still be referred to as specialists in many cases.

SPECIAL THANKS

Special thanks to my brother, Sean Sheehan; my neighbor, Scott Gage; and my son, Patrick Sheehan, for being there through all my pre-reads as the book took form, chapter by chapter; to my high school valedictorian of valedictorians, Ruth Van Deusen, for proofing literally *everything*; my new military advisor, Patrick "Randy" Manchego, for keeping me straight on military ranks prior to getting the draft manuscript to my awesome-most, soccer-family editor, Annie Dawid.

I am extremely grateful to Michael and Steve at WildBlue Press for publishing my second novel and allowing me to continue the Blake Thompson "Happenstance" series.

IN HONOR OF

All of our brave and selfless first responders: military personnel, firefighters, police officers, smokejumpers, emergency search and rescue, medical responders and hospital personnel, and anyone else I've missed. Based on heart, selflessness, dedication and actions, all should be granted automatic membership to the era of heroes best known as the Greatest Generation. We thank you for everything you do and the sacrifices you make. In many cases, your heroics go unheralded, or even unfairly stereotyped and debased in today's world, but that does not diminish the true greatness of your efforts, nor the appreciation I, and so many others have by simply knowing you are there if and when we need you. Thank you.

CHARACTER NAMES

Cmdr. Blake Thompson–Main character

SEAL Petty Officer First Class Diego Velasquez

SEAL Lt. Sean O'Rourke–Pilot and sharpshooter

Spc. Rakesh Deshpande–Indian team member from the Armstrong I flight

Spc. Klaus Schneider–German team member from the Armstrong I flight

Maj. Vladimir Popov–Russian team member from the Armstrong I flight

Cmdr. Jack Pavlik–Commanded and piloted the Armstrong I

SEAL Warrant Officer W-5 Harry Lundrum–Team brainiac

SEAL Warrant Officer W-3 Li Zheng–IT specialist

Jimmy Decker–Reagan I engineer

Robert Stern–University of Houston student

SEAL Warrant Officer W-3 Patty Myers–Linguistic specialist

Fred Johnson–Clear Creek sheriff in Georgetown

President Andrew Callahan

Vice President Annie Murphy

Carrie Bowers–Two-star general commandant at USAF Academy

Ben Tellinino–National Security Council (NSC) secretary

Brad Martinez–Director, NSA

Army General Landon McMullen–Chairman of the Joint Chiefs of Staff

Frank Pelino–Chief of staff

Joe Foster–Colorado Springs FBI agent

Dave Pangman–Georgetown trooper

Ataullah El-Hashem–Member of Armstrong I flight crew

Sen. James Harley from Arkansas–Anti-SETI group leader

Sen. George Blasio from New York–Anti-SETI group

Sen. Mary Celeste from California–Anti-SETI group

Sen. Jerry Pinkerton from Montana–Anti-SETI group

Sen. Ronnie Dempsey of Michigan–Pro-SETI group leader

Sen. John Strong from Maine–Pro-SETI group

Sen. Julie Stiles from Louisiana–Pro-SETI group

Sen. James Colburn of Oregon–Pro-SETI group

Lt. Thjars Chjssiast ("Thars Chiss-e-ast")–The senior remaining officer on Jarisst I

Capt. Zyles Blissiart ("Ziles Bliss-e-art")–Captain and designer of Jarisst I (deceased)

Jarns Blissiart ("Yarns Bliss-e-art")–Brother of Zyles and a military scientist

Qulys Plyenysst ("Que-Lis Ply-en-ist")–Jarisst I sergeant at arms

Juulys Lystnyng ("Jewels List-ning")–Jarisst I linguist, the only surviving female from the original crew.

Knarls Rjissist ("Gnarls Rye-jist")–Private first class on Jarisst I

Jenysys Thalysst ("Jen-e-sis Thal-ist")–Jarisst I medical officer

Cryells Elysst ("Cry-lls E-lee-ist")–Jarisst I engineer

Allympht Allsysst ("All-leem-fit Alls-ist")–Jarisst I engineer

Zalmyt Wylmysst ("Zawl-m-it Will-mist")–Jarisst I technical specialist

Platsys Flysst ("Plate-sis Fyl-ist")–Jarisst I technical specialist

Nylsst Volysstmyn (Ni-list Vole-ist-min")–Jarisst I technical specialist

Dimitri–Russian communicating with moon base Pink Floyd

Boris–Russian communicating with moon base Pink Floyd

Bob Waters–Colonel, Pentagon.

Brandon Talley, Roger and George–Three University of Houston football players

Sara McClelland–Robert's girlfriend

Claude Coleman–Houston football coach

Cmdr. Rachel Joslin–Night Star pilot

Gen. Pete Pfisher–Army one-star general

Gen. Tom White–Air Force three-star general

Dr. Beth VanDeusen–Chancellor, University of Houston

Dr. George McDearmon–Medical doctor and PhD in biomed engineering, University of Houston

Anton Titov–Prime Minister of Russia

Sergei Tolstoy–Russian chief of staff of the Presidential Executive Office

Mikhail Yeltsin–The Russian director of Foreign Intelligence Service of the Russian Federation or SVR RF

Igor Yakovlev–The Russian military chief of general staff/president

Andrei Grigorov–Titov's top adviser

Cmdr. Joe Garrity–Commander, Space Dock

Gen. Mark Beckman–Pentagon

Gen. Louis Whittler–USSTRATCOM

Chris Jones–Space Dock PFC

Paul Belvedere–Space Dock PFC

Master Sgt. Joe Penske–Space Dock Armory

Gen. Ryan Cobb–Head of U.S. Space Forces

Lt. Jane Peters–Security detail lead at docking bay

Gen. Boris Vasiliev–New Russian Military chief of general staff

John McCallister–NASA administrator

Rear Adm. Bill Pendleton–Commander, Submarine Force, U.S. Pacific Fleet (COMSUBPAC)

Cmdr. Jake Ridder–COMSUBPAC

Capt. Ricky Perez–South Dakota submarine, Virginia class

Capt. Ted Lambert–Utah submarine, Virginia Class

Capt. Tony Chaparral–Colorado submarine, Virginia Class

Maj. Pat Sullivan–F-18 pilot

Maj. Zhang Wei–Chinese major

Lt. Wu–Chinese lieutenant

I.Y.–Russian moon contact

Alek Townsend–Texas governor

Capt. Nikolaev–Russian captain on the Kazan

Ensign Johnson–On board the USS Dakota

Capt. Petrov–On board the Russian Kazan

Adm. Sokolov–On board the Kazan

Rear Adm. Matt Browning–on board USS Kennedy

Cmdr. Ryan Phillips–Commander, USS Kennedy

Capt. Lee Spaulding–Commander, USS Galinis

Capt. Trent Moore–Oregon State Police

Inspector Clauson–Oregon State investigator

Chief Baker–Chief of State Police in Redmond, Ore.

Zhou Qiang–General secretary and president of China (succeeded Xi Jinping), the People's Republic of China

Aleksei–Aide to Russian Gen. Boris Vasiliev

Col. Brian Watts–Commander, Holloman AFB, 49th Wing

President Jin-Lin–President of Taiwan, the Republic of China

Chia Ling–President Jin-Lin's secretary general

Gen. Oleksiy Dombrowsky–Ukraine minister of defense

President Fedir Chevchenko–Ukraine president

President Nikita Makarevich–Belarus president

Gen. Ilya Morozov–Belarus defense minister

Allen Hayes–Curator of the New Mexico Museum of Space History

Capt. Ed Jones–Military police who accompanied Harry to Alamogordo

Riddhi Khatri–Prime minister of India

Adm. Mack Young–Leading combined US/India forces in Philippine Sea

Maj. Aztgar–Descendent of Gen. Aztgar

CHAPTER 1

Colorado Springs, Colo.
Tuesday, Sept. 11, 2029

Cmdr. Blake Thompson was sitting on a bench at the scenic Broadmoor Seven Falls attraction in Colorado Springs. The morning was still young and the air was a crisp 58 degrees Fahrenheit. The throngs of hummingbirds that frequented the waterfalls all summer long hadn't yet headed south for their annual migration trek. The tiny birds were beginning their daily sprints, filling the sky with their high shrill sounds as they darted to and from the sugar-laden feeders lining the nearby buildings. The sounds of multiple waterfalls, although greatly diminished from their typical flow levels, added to the calming sounds of the secluded location.

Blake, now 42, was enjoying the untainted serenity of the moment and readily let it flood his senses for a few quiet moments. As he had done annually for nearly three decades on this exact date, Blake intentionally sought out a quiet location where he could contemplate the world by himself. On this date, exactly 28 years ago, his dad, one of New York City's bravest, had lost his life at the World Trade Center during the 9/11 terrorist attacks, along with 411 first responders and more than 2,580 other innocent people.

Blake had experienced a lifetime since that fateful day, but had chosen never to forget the pain or loss associated with the events of that day, instead using it to fuel his passion for success in the military, and now in the Space Force. Over the years since 9/11, Blake found that the best way to honor his lost friends and family was to remind himself of what each one of them represented to him and how they'd helped define who he'd become. After that,

Blake retraced the steps of the journey he'd taken since that horrid day. Blake found the process to be both therapeutic as well as a technique to sustain focus on what he wanted to accomplish in the year ahead.

Blake began fast-forwarding through the growing history he had collected over the past three decades. The journey started with the multitude of funerals for his father and the many firefighters and police officers his family knew, acknowledging each family friend by name. Followed by his move, with his mom and sister, Cindy, to the small town of Cobleskill, in rural upstate New York, where he mastered playing goalie on his high school soccer team. After graduating from high school, he proudly started his military career at the prestigious West Point Academy, followed by his obligatory tour of active duty, reenlistment, attainment of the coveted SEAL trident pin and the many Special Ops he'd participated in throughout the next two decades–all while attempting to quench his hatred for the radical Muslim sects around the world he still blamed for the deaths of his father and friends.

Then came that incredulous day after he joined the U.S. Space Force and learned of the *object* near Pluto. The long, challenge-filled trip to Pluto on the Armstrong I, the object on Mars discovered by the Reagan I crew and the unprecedented realization that we were no longer alone in the universe. The Cjarians and their Jarisst I spacecraft would rewrite history once the rest of the world learned of the events. The Cjarians and the Armstrong I crew had helped each other safely return to Earth through a staggering chain of events that remained cloaked in secrecy from the rest of the world. The culmination of these events was reached when the Cjarians helped Blake deliver a lethal blow to the terrorists that had attacked the U.S. An amazing journey to date, but Blake hoped he was on the precipice of much more to come. The Cjarians had soon after departed and not been heard from since. Blake thought daily of all 11 surviving members of the Cjarian crew, but especially for Thjars, Juulys and Qulys, who'd become the ship's leaders after the unexpected deaths of their captain and first officer.

Blake ruminated for a few more minutes before returning to the reality of the current day, where he was vacationing in

Colorado with two of his longtime SEAL teammates: Diego Velasquez and Sean O'Rourke. The three men had plans to enjoy the mountains and then watch the U.S. Air Force football team's home game against the Notre Dame Fighting Irish. Both teams were ranked in the NCAAF top 25 poll, and the game was already being billed as one of the biggest games of the year. Notre Dame came in ranked number four in the nation, while the Air Force ranked a respectable 17–the first time the Falcons had cracked the top 20 in more than a quarter of a century. The last time the Falcons had been ranked this high was in 2002 under legendary Air Force head Coach Fisher DeBerry.

For the past week, Sean and Diego had been challenging Blake to sneak into the Air Force locker room and suit up for the game, teasing him that other than his leathered face, he could easily look the part of a Division I tight end. At 2.1 meters (6 feet, 6 inches), 111 kilograms (245 pounds), and in an athletic condition that rivaled the best professional athletes, Blake had always been considered a "specimen" by his friends. Diego and Sean were quite confident Blake could make it work, but as much fun as that would have been, they also realized what a disaster it would have caused for the Academy once uncovered, so they simply enjoyed the laughs and camaraderie by making it their own private shtick for the weekend.

In addition to his size and fighting skills, Blake was also well known within the Pentagon for his innate expertise in military logistics and ops planning and he was especially adept at re-scoping and re-planning an op when things went wrong, as they so often did during military ops. This skill had turned out to be Blake's most valuable trait during his military career. It had also turned out to be crucial during his journey to Pluto and the fight against the terrorists.

Petty Officer First Class Diego Velasquez, 28, at 1.8 meters (5 feet, 6 inches) and 63 kilograms (140 pounds) was perhaps, pound for pound, one of the best hand-to-hand combatants in the U.S. Special Forces inventory. Diego had crossed the U.S.-Mexico border as a 5-year-old child with his mother and three siblings and grew up in a tough, gang-invested L.A. neighborhood. Soon after graduating from high school, Diego joined the Marine Corps, where he quickly adapted to the Marine Corps theme of "no rules barred, meanest sons of bitches in the world." Diego had obtained a third-degree black belt before graduating from high school, but continued to elevate his fighting skills by picking up boxing, judo and Brazilian Jiu Jitsu after joining the Marines.

Lt. Sean O'Rourke, 34, was Blake's primary pilot whenever they were required to transport themselves into or out of a target area. Sean was one of those uncanny guys who could fly anything, and was also among the best sharpshooters in the military. Sean's family traced its roots to Shannon, Ireland, and he could talk with a brogue so heavy you could spoon it, but usually only when he was hell-bent on antagonizing his closest friends.

The three had arrived early for the game in hopes of hiking the famous Pikes Peak Barr Trail and planned on heading into the mountains for three days of scenic jeep rides and outdoor camping, closing the week out with the highly anticipated football game–a vacation they had been looking forward to for quite some time.

They'd completed the Pikes Peak hike yesterday, then enjoyed dinner and a few beers at the Phantom Canyon Brewery on East Pikes Peak Avenue in downtown Colorado Springs. The hike had been everything it was billed to be. The trail was 34.3 kilometers long and covered an altitude climb of 2,256 meters. They'd taken a little less than six hours to complete the hike and then took an extra hour enjoying the stunning panoramic views from the 4,302-meter summit. Blake recalled the history signs he'd read at the summit describing how Katharine Lee Bates's first visit to the peak in 1893 inspired her classic song, *America the Beautiful*. Until one saw the view from the peak, they would never appreciate how perfect her lyrics truly were.

Suddenly, the quiet serenity was rudely shattered by a loud car horn and an even more obnoxious yell coming from the direction of the parking lot–the voice had a distinct Irish accent.

"Warr 'r' ye Mister Blake? Git yer arse in gear, laddie, or we'll miss 'r hook up fer 'r jeep ride. Shake a leg, mate!"

Back to the real world, he thought as he started heading back toward the parking lot. "OK, I'm coming, Sean," Blake yelled as he rounded the building and saw the duo in their Jeep. "Diego, can't you put a muzzle on that Irish mutt of yours?"

"Yeah, right, been trying to do that for years, but I think he might be a bloody ventriloquist–nothing shuts him up!"

"Ahh, you guys wouldn't know what to do without me," Sean bounced back. "Come on, let's go–no way am I gonna miss this jeep expedition; it'll be the best vacation ever!"

"Amen!" Diego added. "Speaking of vacations, where did all of your Armstrong I crewmembers disappear to, Blake? We haven't heard anything since, what, three months ago?"

"Good question. The last I knew, Vladimir was the only one truly on vacation; he's on a yearlong fishing retreat somewhere in Russia. Klaus signed on with a German deep-space telescope team that co-launched a telescope with Russia back in 2019. Rakesh returned home to India to become a full-fledged professor at the prestigious Indian Institute of Technology-Bombay, better known as IIT-B. Ataullah is home with his family, still recovering from his injuries. And Cmdr. Jack Pavlik accepted a position in Washington within the U.S. Space Force administration."

"Are you still keeping contact with them?" Sean asked.

"Maybe once a month, nothing frequent," Blake replied.

"So, if you don't mind me asking …" Sean started to say.

"Would it stop you if I said I did?" Blake laughed.

"Aww, I'm being genuine this time, really. You always disappear on this day, every year. I know the significance of the day, but … not being nosy, but just trying to be there for ya, mate. You never talk about it."

"Now you sound like my sister," Blake smirked. "Thanks for asking, but I'm good. Plus, I think you already have enough of the share-my-opinions-and-feelings commentary to cover all of us!"

"We're comrades, teammates and best friends, but …" Sean wasn't quite ready to give it up yet. "To be honest, we know all the challenges you've been faced with, the ops we've conducted together, but other than that, you're a pretty private dude, man– sometimes to the point that we wonder if we actually do know who the real Blake Thompson is." Sean paused. "Come on, try it. Tell us something deep that you've never shared with anyone before … anything …"

"Like I said, I'm good. I really am. Sean, if I ever need a shrink, you'll be the first person I call. Does that work?"

"Sure," Sean responded sarcastically while looking over at Diego.

Diego simply shrugged.

"Well, gents, what do you say we get at it? There's a big, wide-open countryside just waiting for us to explore and conquer," Blake said, changing the topic.

"Oorah!" both men replied simultaneously.

Twenty minutes later, the trio exited I-25, just north of Colorado Springs and pulled into the Kum & Go gas station on Interquest Parkway. Blake pumped gas while Diego and Sean headed into the store. Their SUV was already loaded with plenty of supplies for the trip, but Diego wanted some bottled waters and beef jerky for the drive.

Blake finished pumping gas, holstered the gas nozzle into the pump's holder and leaned back against their 2028 Jeep Wrangler rental, waiting for the duo to return. Glancing over at Pikes Peak, Blake found himself still in awe of its grandeur, even more now that they had climbed it. He was convinced he could get used to living in the Fourteener state, as Colorado was known due to its possession of more than 50 peaks that topped 14,000 feet, or 4,267 meters–the most of any state in the United States.

Two minutes later, Blake heard the banter of Diego and Sean returning from the store.

"Did you get a load of that guy in the denim jacket?" Sean asked Diego.

"Sure did. I was waiting to see if he was going to try something, but I think he was on to me."

"What's that?" Blake queried.

"Some little weasel in the store. Looked guilty as sin, as if he was going to rob the place or do something else. He looked crazy nervous," Sean replied.

"Or high on something," Diego added.

"Or likely, both," Sean laughed.

"Hmmm, that guy?" Blake pointed to a man in a denim jacket.

"Yeah, that's him," Sean replied, "and it looks like he's hitting on that girl who just got out of that pickup truck."

"Maybe, but she sure doesn't look too thrilled about it," Diego replied.

"Neither does the cowboy getting out of the driver's seat," Blake added as the cowboy rounded the hood of the truck and headed toward the man in denim.

"Holy crap!" Sean stammered as the man in denim dropped the cowboy with a vicious jab to his nose.

"Hey! Stop!" Diego hollered as he started moving across the parking lot.

The man immediately started running.

"What the hell?" Sean stammered.

"Come on, let's follow him!" Diego hollered as he took off sprinting after the man. Sean joined in, but Blake paused long enough to talk to the woman in the car next to their Jeep.

"Ma'am, I'm assuming you're the nurse behind that decal on your car?"

"Yes …"

"Please check on that cowboy," Blake directed, "and we'll be back as quick as we can. Thank you."

Blake immediately began running after Diego and Sean, as the nurse hung up her gas pump and headed over to the young couple.

"I think he's heading for that Taco Bell. Catch him, Diego!" Sean yelled. "Damn, that Diego is one fast little Mexican," Sean laughed as he ran.

"Yeah, and you're just a slow white boy. Keep up cracker!" Diego countered over his shoulder.

The three men weaved around a number of parked cars and sprinted across the parking lot, following the man as he ran across the street directly behind the gas station and into the Taco Bell parking lot on Rampart Hills View, where he jumped into a dark blue sedan and drove out of the parking lot, heading west.

"Ahh, crap!" Diego yelled from ahead. "Go in front of the Taco Bell and cut him off in case he tries to head back to I-25. I'll follow around the store."

"On it!" Blake yelled back as he sprinted to the street.

"Come on, Sean!"

"Right with you, Blake!"

"He turned north, Blake; he must be heading to that hotel, the Great Wolf Lodge," Diego yelled.

"Dang it! We would've had him if it wasn't for his friggin' car!" Sean stated what all three men clearly knew.

"Diego, see if you can cut through the Dunkin's just past the movie theater," Blake yelled. "We'll keep going up the street."

"Ten-four!"

The car disappeared from view as the road ahead curved left.

Blake and Sean continued sprinting up the street, while Diego disappeared into the Dunkin Donuts shop to shorten the gap by cutting off the curve in the road, thereby coming out nearer the hotel.

Blake and Sean cleared the bend in the road just in time to see the man, across the hotel parking lot, talking on his cell phone as he exited his car. A split second later, the man looked in their direction and then started running toward what looked like a back entrance to the Great Wolf Lodge. Simultaneously, Diego burst out of the Dunkin Donuts shop, with an opportunity to close on him, but the man had started with a substantial lead. As hard as Diego tried, the man in the denim jacket still managed to enter the hotel before Diego could catch him, with Blake and Sean not far behind. All four men were running down the hallway. The man in denim was heading toward the elevators, pushing people out of the way as he ran. It was going to be close.

"Get him, Diego!" Blake yelled.

They rounded the corner just in time to see the elevator close and Diego slam into the doors.

"Damn it!" Diego yelled as he kicked the door.

"Wait, watch the floor numbers and see where it goes," Blake directed, looking up at the display above the doors.

"Good catch, Blake. Hit the stairs, Diego! I got 20 bucks says you can't catch 'im!" Sean yelled.

"Hand it to Blake for safekeeping. I'll collect later!" Diego yelled back. "Call and tell me what floor he stops at!" Diego added as he disappeared through the door to the stairs.

"I'll take the next elevator; tie us both in with your cell," Blake ordered.

No sooner did Sean get the three of them connected by cell, when the man in denim's elevator stopped at the fifth floor.

"It stopped at five! Diego, are you there yet?"

Diego broke through the fifth floor door, breathing hard.

"Just got there. It's a feint. No one got out. Sean, tell me where he goes next," Diego said as he ran back into the stairwell.

The second elevator opened and Blake jumped in, leaving Sean downstairs to watch the elevator movement.

"Hang in there, Diego, there's only nine floors in this place," Blake replied.

"Thanks."

"Haha, admit it, Diego, you lost him, didn't you? Twenty bucks, I'm kind of liking this. How're ya holdin' up, buddy?" Sean goaded.

"Don't sweat it. I've still got enough to kick your skinny green ass when I get back down there, ya bloody Irishman!"

"Keep climbing, Diego," Sean said more seriously. Sean could hear Diego's breathing, squeaking shoes and thumping steps as he sprinted up the stairs.

"He's at nine, Diego, nail him!" Sean yelled just as Diego exited the stairwell.

Diego surveyed the hallway. There were only two people: himself, and the man in denim. The two men were facing each other with approximately 20 meters between them; both were sweating and breathing hard from the unplanned exertion.

"Yo, dude, what's the big rush?" Diego asked, between heavy breaths.

A pregnant pause ensued as the two men evaluated each other, the man in denim still clearly agitated, but not sure of his path of action. Neither moved.

Then a door to the man's right opened and a smile began to spread across his face as four more men joined him in the hallway. He crossed his arms and looked at Diego with a smug expression as the men spread out, slowly moving in Diego's direction as their room door closed behind them.

"That's your second mistake," Diego said emotionlessly.

"What the hell you talking about, spic?" one of the new entrants taunted.

"Your first mistake was this guy running away from me," Diego said, pointing to the man in denim. "Your second mistake was letting your room door close just now."

"Who the hell do you think you are, Shorty?" the man spat out, just as the second elevator door opened behind them and Blake stepped out.

"Is this an invite-only party, Diego?"

"Yeah, and you're invited."

"Well, boys, I hate to break this to you, but he really hates being called that," Blake said calmly.

"Shorty?" the man laughed.

"Rough business, this movie business." Diego said without removing his gaze from the group's spokesman. "Just to be clear, gents, I'm not Dustin, Martin or Danny."

"Hmmm, 'Get Shorty,' right?" Blake added as he moved to the middle of the hallway, less than seven meters behind the men.

"Bingo. Score it, Big B."

"Well, Diego, I'd say that these look like good odds for any Greek, don't they?"

"Ahh, yes they do … the Spartans in '300'?"

"That evens the score."

"Movies? What the hell is wrong with you morons? We're about to kick your asses back to the Stone Age and all you can do is quote dumb ass movie lines?"

"I'll take that bet and raise you 20," Blake replied to Diego, while smiling at the man like a cat about to pounce on a cornered mouse.

"First one to take down two gets the fifth as a reward, deal?" Diego proposed.

"Deal."

Diego and Blake approached the five men from opposite sides.

"You guys are even more screwed up in the head than I thought. Let me do the math for you idiots. There's five of us, and only two of you." The man laughed and turned to one of his buddies before continuing. "You deal with Shorty and I'll take care of the old man, or should I say, the old Greek?"

The man was grinning from ear to ear as he turned back toward Blake–learning the hard way never to turn your back on a trained killer. Blake had already picked out his first target, him– the biggest guy in the group. He was a little shorter than Blake, but big. Definitely a body builder with plenty of bravado. The loud mouth. The cocky one. Most likely their leader. Two options, Blake thought. Take the leader out and then gauge the appetite of the rest of the group, or keep the momentum going from the initial offensive. Yeah, Blake thought, no doubt–option two was on today's menu. Take the high ground and wipe out as many as you can on the first strike. Why risk giving them a chance to recover and regroup?

Blake headed straight toward the group of men, like a bull bearing down on a matador. The man-turned-target was three quarters through his turn, fully exposing the right side of his rib cage, just in time to catch Blake's foot, powered by more than 110 kilograms of raw, rolling power, squarely in the middle of his rib section. Blake lunged forward with his full weight and momentum, thrusting his right foot into the man's midsection as hard as he could. He never saw it coming. The sound of cracking ribs was audible as the man folded over Blake's boot. The impact was like a car wreck ... the momentum of the first car instantly transferred to the second car, which caused target number one to accelerate backwards into the individual immediately behind him, who just happened to be the now infamous man in denim. Both men crashed against the opposite wall and fell to the floor in a heap.

"Old man, my ass," Blake said as he continued moving in one fluid motion to the left. Blake squared his shoulders to the next man, whose mouth was wide open in dismay, still looking down at his leader and evaluating how quickly he'd been dispensed with. The man clearly had not learned his lesson, either, as he should have been focused on the freight train heading straight toward him. Blake believed in the old adage that the shortest path between two points was a straight line. There would be no wasted energy or time with a swinging haymaker punch. Instead, Blake took a play straight out of Mike Tyson's winning recipe in his famous 1988 title defense against Michael Spinks. Blake tensed his back and shoulders and waded straight into the second man before he could start back-pedaling. Blake drove his fist directly into the man's jaw with the force of a pile driver and the second man flew backwards, landing on the floor a solid two meters behind, flat on his back. Lights out.

"Blake! Save some for me!" Sean yelled into his phone from inside the elevator as he was now heading to the ninth floor–the commotion from Blake and Diego's mics clearly told him the fight had started without him.

Never one to miss a good brawl, Diego had already closed his gap with the group as soon as Blake's foot began traveling toward his first target. With two more quick steps, Diego was within striking distance of his first target, who was also distracted by Blake's action. Diego launched a vicious Jiu Jitsu kick to the side of the man's head directly in front of him and dropped him to the floor like a sack of potatoes. The fourth man to leave the hotel room had seen enough and immediately put his hands up and backed against the wall, leaving two unconscious men on the floor, one man writhing in pain from what was likely multiple broken ribs and the original man in denim now quaking with fear, also still on the floor.

The elevator door opened and Sean stepped out.

"You actually saved one for me?" Sean quipped with a big smile.

"Yeah, the four on the floor. Frisk them and make sure they're clean."

"That's funny, four on the floor … looks like these gearheads lost that race," Sean laughed as he approached the group. "After all that time cooped up on the spaceship, I guess you were kind of overdue for a good brawl, weren't you?"

Blake ignored Sean's comment and looked at the lone man still standing with an intensity that clearly communicated his expectation for one hundred percent cooperation–immediate and without delay.

"Give me your room key or I'll use your head to open the door," Blake ordered.

The man reached into his pocket, pulled out his room card and gingerly handed it to Blake while he stayed firmly planted against the wall.

"Diego, call 911."

"On it," Diego replied as he pulled his phone out of his pocket.

Blake opened and entered the door that Diego said the men had come out of, ignoring the Do Not Disturb sign hanging on the door handle. Thirty seconds later, he emerged back into the hallway.

"Sean, are they clean?"

"Yup, surprisingly, they weren't carrying any weapons. Did we just screw up?"

"No, they were definitely carrying, but not exactly on them."

"Diego, we don't know what else is connected to these guys. For all we know, there could be a second room. Tell them to bring SWAT and call the FBI as well; this is going to get interesting real fast. Sean, keep your pistol at the ready in case someone other than the local authorities decides to show up. Sorry, buddy, but it looks like these guys just postponed your mountain Jeep ride."

"What the hell did you find, Blake?" Sean asked as he glanced over Blake's shoulder into the room.

Blake simply pointed.

"Holy mackerel! It's the mother lode!"

*****

Ninety minutes later, after the suspects had been taken away and the room photographed from every angle, Blake, Diego and Sean were finally "released." They had answered an endless stream of questions before Blake remembered their Jeep. Hoping it had not been towed away from the pumps yet, he tossed the keys to Sean and asked him to retrieve it from the gas station while Blake continued talking with the FBI agent in charge, Joe Foster. Once Joe had verified they really were who they claimed to be, he'd quickly changed his demeanor from that of an investigator to that of an intrigued and thankful brother-in-arms.

"Blake, thank God the three of you just happened to show up when you did and decided to call that guy out; who knows what could have happened otherwise? I'm guessing you know guns even better than I do, but this looks like a pretty lethal set of rifles. What are they?"

"Barrett M82/M107 military-issued sniper rifles. All three of us are familiar with them and trust me, they are quite effective. But these look like they have been modified and modified by someone who knows a lot about guns."

"The next question is: What the hell would they be doing here? There's nothing even close by to shoot at."

"Actually, there is." Blake said pointing out the window, directly at the U.S.A.F. football stadium.

"Good grief, that has to be, what, a couple of miles away?"

"Correct, Joe, but still in range from this vantage point and with those weapons," Diego acknowledged, pointing to the sniper weapons.

"The U.S. Army M107 operator's manual estimates the maximum range of the M107 to be 6,800 meters, or about 4.23 miles, using a standard 660 grain bullet," Blake added and then pulled his phone out. "Google Maps estimates it's approximately 2,750 meters from here, or about 2.74 kilometers, or 1.7 miles away. But realistically, even the best snipers in the world struggle at distances over a mile, especially if there's any wind or significant altitude changes to the target."

"So, you're saying the target must have been something else then, right? Maybe not even from this room?" Joe asked.

"You may be right, but that is not what I was suggesting. To be clearer, the top snipers in the world find *single* shots at ranges over a mile quite challenging, but given the opportunity for multiple shots, a good sniper with a spotter can home in on the target within a few shots. If you watched the movie 'Hurt Locker,' recall the scene where Jeremy Renner, playing Staff Sgt. Will James, spotted for Anthony Mackie, who was playing Sgt. JT Sanborn–he nailed an enemy sniper in an abandoned house from over a mile away after missing the first few shots. The same holds here for anyone who has time. Sean could easily do it within five shots on a calm day. But what concerns me more in this situation, assuming this was their target, is that they may have been waiting until the stadium would be full of people."

"Oh, my God …"

"Yes, they wouldn't have to aim. They could simply lob bullets in randomly, one after another. People would have no idea of what was happening or where it was coming from. There would be mass panic and many casualties."

Sean walked back into the room just in time to hear the last few exchanges between Joe and Blake.

"Blake, where are our seats located?" Sean asked quietly.

"On the west side of the stadium," Blake said calmly and then paused. "And, yes, you are correct, Sean–directly within the target zone."

The four men looked grimly out the window until Sean broke the silence.

"What the hell is going on, Blake? Do you think they were actually after *us*?"

"Good question, Sean. I don't know why they would be, but anything is possible–especially as you said that guy got so spooked when he first saw you in the store, almost like he may have recognized you. Maybe there was more going on than you first realized."

"That's crazy," Sean replied.

"Trust me, Blake, these guys will talk. We'll find out what they were planning," Joe responded sternly.

"Well, I expect you'll find a way, but I'm concerned that the Air Force football game, the one we have tickets for, is only a few days away. Was there anything of interest in the room other than the rifles?" Blake asked.

"Actually, there was one other item; we found this map."

"May I see it?"

"Tell you what, how about I hold it and you take a picture of it. Looks like the circle they marked on the map is in the mountains just a couple of hours from here. Want to check it out?"

"Absolutely!" Sean piped in. "We were planning on going to the mountains as it was. The trip is back on, gents!"

"Whoa, before you get too far, we have no idea what is out there. Blake, do you want us to go with you, or would you prefer we spice up your supplies with some higher grade equipment?"

"Your assumption is correct, Joe; we pack no matter where we go. You know, as American Express says, 'never leave home without it.' But in this case, 'it' means a fully loaded pistol and our concealment and right-to-carry papers. That's about it, so we'd greatly appreciate Uncle Sam's endless generosity." All four men laughed.

"Knowing what we are up against now, three long-range rifles, three lightweight semi-automatic rifles like an AR-15 and plenty of ammo might be a great start. Any chance you have some extra body armor that might fit us?"

"I'm sure we can work something out between our office and the Colorado Springs SWAT teams. How about we meet at my office at 111 S. Tejon St., number 600, in downtown Colorado Springs in, say, two hours?"

"Sounds like a plan. See you then, Joe. Thanks a million."

"You're welcome. It's the least I can do."

"How about one more thing then?"

"Sure, Blake, what is it?"

"Have your ballistics lab check out the ammo these guys had. There are boxes of normal military issue ammo, but then there are some other ones that I don't recognize."

"Are you thinking they may be foreign?"

"Actually, no … worse. A few years back, I recall meeting an ammo rep that talked about a research project they were working on to develop bullets that would fragment at the end of the intended trajectory, kind of like a miniature artillery shell. The technology seemed pretty far out at the time, almost like a sci-fi write-up, but … some of that ammo looked really different. Imagine if they somehow had those. And then imagine what that weapon would allow them to do to a densely packed group of people–like in a football stadium."

"Holy Toledo …"

"Correct."

"Great catch, Blake, I'll get the lab guys on it ASAP and keep you posted."

*****

Five hours later, the SUV was loaded up with a new sporty, aerodynamic, roof-mounted luggage shell that was well stocked– courtesy of the local FBI and SWAT offices.

Blake, Sean and Diego shook hands with Joe, thanking him one more time, especially for the three military issue Iridium Extreme 9575 Rev C satellite phones that he threw in for good measure. Joe forewarned them that cell phone reception could be pretty spotty in the mountains and they would definitely need the Sat phones to make sure they could check in each day at agreed times. Joe also told Blake that he needed to thank his fellow Army brothers over at Fort Carson, home of the 4th Infantry Division and the 10th Special Forces Group. The Special Forces Group provided the Sat phones without question as soon as they heard what had happened that morning and that three SEALs were involved. They also threw in three Enhanced Night Vision Goggle (ENVG) IV headsets and a bunch of miscellaneous supplies. The staff sergeant who delivered them to the FBI office only made one request: "Tell our buddies happy hunting and if they need backup, call, we'll bring it."

As a parting gift, Joe also gave each of them a formal FBI card that could be presented to any law officer they encountered, just in case anyone needed a little extra convincing. Joe's cell phone and signature were on the reverse side, along with a hand-written note:

"Please provide any assistance you can to my friends Blake, Diego and Sean. They're on a special mission for the FBI."

With that, the three friends set out for the mountains. Target location: a small collection of buildings in the mountains, just north of Resolution Mountain, identified with the map and satellite imagery from none other than NORAD, buried deep within Cheyenne Mountain.

*****

With the unplanned events of the morning and subsequent afternoon activities in Colorado Springs, Blake, Sean and Diego knew they wouldn't make it to their mountain target during daylight, so they planned on driving as far as Frisco, and staying overnight. Knowing they had plenty of time for the shortened trip, Sean proposed they stop for dinner at the Red Robin Gourmet Burgers and Brews restaurant near the intersection of CO 470 and South Broadway in Highlands Ranch, just south of Denver, claiming they had the best burgers and fries in the business.

By 8:30 p.m., well after sunset, the trio was on the move again, heading west toward the CO 470/I-70 interchange.

Twenty-two minutes later, Blake turned onto the I-70 west ramp for the one-hour drive to Frisco.

Thirty minutes later, and almost halfway to Frisco, a flurry of state trooper cars screamed past the trio at speeds in excess of 160 kilometers per hour.

"Dang, they're in one hell of a hurry! I wonder what happened." Sean vocalized what each man was thinking.

"Must be a whale of an accident scene. Better keep an eye out for ambulances, too," Diego returned. Sean and Blake both nodded.

They didn't have to wait long. A few miles later, as they crested a large hill, passing the route 40 exit and Douglas Mountain, they were greeted with an eerie sea of red tail lights in front of them in the westbound lanes and a long double line of white headlights facing them from the eastbound lanes, broken only by a darkened section of highway on either side of a group of trooper cars with blue strobe lights. Additional trooper cars had arrived from the west, based on the direction they were pointing, as well as what must have been every available police car from the small nearby community of Georgetown. It looked as if the cars were lined up to watch a drive-in movie, with cars waiting to enter from both directions. If it really had been a drive-in theater, the screen would have been located south of the highway, facing north, but Blake knew there would be no movie screen in this setting.

"Diego, look at the way those police cars are fanned out … looks more like a protective ring than an accident scene, or even a barricade, doesn't it?"

"Sure does, Blake. What do you think?"

"It looks like they're all focused on something in the eastbound lanes and the lanes in both directions are clearly shut down," Blake responded.

"And there's a crap-ton of cops–look at them all!" Diego echoed.

"Whatever it is, it looks pretty serious. I'll drive up to the blockade along the side berm and see if there's anything we can do to help. Open the windows and turn all the lights on so we don't make any of those troopers trigger-happy. I'll put the flashers on; too."

Two long minutes later, Blake reached the blockade; sporadic gunfire could be heard ahead. Blake handed their IDs and Joe's FBI card to the troopers, letting them know they could help and that they had appropriate military gear with them as well. The trooper ran to his patrol car and got on his radio. Seconds later, he motioned Blake over to the patrol car. When Blake reached his car, the trooper returned their IDs and handed Blake the radio mic.

"Thanks for the offer to help. Whatever is going on up there is more than we came prepared for and the Denver SWAT team is still 30 minutes out. It'd be great if you guys could level the playing field a bit until they get here."

No sooner had the trooper ended his statement than automatic gunfire again erupted near the patrol cars up ahead, quickly followed by pistol shots from the police cruisers. The sound of metal on metal and breaking glass was unmistakable. Blake spoke into the mic and then listened intently to the trooper on the other end.

"OK, I think I have the gist of it. Do you have a cell phone on you?"

"Yes, of course, why?"

"What's the number?"

"972-245-2386, why?"

"We're on a police channel, right? I need to make sure our next steps are not monitored. I'm Blake–your first name?"

"Johnny."

"OK, Johnny, I just typed your number into my cell phone. I'll call you right back." Blake handed the mic back to the officer and then called Johnny's cell.

Blake laid out a quick plan, specifically identifying where the three of them would be firing from to ensure no friendly-fire accidents.

The background gunfire continued. Whoever these guys were, they were well armed.

"Keep your heads down. I'll be back to you in a little bit."

"Will do. Thanks for the help, Blake. Over and out."

Blake returned to their SUV and updated Sean and Diego as they unloaded supplies from the storage shell on the Jeep's roof.

"Officer," Blake commanded the man he had first talked to. The man trotted over.

"I need you to maintain guard of this car until we return; there are weapons in here that you do not want in the public's hands."

"10-4. Cisco, Pete, over here! By the way, the name is Sgt. Dave Pangman. Anything you need, you got it."

"Thanks, Dave. Have someone else get word to the cars on both sides of the highway to kill their headlights."

The troopers fanned out around the SUV with their guns drawn, each glancing back over their shoulders in awe of what they were seeing. Blake, Diego and Sean were donning full body armor, headsets that included night vision goggles and mics to communicate with. Sean was loading his Barrett M82/M107 sniper rifle while Blake and Diego loaded Heckler & Koch HK416 assault rifles. Each man also loaded two Sig P320 modified pistols and placed additional ammo into their vest straps while sporadic gunfire continued at the police blockade. Nearby car lights were quickly going out and darkness was gaining the edge that Blake wanted.

"Sweet! These sniper rifles already have night scopes on them. We really need to buy some beers for those Fort Carson guys," Sean volunteered.

"Oorah," Diego replied as he finished painting himself with camo face paint.

The discussion was suddenly broken by the unmistakable sound of a grenade explosion, followed by the flaring light of a burning trooper car. Unintelligible yelling followed from where the bad guys were holed up. Whoever they were, they had multiple cars, two heavy-duty Ford pickups, one tractor trailer and one U-Haul truck providing significant cover for them.

"Good Lord!" Dave whispered. "They have grenades, too? Those poor guys behind the cars don't stand a chance. Sure hope you can help them. I know more than a few of them. What's the plan?"

"Sit tight. You'll see shortly. Keep that car protected."

The time for idle chat was over and the time for action had arrived. The three men, now transformed into full combat soldiers, huddled together.

"Based on what the trooper at the scene relayed, there are at least six bad guys, but there could be more. They have multiple officers wounded and at least two KIAs, including one civilian, so we need to move fast before there are more. They also have multiple hostages according to the trooper. Apparently, a local cop stopped to check them out and it turned out to be a fully armed drug convoy."

"Gotta be a huge haul to carry this much firepower," Sean chimed in.

"He also said that the bad guys are not on the highway. They're in the parking lot next to the lake on the south side of the highway. From what I could recon with the night glasses, as well as what I can see on Google satellite, there's a building and a couple of large tanks on the north end of the lake, just off the eastbound lanes. Sean, you're our sharpshooter, get up there and find a good position to fire from. You should be within 500 yards and have a great angle on their position based on how the road curves. See if you can ID the bad guys before we get in position."

Sean nodded.

"Diego, I need you to re-enforce the troopers. They know you're coming, but you can tune into their system on channel three to make double sure. Don't give away any tactical information on the police radio."

Diego acknowledged with a thumbs up.

"Where are you going, Blake?"

"Swimming–looks like those guys back in Colorado Springs thought of everything," Blake said as he held up a snorkel. "I thought I might just pay them a visit from their unprotected backside. I expect they think that side is safe and are totally ignoring it. Once I'm in position, I'll let you know. When I do, that will be your sign, Diego, to tell the troopers to huddle down as I'll be firing in your direction, straight toward the highway. Get yourself at a safe angle on the west side and when they start to reposition to protect themselves from me, you'll attack their flank. We should have them in a good pincer move and they won't have time to react before we take them down. Sean, you'll have ample time to scan for targets. Make sure you keep an extra eye on those trucks in case they have reinforcements inside. Let us know immediately if you see any. Also see if you can ID the leader or the most heavily armed guy. I need you to drop him and at least one more of them before I open fire. Once I signal, light 'em up. Oorah."

"Oorah," Sean and Diego answered simultaneously. The three men knuckle-tapped then disappeared into the night, Sean and Blake toward the building on the north side of the lake and Diego southward into the endless line of cars.

A helicopter, likely from a Denver news organization, arrived on the scene and was immediately shot at from multiple rifles. The copter quickly retreated to a safer distance.

Ten long minutes later, Diego was in position with the troopers, just west of the target zone. He could easily see movement through his night goggles that validated where the bad guys were holed up. Sean was in a prone sniper position on top of the primary building where he was also able to watch Blake slip into the dark water and disappear. Sean relayed to Diego that he could make out six bad guys and no fewer than ten hostages–all of whom were clearly being used as human shields.

"Blake called it; their lakeside is wide open. These POSs need to go on a one-way ticket," Sean whispered into his mic.

"Roger that," Diego responded. "Guessing Blake is still underwater. Can you ID the leader?"

"Oh, yeah. Clear as a bell based on how he's treating the hostages and laying out hand gestures. That A-hole has earned first shot."

"Do him, Sean, and we'll call it even on the 20 bucks you still owe me."

"You're on, as soon as Blake gives the word."

"The trooper next to me claims they demanded an armored personnel carrier and the feds are sending it with hopes of saving the hostages. We've got less than 20 minutes before it arrives and the bad guys know it's coming. They made the troopers keep an open mic with the feds and they're reading off the mile marker every five miles. The guy next to me is calling it out on his bullhorn. We gotta clean this up before that APC gets here."

"Oorah."

Two additional minutes passed before Blake was ready to rejoin the conversation. He rose slowly, only partially emerging from the dark water–night goggles on, dripping water, with his HK416 assault rifle raised and ready. He slowly panned the area in front of him. The good news was that his guess had been correct– no one had expected company from the rear and all eyes remained riveted on the police cars on the highway.

"Tell the troopers to stop shooting. I count six bad guys, plus 11 hostages. Sean?"

"Ditto on the bad guys. I only saw 10 hostages, so we'll go with your 11."

"Sean, targets selected?"

"Roger," Sean whispered back and detailed out each target, assigning each with a number from one to six.

"Diego, ready?"

"My whole life, Chief, oorah times 10."

"Get those troopers down."

"They're already down and out of the line of fire."

"Sean, you ready?"

"Locked in and ready."

"Light 'em up."

Sean had already let all the tension drain from his body. He'd become one with the eyepiece and the trigger, a continuation of the gun itself. No wind was present, so he only needed to adjust for distance and the height difference from his perch. The figures were bright green in the night scope. Sean zoomed in. Nothing existed except the leader. Sean took three slow, rhythmic breaths and then exhaled. His finger tightened on the trigger. He pulled back ever so lightly and squeezed–all of his focus on the single finger to avoid any other movement of his body. A loud rifle shot echoed across the canyon and a second later, the leader's head disappeared in a cloud of green mist.

This was clearly a new sound and the remaining five men had no idea where it came from. The now leaderless group sat stunned for three long seconds as their leader's headless body flopped to the ground. One second later, a second rifle shot echoed across the mountains and another man fell, struck high in the chest and knocked backwards a good three feet.

"Targets one and three eliminated. I don't have clear shots on the other four. Target six in the Hawaiian shirt is surrounded by hostages. It's going to be hard to avoid risk to the hostages on him, but we're committed now," Sean summarized.

"Great shooting, Sean. Our turn. Diego, I've got target four and five, you have targets two and six. Ready?"

"Oorah."

"Three, two, one, now ..."

Blake fully emerged from the water and let loose two quick bursts from his HK416 assault rifle from less than 50 feet away.

Two more bad guys down: number two with a burst to the head, number five with a burst to the back. The remaining two men turned toward the unexpected action behind them just as Diego sprinted through from the west side and slayed his first target with a single burst to the head. Unfortunately, Sean was correct about target six, the one with the Hawaiian shirt. He was surrounded by four hostages and well protected from a safe shot from any direction.

"Cover me, Blake. Too many friendlies. Going in over the top."

"I'm in position, go!" Blake threw a stun grenade between the water and the collection of hostages and fired a quick burst into the air to draw the remaining target's attention toward him and away from Diego.

Diego slung his rifle over his shoulder, sprinted to the side of the car separating him from the remaining attacker, vaulted over the parked car roof and slammed into the circle of people, both friend and foe, bodies flying in different directions. The force of his impact drove target six sideways as he pulled his gun's trigger, sending a stream of bullets into the night sky. In one fluid motion, Diego pulled his Ka-Bar from his right bootstrap and plunged it deep into the man's chest while holding the man's gun vertical with his left hand. As the man's grip loosened on his weapon, Diego let go of the still implanted knife, wrestled the AR-15 from his grip and exploded his head with a short burst from the man's own weapon.

"Targets two and six down for good."

"Hold positions. Sean, do you see anything else?" Blake responded

"I've got lots of friendlies. Tell them to sit tight," Sean ordered.

"No one move," Blake bellowed into the night. "Stay where you are. Do not move! We're here to help."

"Sean?"

"One unknown under the western-most Ford pickup and one possible bad guy we missed in the U-Haul."

"I've got visual under the Ford; it's a friendly, no doubt," Diego answered.

"Good. Sean, are you positive on the U-Haul?"

"No, can't confirm. It sure looks like he has a pistol, but he hasn't fired. Better verify."

"On it," Blake whispered back.

Fifteen seconds passed before Blake spoke again.

"We're clean, but I've got one scared U-Haul driver now packing more than his own gun. Definite friendly. Call the troopers in to get the hostages to safety. Diego and I will double-check the vehicles."

"Roger that."

*****

Three hours later, the trio was at the Clear Creek County Sheriff's office in Georgetown drinking coffee and completing the necessary debriefs and paperwork. It had been quite a day so far and it was becoming clearer by the hour that their planned vacation to the Fourteener State was definitely providing more surprises than they planned on. One officer had been killed, the local police officer who had first stopped the two Ford pickups and the tractor trailer, as had one civilian, who had been caught in the crossfire. At least six troopers were injured, three seriously.

Blake passed on condolences to the local sheriff, Fred Johnson, who in turn deeply thanked Blake and his friends. The sheriff knew there would have been many more funerals for both troopers and innocent bystanders had the trio not showed up when they did.

"The fact that you guys happened to be in the right spot at the right time was a pure miracle from heaven. Having said that, what the three of you were able to do in less than 15 minutes is the stuff they make legends out of around here. You guys will be the talk of the state for a long time."

As it turned out, the two Ford pickups had been providing protection for the tractor-trailer. The trailer would require a more extensive investigation before they knew what was really in it, but initial estimates tagged the value of drugs in it at over $500 million and it also included a cash hoard that easily exceeded $250 million, let alone the huge cache of recovered weapons. The thugs all carried false IDs and hadn't yet been identified, in part, as one trooper was heard to say, because the SEAL attack left precious little facial data to analyze. Regardless, the state troopers were pretty confident that it was the work of the Russian mafia that had made Colorado their home over the past decade. One trooper told Blake that ever since 2014, when recreational marijuana had first been legalized in Colorado, unlike the safer environment that had been promised by many state and local legislators, they'd seen a significant increase in illegal activities by both the Mexican cartels and the Russian mafia. Ironically, the new Colorado laws actually made both the legal *and* illegal drug activities easier to operate due to Colorado's wide-open spaces being harder to police and the fact the drug traffickers no longer had to deal with U.S. Customs agents at the Mexico-U.S. border crossings. State-to-state crossings were easily and frequently carried out with little fear of ever being caught. This incident in Georgetown had simply been a lucky hit by the local trooper, which unfortunately turned out to be very unlucky for him and his family. Sadly, the officer left a wife and three young children behind.

Blake, Sean and Diego cleaned their gear and reloaded everything into the SUV. As they drove away, they were greeted with what looked like an endless line of troopers who wanted to express their gratitude and respect as they drove by. Sean broke the silence once they passed the last car.

"Blake, I'll never forget that … All those troopers lining up like that. It's not like they don't put themselves on that same line every day."

"It's a brotherhood," Blake responded reverently. "Anyone that puts their life on the line for someone else is part of it. That line includes firefighters, police officers, smokejumpers, soldiers, rescue personnel, hospital personnel and others. It's the respect you give to a brother or sister in any service, no different than we do for a fallen SEAL." Blake paused before continuing, "It's what I saw a hundred times over during all the 9/11 funerals. It was humbling, honorable and powerful at the same time."

"Amen, Blake," Diego responded softly. The three men remained quiet for the next couple of kilometers. A storm was rolling in over the mountains and lightning flashed. After a few minutes, Sean broke the silence again.

"We go looking for trouble every time we go on a mission. I understand that, but …" Sean paused, clearly agitated. "Why the hell does crap like this follow us even when we aren't on a mission? You ever wonder about that? For cripe's sake, we're on vacation in Colorado, not on patrol in Somalia or Kabul!"

"Fair question, Sean," Diego responded first. "I guess it's just what we were made to do. It's in our DNA to fight and protect others who can't protect themselves. I'm not being righteous, just stating the facts."

Until that point, Blake had remained silent, pondering the words of both of his longtime friends.

"The trials you talk of, those are our trials. Tribulations that were birthed from evil, greed and hatred. Like Diego said, we made it our mission to protect the people who can't protect themselves–no matter where it takes place. Colorado is frequently referred to as God's country, so I'd like to think He just used us to clean it up a little more. If so, I'm OK with it. Given a choice, I'd rather it was us than some random John Q. Public and his family."

Both men responded with a whispered "Oorah."

The three men fell silent again, listening to the rhythmic sound of the tires. It was 12:30 a.m. and they were making fast work of the remaining drive to the Holiday Inn in Frisco. It was 30 minutes away, still leaving plenty of time for Blake to reflect on the day's events. Eight people dead, two of whom didn't deserve it, one who put himself at risk every day to keep others safe. Both left loving families behind. For those two, Blake would grieve. For the other six, not a single thought of loss. Those six men had put the lives of others at risk without any hesitation at all, and all for greed. That crossed a line with Blake, one that quickly separated those men from society and the rights and protection society offered. To Blake, it was no different than putting down a pack of rabid dogs. He would lose no sleep for those men, and he knew the world would be a better place because of it.

Blake's thoughts then reflected back to what the local sheriff had said relative to "a miracle from heaven." Were they? Did He truly orchestrate their "random" encounter? If so, then why did the two innocents have to perish? Why did any innocents have to die? Blake's mind quickly connected back to his trip to Pluto on the Armstrong I and his fellow crewmember Col. Ataullah El-Hashem. Blake had initially distrusted Ataullah and his Muslim roots, but gained great respect for him during their months-long trip and the challenges they encountered, even though their religious beliefs were significantly opposed in many ways. But one comment that Ataullah made still resonated with Blake. The two men had been talking about God's will when Ataullah replied, "That is not mine to question, Blake. There is no way I or any man can understand the perfect and infinite knowledge of Allah. It is the will of Allah." Allah, in Ataullah's belief system, God in Blake's belief system; it was a similar reverence, even if Blake did not agree with the overall teachings Ataullah believed in.

Blake had been raised in a Baptist church and had maintained his strong faith ever since, but he'd always struggled with the statement that "Everything is God's plan." He believed he had God-given talents he should utilize to the fullest. He believed that God's ability to impact anything was limitless, but he simply didn't believe God worked that way. Blake believed part of his test and responsibility was to determine how and when to use his God-given abilities to his best. It was a debate he still struggled with and one he knew he wouldn't find an answer to tonight. He did, however, find solace in the realization that regardless if today's events had been a random intersection of events and people or had been orchestrated by a greater power, both paths resulted in the same answer: two innocents lost and six animals eliminated from the food chain.

Yes, he could live with the latter.

*****

"Sen. Colburn?"

"Yes, who is this?"

"Stop your support of the aliens or suffer the consequences. This is not an empty threat. You are running out of time."

The call disconnected.

Sen. Colburn called the Secret Service and registered another threat call. The same as all the others: no caller ID, a short call and a voice modulator. He wondered how many of these calls he would get before they finally quit.

*****

CHAPTER 2

The White House
Wednesday, Sept. 12, 2029

In the seven months since the Cjarians' departure, the initial atmosphere of celebration and jubilation that prevailed throughout the Senate chambers, the House of Representatives and the Oval Office had changed significantly, and quickly, but nowhere did it change as much as within the Senate. The initial excitement was replaced by fear and anxiety toward the relatively unknown aliens. President Andrew Callahan had been caught off guard when the fiery debates first arose. He had attempted to calm their fears and growing anger, but instead of quelling the disturbance, it blossomed further. After three months of growing discontent, in an attempt to placate the growing discord on the topic, President Callahan formed a top secret, special presidential commission on the existence of extraterrestrial life that consisted of eight key senators, four from each side of the debate. The two sides quickly became known as the Pro-SETI and Anti-SETI groups, where SETI was in reference to the long-standing Search for Extraterrestrial Intelligence organization. Surprisingly, and uniquely for Congress, there appeared to be no party line separation between the two groups, as both sides included Democrats and Republicans–a rarity in Congress.

The core argument of the Anti-SETI group was that of distrust and safety over a range of topics as far ranging as the risk of new diseases to the fear associated with the potential for interplanetary war. In the case of the Pro-SETI group, the primary interests included the opportunity to gain new technologies and trade, the ability to travel to the stars and the simple excitement of finally proving the existence of extraterrestrial life.

President Callahan hoped the special commission would help calm the Anti-SETI group and perhaps develop some common ground. Unfortunately, it did the exact opposite, further fueling the flames of dissention while providing the Anti-SETI group with a formal platform to push their agenda deeper into government circles. The continually building rhetoric elevated to the point of actual physical threats, creating safety concerns for elected U.S. officials not seen for decades.

During the previous week, Sen. James Harley from Arkansas, the leader of the Anti-SETI group, initiated a yelling match in a closed Senate chambers meeting with Sen. Ronnie Dempsey of Michigan, the leader of the Pro-SETI group. Emotions elevated on both sides to the point where the hurling of insults and threats elevated to an actual physical pushing confrontation. Security was called in and the opposing groups were separated and escorted from the chambers. Unfortunately, the damage was further magnified after a senator's aide leaked his cell phone video of the episode to the Washington Post, leaving everyone to theorize what topic could have possibly brought the two sides to a physical altercation.

The growing division in the Senate was growing more contentious by the day, with fewer Senators remaining undecided. This singular issue had become as divisive as the congressional left-vs.-right attacks that had so negatively divided the country a decade ago. It was also becoming clearer that Sen. Harley saw this opportunity as a vehicle to attempt a major power grab, predominantly at the expense of President Callahan and his followers, as everyone knew that President Callahan was a strong supporter of the Pro-SETI group and the newly discovered aliens.

President Callahan looked at the four people standing in front of his desk in the Oval Office. The foursome consisted of Ben Tellinino, National Security Council (NSC) secretary; Army Gen. Landon McMullen, chairman of the Joint Chiefs of Staff; his own chief of staff, Frank Pelino; and Vice President Annie Murphy.

"What the hell is going on?" He challenged the group. "It's as if Congress has lost its collective ability to think or reason! I didn't think we'd ever get more divided than what we saw a decade ago when the Democrats and Republicans refused to agree on anything. Government officials–even actual members of

Congress–were literally lying and making up some of the craziest crap you could imagine for no other reason than to simply make the other side look bad. But this … this is not only crazy; it's downright dangerous. This issue has divided Congress to a level our country has rarely experienced, but it's happened in only seven months … Who knows what it will be like in another seven months?" The president paused. "Good Lord, what would happen if the Cjarians actually did return? Our only saving grace is that the general populace has no idea of what is going on, only NASA, the military brass and Congress are aware of the Cjarians."

President Callahan paused again, stood up from his desk and turned to look out the window at the White House lawn. His four trusted advisers remained silent and shifted their positions, knowing the president needed to vent and would make it clear when he was ready for discussion.

"Think about it; we may be looking at the greatest historical, cultural and scientific event since the birth of Christ–and yet there are some that want to treat it as a threat." President Callahan turned to face the foursome. "Some of these senators are actually talking about regulations that would *prohibit* contact with the Cjarians and even *attacking* them if they decide to pursue additional contact with us. This is absolute insanity. Gentlemen, ma'am, I need ideas."

Frank Pelino responded first.

"Sir, I think we need to focus on Sen. Harley. He's their clear leader and he's whipping everyone else into this frenzy. Take him out and I think this mess has a chance to settle down, but keep in mind that he also chairs the Senate Armed Services Committee, so he already had a significant power base before this SETI thing even started."

"Sir," Gen. McMullen jumped in, "I believe it may be too late for a compromise. As Frank suggested, Harley has already built an extensive support system within the powerful Armed Services Committee and I'm concerned that he has also convinced some within our military complex that he, and he alone, stands for the only acceptable option: that of no aliens."

"The military complex? Do you mean suppliers or our actual military leaders?" the president asked incredulously.

"Both, sir," Gen. McMullen replied.

"Good God." President Callahan sat down and paused, tapping his pen on his desk.

"So what are you proposing? Do you want me to have him assassinated? Is that what you mean by 'take him out'? Or do you want me to initiate a drive to impeach him? What specifically are you suggesting?"

"Kill him? No, this is still the United States–we all know that's not an option in this country. But impeachment? That's not a bad idea, sir, but I'm afraid it will take too long."

"Then what?" the president stammered.

"We've been discussing another option, sir," Frank Pelino interjected.

"Continue."

"In a nutshell, sir, we come clean. We share the news with the world."

"Really, Frank, are you serious? Is that the best you can come up with? You want me to tell the country that I've been dishonest with them?"

"Yes, sir … well, maybe not exactly …"

"What the hell does that mean, Frank?"

Frank looked cautiously at the others before he continued.

"Mr. President, think about it. We invite the other world leaders that were part of the Armstrong I investment team to an internationally televised, global conference in a neutral country, say for example, Switzerland–then we break the news to the world. We share how the various countries all helped finance and build the Armstrong I. We highlight the incredible investments these countries made with the hope of gaining access to new technologies that the entire world could benefit from, and centuries earlier than we could have done by ourselves. We share the fact that we investigated the object near Pluto in secret because we had no idea what to expect, and then tell them how we saved the Cjarians and how the Cjarians, in turn, helped save our astronauts. We talk upbeat about the potential for new friends, new markets and the ability to travel to the stars. We create confidence in how we'll ensure safety against new diseases and how we will avoid the risk of any unexpected pandemics. We …"

"What about how we just convinced the world last January that the hand of God reached out and destroyed the terrorists that were threatening to detonate a nuke in the U.S.? Let me remind you that was the cornerstone of the story we sold the world. We could lose face for lying, or worse yet, we could end up rejuvenating terrorist fervor. Have you considered this?"

"Yes, we have, sir," Gen. McMullen answered.

Frank decided it was time to provide additional support for Gen. McMullen and jumped back in.

"Could it rejuvenate the terrorist organizations around the world? Yes, it could, but sooner or later, this news will break out–especially if the Cjarians actually do return. In other words, sir, it's not an *if*, it's a *when*, so we are simply accelerating the inevitable."

President Callahan nodded his understanding as Gen. McMullen continued.

"Sir, in addition to what Frank just mentioned, the truth is that the major governments of the world have made tremendous progress reducing terrorist capabilities around the globe the past seven months. The summit you held in Helsinki, last February, will go down as a historic watershed decision that resulted in the unification of the world powers against terrorism. Since then, it has arguably led to the biggest impact on global terrorism in history. The nations of the world came together like they haven't done since World War II, at least on the topic of terrorism. They shared critical information and resources that led to the elimination of most of the key terrorist cells, training centers and most importantly, financial pipelines around the world. The threat of global terrorism is now the lowest it has been in decades, if not more than a century."

"I agree that the risk of reigniting terrorism fervor is pretty low, but unfortunately, history has proven that we will never exhaust the human proficiency to birth an endless supply of new lunatics and fanatics. It's only a matter of time before some other maniacal idiot with boldness, charisma and a message of his or her vision can rally a group of wronged individuals somewhere in the world that believes their only answer is through violence," the president ended solemnly.

"You are correct, sir," Frank resumed, "but as we said, it's a *when*, not an *if*. So our timing is as good now as any time, perhaps even better. We are also recommending that we take the offensive on Harley and start to discredit him publicly by identifying the negative aspects of his views and those of the Anti-SETI group. We accuse them of trying to rob the world of new technologies, space travel and the ability to interface with alien civilizations. In addition, we found some dirt on Harley ..."

"Don't even tell me about it, Frank, I really don't want to hear it—you know I won't tolerate mud-slinging campaigns," President Callahan interrupted his chief of staff.

"We knew you would say that, sir, but the truth is that he's already been slinging it pretty heavy relative to the Pro-SETI group, and you. We all know he plans to make a run at the White House in '32 and will use anything he can to discredit you and promote himself. We need to start fighting back before he gains more credibility with the voters and we need to start working more openly with Sen. Ronnie Dempsey of Michigan, the Pro-SETI leader. Sooner or later, you ..."

"Make it later. I'm serious, Frank ... all of you. I'd rather win this the right way. We all have dirt of some kind in our closets, but more importantly, the divisive far-left-ultra-liberal versus the far-right-ultra-conservative battles that occurred just one decade ago fractured the very fabric of this country. I do not want to see anything take us back to that nightmare. It has taken us years just to start the recovery process—and we're clearly not done yet."

"We agree, sir, but with all due respect, you are being a little naïve. It can, and likely will occur again, regardless of what you want, or attempt to prevent. It's another unfortunate part of politics and human DNA, and Harley is already focused and actively doing exactly what you are afraid of doing. He wants to create total chaos and then thrust himself into the center of it as the only person that can possibly save the nation, and perhaps the world. Relative to a legitimate solution, it's total bull, we all know that, but we also know how that can be used to swing the popular vote. It's like bees to flowers—it works."

"I hear you, gentlemen, but I don't have to like it and I can still stave it off for a while longer—that's an order. But, I will make one new request."

"What's that, sir?"

"I want Harry Lundrum on the SETI Commission. We need someone who can present factual positions and articulate them in a manner that's hard to object to."

Ben smiled. "We were hoping you would say that. We already took the liberty of opening communication with Harry. As you would expect, Harry was excited, in his low-key manner, of course. No one can out-debate or out-science Harry."

SEAL Warrant Officer Harry Lundrum, now 30, was the brainiac of Blake's SEAL team and one of the smartest people any of them had ever met. Blake commonly referred to Harry as "Einstein" due to his ability to conceptualize the physics of a problem and construct mathematical models in his head. Harry had graduated from Harvard with a dual PhD in chemistry and mathematics at the age of 21, then followed up with a third PhD in astrophysics from MIT by the time he was 24. Yet, with all of that intellectual pedigree, the most enduring characteristic of Harry was that he simply lacked any arrogance at all. Harry could hold a conversation with leading scientists as easily as he could with grade school students. But God forbid, if Harry saw anyone belittling someone else on an intellectual level ... it was game on– and Harry had never been known to lose an intellectual challenge.

Harry had played a key role in helping to save the Armstrong I astronauts and defeat the terrorists that threatened the United States with a nuclear holocaust. Those same terrorists had also killed hundreds of civilians with high-visibility attacks across the nation and forced President Callahan to institute martial law less than a year ago–an emergency state thankfully lifted once the terrorists were defeated.

"So, what's next?" President Callahan asked his trusted advisers.

The group spent the next 20 minutes discussing facts, rumors, ideas and opinions until the meeting ended, simply because of the need to attend the next planned meeting on President Callahan's schedule.

Most people were unaware of how scripted the daily life of the president was. The most powerful man in the world was captive to the demands of his own title and office. Everything was scheduled and timed to the minute, with multiple people ushering events to start and end on time to ensure continuity of the all-important and all-controlling schedule. The daily agenda included critical events such as the current meeting, and others such as the president's daily debrief meeting, but a great deal of the day was for mundane things such as meeting "special" people, bestowing honors, acknowledging dignitaries or special events. Some of the president's pressing priorities were as mundane and unimportant as announcing National Clean-Off-Your-Desk Day, but they still demanded the president's time–all while the most pressing matters of the world were put on hold until the schedule allowed them an opportunity to return to the discussion table.

*****

Frisco, Colo.
Sept. 13, 2029

By the time Blake, Sean and Diego finally checked in and opened the doors to their rooms at the Holiday Inn in Frisco, it had been just shy of 1 a.m. The trio had agreed to meet for breakfast at 7 a.m. and finalize their plans for approaching the cabin identified on their map.

What was left of the night passed quickly and the men woke, showered, checked out of the hotel, loaded the car and headed for the Log Cabin Café at 121 Main St., just a short distance away. Diego had identified the cafe after a quick internet search and wanted to check it out as it highlighted hearty American and Mexican cuisine.

They drove over to the restaurant, ordered their meals and then spread a map of Colorado out on the table.

"That's nuts," Sean piped up.

"What is?" Blake responded.

"Look, it's obvious we go on to Copper Mountain, but once there, we have to make a choice … but really? Could they have picked a more out-of-the-way, no straight-line location? It looks like Copper Mountain is less than 15 kilometers from Resolution Mountain as the crow flies, but it's at least an hour drive no matter which way we go to get there: West on Interstate 70 and then south on 24, or south on 91 and then north on 24. At its closest point, I-70 actually looks like it gets within just seven or eight kilometers of the cabin–yet we have to drive for an hour! Might as well park on the roadside, get out and hike it."

"Tell you what, Sean," Diego laughed, "Let's drive a few kilometers so you can get a better look at the terrain around here before we buy into hiking it. For example, that *little* hill we saw from the hotel parking lot this morning. The map says it's called Wichita Mountain and it's over 3,300 meters tall. And in this state, that's small! I'm betting the car ride will be quicker, although I do agree, it sure looks like their location is oddly, but perfectly located midway between the two driving options."

"Feels like they looked hard to find a place like this, doesn't it?" Blake added.

"Sure does, Blake," Diego responded. "Three ways in on ground and three out, but most people would only see two, with no clear winner–and that doesn't include access from the air."

"Well, which way do you guys want to go ... west or south?"

"I've heard about Vail, the home of the rich and famous, but I've never seen it before. How about we go west and at least see how the rich folk live?"

"Works for me," Diego said.

"West it is, and just in time–breakfast is served!" Blake added with a smile.

Forty minutes later, the trio had finished their breakfasts, paid and were on the road again, taking the I-70 onramp at exit 201, heading west toward Copper Mountain.

The scenery was stunning–mile after mile of it. Although it was too early in the fall for the majority of the famous Colorado yellow aspens to show their colors, they were still able to enjoy some early turning, brilliant yellow trees at the top of Vail pass, above an elevation of 3,200 meters. Then came the long drive down Vail pass and they were finally in the world-renowned Vail Valley, elevation 2,445 meters–still high, but a surprisingly 320 meters lower than where they had eaten breakfast in Frisco.

"Wow," was about all Sean could mutter as they passed by the Vail golf course and then a minute later as they passed by downtown Vail and the nearby ski runs where he piped up again.

"Holy Toledo, that's how the other side lives, eh? Pretty darn nice …How much do you think those homes go for?"

Diego looked down at his phone and hit a few buttons.

"*Muy caro*! According to Zillow, the average house is listed at just over $2 million. I don't know, Blake, but if we pooled our retirement funds, we just might be able to buy an outhouse here!" They shared a quick laugh as the Jeep continued westward on I-70 and exited Vail Valley.

"So how does this compare to upstate New York, where your sister lives?" Sean asked Blake.

"That's a different kind of beauty, but no less spectacular than this is, just in its own way, of course. And it's *way* cheaper than this place! My sister, Cindy, and I both graduated from the Cobleskill-Richmondville High School, halfway between the two towns. It's a rural area of rolling, tree-covered hills, dotted with small family farms, streams, ponds and lakes everywhere. And in the fall, the mountains are on fire with the most beautiful kaleidoscope of red, orange, yellow, purple and pink colors from the sugar maples and ash trees that you'll ever see. It's beyond anything you can imagine without seeing it with your own eyes. Similar to the Grand Canyon, a camera just doesn't do it justice. It looks like it came straight out of a Norman Rockwell setting."

"Is that where you played soccer during high school?" Diego asked.

"Yes."

"What the heck did you do for fun out there in the middle of nowhere?" Sean asked.

"There were outdoor activities to enjoy all year long. In the spring, summer and fall, we fished, hunted, played pick-up sports, climbed the hay mows in the big dairy farms, chased Bigfoot sightings and picked apples and berries. In the winter, we made snow forts and went tobogganing. On top of that, we also went spelunking in the abundant limestone caves and then, of course, there were the infamous cow-tipping stories. It was pure heaven for a kid. I can still remember our mom telling us that people didn't fully appreciate the beauty of that area until they left. I still miss it."

"Cow tipping?" Diego queried. "You're kidding, right?"

"Between us and the fence posts," Blake laughed.

"Yeah, it's really what some would refer to as an urban legend, but we're quite guilty of spinning many a tall tale on that topic," Blake said.

Five minutes later, Blake turned south on U.S. Route 24, heading toward the Camp Hale exit and Resolution Road #702.

Camp Hale was an old WWII site where the 10th Mountain Division soldiers trained in 1942 for alpine and high altitude combat against the Nazis. It was also used in the early 1960s by the CIA to train Tibetan guerrillas. To this day, it was still possible to find unexploded ordnance in the surrounding areas left over from both eras of military use.

Ten minutes later, Blake exited near Camp Hale and found his way to Resolution Road #702. They were approximately five miles from their objective by road, but from here on out, travel would be much slower over the small dirt roads, similar to the thousands of other dirt roads that snaked their way through the various mountain passes and valleys throughout Colorado. These roads were used mainly by hunters, campers and recreationists using SUVs, pickup trucks and four-wheelers. Their Jeep Wrangler was a perfect fit and looked the part of the weekend warrior they had initially planned on being. No one would even give them a second look. Blake decided it was time to outline the plan he had been mulling over.

"Here's what I'm thinking. Once we clear Ptarmigan Pass we should be within a mile of the cabin. We'll keep our eyes peeled for a secluded spot where we can park for a few minutes to break out our gear. That way, we'll be better prepared just in case those guys still have some friends here. We'll drive by in case we can see anything from the road. If not, we'll park about a half-mile past the cabin and hike back through the trees to take a closer look. Agreed?"

"Sounds like as good a start as any," Diego responded.

"Good here. Heck, it's been almost half a day and we haven't had to fight or shoot anyone yet; we're overdue for some action!" Sean chuckled sarcastically.

"Well, here's hoping the only living creatures we see are of the four-legged variety. To be honest, I'd really like some quiet time to enjoy the mountains," Blake responded.

"Amen, brother," Diego replied.

*****

A full hour later, after the men had donned their gear, they'd driven by the cabins without seeing anything through the trees. As agreed, they parked the Jeep north of the site and hiked in by foot. Blake led the trio in, fanned out in a wide, point-first arrow shape as they approached the cabin. Trees, boulders and scraggly brush covered the terrain.

Blake held up his hand, wordlessly signaling the others to stop and listen. After a solid two minutes, Blake motioned for Sean and Diego to join up with him and the trio slowly approached the buildings with guns at the ready. Blake had originally considered the option of approaching like a trio of hunters, but after the events of the last couple of days, they all agreed that the safest option would be 100 percent battle readiness.

"Anyone see or hear anything?" Blake whispered.

"Nothing. It's pretty quiet and I don't see any vehicles or signs of recent occupation," Diego responded.

"I've got two buildings, one outhouse and one shipping container. Either of you see anything else on the way in?"

"That's a match," Sean whispered back.

"See any cameras anywhere?"

"Good question. None that I can see from this side, but it wouldn't surprise me if there were."

"OK, you guys cover me while I check out the cabin."

"Roger."

Blake sprinted to the north side of the larger cabin and turned with his back against the cabin's wall, looking toward Diego and Sean. Sean was looking through his riflescope, scanning the site. Twenty seconds later, Diego gave Blake the thumbs up.

Blake slid up to the window, with his Heckler & Koch HK416 assault rifle in position, then rotated 180 degrees to look into the window and scan the interior. Nothing. He rolled to the other side of the window, looked back at Diego and was rewarded with a second thumbs up while Sean continued to scan the area through his riflescope. Next stop, the front door on the west side of the cabin. Blake motioned for Diego and Sean to change positions to get a better view of the cabin door. Once in position, Blake tried the front door. Locked.

"No need to destroy any property yet," Blake whispered into his mic. "Let's try the second cabin, but first, I'll make sure the other sides of this cabin are clear."

Blake completed a 360-degree sweep of the cabin's exterior and checked out two more windows while doing so. He gave Diego a thumbs up and pointed to the second, smaller cabin. Just then, the sound of a cracking branch broke the silence, coming from the direction of the shipping container. The three men froze in place, guns raised, their eyes scanning the area for any signs of movement. Nothing. Blake hand-motioned Diego and Sean that he would approach the shipping container straight on.

Blake sprinted across the opening to the shipping container. It had been hidden from aerial view by a clump of pine trees so they had no idea what might be behind it. As he started to slide along the side of the container, another branch cracked on the opposite side and he froze again, looking back toward Sean and Diego.

Diego tossed a small rock over the back of the shipping container and was immediately rewarded by a thud and a quick scuffing sound against the container wall that sounded hard and non-natural.

"Bull's-eye," Diego whispered into his mic. "Keep your eyes open. Sean, there's definitely someone over there."

"And likely armed," Sean whispered into his mic. "If I had to guess, someone backed against the container wall when they heard your rock hit and the scrape was his rifle butt. Blake, watch the left side of the container. I've got the topside and Diego is about to spring the trap from the right. Take him, Diego."

Blake eyed Sean intently. Sean was one of the best sharpshooters he'd ever known and he was confident Sean could shut down any threat before they could get a single shot off—assuming whoever it was moved into his field of view.

Diego was holding his hand up, signaling Blake and Sean to remain still. Whoever it was, Blake knew they were about to be in for a very rude awakening. Diego moved farther to his right in an attempt to expose the threat.

For almost a full minute, the world remained silent. Then another branch crackled under foot. Diego froze, his pistol in a two-handed grip pointed straight ahead at the shipping container.

"Show yourself, buddy, but real slow. We have you covered. Move to my voice and hold your weapon above your head with both hands," Diego ordered as he started moving again, very slowly to his right.

No reply. Not a sound. Nothing.

"Dude, this won't end well for you, trust me," Diego yelled as he tried to coax the man out.

A distinct, metallic sound echoed across the opening–the unmistakable sound of metal on metal

Diego froze.

"Did that idiot just rack a pistol?" Sean asked, loud enough to be heard without the mics.

"Sounded like it, but I still can't see him," Diego replied softly into his mic. "Blake, move to the left in case he tries an end around. Sean, move toward me, but only as long as you can still cover the top of the container."

Diego stopped. His stance changed and he sat backwards, as if he had been pushed back.

"What is it?" Blake asked.

Then Diego's pistol rose vertical and he started chuckling.

"Diego?"

"Bambi just joined the hunt, and with a rather nice rack! Looks like a 12-pointer."

Blake smirked, "OK, looks like we can stand down. Let's let Bambi have his day, but how about you scare him off. I'd hate to have to shoot him because he wanted to tango with those antlers."

Diego stood up, smacked some nearby branches and waved his hands wildly while Sean continued to scan the site. The buck bolted back toward the south. Diego walked over to where the deer had been.

"Wow, check this out. Looks like a fox trap–guess that must have been the racking sound we heard. Good thing Bambi kicked it instead of stepping into it," Diego said.

"I'm pretty sure this place is deserted," Sean replied, still surveying the area, "but let's complete the sweep and then we can talk. Venison sounded mighty good, Blake, heck of a wasted opportunity."

"Sean, do you ever *not* think of food?"

They all shared a laugh.

Ten minutes later, the three friends stood together, alone in the clearing.

"Everything is locked up tight, except the outhouse, of course. I don't think this place has seen any use for quite some time. Looks like it's also wired for a generator, but I don't see it. Best guess is that it's in the shipping container. That must have been fun getting here. Let's check out that dumpster and see if it has anything of interest. Sean, you keep watch just to be safe. Diego and I will see if there is anything that might give us a clue to who owns this place," Blake directed.

The dumpster only required a few minutes to search. The only item of interest was a receipt inside a microwave box buried at the bottom; well protected from the elements. The microwave had been purchased a few months earlier at the Walmart store in, of all places, Frisco. No name was on it, just the last four digits, 7843, of the credit card used. Blake folded it neatly and placed it in his chest vest pocket.

"Well, that's a cut; time to call Joe Foster and let them know all is quiet out here," Blake summarized.

"Agreed. You make the call, Blake, and we'll get this gear packed up. It's time to get some jeepin' underway," Sean said excitedly.

"Oorah!" Diego echoed.

*****

CHAPTER 3

The White House
Sept. 13, 2029

The SETI Presidential Commission meeting was under way in the President's Cabinet Room, adjacent to the Oval Office. The two opposing teams were literally sitting on opposite ends of the long table. The Pro-SETI team, at the far left end, was led by Sen. Ronnie Dempsey of Michigan. Sen. Dempsey's end of the table included Sen. John Strong from Maine, Sen. Julie Stiles from Louisiana and Sen. James Colburn of Oregon. The Anti-SETI group, on the far right end of the table, was led by Sen. James Harley from Arkansas. Sen. Harley's end of the table included Sen. George Blasio from New York, Sen. Mary Celeste from California and Sen. Jerry Pinkerton from Montana. In between the two groups sat President Callahan, while the opposite side of the table was manned by Frank Pelino and Vice President Annie Murphy. Although the table was large enough that it could accommodate twice the group's size, the empty chairs between the two opposing groups provided a stark reminder of how polarized the two groups had become. Harry Lundrum, Gen. McMullen, Ben Tellinino and two recorders sat in chairs alongside the walls of the conference room.

"Who is this and why was I not informed of a new attendee to this meeting?" Sen. Harley bellowed pointing at Harry. The President nodded to Harry to introduce himself.

"Good morning, my name is Harry Lundrum."

"OK, that and five bucks might get you a good cup of coffee in this town. Would you like to give us a little more to go on?"

"Sure. I'm 30 years old. I graduated from Harvard with a dual PhD in chemistry and mathematics, and then followed up with a third PhD in astrophysics from MIT. I served with Cmdr. Blake Thompson's SEAL team for a number of years and was part of the group that helped the Reagan I and Armstrong I astronauts' return to Earth. I did not get to personally meet the Cjarians, but from what Blake relayed to me as well as their actual actions, the initial data would suggest that they're friendly. Other than that, I read a lot. The president had previously asked me to be his scientific adviser, but I wasn't quite ready to give up the other pursuits in my life."

"Oh? Then why did you come now?"

"Because the president requested my assistance."

"Great, so now we have another of your friends amongst us," Harley shot back sarcastically. "You still should have gotten my approval, Mr. President."

"He doesn't need your approval, Sen. Harley," Harry responded flatly. "This is a presidential commission, which means he has the full right to start it, cancel, or modify it at any time he desires."

President Callahan smiled as Harry finished.

"Oh, so now I suppose you're going to tell me that you also have a law degree from George Washington University and that you specialized in Congressional activities, right?"

"No, but as I mentioned, I read a lot."

"Good grief, so now you've brought Rain Man," Sen. Harley expressed exasperatedly as he looked over at President Callahan.

"Ahh, yes, the 1988 movie with Tom Cruise and Dustin Hoffman. Some have called me a savant, although I don't claim to be one. Just to make sure we're on the same page, a savant is defined as a learned person, especially a distinguished scientist, so thank you for the compliment. Having said that, Dustin Hoffman's character, Raymond, was actually an autistic savant, something I can prove I am not. I recommend you read a book by Trevor Clark called "Exploring Giftedness and Autism: A study of a differentiated educational program for autistic savants." In chapter one he talks about what he calls the 'paradox children.' I think you may find that of interest if you would like to pursue this discussion further."

"So he has a photographic memory as well?" Sen. Harley was still trying to steer the conversation back to President Callahan.

"Many have claimed that, Senator," Harry stated dryly. "But I really doubt we're all here to discuss my background, so may I suggest we get back to the intent of the meeting?"

"Thanks, Harry." The president smiled and nodded at Harry. However, the smile quickly disappeared as President Callahan looked back at Sen. Harley.

"I am confident that you will find Harry's addition to this team very beneficial. Harry is a totally unbiased individual who will back statements or dispute them, but always with unquestionable facts and analysis. His ability to break down a problem and craft solutions is unparalleled. What I witnessed this man do during the Armstrong I and terrorist struggles goes beyond what the rest of us in this room were able to do in aggregate. So, he has my full, unrestricted support. Gentlemen, are we ready to start?"

Sen. Harley shifted his weight and grimaced, nodding his concurrence.

"Sen. Dempsey, how about you?"

"Yes, Mr. President, I am ready as well."

"Alright, Ben, I'll turn it over to you. Take it away."

The debate remained highly spirited throughout the next 55 minutes. It was clear from the written comments that each group provided there was a growing percentage of the Senate members who were taking distinct sides in the debate. No fewer than 28 of the 100 senators were now siding with Sen. Harley. Thirty-nine were siding with Sen. Dempsey and President Callahan. The remaining senators remained undeclared, but were all in high demand for one-on-one discussions in an attempt to get them to commit.

Sen. Harley continued to escalate the risks associated with alien diseases, claiming that it could risk all life on the planet, but he also continued to raise concern over the threat of an alien war if the Cjarians were found to be unfriendly, or possibly in serious need of the resources that Earth possessed. Harry decided to address Harley's last comment relative to the risk of war.

"Sen. Harley, regardless of your legitimate concern for war, the truth is that it is out of our control now that they know we are here. Even if we don't invite them here, or allow further communication with the Cjarians, they can still pursue that path, so technically, we are wasting our time debating that aspect. If it helps, I'd propose that we have a better chance of knowing what they are doing if we actually *do* keep them close. If Cmdr. Thompson was here, I am quite confident that he would concur and likely quote Al Pacino in 'Godfather II,' who said: 'Keep your friends close and your enemies closer.' Both paths support keeping close contact with the Cjarians to make sure we don't get surprised–that's without even considering the potential benefits of learning about their technologies."

"Cmdr. Thompson? He's just a simple commander, Mr. President. Are we really listening to this garbage?"

"I'll answer that question," Gen. McMullen joined in. "As far as I am concerned, Cmdr. Thompson speaks for me. And for that matter, so does Harry. As President Callahan mentioned, their credibility has already been proven beyond question. Don't get me wrong Senator, your concerns are real and legitimate, but in this case, what other options do we have?"

"Assuming what they told you is true, they have not been able to contact their home planet. Given that, we could destroy their ship and eliminate the risk altogether," Sen. Harley replied with a cold edge to his voice.

The room went silent as the Pro-SETI group and the president looked at each other in total disbelief before all turned back to face Sen. Harley.

"How could you possibly even consider that option?" President Callahan asked. "They have done nothing wrong. They actually helped us if you recall the events that took place earlier this year. Senator, perhaps *you* would end up starting the war. Is that what you really want? By the way, at this point, I have to assume that their weapon systems, like their spacecraft technology, also have a high probability of being far superior to our own."

"They helped us because they were helping themselves. You people are playing with fire. Emotions are rising and someone is bound to get hurt if this keeps up," Sen. Harley replied, anger in his voice.

"Is that a threat, Senator?" President Callahan asked. "The senators on the Pro-SETI side of this table have already received numerous threats by mail and phone. Seeing as only Congress, our military leadership and NASA know about the Cjarians, how is that possible, unless it's coming from someone within Congress, and specifically from someone on the Anti-SETI side of the debate? I shouldn't have to remind you of the illegal nature of threatening a Congressman, do I?"

"Would I like to threaten you idiots? Hell, yes. Am I that stupid to do something like that? Hell, no, so quit wasting my time. Drop the theatrics and get back to the facts. If you don't have the stomach to protect the people of this country, and that of the other people around the world, then perhaps you should consider stepping down, sir. There are other world leaders who clearly agree with me." Sen. Harley was looking directly into President Callahan's eyes. "What do you think your constituents would say if I were to let the world know about the secrets you've been keeping? That your intent, all along, was for your own political posturing and grandstanding so you could say that you resolved the financial predicament this country has been in for decades. That this effort was pursued solely to collect financial commitments from other countries and to lay the groundwork to use the alien technology to promote U.S. interests and debt reduction–all at the risk of war and disease like the world has never seen before. I don't think that would come across very well, now would it Mr. President?" Sen. Harley sat back in his chair and crossed his arms with a rather smug look.

"Are you blackmailing me? I could have you arrested for treason, Sen. Harley."

"Right. How, and on what grounds?"

"For releasing top secret information and for attempting to blackmail a sitting president. Is that what you want?"

"So, you would turn me into a political prisoner, is that it? Someone disagrees with you and you throw them in prison for wanting to share the truth. The truth would favor me. The Russians would love it. How do you think your friends at the Washington Post, CNN and the other major news channels would respond? No, Mr. President, I believe I have the upper hand. Threats of war and deadly diseases against your dream of unknown technologies and empty promises of U.S. debt reduction."

"You're forgetting one thing, Mr. Harley," Gen. McMullen interrupted.

"Am I, General?"

"Yes, the military still reports to the president."

"As long as you say so, General."

Sen. Harley crumpled up his agenda copy and tossed it across the table in the direction of Gen. McMullen as he and the other three senators in the Anti-SETI group stood up and departed the room. The crumpled ball of paper bounced off the conference phone and landed in Harry's lap.

President Callahan ignored Sen. Harley and turned to the Pro-SETI group.

"Sen. Dempsey. You may also leave with your group, but please keep this quiet for now."

"Yes, sir."

The Pro-SETI group left quietly, concern still showing on their faces. Harry started to get up, but the President ordered him to stay put. Once the door closed the president spoke again.

"He truly thinks he has the upper hand, but the comment that bothered me the most was his parting comment relative to the military. If this wasn't the U.S., I would truly be concerned that he was attempting a coup. Gen. McMullen, what the hell is going on?"

"I don't know, Mr. President, but I feel like the debate stage has ended. We may now be in a fight for our political futures, and possibly much, much more," Gen. McMullen responded. "This feels like the beginning of another possible threat to the stability and future of the country, but worse yet, it's from the inside, not some rogue terrorist group. It's from the heart of our own government."

"Mr. President," Frank chimed in, "I think we need to continue the discussion we had earlier about coming clean and taking the story to the people, before Harley does. And we make it clear what Harley is trying to do. Paint him into a corner."

"What if he's trying to make us do that, Frank? I have this nagging feeling that he's baiting us. It feels like he has something up his sleeve we haven't seen yet," Annie added.

"Harry, what do you think?"

"First off, I don't trust the man at all. He is manipulative and hits me as a total psychopathic narcissist. He fits too many characteristics of a dark personality; one that may truly have evil intentions. According to one Paul Ratner, it has to do with 'the basic tendency to maximize one's own utility at the expense of others, accompanied by beliefs that serve as justifications for one's malevolent behaviors.' These people are highly intelligent and have a total indifference to the safety and well-being of others, putting their own success over anything else, including other people and their very lives. I detest people like that."

"OK, Harry, I think it's clear that you don't like the senator from Arkansas–join the club. I'll keep it simple and just stick with *psychopathic narcissist*. What do you recommend?

"I need to think about this one. I agree that we should release the information about the Cjarians, but I also agree with the vice president that it feels like he's baiting us to do just that. He appears to be one step ahead, and we need to be one step in front of him. Let me think about it. Can I have until later in the week?"

"I'd like it sooner, Harry, but if you need time to think, then it's granted. Let's meet as soon as you're ready, set it up through Ben. Gen. McMullen, I can't believe I'm going to request this, but I am. Create a list of who you trust and who you don't within your military circles–just in case he really does have backing that we're blind to. Any other questions?"

No one did. The meeting broke up and Harry was left to ponder what he had just witnessed. His first thought was to call Blake and simply have this idiot taken out, but he knew President Callahan would not agree with that proposal. Harry needed time to think, but he was woefully short of data to work with.

*****

On Board the Jarisst I
Sept. 13, 2029

Last winter, soon after departing Earth orbit, the Jarisst I headed straight for the outer edge of the solar system, far from any gravitational fields in order to safely engage the ship's Quantum Physics AntiMatter Space drive, or Q-PAMS, that would allow them to speed through space faster than the speed of light. Without it, the ship was limited to near light speed travel. The flight to the edge of the solar system had been quick, and full of hope and expectation that they would soon be freed from their unplanned captivity and could finally start their search for Cjar.

Although the ship appeared fully functional and the ship's fuel stores had been refilled prior to departing the space dock above Earth, the Q-PAMS drive would not engage and remained nonoperational, or at a minimum, unresponsive. The crewmembers were at a total loss; it was one more challenge in what seemed like an endless sea of challenges.

Those challenges had started almost a year ago with the realization that the ship's captain and most of the original crew had been tragically lost in an accident that somehow brought them to this distant, unknown star system. They still didn't know where they were, or exactly how they'd arrived in this small star system, nor had they been able to raise contact with their home world, Cjar. It had been even more devastating when they came to the realization that the 11 surviving crewmembers had been in a suspended sleep within their specially designed G-Cells for more than 500 years! Everyone they'd known back home was long dead. They didn't even know if Cjar had survived the war with their hated foes, the Klaxx.

Lt. Thjars Chjssiast was the senior remaining officer on board and had, therefore, assumed responsibility for the ship and the surviving crewmembers. His unexpected promotion, as challenging as it was, was made even more daunting as he lacked full access to the ship's flight computer and controls. Security protocol restricted access only to the previous ship's captain and chief designer, Capt. Zyles Blissiart, and his first officer, both of whom died centuries ago. Zyles' brother, Jarns, also a military scientist, was one of the 11 survivors, but he was not cleared for his brother's access codes, either. Jarns had been working feverishly over the past eight months to re-establish access for Thjars and himself, but had yet to achieve even a sliver of success.

Thjars relied heavily on two other veteran Cjarians during this ordeal: the ever-dependable sergeant-at-arms Qulys Plyenysst and linguist Juulys Lystnyng, the only surviving female from the original crew. The remainder of the crew included Private First Class Knarls Rjissist; Medical Officer Jenysys Thalysst; two engineers, Cryells Elysst and Allympht Allsysst; and three technical specialists, Zalmyt Wylmysst, Platsys Flysst and Nylsst Volysstmyn.

Their ship, the Jarisst I, was a one-of-a-kind spaceship: a technological breakthrough developed for the centuries-old Cjarian war with the Klaxx. The ship, and the Q-PAMS drive that powered it, had been designed and built in secrecy on Secretorum, a moon that orbited the fifth planet in Cjar's home system. The Q-PAMS drive was a revolutionary drive system that could propel a ship through space at more than 200 times the speed of light.

Since departing Earth months ago, and realizing that their ship was still not capable of regaining faster-than-light operation, the Jarisst I crew had spent the majority of their time exploring the planets within the Sun's planetary system. The exploration was a means of learning more about the solar system they were currently marooned in, but more importantly, it was a vehicle to keep the crew actively engaged–attempting to maintain some level of normalcy within their lives, as well as to provide time to continue work on the Q-PAMS drive and access codes. That, however, did not hinder their continued attempts to establish connection with Cjar, as well as to keep monitoring space for any messages that might provide a clue to the whereabouts of other Cjarian ships.

The crew had initially agreed not to tell anyone on Earth about their current Q-PAMS predicament, but over the past few months, the topic had evolved into a continual debate, attempting to choose between returning to Earth for help versus heading out to the stars in hopes of making a lucky contact with a Cjarian ship or outpost. The latter option Thjars found to be tantamount to suicide. Space was simply too vast, with individual star systems separated by endless light years of distance, to hope that they would be lucky enough to make contact. Furthermore, they had no way to know which direction to go in or how long they would remain lost in space, especially as they were currently limited to less than light-speed velocities without the Q-PAMS drive and would very likely run out of fuel before they could ever find anything.

The ship was currently orbiting the planet Saturn, as the earthlings called it, and mapping its gigantic rings and the various moons that orbited the planet. So far, they had identified no fewer than 53 moons of various sizes. Some were as small as asteroids, but one was big enough to be considered a planet in its own right. Saturn's rings were, by far, the highlight of the planets they visited.

"Thjars, have you ever seen anything as beautiful as that?" Juulys asked.

"It is stunning, Juulys, especially when you're in the right position to see their star's light reflected off, and through the rings," Thjars responded. "It's hard to believe its ice way out here in space, but Platsys said he validated it with his scans."

"Platsys."

"Yes, Juulys?"

"You're our best astronomer ..."

"And I'm your *only* astronomer, which means ..."

"Yes, the worst, too!" They all laughed. "Let's stick with the best," she concluded with a smile. "Have you ever heard of a planet like this before? They call it Saturn, correct?"

"No, Juulys, I haven't, at least, not on this scale. And, yes, they do refer to it as Saturn. It's almost 10 times the diameter of the third planet they call Earth. Although still smaller than that giant planet they call Jupiter–that planet's mass is more than double all of the other planets put together!"

"It's still a stunning sight, but, Juulys, Platsys ... we're avoiding the real topic we need to be discussing. I need you all to get back to the reality of our situation," Thjars interjected. "We still haven't agreed on what to do next."

Heads lowered and the electricity of the moment vanished, replaced with the weight of a pending decision and its associated gloom. Thjars saw it and felt it.

"Look, I don't mean to ruin the day, but not making a decision *is* making a decision: one that may condemn us to remain in this system for the rest of our lives. We need to come to an agreement, and soon. I really don't recommend we wait any longer."

"Make the decision, Thjars," Qulys stated respectfully, but firmly, like the soldier he was.

"Qulys, we've been through this before. Yes, I can make the decision, but our very lives are at stake, so we all have a say in it. On the positive side, there are very limited options–we just need to agree on one."

The highly experienced, war-tested, ever dependable and tough-as-nails Qulys finally decided that the rookie, didn't-ask-for-this-but-got-promoted-anyway Thjars, might just need a little extra push to grow further into his recently minted leadership role. Qulys stood up and walked to the middle of the room where all could see him and he spoke with the voice that only a seasoned sergeant-at-arms could muster–it demanded immediate attention.

"Cjarians, your captain has requested your input. No more debating, no more whining. You each get one vote and the outcome of that vote is what we will do–and we are voting now! Thjars, give us the options."

"Thanks, Qulys, or maybe I should say, *yes, sir*!" Thjars smiled as he saluted Qulys in an exaggerated manner. Most of the crew joined in the chuckle, but only Qulys and Juulys were truly aware of what Qulys did. Not only was Qulys attempting to pull them back from the growing gloom, but they also knew that Qulys was trying to openly reinforce Thjars' role as captain. It was critical that the entire crew confidently and unquestionably support a single leader during a crisis. The last thing the ship needed was a split crew, or worse yet, a mutiny.

"As I see it, we have three distinct options. The first is to avoid contact with the earthlings and remain in their star system until we can fix the Q-PAMS drive, or wait for Cjar to find us. The second is to strike out into space, at sub-light speeds, and pursue a random path that hopefully crosses paths with Cjar or another Cjarian vessel. The third is to contact Blake and ask for their assistance. I'm going to poll each one of you for your vote. Option one, two, or three."

"Wait, Thjars," Juulys interrupted him. "I respect your willingness to make this fair for all and to drive to a quick answer, but we don't all have equal understanding of the potential outcomes. Please give us a short summary of what you see as the pros and cons of each option before we vote." She finished and winked at Qulys. They were both on the same page relative to helping to push Thjars forward.

"OK, Juulys, I'll give you my honest assessment. Let's discuss option one first." He stopped and looked over at Jarns.

"Jarns. What do you estimate is the probability that you can fix the Q-PAMS drive within, say, the next year?"

"A year? Honestly, Thjars, I'd be happy if I could figure out what the actual problem is in that timeframe. I've been working it hard for seven months and I literally have nothing to show for it. Even if I could figure out what needs to be done, that doesn't mean we have the ability to actually fix it without a capable Cjarian space dock. I'm sorry, Thjars, but I'm not feeling too optimistic about repairing the Q-PAMS drive any time soon."

"That's OK, Jarns, and it's nothing to be discouraged about. You've given it a lot of heart and sweat–better than any of us could have done, and we thank you for that."

Thjars stood up, patted Jarns on the back and walked into the middle of the room next to Qulys. Qulys smiled at Juulys and flashed a quick thumbs up sign they had learned from Blake. Juulys had to cover her mouth so she wouldn't laugh as Qulys found a chair to sit down in and give Thjars command of the stage.

"So, would it be fair to say that your expectation for success is … maybe less than 20 percent?"

"Honestly, Thjars … umm … sir … I would say with confidence that it's less than 10 percent. I've exhausted every idea I had."

"Thank you, Jarns. Now for option two. I don't know how to say this nicely, so I'll just say it. I just don't see it as a viable solution, in any form or stretch of the imagination. Knarls, I know you have pushed for this option, but I honestly see it as nothing less than a suicide mission. We have no idea which way to go, and the nearest star–which we know isn't Cjar–is more than four light years away. That would take us at least five years just to reach it without the Q-PAMS drive, and the chances that we would find help there is likely zero–definitely less than what we know is already here on Earth. Think about what would happen if the ship broke down or ran out of food and/or fuel, which will happen, sooner or later. I see option two as a death warrant for all of us–to die in space, alone. Granted, we could all jump back into our G-Cells and hibernate until someone finds us, but would that really help? Would we be better off than where we are now? "

"We could program the ship to wake one of us after a set number of years or if it detects a nearby celestial body, couldn't we?" Knarls asked.

"Yes, we could, but we would be rolling the dice assuming that we might be near life that could actually help us, or moving even farther from help. I don't think that is worth risking when we know we have potential help right here, right now," Thjars responded gently. "Juulys, what was the comment Blake made about the birds?"

"The one about a 'bird in the hand is worth two in the bush'?"

"Yes, that's the one; thank you, Juulys. I understand that phrase even better now. Earth is our bird in the hand. Space is our bush–and it's a pretty big bush."

"So, the bird, or option three, is left. Option three scares us all because we still don't know which governments on that planet we can truly trust, and the idea of turning this technology over to an immature civilization borders on the unethical, as well as being potentially very dangerous–for them and for us. However, we do know Blake and I think we all trust *him* at least. Option three also provides an immediate path to gaining access to more technical and manufacturing capabilities; both of which would significantly increase our probability of success for fixing the Q-PAMS drive."

"I would throw out option two as non-viable, which means it comes down to a very low probability, wait-and-see option versus a higher probability, but more dangerous option where we ask for help. Personally, I want to see Cjar again. Option three is my clear winner."

"Thank you, Thjars. That was an excellent summary." Qulys stood up first. "I share your vote, Thjars, I like option three. Juulys?"

"Ditto, Qulys. Thjars, we just needed you to provide a confident path for us. You just did. You are our captain and I propose we cancel the vote and go with your recommendation." The room broke into murmuring discussion until Qulys' bellowing voice commanded silence.

"Cjarians! Whose butt do I need to kick out of the airlock first? The captain has made a decision and any disagreement will be treated by this sergeant-at-arms as a mutiny. Do I make myself perfectly clear?" Qulys smiled as he finished, but his point was clear to everyone.

Jarns stood up. "If my brother was still alive today, and still captain of this ship, he would have simply made the decision–and we would have followed him without question. We owe Thjars that same respect. Without it, we will fall apart and die."

The room went silent for a few long moments until Thjars spoke.

"Thank you, Jarns. The more I get to know you, the more I can see your brother Zyles in you, and I greatly respect that. As for me, I am your captain, but I will never be Zyles. I will always give my best for you and for Cjar, but I am different from Zyles. You all need to realize and accept that fact." Thjars paused and surveyed the rest of the crew. "OK, friends, this is your last opportunity for input. If you cannot convince me that there is a better option than number three, then I will contact Blake. Your thoughts?"

The room remained silent as Thjars looked directly at Knarls.

"Thjars, everyone knows that I've been the biggest advocate for option two, but ... I apologize for my lack of support. I will agree with and support your decision."

Once Knarls capitulated, the rest of the crew quickly joined in.

"Thank you, Knarls. Thank you, everyone. Juulys ... Qulys ... we've got a lot to sort out before we make our next move."

Juulys and Qulys again exchanged smiles. Their young captain was definitely different than Zyles, but it was a good different–and he was growing up quickly.

*****

Colorado
Sept. 14, 2029

"Hello?" Blake answered the unexpected call on his Sat phone.

"Blake?"

"Yes ... Who's this?"

"Joe. Joe Foster, FBI. Do you remember what we recovered in the hotel room?"

"Yes ..."

"We need to talk. ASAP. Where are you?"

"We're at Lizard Head Pass."

"Lizard Head what? ... What and where the heck is that?"

"Off of route 145 … maybe a half hour south of Telluride."

"OK, I hate to do this to you, but get back to Telluride quickly. We'll have a copter waiting for you."

"That hot?"

"Yes."

"OK, Joe. We'll make it work. We were planning on driving back tonight anyway to make sure we didn't miss the Air Force game tomorrow. It starts at four o'clock, but I hear the tailgate parties are as good as the game. Based on this copter ride, I'm guessing that's off, correct?"

"Blake, we need you at the game even more than you want to be at it. Trust me, you'll be there."

"Well, I guess vacation is over, but it was a great ride while it lasted. We're turning around now and Diego is checking his phone … hang on … looks like we should be there in approximately 30 minutes according to Google. Does that work?"

"Yes, thanks, Blake. You'll understand once I get you up to speed on the latest info. Until then, I do have to ask you one more question."

"Shoot."

"You've only been in Colorado for, what, just a couple of days? Never before that?"

"Correct, first time ever."

"Lizard Head Pass? … With all the ski resorts and famous mountain passes, how the hell did you pick that place out?"

"That was actually easy," Blake laughed. "Sean saw the name on a map and said, 'With a name like that, it has to be good.' Then Diego replied with a simple, 'Smucker's Jelly! I'm in,' … How could I argue? Heck, after all, I'm just the driver."

"Guess that will have to work," Joe laughed back. "See you in 30 minutes."

"You're out here, too?"

"Not yet, but I'm on the chopper heading your way right now. We've got a lot to cover, but before I sign off, I heard about your unplanned tour of duty in Georgetown. Glad to hear you guys are OK. Sounds like your timing couldn't have been better. Even though we were told to keep your involvement under the radar, there were too many witnesses. You guys may be nameless so far, but you're on every news station. They interviewed the witnesses in their cars as well as some of the actual hostages; all talked about some kind of ninja ghosts that showed up out of nowhere and saved the day."

"Thanks, Joe. We just did what we were trained to do, but we couldn't have done it without the supplies you guys gave us. Unfortunately, one cop and one civilian never got a chance to go home."

"I hear you, Blake, but you still saved a lot of other people that night. See you in a bit. Over and out."

*****

Thirty-three minutes later, Blake reached up and shook hands with FBI Agent Joe Foster as he instinctively bent down to avoid the rotor blades and board the Black Hawk helicopter that had just arrived from Fort Carson. Sean and Diego followed right behind him.

"Don't worry about your Jeep or your stuff; it'll be taken care of," Joe yelled against the noise of the rotors. "Agent Randy Jones, the guy that just jumped down, will drive it back for you. Toss him the keys," Joe directed.

Blake pulled the keys from his pocket, tossed them across the copter cabin to Sean, who in turn tossed them out the side door next to him, into the waiting hands of Agent Jones.

"Don't scratch it, or Uncle Sam will make you pay for it." Sean laughed and gave the agent a double thumbs up sign.

Agent Foster handed each of them a headset so that they could better communicate during the flight back to Fort Carson.

"It's your dime, Foster." Blake clearly wanted to get at it, and quickly. "So, what's up?"

"Remember your reaction to the ammo? You said it reminded you of a discussion you had with an ammo rep and some research project they were working on years ago?"

"Somehow, I don't think I'm going to like this," Blake replied.

"Correct, Blake. I had no idea anything like this even existed. They are from a top secret Army program, codenamed Starburst. It's so black that I can't even get clearance to know who makes it. From the sounds of it, it's still not in the general military inventory. That guy must have been drunk to tell you about it."

"Well, that's at least good news, right?" Sean jumped in.

"Actually, no," Foster replied. "That means it should be even harder to get. How these guys got a hold of something this secret is a huge concern for the military–and those guys you collared still aren't talking."

"Give us an hour; we'll make them talk," Diego replied coldly.

"I'd like to agree with you, Diego, but these guys are a different breed. Three of them are clearly mercenaries, but they act like they would happily go down as martyrs as long as their cause remained intact. The other two are definitely not fighters, but they are in so deep they won't talk. It reminds me of how scared some of the local drug dealers are of the Mexican cartels and the Russian mafia–both are operating out here, and with more freedom than the nightly news ever reports. Those guys know they're at constant risk of being taken out by the police, or even another rival group, but they're more afraid of the way they would die from the drug lords, as well as what might happen to their families if they did talk. The cartels and mafia are brutal on traitors … beheadings ... skinning people alive … burying or burning people alive … women and kids alike …" Joe paused, like he was reliving a nightmare. "You can't believe some of the things we've seen that never make the news. Their goal is to make the fear of retribution so extreme that it absolutely guarantees their loyalty. This feels like that same kind of control–and, believe me, it works."

"That's pretty extreme, and scary as hell. Do you still think we were their target?" Sean asked.

"Like I said, they aren't talking, but yes, we still think they were after the three of you. And if it is them, then it's even more important to keep your names out of the news. If they were pissed off at you guys before, I can only imagine the bounty that's on your heads now, given what you spoiled in Georgetown."

"Just to test the other venues we've operated in, do your guys think this could be terrorism?" Blake asked.

"Hard to say, but my gut says no. Everything I've seen has 'target' written all over it, and that would suggest it's not terrorism because they typically don't target single individuals in the West. Whoever it is, we think you guys were their target, but we simply can't guarantee that yet, nor give you a motive for why they were targeting you."

"Joe," Blake said softly, with concern in his eyes.

"What, Blake?"

"Remember Patty, Harry and Li? We have other members of our team that aren't here. Maybe even the members of the Armstrong I and Reagan I crews, depending on what these guys are truly after us for. They all need to be notified of the potential danger immediately, and also provided with federal protection."

"That may be one area where we're ahead of you, Blake. We already have agents watching Harry, Patty and Li, but we haven't told them anything yet. I was worried about that as well."

"Thank you, Joe, but you better tell them what's going on, and tell them today. Knowing those three, they've already picked up on the fact that someone is watching them. By not telling them, you're actually putting your agents at double risk–from both the bad guys, and the good guys."

"Great point, Blake. We were focused on not upsetting anyone. Will do. We also hadn't considered the astronauts. I'm having a hard time convincing myself they are at risk, but I'll call in a request to expand our nets to include them as well."

"Thank you. Now, tell us a little more about this ammo. What's it really capable of?" Blake asked.

"It's hard to fathom that we have technology like this, Blake. Although I'm not cleared to know who makes this stuff, I was cleared for the information I'm about to share with you, but I have to get your agreement that you don't share it further."

All three men nodded, but Blake had to add one caveat.

"Joe, we will need to include the others on our team as well."

"Agreed, but keep it to them only–the need-to-know status on this information is extremely tight."

"Roger."

"Blake, the miniaturization is incredible. Each round has a small built-in radar altimeter, programming capability, speed sensors, distance sensors and a burst timer. As you suspected, the rifles were also modified, both for the larger round as well as with a software interface that provides distance and height commands to the round. The two settings are selected by the user via two dials on the side of the rifle. The first dial adjusts for burst altitude, from off to as much as five meters. The second dial, when turned on, adjusts for distance to the target. Together, the user's selections preprogram the shell for a specific burst height and distance. You had talked about a sniper's accuracy versus simply lobbing the bullets in. It looks like the latter was their plan."

"That would have changed many of the battlefields we were in, and significantly," Sean replied.

"Correct, Sean. As I understand it, the concept was initially developed to strengthen small mobile teams, like your SEAL teams, that were out in the mountains against superior numbers. Think about how quickly and accurately you could begin to even the odds. Not only that, but the burst function would allow you to accurately hit targets behind rocks or buildings. As lethal as your SEAL teams are, it would easily double or even triple your current lethality levels."

"Good, Lord. We never would have had a chance … but with a packed stadium," Blake paused. "What kind of carnage do your guys think they could have achieved?" Blake asked.

"The stadium seats over 46,000, most of which are on the west side where the trajectories would have carried. Casualties would have been in the thousands if the intent was to maximize damage, but I don't think that was the case."

"How so?" Diego asked.

"Their ammo supply and setup looked like they were planning on leaving, not making a fight-to-the death stand. That suggests they were planning just a few shots each into the target zone and once the target, or targets, had been neutralized, they'd pack up and leave. The authorities would be consumed with the immediate chaos of the actual crime scene and the many casualties. Worse yet, the nature of the injuries would suggest a hand grenade, not a rifle shot. By the time they could even start thinking about a gun or where the shots came from, these guys would be halfway through Wyoming as the state border is less than three hours straight north from here."

"That gets us back to determining who or what their target was," Blake responded. "Until we know otherwise, I think we have to continue to assume it's us."

"Even though we lack a specific motive, the FBI agrees with you, Blake. Think about it: you've got Special Operations history around the world–lots of people and organizations that might want revenge, including some key drug organizations. We're leaning toward someone wanting revenge, so you need to start thinking about who the hell you pissed off that much."

"Well, that's a pretty long list, Joe, but most of the time we were undercover as a SEAL team. That should not be information that is easily obtained."

"Whoa! You're saying it's an inside hit?" Sean piped up.

"Not necessarily," Blake answered. "But, it's a legitimate possibility that we need to consider, or more likely that our data systems have been compromised."

"How these guys knew you three would be at the game is also a key mystery. And one that you will have to help us figure out based on who you shared your Colorado plans with."

*****

A little over an hour later, the Black Hawk helicopter touched down at Fort Carson and unloaded its human cargo. The foursome had spent most of the flight asking questions and exchanging ideas, but nothing had yet captured their attention to a level that defined an investigative nugget worth pursuing. Halfway through the flight, Blake called Harry and gave him an update. Harry acknowledged seeing a couple of formal-looking men who seemed to show up wherever he'd been, but never felt threatened by them. It all made sense now. Blake also asked Harry to pull in SEAL Warrant Officer Li Zheng, a fifth member of their original SEAL team. Li was a 27-year-old Chinese-born computer specialist who had worked with Blake for the past five years. Blake considered him both a personal friend as well as the best computer hacker the CIA ever encountered. The man simply thought in bits, bytes and electrons. Li had also been an accomplished marathoner in college and won the famed 4,302-meter-high Pikes Peak marathon–a now ironic fact as passed it on the way in. Harry told Blake that Li was actually at the University of Houston with him, working with their newest non-combat teammates, Robert Stern and Jimmy Decker.

Robert Stern was a senior aerospace engineering student at the University of Houston and also interned at the Lyndon B. Johnson Space Center in Houston. Robert had identified the object buried in the red Martian sand while he was working on the Mars Rover program last year. The object turned out to be a communication pod, or C-Pod, that the Cjarian spacecraft had launched when it first entered their planetary system hundreds of years ago. Robert also turned out to be a legitimate software prodigy, a common interest area with Li and Jimmy Decker that led to the creation of a circle of very capable friends.

Jimmy Decker was the engineer on board the Reagan I. He'd helped excavate the C-Pod from the Martian landscape, then spent weeks analyzing it during their long and harrowing trip home to Earth. Jimmy was also quite adept at programming, and was a fun-loving technical geek at heart.

The only remaining member of Blake's SEAL team not present was SEAL Warrant Officer Patty Myers. Patty had been kidnapped last year in Yemen as they attempted to track down sources of the sabotage associated with the Armstrong I– sabotage they wrongly thought was connected to the Armstrong I crewmember from Saudi Arabia, Col. Ataullah El-Hashem. Harry, Sean and Diego had saved her from what likely would have been a brutal death at the hands of the terrorists.

A month after the terrorists had been defeated, and the country was able to get back to a more normal routine, Patty had approached Blake to talk privately. She'd been at a crossroads and wasn't sure if she wanted to continue on the SEAL team. Blake suggested she take a year off and then reassess, but he knew he would sorely miss her expertise, especially with the chance that the Cjarians did return. At the age of 32, Patty was already one of the most accomplished linguists in the military. She had ratcheted up the ranks within the CIA special request rooms, as she was fluent in English, Arabic, multiple Chinese dialects, Russian, German, French and Latin. The CIA quickly realized that Patty was also a natural cryptanalyst and pushed her into a PhD-equivalent program that paid off handsomely in their continuing efforts against the Taliban and Al-Qaeda networks. The combination of Li and Patty had opened up all kinds of options when it came to cracking electronic security systems and encrypted codes.

Although Blake was personally and professionally disappointed over the loss of Patty, he also knew that a SEAL had to be 100 percent engaged at all times, or they would greatly increase the risk of failure and death to themselves, and their teams. He knew he had no choice, so he bid her good luck, but requested that she keep in contact so that he knew she was doing

OK. He also made her promise that if she needed anything, to call and they would come to her aid. Patty had hugged Blake, professed her gratitude and promised she would stay in contact. She also said she wanted to keep studying the Cjarian language, but off the government's radar, and would appreciate any new information that Blake could pass her way.

*****

CHAPTER 4

United States Air Force Academy, Colorado Springs
Saturday, Sept. 15, 2029

Blake woke up at 5 a.m. and headed over to the Air Force Academy Fitness Center to hook up with Diego and Sean for a quick workout. They had originally planned on staying at the Great Wolf Lodge, where the incident had occurred just a few days earlier, but had decided to stay at the Air Force Academy after they received a personal invite from the commandant, two-star Gen. Carrie Bowers, the fourth woman to lead the prestigious facility. Gen. Bowers had heard about the plot to attack the weekend football game and personally drove to Fort Carson to meet the trio when they returned, thanked them, and invited them to stay on campus as her personal guests. It was an invite the trio knew couldn't be turned down, but in this case, it was also one that all three were eager to accept.

The trio completed their exercise routines and returned to their rooms to shower. When Blake finished, he noticed a note under his door from Gen. Bowers herself, asking if they wanted to join her for a private breakfast. Blake smiled, again knowing that the invitation was not really optional. He picked up the phone and dialed the number on the letterhead.

"Gen. Bowers?"

"Yes."

"Good morning. This is Cmdr. Blake Thompson. The breakfast offer is outstanding, and we would be honored, thank you. If I could be so bold, could I propose that we all sit with the cadets at Mitchell Hall?"

"Absolutely, and it appears that Gen. McMullen knows you as well as he claims."

"How's that?"

"I talked to him yesterday and he predicted you would do exactly what you just requested. I believe his exact words were: 'Blake will never place himself above anyone else, or even allow the appearance of it. Not because he wants to look the part, but because he lives the part. There are none better.' Based on that summary, I believe it is I who should be honored. I will see you there shortly, but I will request that you still sit at my table so that the cadets know you are my guest of honor. Is that acceptable?"

Blake laughed; he was beginning to like her.

"Yes, General, I find your terms acceptable. See you shortly."

Mitchell Hall was dedicated in 1959 and named in honor of Brigadier Gen. William "Billy" Mitchell, commonly called the father of the U.S. Air Force. The mess hall was a cavernous, three-and-a-half story building covering a full 1.7 acres. It could serve more than 4,200 people at one time and within 30 minutes– an efficiency that brought great pride to the Academy as it was recognized as one of the most advanced mass dining facilities in the world.

As Gen. Bowers entered with her guests, the cadets all jumped to stand at attention.

"At ease, cadets, please continue." The room sat as one. "We are joined by three guests today, all three of whom are distinguished SEALs, among many other contributions they have made to our country with their dedicated service. I am honored to have Cmdr. Blake Thompson, Lt. Sean O'Rourke and Petty Officer First Class Diego Velasquez join us for breakfast."

The three men saluted the room and followed Gen. Bowers to her table as Blake yelled, "Beat Notre Dame!"

The room broke into a bedlam of cheers and then quickly returned to the meal at hand.

"That was incredible. Thank you, General. I will remember this for a long time."

"You are most welcome, but I need to thank you three much more. As I understand it, today could have gone down as the worst day in the history of any of the military academies had it not been for you three."

"We were at the right place, at the right time, and we did what we were trained to do. I'm just thankful we were given the opportunity to intervene. Let me also remind you that the day isn't over yet."

"Fair point, Commander. Let's eat."

Forty-five minutes later, they shook hands as the trio departed to go prep for the game. Agent Foster had requested that they meet at his downtown Tejon Street office by 11 a.m., but that unfortunately gave them little time to cruise the campus and see the sights. Regardless, they made the most of what they had. The Academy was located in a spectacular setting at the base of the mountains, just north of Pikes Peak and below Ormes Peak, with the iconic Cadet Chapel as its centerpiece–exactly where they headed to start their tour.

*****

FBI Office, Colorado Springs

"Foster! What up?" Sean asked as he walked in the door and patted FBI Agent Joe Foster on the shoulder. Blake and Diego walked in right behind him.

"Well," Blake added, before Joe could respond to Sean, "those guys obviously had connections with someone. Were they able to get a call out that they had been busted?"

"So much for small talk, eh, Blake? Right to the point as usual. No wonder you can't ever get a date!" Sean chided his *always business* buddy.

"No, we're pretty sure of that," Joe answered, ignoring Sean's jab. "You guys stopped them before they could do anything, and it's not like some of them were in a conversational mode by the time you were done with them," Joe chuckled. "But we've made sure that they've remained 'disconnected' since then, if you get my drift. Unfortunately, there's a pretty good chance that an operation like this would've required contact at a set frequency for them to report status. Assuming that was the case, then whoever is paying them likely knows something is up just by the simple lack of contact. In addition, even though we're still trying to keep a lid on this, they were already granted court-assigned lawyers, and now that community is talking, so word is starting to get out."

"Do you expect they have a backup plan?"

"I don't think so, Blake, but we can't take any chances."

"You're not thinking of canceling the game, are you?" Sean jumped.

"Absolutely not, but we are planning some surprises for anyone that even attempts to carry out their plan."

"How about you just let us talk to them like we suggested earlier? Especially that squirrely leader … just say yes, and tell him I'm going to make him an offer he can't refuse. He'll talk, I'll guarantee it," Diego replied, even more coldly than the first time.

"'Godfather,' 1970s, very appropriate, Diego. Count me in," Blake responded.

"Trust me, guys, I would enjoy saying 'yes' to your proposal, but I can't," Joe added. "We're no longer under martial law like we were a few months back, so the law of the land is once again back to the Fifth Amendment and their right to remain silent, as well as the fact that they *are* innocent until proven guilty. They'll claim they were going hunting in the mountains and randomly bought the special ammunition from some guy they ran into without knowing what it really was. You know how it works, once they finalize their team of fancy lawyers, the suits will back them to the hilt."

"You have to be friggin' kidding me! Who in their right mind would defend this trash?" Sean voiced angrily.

"Amen, Sean. I wish we could take down the f'in' lawyers, too; sometimes I think they're worse than the crooks. Until then, we'll hold them on probable cause and improperly obtained military weapons for as long as we can."

"That's good to hear. So what's the plan and what would you like us to do?" Blake countered.

"If you're willing, we need you in the stadium. Assuming you guys were, and still are the target, we need to keep the trap baited."

"No problem," the three men answered in unison.

"Good. But you should know that we have some outlandish outfits for you … just in case you want to reconsider," Joe laughed. "These are lightweight, bullet-proof vests to wear under your jackets. In addition, we made up these three metal Air Force helmets with F-16 and *Beat Notre Dame* decals on them, as well as beer cup holders. It'll help make you guys look like three more die-hard, nutty Air Force football fans. They also come fitted with a mic system so that we can talk with each other."

"This is great!" Sean aped as he put on the bright silver helmet closest to him. "Do we get to keep them?"

"How about something else to pack under our coats," Blake asked, ignoring Sean. "We need something in case we actively need to take someone out, something that we can get through the gates."

"Yes, Sean, you can keep the helmets," Joe smiled. "Blake, absolutely. You'll be carrying the same Sig pistols we gave you earlier. As for the gate, no worries. We'll be bringing you in with one of the ESPN trucks, right into the stadium."

"How did you convince ESPN to work with you without telling them what was actually up?" Blake asked.

"You might be surprised, Blake. We actually do this as standard protocol at most of the big college and professional games, ever since 9/11. We don't advertise it and the networks have gotten pretty used to it, almost like seeing an ambulance pull up to the gate for a big football game. And yes, we also use the ambulance option as well from time to time. And just for added measure, we typically have a half dozen or so federal agents spread throughout the crowd."

"Bet you have to win the lottery to get one of those gigs, eh?" Sean laughed.

"Pretty much," Joe responded, "but there are a lot of games to go around and we do try to spread the wealth."

"That's actually good to know. So how do we know who the good guys and the bad guys are?" Blake asked.

"You guys are easy–that's why we gave you the bright shiny helmets," Joe grinned.

"Smart wrasslin'," Diego grinned back.

"As for the other agents, you'll get to meet them ahead of time, but they're all seat ushers. And for this game, we actually have a couple of agents with some heavy duty gear in a couple of the food booths."

"How about outside the stadium?" Blake continued.

"We have a number of officers at the Great Wolf Lodge, both in front of the building so that they can see anyone that attempts to open a window, as well as two more on the roof. We really doubt they'll attempt the same location, but it was a great spot–knowing what we know now. We have no fewer than six Air Force parking lot attendants that are packing as well."

"How about the mountains?" Blake was still analyzing the setting.

"Two sets of three UH-60 Black Hawk helicopters each will provide alternating air support of the entire area. All six will be armed with standard 7.62mm machine guns and live Hellfire missiles–anyone that opens fire from a secluded position will be dealt with quickly and lethally. We have the top three sharpshooters from Fort Carson stationed at various points on the hills and mountains to the west of the stadium, all in full camo with dual spotters. We have five more Fort Carson canine teams dressed as security personnel stationed strategically around the stadium; they'll be scanning the mountains and wooded venues during the entire game. This way, if they try to lob in shots from the woods, we should still be able to stop them quickly. And to top that off, your Special Forces buddies from Fort Carson will be sitting in Humvees at three pre-determined locations for quick response if the attacking forces are too close to the stadium for the Black Hawks to take out."

"I'm impressed. Seriously, Joe, very impressed. I can't second-guess anything. Looks like we might get to enjoy a football game like we originally planned," Blake stated sincerely.

"For what it's worth, your man Harry already called the office. He seems like a great guy, but he said that if we didn't plan it out to this detail level, you would do it for us. In all fairness, more of this plan is his, than mine," Joe added with a somewhat embarrassed shrug of his shoulders.

"Don't sweat it, Joe; we've been doing things like this for a long time. I'm still impressed that you pulled it off this quickly. Thank you."

"Blake, your light is on," Diego said sternly as he pointed down to Blake's satellite phone on his belt. Blake picked it up and answered.

"Blake here."

He listened intently for a couple of minutes, turning to face the window so no one could see his expression.

"So, it's not an emergency, correct?" Blake asked into the phone. Another minute passed. Diego and Sean exchanged glances. Agent Foster looked clueless.

"We're heading to a football game shortly and it will be late before we get back tonight, assuming everything goes to plan. I'll check back in at 7 a.m. Colorado time tomorrow. Call me back if that's not workable. Thank you."

Blake disconnected the phone, but remained still, looking out the window.

"Blake ... you OK?" Sean asked quietly.

A few long seconds later, Blake turned around, with a smile from ear to ear.

"Spill the beans, Blake," Diego demanded. "What's up?"

"Our long-lost friends just made contact. They want to talk," Blake answered, trying not to give away anything to agent Foster.

"What? You're kidding us, right?" Sean said, almost coming out of his skin.

"Nope. Straight up. More to follow tomorrow, gents, but it appears that not all those who wander are lost."

"J.R.R. Tolkien, 'Lord of the Rings,' right?" Sean questioned.

"'Fellowship of the Ring' to be more specific." Blake answered.

"What are you guys talking about?" Foster interjected, looking totally lost.

"Nothing!" All three men answered simultaneously.

"Sorry, Joe, but it's a totally different topic. I wish we could, but we can't," Blake added as he made a silent zipper motion across his lips.

*****

Del Frisco's Double Eagle Steakhouse, Washington, D.C.

"Callahan is on the ropes. We need to up the ante fast and go for the political knockout while we have the opportunity. If we can't find dirt, then make some up. Pay some tramps to come out of the woodwork and make some outrageous claims. Find some shady loan shark that'll claim he lent him money 20 years ago. Come on, get imaginative. You're getting paid a crap ton of money; start earning it."

"Understood. I'll tell the guys to open up the playbook some more," the other man responded. "But, if you don't mind me asking, what are you doing? Just because you're sitting in the ivory tower doesn't mean you can't take risks like the rest of us. Don't hang it all on my guys."

"You don't think I'm taking any risks? You have no clue. I've got multiple channels I'm working, but my primary focus is to scare the bejesus out of his primary supporters. Trust me, pretty soon they'll think twice before opening their mouths in support of the aliens and Callahan. You work the dirt on him, I'll take care of his base. Without his base, he's done."

*****

USAF Football Stadium

As planned, Blake, Sean and Diego arrived unobserved, riding in an ESPN crew van two hours before game time while the majority of the fan base was still engrossed in tailgate parties that dotted the grassy parking lots.

"This 'ere is friggin' awesome, laddies!" Sean quipped with a heavy brogue.

"It sure is. I've never been to a big game like this before," Diego added.

"Well, that makes three of us, gentlemen," Blake said as he jumped into the conversation. "This has to be as good as it gets. With Pikes Peak and the surrounding tree-covered mountains, it's as beautiful a backdrop as any stadium in the country. Cadets in full dress everywhere you look, in addition to the famous Notre Dame Fighting Irish. Pomp and circumstance to the max by two teams built on honor and tradition–one that stands on commitment and service and the other being one of the most storied college football programs ever." The three men looked out over the stadium, absorbing every view as if they would never see it again, until Blake broke the silence.

"The only thing better would be if Sean was in the Notre Dame mascot suit!" Blake laughed.

"Darn straight, laddies! You guys take him out when he heads to the restroom and I'll slip into his outfit and hit the field!"

"As much as I'd pay money to see that, I'm afraid it would take Notre Dame decades to recover their good name if you did," Diego quipped back.

"Ahh, man! I thought we were friends, no?" Sean acted as if he had lost his best friend. "The heck with y'all, let's go check out the food courts."

"Now that's something we can agree on," Blake responded. "I'm starving. Too. Let's go."

Fifteen minutes later, after checking out their options, Blake grabbed a massive sausage sandwich overflowing with peppers and onions, Sean nailed a Reuben sandwich stuffed with corned beef and Diego corralled a monster burrito. Diego struck up a friendly discussion with the lady behind the counter and when he spoke to her in Spanish, she immediately became awestruck with the handsome Diego.

"Tu comida se ve deliciosa!"

"Espere usted aqui. Tengo algo especial para usted," the lady said as she held her index finger up.

She disappeared into the back and returned proudly holding a homemade tamale that she handed to Diego as she curtsied.

"Gracious, eres un ángel!" Diego bowed deeply and then turned to join his friends.

"You suave Mexican! The game hasn't even started and you already have a girlfriend?" Sean gasped.

"I'm just being polite, you dumb Mick. Maybe you ought to try it some time."

"Don't worry, Diego, I think the world is still safe for the foreseeable future," Blake laughed.

"Hey, Diego, you want that tamale? I love tamales," Sean begged. "Slap some peanut butter on it; that's the bomb!"

"Peanut butter? Are you out of your mind? No good, self-respecting Mexican would ever put peanut butter on a tamale!"

"Hey, if you haven't tried it, don't knock it."

"Ya know, Sean, a friend of mine, TonyG, used to always tell me there was a special place in Hell for gringos like you. I think I finally understand him now."

The three shared a good laugh and continued jabbing at each other until they located an open table to sit down and enjoy their first round of stadium food. Blake topped it off with a round of root beers to wash the food down.

"Sorry, gents. Some good Colorado brew sounded better, but we're on duty so we need to be at the top of our game."

"Ugh, yeah, thanks for the reminder," Sean responded.

"Well, on that point, how about we find our seats and start looking the part of the rabid Air Force fans we're supposed to be?" Diego added.

The game started an hour later. By halftime, it was already turning out to be everything the networks had hoped for. Notre Dame was definitely a powerhouse this year and had already scored 24 points in the first half, but Air Force was still in the game, down by only one touchdown.

Blake's cell phone beeped. "Hello?"

"Blake, it's Joe. Anything of concern there?"

"Nothing here, Joe, but I'm more worried about things from your side of the stadium. Have your guys spotted anything?" Blake countered.

"Nope, pretty quiet so far. How's the game?"

"Worth every penny and every minute. Did you see the B-2 flyover before the game started? That was phenomenal; it was so low I swear you could see panel joints. And those F-22s … ahh, the sound of freedom!"

"Well, keep watching. The halftime show always has a demonstration with their trained falcons. You haven't seen anything until one of those birds whizzes by your head at over 200 miles per hour! Good thing we gave you those helmets, eh?" Joe laughed.

"Yeah, thanks, man. You always have our backs and heads, too, right?" Blake chuckled.

The halftime show was indeed something to remember. Between the marching cadets, the falcon demonstration and the mighty Notre Dame marching band, Blake almost forgot they were there to conduct surveillance, as well as being under surveillance for their own protection. The second half continued the excitement of the first half and although the crowd cheered the home team on, Notre Dame was just too powerful and deep in talent. The final score was Notre Dame 45, Air Force 27.

*****

Sunday, Sept. 16, 2029

At exactly 7 a.m., Blake's Sat phone buzzed.

"Cmdr. Blake Thompson here."

"Cmdr. Thompson, this is Col. Bob Waters, Pentagon. I have a special call for you, and you only. I've been instructed to get your acknowledgement that this is a top secret call and that you will be connected directly with President Callahan once you have ended this call. Is that understood and acceptable?"

"Yes and yes."

"Are you where you can talk alone?"

"Yes."

"Please hold."

Ten seconds passed and Blake heard a couple of clicks suggesting the call was being relayed to him.

"Hello?"

"Thjars? This is Blake."

"Juulys wants to make sure it's you. She wants to know what finger she is holding up and who her favorite person is, a person who really isn't."

"I think I can safely answer that, Thjars. Juulys is holding her thumb upward and she is asking about Roger. Would that be correct?"

Blake smiled, recalling her confusion over Blake's use of the thumbs up sign to acknowledge that all was OK during their rendezvous near Pluto. She'd become further confused when Blake signaled his acknowledgement to the Armstrong I crew by saying "Roger," to which Juulys had replied in fear, "Who is Roger?"

"Thank you, Blake. We had to be sure."

"No problem, Thjars. Say 'hi' for me."

"You just did yourself, I have you on speaker."

"Hello, Blake."

"Hi, Juulys, it's great to hear from you two again. Is everyone OK?"

"Yes, we are fine, for the most part."

"Hmm, what part isn't?" Blake said with mild concern in his voice. "Where are you?"

"We're orbiting Earth at approximately 750,000 kilometers, about twice the distance your moon is from Earth. We are OK, but our ship has a problem."

"The Jarisst I? Is it an emergency?"

"No, but it is a major issue. Are we sure there is no one else on this line?" Thjars interjected.

"To be honest, I would be surprised if we are not being recorded, or that someone high in President Callahan's administration is not listening in right now. I would direct it to be done if I was in his position. As for others, this is a military satellite connection and I feel pretty confident that only the U.S. government has access. Even then, it would be on a need-to-know basis only, and I expect the list of people approved to listen or to review this discussion afterward would be a very small list approved directly by President Callahan himself. Does that help?"

"Yes, it does. Once again, you have demonstrated your honesty, and reinforced why we trusted you. You could have just said 'No one else is on,' but you didn't. Thank you," Juulys replied.

"I had to trust you as well if you recall my one-way spacewalk, as well as the assistance you provided to our crew after our light sail was damaged. It's definitely a two-way street. So what seems to be the problem?"

"The Q-PAMS drive is not working. You replenished our fuel storage, but the system simply won't run."

"Is it on and not working, or dead?"

"Good question, Blake. It comes on, but nothing happens, so we really don't know. As a result, we remain limited to our sub-light speed drives without it."

"Which means you have no way of getting home, correct?"

"Correct," Juulys replied.

"How can I help?"

"This is very hard for us, Blake. We are concerned about protecting the Q-PAMS technology and what could happen if it gets in the wrong hands," Thjars interjected again. "You mentioned your friend, Harry, and many other scientific organizations on Earth that might be able to help. Are those options still available?"

"I'm sure they are, but I can't speak for the United States. In fairness, President Callahan needs to make that decision."

"We anticipated that, Blake; please ask him for us," Thjars responded and then went silent.

"You're quiet, Thjars; is there more?"

"Yes, Blake. I'm not sure how to say this without you taking it wrong."

"Sometimes, it's best to just say it and get it out of the way, so let me try for you," Blake paused. "You're concerned that we will attempt to steal your technology, and worse yet, seize your ship and hold it, possibly even hold you and your crew captive. Am I correct, or at least close?"

Audible gasps could be heard.

"Blake! How could you think that of us?" Juulys responded shocked, and then fell to a whisper. "How did you know?"

"I meant no insult. It's exactly what I would be thinking if our positions were reversed. Like I said, sometimes it's better to just get the issue out in the open."

"OK, but we just weren't ready for it to be stated so bluntly. So, now that you have identified our concern, what do we do?"

"I wish there was a way to guarantee an outcome and provide you with an answer that was 100 percent reassuring, but there isn't. You have a critical problem, and if you want to increase your chances of getting back home, I'm afraid you simply have to trust us. There is no other way. The mere fact that you are asking makes me think you've been trying hard to resolve the problem for the past seven months, but feel it is now out of your ability to resolve. Is that correct?"

"Yes, Blake, exactly," Thjars replied.

"Let me try to ease your fears then," Blake responded. "I promise you that I will put my life on the line to protect you and to protect your freedom. I can also make that same promise for my team members, most of whom you've already talked with or have at least heard of. They will not hesitate to do likewise. I'll remind you that you have seen enough from President Callahan to know he is an honest man. Let me also remind you that he is the leader of the most powerful nation on earth, and he also has the most powerful military in the world–one that will definitely be able to help protect you. To be blunt again, if he had wanted to take your ship and imprison you, couldn't he have accomplished that while you were being refueled at the space dock months ago?"

"We thought about that as well, Blake, but a man can always change his mind when a second opportunity presents itself."

"Fair point, Thjars."

"We know you are honest, Blake, and you've made very valid points. Furthermore, we do trust both you and your President Callahan to hold true to your word, but it doesn't mean this still isn't scary. We are entrusting the top military secret that Cjar has, or had anyway, to a people we really don't know, and to a people that continue to demonstrate their penchant for war and destruction."

"I can't disagree with you, Thjars; that's why it has to be your decision. If it helps, we could arrange for the meeting to occur at the space dock. Harry, myself and perhaps select others from Earth's technical community could fly to the dock to meet with you there. As long as you are in your ship, you have your weaponry available to protect yourselves–if you really felt that was necessary. Think about it, Thjars. You're concerned that we might attempt to take over your ship, but ..." Blake paused. "Shouldn't we be equally concerned that once we've helped fix your ship that you might decide to disable the space dock as a means to protect your technology and escape us forever?"

"Blake! We would never do that!" Juulys expressed in horror.

"I know that, Juulys, but many on Earth's side of the equation do not. I'm trying to make you see that this trust issue is equally large on both sides–just like it was when we met for the first time near Pluto."

"Blake, you speak with great wisdom," Qulys interjected. "I see your point, and I agree. Let us get past this fear, Thjars. Blake, when could Thjars talk to President Callahan with you?"

"I almost hate to interrupt," another voice interrupted their conversation, "but I have to. This is President Callahan."

"What ...?" Thjars stammered.

"Whoa, good morning, sir." Blake added. "Did I break any rules?"

"No, Blake, quite the contrary. I can validate that you and I have not talked for quite some time, yet you predicted everything I would do or say. Thjars, Qulys and Juulys, I apologize for secretly listening in, but I have a duty and a responsibility to protect my people, just like you do yours. I give you my word that I will not do anything without your permission and that the full power of my office and government will be used to ensure your protection and the repair of your ship."

"Thank you, Mr. President, I accept your offer and although you surprised us, I do understand why you were listening in. What do we do now?" Thjars asked.

"Let me work out the details and make sure we are properly set up for your arrival, then I will contact you. I expect I can get back to you later this week. Is that acceptable?"

"Yes, thank you, sir."

"Until then, are you in need of anything, any supplies?"

"No, Mr. President, we are fine. Thank you for asking.

"I look forward to seeing you in person someday, Thjars. Until then, take care."

"Thank you, but thinking further, I would like to make two requests."

"Yes, Thjars, what is it?"

"To ensure continuity, can we request that all communication go directly though Blake, or of course, yourself if desired?"

"Absolutely, consider it done."

"Also, can we limit this first visit to just Blake and Harry, and perhaps select people only from his Armstrong I team? I realize that we may need to bring additional experts in, but I would like to start slowly."

"OK, now it's my turn to support a proposal," Blake interjected for the president. "If our positions were reversed, I would have requested the exact same limitations. President Callahan, I am confident that Harry, myself and a couple of crewmembers from the Armstrong I, and perhaps even a couple from my SEAL team would be adequate to assess potential next step options."

"If you two both find that acceptable, then so do I," President Callahan added.

"Thank you," Thjars answered. "I'm also good with Blake making the proposed selections."

They talked for an additional 15 minutes on various topics including their tour of the solar system, ship status, crewmembers and other topical interests before disconnecting from the Cjarians. Blake stayed on with President Callahan to outline his plan to visit the Cjarians at the space dock. As they finished, President Callahan ended with one final comment.

"Blake, whether you planned on accepting this responsibility or not, the weight of this extraordinary new relationship continues to reside on your shoulders. For what it's worth, I have total faith in you. I just wish I could join you there."

"I believe you do, sir, and I wish you could, too. I'll keep you posted as frequently as I can, Mr. President."

"Thank you, Blake," President Callahan replied and the connection went silent.

Blake called Diego and Sean.

"Pack up, gents. We leave tomorrow for Houston."

*****

Moon Base, Pink Floyd

"The satellite is in position to exchange messages, Dimitri."

"Then send it, Boris."

Two short minutes passed.

"Done. The message has been echoed back, acknowledging it was received, and includes a short response."

"Full power in the new wing has been completed. Lights are on thanks to your recent deliveries. We are now prepared to take on additional visitors. Let me know when you are ready."

Stop.

"Good to hear. Do not give up my friends. I will see you soon. Supplies will be delivered tonight - I.Y."

Stop.

*****

CHAPTER 5

Colorado Springs Airport
Sept. 20, 2029

The time went way too slowly for Blake. He was eager to see the Cjarians again even though he knew it would still be days or even weeks before a launch to the space dock could be readied. In the interim, Blake decided to go to the Houston Space Center to meet up with Harry, Jimmy, Li and Robert to begin preparations for the upcoming visit to review the Q-PAMS. Thjars had still been hesitant to forward any detailed technical information on the Q-PAMS drive, but he'd shared that its overall design integrated an extensive array of quantum physics, antimatter and particle accelerator technologies, about which Harry immediately began reading everything he could get his hands on.

The trio was booked on the 8:15 a.m. American Airlines flight from Colorado Springs to Dallas for the first leg of their trip to Houston. With 40 spare minutes before boarding started, Sean was quick to point out that they had more than ample time to find some grub at the airport. A short time later, they were digging heartily into their breakfasts at the Monte Vista Bar and Grille restaurant, simultaneously enjoying their last sights of scenic Colorado. The panoramic view of the Pikes Peak and Cheyenne Mountains was absolutely magnificent.

"I could definitely handle living in this state," Sean volunteered as he chewed on a slice of bacon and snapped a photo. He then called the waitress over and asked her to take an additional picture of the three of them at the table with the mountains as their backdrop.

"That's a keeper," she said, looking at the phone display. "Have a safe trip today, gentlemen."

The three men thanked her in unison as she handed the phone back to Sean.

Blake looked at his watch: 10 minutes until boarding. They paid their bill, left a healthy tip and headed to their gate. As they walked, Blake reflected on his attempts to make air travel reservations the night before. He had been unable to reserve a single seat on the flight as the Embraer 190 was already overbooked. He researched other options for flights the next day, but every flight to Dallas for the next two days was equally overbooked. Blake texted Frank Pelino, President Callahan's chief of staff, to let him know they were having trouble getting flights and that he was going to look into renting a car if Frank couldn't arrange a military flight. It was a 720-mile drive to Houston, but with three drivers, they could easily cover the distance in less than 12 hours. Frank told Blake to give him 45 minutes to check on other options and then he'd get back to him.

Forty-one minutes later, Frank called back and told Blake they not only had three seats on the morning flight, but they were all booked in first class. Frank chuckled as he shared how he told the CEO of American Airlines that it was a national security issue and directed the executive to notify and reimburse the "unlucky" previous seat owners with a free round trip to Hawaii with two first class tickets–and forward the bill to the White House. One could easily get used to having a travel agent like Frank, Blake mused.

Just then, Blake's phone vibrated.

"Blake, here."

"Blake, it's me, Harry."

"Hi, Harry. We're just getting ready to board, so I only have a couple of minutes. What's up?"

"OK, I'll keep it short, but when you get here, we need to talk about Harley."

"Who?"

"You know, the senator from Arkansas, the one that heads up the Anti-SETI group?"

"Oh, yeah, I remember. Can't say as I like the guy, but then again, I really haven't met him in person yet."

"Well, I have, and I definitely and definitively don't trust the man. We need to talk."

"OK, Harry, we should be there in about six hours, we can talk then. Do you have anything you can send me to read on the plane to give me a head start?"

"I distrust the man enough that I'd prefer not to email you anything. Keep in mind that he also chairs the Senate Armed Services Committee so he has some pretty powerful connections. To be honest, I'm even hesitant about using the phone. We'll talk when you get here," Harry said eerily and disconnected the call.

"You look concerned. What was that all about, Blake?" Diego asked.

"It was Harry. He wants to talk about Sen. Harley, you know the Anti-SETI guy in Congress?"

"Yeah, he's also the head of the Senate Armed Services Committee, a pretty powerful player. But I saw him give a speech once, and I can detect a pontificating, bull-shitting weasel from a mile away. Worthless, pretentious, self-centered hot airbag, if you ask me," Diego added.

"Well, you may be right. Harry wants to talk to us about him as soon as we get to Houston. He's concerned enough that he didn't want to have the discussion on the phone."

"Hmm, that seems like a pretty strong response, especially from Harry," Sean interjected. "Well, they just called our boarding group. Let's get to Houston and see what's bothering Harry."

*****

Six hours later, the trio exited the George Bush Intercontinental Airport in Houston, near the American Airlines baggage claim area in Terminal A, and climbed into Harry's waiting car.

"How was the trip?" Harry asked.

"Pretty uneventful, which is always good with air travel," Blake replied. "Enough with the pleasantries, Harry, we've got, what, an hour's drive to the Space Center? So, what's got you worried?"

"There you go again, Blake! At least you got one whole sentence out this time before you got down to business," Sean chided him.

Blake just smirked and then focused on Harry.

As they drove away from the airport, Harry summarized the meeting at the White House, the heated discussions and the threat made by Sen. Harley.

"I'll be honest, I believe this guy is crooked to the core, and all of his standup BS has nothing to do with the Cjarians; they're just a convenient distraction that he can use as a vehicle to pursue his goals. I've researched him pretty deeply, and it's clear he's spent his life running over people to get where he is. He's so hungry for power that I don't think he would stop for any reason, and I don't think that anything he did, no matter how unscrupulous it was, would surprise me–he's unconscionable. Unfortunately, he's also very smart and charismatic, which makes it highly probable that he may be a true sociopath–definitely not a person you want running the show. If you have something he wants, you'll be his best friend. If you're in the way, he'll run you over. If you're in between, you don't exist. Scary guy."

"If this was the Middle East or Africa, we'd just waste his ass and move on. Seems like an appropriate option," Sean volunteered sarcastically.

"Yes, but unfortunately, as you well know, Sean, this isn't Mogadishu or Fallujah, so we need to figure out how to fight and beat him on his own turf," Blake responded.

"I know, but it's still an option if you change your mind," Sean laughed mischievously.

"So, what are you thinking, Harry?" Blake returned the conversation to Harry.

"I've spent considerable time looking at options, and I'm convinced part of Harley's plan is to force President Callahan to break the news to the country. He wants that so he can immediately use it against the president. Unfortunately, I don't see an alternative because it'll look even worse if he brings it up first and puts President Callahan on the defensive for hiding worldwide-critical information."

"Is he looking to create panic?" Blake asked.

"I wondered about that as well, and I still think that idea has merit, but regardless of who brings it up first, it will still have the same impact on most people's emotional reactions."

"Fair point. Other thoughts?"

"How about we hack his computer and see what he's really up to?" Sean challenged.

"Actually, I've been leaning toward that as well," Harry answered.

"Whoa! The righteous Harry? You want to hack a senator's computer?"

"Yes, actually, his home wireless system because that will allow us to pick up on both his computer and phone discussions."

"Now you're talking, Harry!"

"Hang on guys, before we attempt anything like that, I need to talk to President Callahan. If the news ever leaked out that we illegally hacked Sen. Harley's house, he'd have the Senate demanding impeachment for President Callahan, and jail for us."

"Details, details. I'll bet Li can get in there without anyone ever knowing," Sean challenged.

"You're likely right, Sean, but if you're wrong, we could end up putting President Callahan at great risk without his knowledge or concurrence, so the answer is 'no,' at least until I talk to him," Blake responded.

"OK, OK, I'll back off, but … what? Did you just say you agreed?"

"Yes, I did," Blake answered with an acknowledging smirk.

"I'm not playing Debbie Downer here, but I'm pretty sure he won't go for it," Harry interjected. "We tried to talk him into getting some dirt on Harley after the meeting and he wanted nothing to do with it. He wants to stay in the Mr. Clean arena."

"Fair point, Harry, but I think I can convince him that this is for a different purpose. There's dirt, and then there's threatening the president–that's a federal felony, correct?"

"Correct, U.S. Code Title 18, Section 871, I believe," Harry replied.

"I'll take your word for that, Harry. Furthermore, this may not constitute something as grievous as an all-out war, but threatening the president is the same as threatening the country. Think about how aggressive the government comes down on people who threaten the country by breaking the Espionage Act–the U.S. government doesn't have much patience for things like that. President Callahan may be more open to a covert operation from that perspective."

"I like it, Blake, especially if you tell him that under no circumstances will Harley's personal information be disclosed, only potential illegal activities–assuming any are found."

"Sounds good, Harry, let's get our favorite hack, Li, and maybe even Robert working on preparations so that they can start as soon as we get a green light. Are they at the Space Center right now?"

"Actually, Li is, but Robert won't be. We'll see him later tonight, much later."

"Where's he at?"

"You'll love this one. Somehow, our good friend Robert has managed to get a date with one of the sorority queens at the University of Houston and they have a dinner date tonight at the Richmond Arms Pub."

"I like his style!" Sean piped in. "She's a keeper if she likes a good pub. Maybe we can quietly stop by and see how he's doing, you know kind of like make sure we think she's good enough for our Robert?"

"Patty would smack you right upside the head if she were here right now, but she's not, so count me in!" Diego said. "How about you Blake?"

"Well, we all need to eat, soooo ... what time, Harry?"

"Six-thirty. It's almost six o'clock right now, so it'll be tight, but we can make it while he's still there. It's about a 40-minute drive from the hotel. You're staying at the TownePlace Suites with the rest of us. We'll drop your stuff off at the hotel, clean up, head out by 6:30 and be there by 7:15."

"Sounds like a plan. It'll be great to see him."

Blake had really taken a liking to the young man. Actually, the entire SEAL team equally liked him; he was like their own adopted kid.

*****

Richmond Arms Pub, Houston

The Richmond Arms Pub was only 15 minutes from the University of Houston, less than a quarter of a mile north of the intersection of Fountain View Drive and Interstate 69, and almost directly across the street from Dave & Buster's and the Prospect Park Sports Pub, an area where college students frequented.

"Seven-fifteen on the spot! Harry, you da man!" Sean said as he exited the car and headed to the pub's front door. He walked through the door and clapped his hands.

"It's a good thing Sir Oliver isn't with us, 'cause I like this place already–even if it is a bloody English pub. Sure as 'ell couldn't admit that to 'im, now could I?"

"And check it out, the EPL is on the main screen!" Blake exclaimed. "Robert's been holding out on us. Liverpool versus Manchester United, live from New York City."

"There's our young man now," Diego stated, pointing to a small table to the back, left of the bar. Looks like he has a few friends with him, too."

"Those are some pretty big boys," Sean added.

"Somehow, I don't think they are friends," Harry stated frankly.

"I think you may be right, Harry," Blake said and started to walk casually toward Robert, with Harry in tow. "Get us four pints of Guinness, Sean."

"Aye, aye, Chief." Sean winked at Diego, "This should be entertaining."

Robert was facing the opposite direction, his attention totally consumed by the three larger-than-average guys flanking his table.

Blake stationed himself in a position where he could watch the game and still overhear the discussion at Robert's table. Sean and Diego walked over with four pints of Guinness and handed one each to Blake and Harry. Harry walked over to an older couple at a table just behind Robert and politely interrupted their discussion.

"Excuse me. So sorry to bother you on your night out, but there's a high probability that the group discussion at the table behind you may get ugly shortly. I recommend you move to the other side of the room and as soon as it's over, I promise this table will remain yours."

The couple quickly got up and moved over to the bar. Sean told Harry that he had alerted the bartender when he bought the beers and also showed him the FBI card Joe had given him.

"I told him we had followed a drug bust suspect here and that we would make sure everyone stayed safe. He said thanks; the beers are on the house." Sean smiled from ear to ear, raised his beer toward Harry and clinked his glass with Diego. Blake continued to watch the game, apparently uninterested in anything else going on in the pub.

"Look, Einstein, I told you to stay away from my girl. You don't seem to understand English, so do I have to put it into a mathematical equation for you, or should I just drag your ass outside and beat it into you?"

"Come on, Brandon, we just came here to enjoy dinner and watch the football game. Please leave us alone," Robert said calmly as he tried to avoid any further embarrassment in front of his date.

"First off, *we* play real football, not that crybaby stuff you call soccer, so knock off calling it football, got it? Now for the last time, she stays here, but you leave, and pronto!" The man in the middle, Brandon, was clearly the main antagonist and he clenched Robert's shoulder, hard. Robert cringed in pain. Blake put his beer down, walked over to the table and placed his right hand on the back of the man's neck and squeezed firmly.

"Hi, Robert. Good to see you. Young lady, pleasure meeting you. Gentlemen, I'm the new bouncer, and I'm asking you to depart now, or should I say *pronto*?"

"Bouncer my ass, who the hell are you?"

"What we have here is a failure to communicate," Sean said with a faked southern drawl as he pulled out a chair and sat down.

"'Cool Hand Luke,' before my time, but I believe the late Sixties," Harry answered without even looking at Sean.

"Correct you are, Master Harry," Sean acknowledged and reached over to knuckle-rap Harry.

"Looks like the show is about to begin, gents!" Diego raised his beer glass, one at a time with Harry and Sean. The man named Brandon looked over at Blake and scowled confidently.

"Sure, the four of you against the three of us?"

"No," Sean answered for Blake, "just him. We're here for the show. But I'm warning you, that hand on the back of your neck … well, it comes with the strongest grip I've ever seen and it's at least as big as Larry Bird's.

"But, I transgress, and you've now been forewarned, so, carry on my good lad," Sean added as he waved his hand in a supportive movement to continue.

"They never learn, do they, Harry?" Diego said.

"Nope, brains are just too small. Too dumb to know when to run."

"Who the f–," was all he was able to get out before Blake's vice-like, oversized right hand clamped down hard on his neck, while his index and middle fingers pushed deeply into his neck, just next to his Adam's apple. As the man began to sink down to his knees, his friend to the right started moving closer to help his buddy out.

"Don't do it, son," Blake said calmly, but the second man didn't listen and started moving around the chair to get to Blake. Blake waited until the man was within striking range, pulled his right hand downward to his lower right, still holding Brandon's neck in his grasp, and struck out a fierce left-hand jab to the oncoming assailant, instantly breaking his nose and dropping him to his knees.

Tables squawked and chairs fell over as nearby people attempted to flee the unexpected commotion.

"Six o'clock, Blake," Harry said as calmly as he was reading the time on a clock. Without looking, Blake spun quickly to his left, with his now retreating left jab coiled into a deadly elbow-first reverse rotation that caught the third member of the uninvited trio squarely in the chin. Lights out as he fell to the ground.

"Oooh, that's gonna hurt!" Sean laughed out loud and sat back in his chair, readying himself to catch the falling attacker. Blake then refocused on the man in his right hand.

"So, my newfound friend, talk. Name and background, or I tighten my grip even more."

"I'd talk quickly bro; this man has a nasty temper when someone causes him to miss his favorite *football* game," Sean chided Brandon, with extra emphasis on the word football.

"Brandon … Brandon Talley … football player at the University of Houston."

"Thank you, much appreciated," Blake replied and looked over at Robert and his date. "I'm so sorry, Robert, I didn't even make an introduction." Blake quickly changed hands on his captive, who remained kneeling on the floor. He shook Robert's hand and then turned to his date.

"Hi, name is Blake, Blake Thompson, a good friend of Robert, and these three are some of his other friends: Harry, Diego and Sean."

"Hi."

"Hello."

"Nice to meet you, Miss. We'll have to straighten young Robert out for not telling us about you, but first we need to get some ice for these two guys." Sean whistled over to the bartender to bring some ice.

"I'm Sara, Sara McClellan. Nice to meet you, too. To be honest, Robert has told me so much about each of you that I feel like I know you already."

"Hopefully, we didn't disappoint," Blake smiled.

"Absolutely not. I actually thought Robert was exaggerating, but clearly he was not."

"Glad to hear it. One more thing," Blake looked back down at the individual still firmly attached to his left hand.

"You owe my friends an apology, and it'd better be sincere."

"Sorry … I apologize," he paused, "Are my other friends OK?"

"They'll be fine, albeit they might be sporting some nasty marks for a few days. Fellow football players?"

"Yes, sir."

"Hmm. They might miss a game or two. What positions do you guys play?

"George, the one you punched in the nose is our center. Roger, the one you elbowed is a running back. I'm a tight end. Sara is, sorry, *was* my girlfriend."

"Interesting," Blake replied, still maintaining his grip. "Well, if you consider what you guys were trying to do tonight as some crazy show of manhood, I hate to break it to you, but you failed miserably. It also suggests that if that's how you handle things, then perhaps Sara made two good decisions: one to break it off with you and another to start spending time with Robert. Do you agree?"

"Seems that way, sir."

"Well, you are talking a little more respectfully now. You won't try to give me any more trouble if I let go of your neck, will you?"

"No, sir. I may be stupid at times, but I'm not that dumb, sir."

"Good man, maybe I read you wrong and there is still a spark of hope in you." Blake released his grip and Brandon began to rub his now very sore and red neck. "I have a proposal for you. How about you, your two friends and I meet tomorrow morning with your football coach and the chancellor for a short meeting? You toe the line and I'll make sure there are no charges and that the coach lets the three of you keep playing. That sound fair?"

"More than fair, sir."

"You keep saying 'sir.' Is there a chance you hail from a military family?"

"Yes, sir. My dad is a career Army man."

"That explains a lot. I expect he might not be too happy to hear about tonight's escapade then—would that be correct?"

"Yes, sir, 100 percent. He'd kick my ass 10 times over. I'll do whatever you want me to do; just please keep my dad out of this."

"I'm beginning to like your family, Brandon," Blake smiled and patted him on the back. "It looks like we have a deal."

"Diego, Sean … how about you help these three gentlemen to their car?"

"Sure thing, boss," Diego replied.

"We'll try to make sure they don't trip and fall again," Sean laughed and then turned to Diego. "See, I was spot on in Colorado about Blake being overdue for a brawl after all that time in space, that's two already! This trip may turn out to be even better than we expected, but Blake sure as heck better let me in on the next one. I'm getting tired of sitting on the sidelines."

"I'm sure you'll get your chance, Sean," Diego chuckled.

Sean and Diego helped the three would-be attackers out the front door just as Harry returned with the two patrons that he had warned away from the table behind Robert.

"We'd be happy to buy you dinner and drinks for any disruption we caused you tonight," Harry said as he held out the chair for the man's wife.

"Thank you, but that's OK, as long as everything is over now," the man replied. "Thanks again for the heads up before all hell broke out."

"You're welcome. Just trying to keep everyone safe," Harry responded.

"Blake, your timing was amazing, and I didn't even know you guys were in town. Brandon has threatened me before and I wasn't sure how far he was going to take it tonight. Brandon and Sara dated for two years before she broke it off and he obviously hasn't gotten over it yet. Thanks again."

"No problem, Robert, glad we could help. I'm pretty confident this may be the last time you have any issues with Brandon. You two enjoy your dinner; we'll finish our beers, have some chow and head out. Sara, again, my pleasure–looking forward to seeing you again."

*****

University of Houston, Chancellor's Office
Sept. 21, 2029

It was 8:50 in the morning and Blake was sitting in the chancellor's office with the chancellor and the head football coach, Claude Coleman. As they waited for the three football players to show up in a few minutes for their requested appointment time, the trio reviewed Robert's and Brandon's history at the university, and then ended with Blake's first-hand description of last night's escapade.

Five minutes later, Brandon, George and Roger showed up, looking quite timid–very different from how they had appeared when Blake first encountered them–as well as sporting the visible marks of their encounter with Blake.

"Gentlemen," Coach Coleman opened the discussion. "How about I hear it directly from you? I understand that you guys were threatening to do physical harm to one of our honor students, although looking at you now, I'm beginning to question who kicked whose butt. Brandon, you can start."

Blake liked the coach's style, no bull crap, straight to it.

"Yes, sir, and it's my fault." Brandon went on to describe last night's incident, in full detail. He apologized multiple times and promised it wouldn't happen again.

The chancellor was the first to speak when he finished.

"Do you realize I could have you expelled from school, Brandon?"

"Yes, ma'am."

"Do you realize there are multiple school codes that should force Coach Coleman to consider kicking you off the team?"

"Yes, ma'am."

"Well, what do you suggest we do?"

"I don't know, ma'am. Let Roger and George go; this was my doing. I really want to keep playing football, but I will do anything to keep from getting expelled–my dad would kill me."

"Roger, George … any comments from the peanut gallery?" The chancellor wasn't done with them yet, either.

"No, ma'am, we're sorry," they said in unison. "It won't happen again."

"Hmm. Well, Cmdr. Thompson has an interesting proposal for you then, and it's one that I think you may find quite attractive. Coach Coleman also found it acceptable, but I'm telling you this straight up: if anything like this happens again, you're out and I mean out fast. Understood?"

"Yes, ma'am."

"OK, here's what you're signing up to–and most of this is Blake's idea, but I like it, too. First, you have to talk to the entire team and explain what happened and why you or they should never attempt something like this again. Secondly, you will spend five hours per week at the YMCA as big brothers–for the rest of the year. Thirdly, you can still play football, but you lose your starting positions. Fourth, you are now Robert's bodyguards; anything happens to him, my first phone call is to Cmdr. Thompson so he can come visit you again. If you agree to the terms, you can remain in school with no formal report and we'll keep this just between us–that means no parents involved. Is this acceptable?"

"Yes, ma'am. You have our word. Thank you," Brandon responded with a spark of relief showing.

"Glad to hear it. One more thing, Brandon."

"Yes, ma'am?"

"The next time you find your emotions getting out of control, try to remember what just happened, and realize that you won't always know the playing field you walked onto. This time, you ran into a formidable competitor, one who also happens to be a commander in the U.S. Space Forces and was previously a U.S. Navy SEAL. Maybe it was bad luck, but regardless, this wasn't one of the most intelligent decisions I've ever seen, would you disagree?"

"No, ma'am."

"Actually, on second thought, maybe it really was a stroke of good luck that you ran into Cmdr. Thompson so that he could teach you a lesson that stops the three of you from doing worse in the future. Yes, that's it, perhaps I should refer to last night as a spontaneous and fortuitous real-life learning opportunity–something we can't teach in the classroom, but still something I would be happy to know that your University of Houston experience helped shape you with." The Chancellor eyed the three young men intently and smiled while she tapped her fingers on the table–clearly not a smile of contentment. She looked at Blake and then at Coach Coleman. "Coach Coleman, anything else?"

"No, just get your worthless asses to practice, and you'd better not be late. George, Roger, you two are excused from drills until you heal, but you'll still support your team in person, in full gear, for all team activities. Brandon, seeing as you got off the luckiest, you'd better play every down as if it's your last and I'll make sure I tell our other coaches that you volunteered for wind sprints after every practice for the next two weeks. Now get the hell out of here before I change my mind!"

The three football players stood up awkwardly and excused themselves. Just as the door was about to shut, Brandon turned and came back to face Blake and extended his right hand.

"Thank you, sir. I won't let you down."

Blake accepted his handshake, looking him straight in his eyes, and was quiet as he held a firm grip on the young man's hand.

"Brandon, by the look I see in your eyes, I believe you. For what it's worth, we all learn best by our bad decisions–so make the most of it, and if you really want to seal the deal, you know what else you need to do, correct?"

Brandon's body tensed, but his eyes never dropped.

"Yes … yes, sir, I do. I'll talk to him, face-to-face when I get home."

Blake borrowed a Post-It pad and a pen from the chancellor's desk and scrawled his name, rank and cell phone number on a sheet and handed it to Brandon.

"Trust me, son, I expect he will take it way better with you telling him, rather than the chancellor. Hand him this and tell him to feel free to call me."

Blake shook hands with Brandon again, turned and thanked both the chancellor and Coach Coleman, then left for the Houston Space Center to meet up with Robert, Li and the rest of the gang.

*****

Li, Jimmy and Robert were in a corner of a conference room at the Houston Space Center, banging away on their laptops, integrating hardware and developing specialized algorithms and subroutines in preparation for the potential approval to hack Sen. Harley's home. They didn't even notice when Blake entered the room and started talking with Diego.

"Those hackers are so intent on their computers that even if the room was filled with smoke and the fire alarm sounded, I'm not sure they'd notice." Blake laughed.

"If you cut their power and zapped their batteries, you might get a reaction, but it might still take a minute or two for their brains to register the disturbance," Diego responded as he shook his head in dismay.

"How was your meeting?"

"Actually, better than I thought. I'm pretty confident that Robert has nothing to worry about any more, and that Brandon might just have a new outlook on life."

"Somehow that doesn't surprise me. Good for you, Chief." Diego smiled knowingly. "So what's next?"

Blake pulled Harry and Sean into the conversation with Diego and reviewed the latest launch schedule with them. Foremost on Blake's action item list was the finalization of team members who would initially board the Jarisst I.

"We leave in three days, so we need to pack and head out to the atoll tomorrow," Blake summarized. "All four of us are going. I've also asked Patty to consider coming out of temporary retirement to spend time with Juulys. That makes five, and with the Night Star pilot, six. We can take two more as Sean has been cleared to be the co-pilot. Harry, you and Jimmy are our science core, so I think we should take Jimmy–that makes seven. Who else should we consider that might help you on the spaceship's drive, as well as be approved for spaceflight in such a short time?"

"That's a pretty small database, Blake," Harry replied.

"I agree. Matter of fact, I came up with a list of one," Blake looked at Harry. "I really didn't want to include the Russians on this trip, but Vladimir is space-worthy and I think he is a legitimate technical candidate with his chemical engineering and rocket knowledge."

"It's a pretty simple decision based on the timeframe, his familiarity with our mission, and his background. I agree, Blake."

"OK, thanks, Harry. I'll get word to President Callahan, and assuming his concurrence, I'll call our good friend Vladimir Popov."

"Just make sure you tell him to bring some more of his Russian vodka." Sean laughed.

*****

One hour later, with President Callahan's concurrence, Blake dialed his phone and waited. After four rings, a click and a voice.

"Hello?"

"Vladimir! Hello. How is my favorite comrade?"

"Blake? Is it really you? Hello! It has been much too long for old friends to talk, da? I am very good. Mother Russia granted me a long vacation. I have not fished this much in my entire life!" Vladimir chuckled. "And how are you, my good friend?"

"Yes, it has been much too long, Vladimir, but I'm still vertical and breathing," Blake responded. Truth was, Blake actually missed his new Russian ally.

"That is good to hear, but you should come fishing with me. Not only can I show you the beauty of my country, and some areas that you have never seen or heard of, but I can also show you how to relax and enjoy life. You work too hard, my friend; you need to take time to unwind and appreciate the simpler things in life."

"Sounds like you've been talking to our Irish friend, Mr. Sean."

"No, but it sounds like he may be smarter than you think. Let me show you how to relax."

"I'm sure you could, Vladimir, and I am quite sure I would enjoy it. Perhaps you will give me the honor of a rain check," Blake added sincerely. "As it turns out, I actually *am* interested in experiencing one of your country's other great treasures."

"Da?" The curiosity clearly present in Vladimir's voice. "And what treasure might that be?"

"How's your vodka supply doing?" Blake asked the single question that they had previously agreed would alert Vladimir that Blake needed to see him in person.

"Ahh, now that is an interesting question. Does that mean you are finally ready to forgo your watered-down American whiskey in favor of my superior Russian vodka?"

"Perhaps, Vladimir," Blake chuckled. "I must admit, your country does have its finer points,"

"I assume you must have a very important engagement, da?"

"You never miss a beat, Vladimir; I most certainly do have such a gathering."

"Well then, I would be most honored to provide your guests with something special from Mother Russia. Let me check my supplies and get back to you," Vladimir answered, and in so doing, also acknowledged that he would return the call from a more protected system. "How quickly do you need the delivery?"

"I am definitely pressuring our friendship, Vladimir, and for that, I apologize in advance, but I need it within 72 hours."

"Seventy-two hours? That will indeed be a challenge! I am not even sure I can get back to my home in time to answer your question."

"Unfortunately, I had no idea that the opportunity would present itself until now. It was pure happenstance, but it is an event of extreme personal value to me and to my family. There is no other beverage in the world that I would prefer to toast with. I would even be willing to fly you here to meet with my family if that is possible." Blake hoped Vladimir would pick up on his hints without giving anything away on a line that was very likely tapped by the Russians.

"You are a tough negotiator, Cmdr. Blake, but I must admit, you have piqued my interest. Your family is my family, da? I am humbled that my Russian vodka is being considered. Let me see what I can do and call you back tomorrow."

"Thank you, Vladimir. I'm looking forward to seeing you again–we have a lot to catch up on and I can already taste that royal fluid." Blake smiled at his phone as he disconnected. Vladimir was one sharp, cool customer and Blake was quite confident Vladimir would find a way to accept his invitation now.

*****

Sept. 22, 2029

It was late Saturday night and the man placed a call on his cell phone. The phone was a prepaid, untraceable Kyocera model that had been purchased at the Briarcliffe, Pa., Walmart store, on the outskirts of Philadelphia.

"All you have to do is arrange for a blown tire, just to send a message. Can you handle that?"

"Of course I can, but there are many ways to do it. If you want it to occur at an exact location, then there are only three ways to do it: shoot it out, attach a blowout device to the car, or lace the road with spikes. The first is the cleanest, but also the most dangerous as it requires a man on location and also leaves a distinctive sound that many people can identify. The second works like a charm, but requires access to the car, which is a risk in itself, and also leaves hard evidence behind. The third might miss the target car, or hit the wrong car. Do you have a preference?"

"Shoot it out; just make sure there are no witnesses. My information suggests he will be traveling soon, so I'll send you a verification message once I'm confident he's on the way. If the blown tire doesn't get him, the message will. No comments to anyone else. Understood?"

"Understood. When do I get paid?"

"Just like before, 35 percent will be deposited upfront tonight. The other 65 will be deposited after you complete the requested transaction. Don't screw it up."

The call ended.

*****

CHAPTER 6

The Johnston Atoll
Sept. 24, 2029

The days passed before the team assembled at the Johnston Atoll, but it had surprisingly only required 36 hours for Vladimir to arrive in Houston and join the team at the atoll. The first thing Blake did after shaking Vladimir's hand in Houston was to request his cell phone, which he immediately exchanged for a new untraceable phone. Blake then turned off Vladimir's private phone and placed it into a steel box under lock and key.

"Sorry, Vladimir, but where we're going, I must eliminate all possibility of anyone eavesdropping on us or tracking your location. I also need you to validate that you don't have any electronic implants in your body."

"You are not smiling, Blake, so I know you are serious–and that makes me even more interested to know why you have invited me. I have a wild suspicion of what it may be, but before I say anything more, I will answer your question. I am clean–no implants of any kind. However, I suggest you consider conducting a body scan to prove it–one never knows what may happen when one is asleep, da?"

"All too correct, Vladimir. And thank you for recommending it so I didn't have to ask."

"Somehow I am confident that you would do the same if our positions were reversed." Vladimir smiled and extended his hand one more time.

The two men shook hands with a grip that said more than words could convey.

Two hours later, with a clean bill of health from the U.S. government, Vladimir walked through the door and into the waiting room where Blake was waiting for him.

"I have one more surprise for you before I tell you why you are really here."

"The anticipation is killing me, Blake, but I am sure you have your reasons."

"Always do," Blake smiled mischievously. "I'd like to introduce you to someone else who just arrived." Blake pointed to a second door that opened on cue.

"Cmdr. Thompson, I am truly honored now. If my eyes do not deceive me, this is the one and only Patty Myers. She was on extended leave, am I not correct?"

"Yes, you are correct, on both accounts," Patty answered for Blake as she crossed the room to meet the smiling Vladimir. "It is a pleasure to see you again, Vladimir. It seems our mutual friend has pulled out all the stops to get us back here. I can only imagine one topic that could possibly justify this." She gave Vladimir a hug and then turned to face Blake.

"So, Blake, when are you going to tell us?"

"Miss Patty, you are as beautiful as ever," Vladimir bowed and then looked at Blake.

"She wastes no time getting to the point, Blake, a skill I suspect she learned from you, and is now applying it back to her teacher. Regardless, I agree, it is now time to talk, or as you Americans say: it's time to spill the beans and put your cards on the table! What has caused you to call us together, my good friend?"

"Ten more minutes and you will know. Follow me," Blake commanded with a smile, turned and headed for the exit.

"After you, Miss Patty." Vladimir bowed again and signaled for Patty to go first. "It appears our Cmdr. Blake is trying to torture us. It is hard to believe that I once called him a friend, da?"

"It'd better be good, or I will take him down for you, Vladimir," Patty replied with a twinkle.

Ten minutes later, as promised, Blake beckoned Vladimir and Patty to enter a room buried deep within the atoll. The trio was immediately met by four other men and one woman. The men were all very recognizable; the woman was new.

"Harry!" Patty squealed in delight and ran to give him a hug. "Diego! Jimmy! Sean!" She hugged each, lingering longer with Sean. "It is so good to see you all."

"Stop it, Patty! Before I start crying," Sean mimed a tear.

"Ha, I thought you didn't care, you rambling Irishman." Patty winked. "I missed you," she whispered to Sean.

"Vladimir!" Diego stuck his hand out to greet his Russian friend, then pulled it back. "Wait, you'd better have some of that Russian vodka with you or I'm calling ICE!"

"Da, da, da … 'friends' my Russian backend! Now I see your true American colors–no vodka and you're already threatening to throw me to the wolves! You Americans are all the same; you just want my country for our natural wonders–and vodka!" The group laughed and started catching up with each other's activities from the past few months–until Vladimir remembered the unknown lady in the room.

"So, who is this lady who stays so quiet in the back of the room? NSA? CIA? Does she not trust me either? I've had body searches and scans, filled out forms in triplicate and answered more questions to more people than I can remember–I say I am clean!" Vladimir feigned sincere emotional stress.

"Must you be so theatrical, Vladimir?" Blake answered, laughing. "Vladimir, meet Cmdr. Rachel Joslin. She's our new pilot."

"My pleasure, Miss Rachel," Vladimir bowed. "Pilot?" he asked as he looked back at Blake. "I cannot stomach the suspense any longer. We're at a launch site we all know well. You have summoned me here to meet your 'family,' and we have a pilot. Blake, please do not disappoint me … I am afraid to speculate further for fear of the disappointment if I am wrong."

"Yes, Vladimir, the time for waiting has passed," Blake said as he walked between Patty and Vladimir, placing an arm around each of them.

"The Cjarians have requested our presence. The eight of us, plus possibly one more, will meet them at the space dock as soon as we can complete our prelaunch health checks and load the Night Star."

*****

Jarisst I

Thjars was agitated. He knew that asking Blake for help was the right answer, actually the only answer, but it didn't stop him from second-guessing himself. The stakes were monumental. Assuming Cjar was even still in existence, he was in jeopardy of going down as the biggest disgrace in Cjarian history for compromising the Jarisst's secrets to an unknown, immature civilization. But what else was he supposed to do? The only other option, without Earth's assistance, resulted in the high probability that they would remain in this solar system, condemned to live out the remainder of their lives within the confines of their ship.

Thjars wished Capt. Zyles Blissiart were still alive so someone who he felt had the appropriate experience could make a decision of this magnitude. Zyles would have known what to do. Who else–Juulys? This really wasn't her charter, but she was a good sounding board … Jarns? No, he was way too inexperienced. Who else? Qulys? … Qulys … Yes! Qulys was perfect. Thjars immediately reached for the mic.

"Qulys, are you available? Where are you?" Thjars called his trusted ally over the com.

"Yes, sir. I'm in the Q-PAMS drive section with Jarns."

"Can you break free and come up to the control room?"

"Yes, sir. Can you give me about 15 minutes?"

"That will work and bring Juulys with you. Thank you, Qulys."

Thjars was still stewing. Maybe it would help if he spent time discussing plans with his trusted friends, especially Qulys, as his sergeant-at-arms was the epitome of strength and control–and Thjars knew he needed some of that right now. Thjars couldn't recall *ever* seeing Qulys unnerved, no matter what they had been up against.

Fifteen minutes later, as promised, Qulys arrived, with Juulys in tow.

"Hello, sir, what can we do for you?" Qulys asked respectfully.

"Qulys, I'm convinced we did the right thing, asking Blake to help us, but to be honest, it's driving me crazy. I feel like I'm betraying Cjar and everyone we ever knew."

"Are you changing your mind, sir?" Qulys asked.

"No, definitely not, but that hasn't stopped me from worrying about it."

"We understand, Thjars; what can we do to help?" Juulys asked.

"I think I would feel better if we strategized a few possible outcomes and then brainstormed what we should do to protect the ship in case our worst fears are realized," Thjars responded.

"That makes sense to me, Thjars," Qulys responded. "So what are you thinking?"

"I don't know, Qulys, to be honest, I'm not even sure where to start."

"Hmm … OK, how about this … let's start with what worries you the most?"

Thjars looked out through the control room window into the quiet expanses of space for a few seconds before responding.

"I know I trust Blake, but … he is not the ultimate ruler of the planet. He isn't even the ruler of his own country. What if their President Callahan really does want the ship and all of this has just been one big masquerade, waiting for us to lower our guard so that he could steal the ship and its technological secrets?"

"So you still don't fully trust *them*; is that a fair conclusion, sir?"

Thjars paused and then answered, sounding somewhat embarrassed.

"Yes, I believe you are correct, Qulys. It's not Blake I distrust; it's all of the unknown people and organizations across their world I don't know and therefore can't trust."

"I understand, sir. So let's simplify it then. Let's just assume that they will wait for us to let our guard down and then attack. In that case, we know they aren't going to destroy the ship, because that would defeat their goal, so the ship is basically safe."

"So, it's us …"

"Correct. Therefore, we can downsize the issue a bit, we just need to know how to protect ourselves."

"Qulys, are you recommending we carry guns?" Juulys responded with consternation.

"That is a legitimate option, but it isn't the only option, Juulys. It depends on what message Thjars wants to send, and what response he expects to elicit."

"I think I see where you're going, Qulys, please continue," Thjars interjected.

"If we show up with guns, then they'll likely feel that they need to carry guns. Then you'll have everyone with itchy trigger fingers, but worse yet, everyone is thinking the other side doesn't trust them, so no one will trust anyone. That's a highly dangerous environment."

"Great point, Qulys. For what it's worth, this discussion is definitely helping me," Thjars volunteered. "I don't want to alarm them, so I would prefer we do *not* carry arms to our first meeting, but how do we protect ourselves then?"

"We'll use the ship to protect us, sir. Knarls and I could remain locked in the weapons bay with our main cannon trained on their space dock. Anything of concern comes up and you can put a stop to everything and tell them to leave or we'll open fire on the dock. That space dock is their crown jewel right now and I highly doubt that they would want to risk that station in a fight. We then escort them off the ship, depart and reassess."

"And kill people on their dock? We can't do that, Thjars! Qulys, how could you?" Juulys shouted in dismay.

"Calm down, Juulys," Qulys put his hand gently on her shoulder. "I have no intention of firing on them–unless they want to start a fight. In that case, they clearly wouldn't be who you are hoping they are. If your intuitions are correct, then there is nothing to worry about."

"Juulys, don't worry, I understand what Qulys is trying to say. I promise you that we will not be the one who crosses that line first. If they do, then we must defend ourselves.

"Qulys, this is just what I needed, thank you. But what if they send a boarding party and take me, or others hostage?"

Juulys had a look of horror on her face, but Qulys was smiling.

"Thjars, now you are thinking like a captain. That's a good question, and a truly viable possibility. My recommendation is that before we even arrive at the dock, you let Blake know our plan so there are no surprises. You tell him that you would like to restrict the initial visit to just him and maybe one or two of his team, at least until we get a better read on their plans. Perhaps just Blake and his friend, Harry. We'll let Blake know that we plan on closing all access to the ship once he is on board. In that manner, we can reduce the risk of additional personnel boarding the ship, or having anyone taking an unguided, unapproved tour of the ship. Prior to entering our ship, we'll ask them to remove their suits in our docking bay. I'll personally search them and their suits for any weapons before we allow them to enter the main ship. Once cleared, they can suit up again and I'll return to the weapons bay with Knarls. If they attempt anything at all, I can either join up with you or we can shoot a warning shot across their space dock. Does that help?"

"Yes ... yes, it really does, Qulys. Thank you. Again, I trust Blake, and even his close friends–it's the ones I don't know that I *can't* afford to trust yet–for the first time, I now know specifically what has been bothering me so much. By limiting the visitors, inspecting them and sharing upfront our plans to have our weapons bay live as protection, I agree we can protect the ship better. I pray to Glysst that we never need the battle cannon."

"I agree, sir, but I won't hesitate to use it if you or the ship is attacked." Both men were quiet for a few long seconds.

"What else bothers you, sir?"

"To be honest, as long as we take this one step at a time, and we talk through my concerns prior to each new step, I think I'm OK. I will contact Blake and let him know. Thanks again, Qulys. Juulys, thank you, too–are you OK with our plan?"

"Yes, I'm OK, but I'm not sure I really helped, other than to provide moral support. I will support whatever you two decide is best," Juulys added with a warm smile.

"You're welcome, sir," Qulys added. "Now, unless you have something else, I need to get back to help Jarns with the Q-PAMS."

Qulys turned to depart and was smiling as he headed for the engine room.

*****

**White House
Pro-SETI Meeting**

"Harry, are you on?"

"Yes, Mr. President, I'm here."

"Good, I have Gen. McMullen, Vice President Annie Murphy, Ben Tellinino, Frank Pelino, Sen. Ronnie Dempsey and the other Pro-SETI members here with me. I want to cover three things. First, Harry's recommendation on how to handle Sen. Harley, secondly, Gen. McMullen's review of his staff risks and finally, new items that any of you may have. Harry, you're up."

"I've chewed on it a bit, sir, and I've even bounced it off Blake. We both think that there really aren't any options. If he releases the information before we do, it could make you look like you were actually hiding something big, and possibly for your own personal benefit. The media would have a feeding frenzy over it and claim that you were secretly doing all of this to reduce the national debt to your advantage prior to the next election. The stories could fuel demonstrations against you in both the U.S. and other nations around the world. Headlines would claim that you are trying to make the U.S. the undeniable world leader–possibly risking a power move to control the planet. Furthermore, Harley could raise fears all over the globe about alien viruses, death and destruction. He would have you on the defensive on multiple fronts and the Cjarians would come out of the gate with the world viewing them as bad. Bottom line: Harley wins."

"Pretty much what we figured, so what does he have up his sleeve if we announce first?" President Callahan queried.

"I'll admit; that's a tough one, sir. Obviously, we can't know for sure, but Blake and I both think he'll pounce on your announcement with the same exact claims, so you'll have to use that to your advantage, and you can easily address that in your speech. Holding the speech in Europe with the other state leaders that were involved will definitely help. Blake and I both think that you need to avoid giving the speech from the White House to help down play the 'it's for U.S. benefit' fears."

"You will also need to be prepared for his counterattacks and take proactive steps to address them in your speech before he can. He will claim that you released the information only because he threatened to if you didn't, which could still be a win for him and the Anti-SETI movement. You'll need to head that off aggressively."

"You want me to start mudslinging; is that correct? Harry, you know my position on this."

"As Blake would say, it's time to draw a line in the sand and fight–not just for your sake, but for the country's sake and for the Cjarians' sake. We can't forget our new friends; like it or not, we are fighting for them as well. If it helps, we really aren't talking trashy mudslinging; we're sharing hard, cold facts, so call it fact-slinging. For example, let's assume the worst, that he's made secret recordings of some of these meetings. He can edit and crop them to make them sound very damning during a 30-second primetime news headline."

"So how do we counter that, Harry?"

"Blake and I are recommending two strategies. One is to show selected highlights of these meetings yourself. Announce the members of the presidential commission on both sides. Show everyone the guidelines that all of the commission members agreed to–including Harley. Then you can acknowledge that Harley threatened to take it to the media–even showing them the video clip where he does it. You would immediately follow that up with the fact that you are trying to avoid a nationwide polarization on the topic so you are declassifying *all* of the commission minutes for that specific purpose. Tell the people that our country has a rich history of debate that traces its roots back to the framers of the U.S. Constitution, and how your desire for healthy discourse still represents the very foundation this country was birthed from. Talk to both the pros and cons of the Cjarians and make this an educational enlightenment speech rather than a divisive speech. Then discuss how you and the government are moving slowly to ensure you can properly manage all the risks involved. Acknowledge how this new alliance will help the U.S., but also explain how it will help the other countries that were directly involved and the rest of the world as well. Take away all of Sen. Harley's arguments so that anything he brings up is something you've already addressed."

"Actually, I like where you're heading, Harry. I think I can work along those lines. My speechwriters can outline something for us to review by tomorrow. What else, Harry? What if he releases video of the threat and how I referred to it as treason? That would make me look like I caved to his pressure."

"That's the hinge pin, sir. If he goes there, you are indeed at risk—he could wipe out your entire speech by undermining your credibility with a simple 10-second video clip. But that's where you have to decide if you are going to fight, or not. Sorry, sir, but this is where you have to show that you can be as ruthless as you need to be to protect this country. Think about it; did you think President Harry S. Truman *wanted* to drop nuclear weapons on Japan? No, he despised it, but he knew he had to do it in order to force Japan to surrender and thereby reduce the likelihood of millions of casualties from a ground invasion of Japan. What we are recommending to you is way less than that. Sorry, sir, but I agree with Blake on this one—it's time to take the gloves off."

"I'm not liking this, Harry, and I'm pretty sure I would not have tolerated a discussion like this from anyone else, but your comments about protecting the country and the Cjarians has me listening, so, I'm going to allow you a little more leeway. What else do you and Blake propose?"

"To quote Blake, 'Show the video and cut his legs out from under him.' Prove to the world what a piece of garbage this man really is. When you show the unedited video, it will clearly show that he wasn't worried about the world; he was in it only for himself. We also recommend that you allow us to bug his house and/or his phone to get more material that will show the world who he is."

"Now you want me to break my campaign promise to the American people and even allow you to illegally wiretap a U.S. senator to gather information for my benefit? I don't like it, any of it. Harry, this is dangerous to the foundation of this country! I promised the American people we would never return to the days of the late twenty-teens, that I would keep it clean."

Everyone remained respectfully quiet, until Harry spoke again.

"Blake was pretty confident that you would say that, sir—and he stated that respectfully."

"Yeah? And what was his proposed response?"

"He said, 'President Callahan needs to accept that it's too late to debate that issue. That it's no longer his decision to control.' He then added that you've already been thrown into the mud pit, whether you want to be there or not. Yes, you made a promise about mudslinging, but you also made a promise to protect the American people. Furthermore, you also promised the Cjarians you would protect them as well. Sir, you simply have to fight, or get out. There are no other choices. By the way, Blake's exact words were 'Tell President Callahan that, like it or not, he only has two options, and only one is viable for success. That means it's time to fight.' He also told me to remind you of last year's nightmare when we decided there were no perfect options as well, so you had to pick the least worst and make the best of it. Well, we're there again. I'll also remind you that the video of Sen. Harley's threat is not mudslinging or grandstanding; it is pure fact, and when presented correctly, will show him as the POS he really is. You *need* to convince the world that it is Sen. Harley who is out of bounds and that he illegally threatened the president of the United States with blackmail. Lastly, knowing how much of a psychopath this guy is, we are fairly confident that we can get some pretty damning material on him if you give us the green light to hack him."

The room went silent. President Callahan was pacing.

"Brad, General, Ben, Annie ... comments?" President Callahan asked his closest cabinet members. Vice President Annie Murphy was the first to speak.

"Mr. President, I've known you for over 20 years, the last couple of years as your VP. You have many attributes that I have always respected, but your most endearing characteristic is your sincere desire to do what's right. So here it is: I agree with Blake and Harry–taking Harley down before he damages this country or hurts the Cjarians is the most right thing to do in this whole crapshoot."

Ben, Frank and Gen. McMullen were all nodding. President Callahan looked at each, one at a time.

"Ben, Frank ... work with my writers and put a draft speech together. I want to see your ideas before I agree to a final. This one speech could make the difference between success and utter failure, so I need the best they've ever done. Let's target no more than a week from now. I'll contact the other state leaders and give them a heads up on what we're planning."

"Sir?" Gen. McMullen spoke up. "What about the wire tapping?"

"I'm not there yet, General. It feels like selfish abuse of my position and power. Right now, it's off the table because I'm not yet convinced it's absolutely required. Let's change the topic and talk about your concerns with your military leaders. What have you identified so far?"

"Yes, sir. I have a hard time believing that anyone in today's U.S. military would consider a coup. Having said that, I have two generals I am not all that fond of."

"You don't trust them, General?"

"I'm not ready to go that far yet, sir, but I just don't have a good feel about either of them. The two are one-star Gen. Pete Pfisher of the Army and three-star Gen. Tom White of the Air Force. To be crystal clear, I have nothing on them that would suggest I should dig any deeper–and I even regret mentioning them."

"Thank you, General, I understand your concern. Let's hold on any action at this time, but keep your eyes and ears open."

"Yes, Mr. President, always."

"Anything else?" President Callahan asked the group.

"One new topic, sir," Frank Pelino volunteered.

"What is it, Frank?"

"We received a call from Klaus Schneider this morning."

"Who?"

"Klaus Schneider. He was the technical specialist from Germany that went to Pluto on the Armstrong I with Cmdr. Thompson."

"OK, now I remember. What does he want that needs my attention?"

"He joined the German deep-space telescope team when he returned from Pluto. Their mission is to monitor deep space for new galaxies and signs of life."

"That seems appropriate," Gen. McMullen interjected sarcastically. "Seems like we've already discovered that there is intelligent life out there, haven't we?"

"Yes, Gen. McMullen, but now that we know about the Cjarians, we also know that they had enemies–enemies that we hope never find Earth."

"OK, so did he find something?" President Callahan asked.

"Yes, but not intelligent life, per se, rather a large comet or asteroid that appears to be heading toward Earth. It sounds like they accidentally stumbled across the discovery as they were retuning the telescope for a software upgrade."

"Software upgrade? Are we sure it's real then?"

"They're convinced it is, sir."

"Great, what else do we need to go wrong now?" President Callahan paused before continuing. "Is this going to be on national news tonight?"

"No, the Germans are keeping it quiet in order to avoid mass hysteria, but they wanted to let a few select country leaders know about it so that others could begin tracking it. He claimed it's bigger than the comet that theoretically wiped out the dinosaurs, so once they identified it, it automatically triggered their extinction event protocol–hence the call this morning."

"Then please pass on my thanks to him. Are we sure it will impact the Earth?"

"No, it's way too early to tell, but it will be close. He thought it might be possible to have the Cjarians take a closer look."

"That's an interesting thought," President Callahan mused. "Harry, I know you turned down my offer to become the White House's science adviser, but that doesn't mean you can't unofficially fill a few gaps here and there. Would that be a fair assumption?"

"That seems like a sound assumption, Mr. President. What do you have in mind?"

"Good! Then how about you contact Klaus and then discuss it with Blake and see what he thinks. Keep me posted if you learn anything new."

"Will do, sir," Harry replied calmly.

"Any other topics to discuss? Anyone?" President Callahan asked again.

President Callahan swept his eyes across the room.

"OK, I guess that's more than enough for one day. Let me know if anything else comes up. Annie, come with me."

President Callahan stood up and left the room, with Vice President Murphy following.

*****

Blake was reviewing flight plans with the Night Star flight team on the atoll when his phone rang.

"Blake, it's Joe Foster, FBI from Colorado Springs."

"Hey, Joe. Anything new on our search?"

"Actually, yes. Are you somewhere safe to talk?"

"Not totally, but I can be somewhere in about 90 seconds, that work?"

"Sure does, I'll just hold on. Let me know when you're ready."

Blake got up from his chair, excused himself for a couple of minutes, headed out the door and down the hall to where he knew there was a cluster of four small meeting rooms available for their use. He picked the first one on his right, closed the door, and let Joe know he was ready.

"Can you hear me, Joe?"

"Loud and clear. Where the heck are you, the Pentagon?"

"Not quite. Wish I could say, but ..."

"Yeah, I know. Never mind."

"OK, so, what's up?"

"That ammunition program I told you about, remember I told you it was made under a black army program codenamed Starburst. Like I said, the level of secrecy is crazy, but I've learned a little more since we talked last time."

"I'm all ears."

"Figured you would be," Joe replied. "It turns out that the company that made them is located in Bend, Ore. They've been running a top secret ammunition lab for the U.S. Army for the past decade."

"There're lots of black programs, Joe. So what's so special about this one?"

"Actually, three things. First, as of six months ago they started reporting directly to the Senate Armed Services Committee. That seemed a little abnormal to me."

"I agree, that is a little odd, Joe. OK, keep going, you've piqued my interest."

"Secondly, it turns out that there are not one, not two, but *three* U.S. senators on the board."

"That sure is a lot of visibility for a small company. Who are they?" Blake was now very interested.

"Sen. James Colburn has been on their board of directors for at least 20 years. He worked there when he first got out of college. Sen. James Harley just joined their board six months ago and quickly added Sen. Jerry Pinkerton to the board as well. According to my source, Harley threatened the company's contract if they didn't include what he claimed were unbiased members on the board because he simply didn't trust Sen. Colburn. The rumor mill is alive and well on this one and there are many anticipating that this new ammo will be the biggest breakthrough in ammo technology and sales in the past 50 years."

"Follow the money, right? Amazing, isn't it?"

"Sure is, Blake, almost nauseating."

"I thought there were restrictions created almost a decade ago that limited the ability of congressional members to sit on corporate boards?"

"Yes, Blake, there were, and still are. The goal was to reduce the risk or even perception of inside trader abuses, but in this case, the government decreed that it was in the best interests of national security and, therefore, allowed the exception."

"You said three things. What's the third?"

"That's the best part. The Pentagon is all over us right now and they demanded we turn over the ammunition so they could quarantine it. Turns out that the first shipment of production was supposed to arrive at the Pentagon a month ago and disappeared in transit. No one knew what happened to it, until they saw the cache you guys found."

"That's good news and bad news, but either way, I can understand why the Pentagon is all over it. That stuff would sell for millions on the black market and would put police and security forces in danger all around the world."

"It sure would, Blake. Unfortunately, there is more bad news– the haul you guys found is less than 10 percent of the shipment that was lost."

"Phew! That is bad news, and let me guess, those guys still aren't talking, are they?"

"No, they sure aren't. The Pentagon hauled them away, but word got out and now the legal hordes are coming out of the woodwork. The sons of bitches are actually getting protection at the cost to the U.S. taxpayers!"

"Due process is one thing, but guilty beyond a doubt is another. Seems like the government could label them as domestic terrorists under the Patriot Act in order to extract them from their lawyers, couldn't they?"

"That's an interesting thought, Blake, but I think that has to come directly from the president. I'll bounce that up the line to see if they've considered that option yet. I'll let you know what I find out."

"So, what else have you found out relative to their motives? Do you really still think we were their targets?"

"I hate to say it, but the FBI still sees you guys as target number one. We haven't figured out why yet, but everything still points to the three of you. The only other option is simply open terrorism and the unlucky chance that you guys happened to be in their target zone, but that just feels thin. Trying to be honest, Blake, but you need to watch your back. Sometimes you really can't tell who your friends or enemies are."

"I know, tell me about it, but thanks for saying it." Blake paused as he thought about his upcoming flight. "By the way, I may be out of touch for a couple weeks. Let me give you a contact number in case you find something really hot. Call 202-456-1111 and ask for Frank Pelino."

"The President's chief of staff? Good grief, Blake. You sure you couldn't just connect me with President Callahan himself?" Joe chuckled. "Take care of yourself, Blake, I'd like to make sure you're still around when we finally figure this out."

"Me, too, Joe. Me, too. Talk to you soon." Blake disconnected the call and headed back to the flight crew meeting. He needed to finish reviewing the flight plan before heading back to the University of Houston for another discussion with the chancellor tomorrow.

*****

Chancellor's Office
Sept. 26, 2029

"Cmdr. Thompson, it's good to see you again. Although I have to be honest, I was more than a little nervous when your message said it was urgent that we meet this morning. I had to cancel a few meetings and I also called Coach Coleman to make sure he wasn't aware of any new shenanigans with his players. Are my football boys in trouble again?"

"No, ma'am," Blake smiled. "As far as I'm aware, they've been walking a pretty straight line since we last met, and I thank you for that."

"You are quite welcome, but I think I need to thank *you* for that," she responded with a sincere smile. "So, it sounds like this meeting must have some critical significance. Do I understand correctly that you took a red-eye flight to get here?"

"That would be correct, ma'am, but it was in a dedicated C-130 flight so I was able to get some shuteye. Did you also get the message about Dr. McDearmon?"

"Yes, I did. He should be here shortly. May I ask what this is about?"

"Absolutely, but I am limited to what I can share, even with you. I'd prefer to wait until Dr. McDearmon is here so I can reduce my risk of slipping up in multiple conversations." Blake smiled and sat back in his chair.

"Would you like some coffee?"

"Black, straight up. Thank you, ma'am."

The chancellor poured a cup of steaming hot coffee and handed it to Blake.

"Thank you." Blake took the cup in one hand and then motioned over to the chancellor's desk. "Chancellor Beth VanDeusen. I assumed you had a full name, but so far, all I'd heard was 'Ma'am' and 'Chancellor.' May I ask where you're from and who you are outside of the university?"

"Absolutely, Commander, although maybe I should say that you aren't cleared for that information, just to level the playing field," the chancellor chided Blake.

"I guess that warrants a formal touché–nice payback." Blake smiled.

"Here's the short version. I grew up in Des Moines, Iowa. I received my bachelor's and master's degrees in mechanical engineering at Drake University. I went on to get my PhD at MIT, held positions at Princeton and then received an MBA at the University of Michigan. I moved here to become the chancellor two years ago. I come from a family with three siblings, I'm 44, single and love the outdoors–that is, when I can actually find the time to enjoy it." She paused and took a sip of her coffee before continuing. "So, how about you, Commander?"

"That's quite impressive, Chancellor, thanks for sharing, and yes, turnabout is fair play," Blake chuckled. "I grew up in New York City as a son of a fireman. He was one of the many who died in the Twin Towers during the 9/11 attacks."

"I'm so sorry; I didn't know."

"That's OK, Chancellor, you couldn't have known, but thank you just the same." Blake nodded. "When the continual stream of funerals finally ended, my mom, sister and I moved to a small town in upstate New York, called Cobleskill. After graduating from high school, I attended West Point to pursue my singular focus–to hunt down and destroy those who killed my father. Following graduation from West Point, I switched military services and pursued a career with the SEALs and traveled all over the world, running ops that I'm still not cleared to discuss. I'm 42 and pursuing my second career with the U.S. government–one that I also can't talk about." Blake paused. "Well, that's the short version of it."

"So, you were in the Army and then joined the Navy SEALs. That seems like an odd switch, isn't it?"

"Many people consider it that way, but I had three uncles who made the Army their career, so it was my way to honor them by starting there. I made it to the rank of major and then joined the Navy to pursue being a SEAL."

"I'm not a military expert, but why not something like the Green Berets or the Delta Force?"

"Good question, Chancellor. The truth was that I was so fixated on destroying terrorist cells that I wanted to be able to attack the terrorists anywhere they showed up: air, land or sea. The

Green Berets and Delta Force are incredible organizations, but I saw a slight advantage to the underwater side with the SEALs."

Just then, there was a knock at the door and a tall, handsome, middle-aged, dark-skinned, athletic-looking man entered.

"Hello, Chancellor, sorry I'm late. Are we meeting here?"

"Yes, please join us, Dr. McDearmon. Cmdr. Thompson, this is Dr. George McDearmon. Dr. McDearmon, Cmdr. Blake Thompson."

Blake reached out to shake Dr. McDearmon's hand. Dr. McDearmon was sporting a quaint bow tie and had that down-home, Southern hospitality air that immediately put everyone around him at ease.

"If it's at all possible, I'd like to drop the formalities. Please call me Blake. May I call you Beth and George?"

"Yes, on one condition," Chancellor VanDeusen responded.

"What's that?" Blake asked.

"Tell us how you found out about Dr. McDearmon, or George, what is it that you need from him and why this is such an emergency?"

"That's a tall order, Beth, but I will tell you what I've been told I can share in these quarters. The actual application is classified top secret and can only be discussed in classified areas and only after the proper paperwork has been signed and approved. Dr. McDearmon has already been vetted by the FBI and is clean as a whistle, but you haven't been vetted yet."

"Whoa! I've been investigated? What are you getting me into? You may be military or ex-military, but I'm just basic John Q. Public. With all due respect, I don't think I'm the right person for a military operation."

"I can promise you that it is definitely *not* a military operation."

"Then why is it top secret?" Beth jumped in to defend George.

"Many things are deemed top secret without having anything to do with a specific military operation. I must also warn you that you will not be able to share this information, with your family–or even the Chancellor. Sorry, Beth, but those are the rules for now."

"So, what can you tell us?" George asked.

"I can tell you that you will take a once-in-a-lifetime-trip to somewhere you have never been to before and meet individuals that you would otherwise never meet. It involves a technological breakthrough beyond your wildest dreams."

"Why do you need my medical background?"

"That, I'm sorry, I can't tell you yet," Blake responded flatly. "You have to join the project before that can be discussed."

"How long will I be gone?"

"Could be as short as one week, could be a month."

"Why me?"

"You have the perfect educational and work background, you're athletic and you're single."

"This really sounds like a military operation, Blake." It was Beth again, and she looked very concerned.

"Look, I know this sounds crazy, but I'm telling you it is absolutely not a military op. And I can guarantee you it will be the most exciting thing you will ever be involved with."

"This is crazy!" George began pacing back and forth in the office. "How long do I have before I have to give you an answer?"

"As of five minutes ago, you had one hour."

"One hour? That's insane!"

"Fifty-five minutes, George. Sorry, but it's an once-in-a-lifetime opportunity and it only gets offered once–now."

"Then the answer is no. I don't believe you. Nothing non-military happens this quickly."

"Tell you what, George. I'm going to ignore your immediate response as just an uncontrolled vocal outburst and give you a little more insight that may help you in your decision-making process. How about I let you talk to one person? One person only. Will you give me that, here and now?"

"Sure, why not? But it won't change my mind. Who is it?"

"Hang on one second." Blake pulled out his cell phone and sent a quick text.

Thirty seconds later, George's cell phone started vibrating.

"Well, are you going to answer it?" Blake asked, pointing to George's phone.

"It says 'likely scam,' why should I answer?"

"The clock is ticking, George. Beth, tell him to answer his phone."

"Blake, this is not the military; you can't order people to do things," Beth replied.

"Forty-eight minutes, George," Blake answered, ignoring the chancellor.

George looked down at the phone in his hand and then back at Blake.

"That's four rings, George. Answer it before he hangs up. You can still say no after you talk, but you won't get a second chance if you don't answer the phone now."

"Fine!" George answered the phone.

"Hello?"

"Hi, George. Dr. George McDearmon, University of Houston, correct?"

"Yes ..."

"This is President Andrew Callahan. You're with Chancellor VanDeusen and Cmdr. Thompson, correct?"

"Yes ... I am. Who is this? How do you know who I'm with?"

"I told you, I'm President Andrew Callahan."

"How the heck do you expect me to believe that?" George stated as he looked at Beth and Blake.

"I don't. Look out the window."

George walked over to the window and looked down from the fourth floor. There was a string of shiny black SUVs and one very large, robust-looking sedan–well known as The Beast.

"I see a bunch of cars and one that does look very official. How does that make you the president?"

"What?" Beth stammered, while standing up. "The president?"

"Try opening the door to Chancellor VanDeusen's office."

George looked at Blake in total disbelief. Beth sat back down in her chair with a bewildered look on her face. Blake motioned toward the door.

"Go ahead, George, open the door," Blake directed in his military voice.

George approached and opened the door as ordered.

"Mr. President ... I'm sorry. I really didn't believe it could be you ..."

Thirty minutes later, Blake left with President Callahan, leaving a pair of stunned academics behind them. George had finally accepted the mission after President Callahan said his country needed him and promised he would not be disappointed. George was told to go home and pack and that there would be a car waiting for him that would then drive him to Ellington Field Joint Reserve Base, where he would be flown to his next undisclosed location.

"Well, Blake, does he measure up to your expectations?" President Callahan asked Blake while they drove away in the presidential limousine. "Honest assessment, please."

"When you put it that way, no. He may meet the technical requirements that you and Harry wanted to the proverbial t, but he lacks the fortitude and inner strength that I know we'll need. We only have a few days to toughen him up."

"Fair points, Blake, but you might need to cut him a little slack. After all, he had no clue of what was coming and still doesn't even know he's heading into space. We caught him cold on all accounts, and this would rock most people to their foundation. By the way, he is a dedicated ironman competitor, so we know he can be physically and mentally tough."

"We'll see, sir; it's just that I'm used to people stepping up to the line without question."

"Blake, the issue may be that you're top of the line, gung ho, oorah and military to the core, so your bar may be just a wee bit higher than the average." President Callahan laughed. "Give him a day to absorb everything once we tell him what's really going on and then you can reassess. If you still feel strongly against it, we'll look at other options."

*****

U.S. Strategic Command, Offutt Air Force Base
Omaha, Neb.
Sept. 27, 2029

It was just before midnight at USSTRATCOM headquarters in Offutt Air Force Base near Omaha, Neb. A cluster of personnel was focused on a 72-inch monitor on the wall. The words "Xichang Space Center, China, Sept. 28, 2029 - 12:57:33" were highlighted above the screen, the last digit changing with each passing second.

"Lieutenant, get Gen. Beckman at the Pentagon on the phone; he's waiting on this update."

"Yes, sir."

Ten minutes passed before the lieutenant responded again.

"Sir, I have him," the lieutenant spoke crisply while extending his hand with the phone in it.

"Gen. Beckman, Gen. Whittler, USSTRATCOM here. We have the situational update from China that we discussed."

"Go ahead, this line is secure."

"The clouds have finally cleared over the Xichang Space Center."

"And?"

"We are detecting activities at multiple launch sites."

"OK, we were aware they were preparing for one or two launches in the coming weeks, correct?"

"Yes, but now it looks like they have four vehicles ready to launch and the payload sections … the payload sections are very different from what we expected."

"How so?"

"One looks like a standard satellite launch, but the other three are quite large. Large enough to carry some sizable payloads."

"Have you been able to get clear photos?"

"Yes, crystal clear. The lab boys are analyzing them now; I'll forward a few to you as soon as we're off the call. Two look like oversized cargo pods and a third looks like it might be a personnel carrier."

"A personnel carrier? Like passengers, or troops?"

"Good question, we also wondered about the possibility of a tourist shuttle based on how much the space tourism industry has grown over the past decade, and there are windows down both sides of the module, but based on what else we're seeing, we're leaning toward it being a troop carrier."

"Why is that?"

"The personnel were not Chinese, which could still support a tourism option, but there was a number of packing crates being loaded that clearly looked like weapons crates and all of the people in the photos were wearing the same color clothing, possibly a uniform."

"Gen. Whittler, are you sure? This is not the time for idle suppositions."

"Look for yourself, General; I'll send some photos right now, hang on for a minute." Gen. Whittler put the phone down, punched a number of keys on the computer and then clicked "SEND."

"The pictures are on the way, Gen. Beckman. They look like northern Europeans from the best shots we could get ... possibly Russian."

"That's the first million-dollar question, Gen. Whittler. The second is *where to* ... the moon, again?"

"Possibly for another lunar module, but why the hell would they need troops on the moon?"

"I don't know, but we need to get this up the line quickly. Thanks for the call, Gen. Whittler; let me know if you see anything else, especially a launch."

"Will do, Gen. Beckman; please share whatever theories you guys come up with."

*****

"Klaus? Klaus Schneider?"

"Yes, this is he."

"Hello, this is Harry Lundrum. I work with Cmdr. Blake Thompson and President Callahan. You may recall that we talked, via Blake, during your flight to Pluto last year. I understand that you called the White House and talked with Frank Pelino about a certain celestial event that might be coming up."

"Hello, Harry, it's good to hear from you. Yes, I did. Is this line safe?"

"Yes, I'm connected through the White House."

The two men spent little time getting acquainted, instead diving into the technical discussion at hand. Ten minutes later, Harry had what he needed so that he could relay the appropriate information to Blake and to NASA's Planet Defense Coordination Office, or PDCO. They exchanged goodbyes and ended the call.

PDCO is part of NASA, with headquarters in Washington, D.C., but utilizes personnel and management resources from across the country. Harry was aware that PDCO monitored asteroids and comets that orbit the sun as well as near-earth objects, or NEOs, but he had to do some additional research to find out that they maintained close relationships with the International Asteroid Warning Network, or IWAN, and the Space Missions Planning

CHAPTER 7

The Johnston Atoll
Sept. 29, 2029

Three days had passed since Blake traveled to Houston to meet with the chancellor. Blake and his team were gathered in the atoll's mess hall, enjoying their last freshly cooked breakfast before heading into space. The expanded group now included their newest minted member, Dr. George McDearmon. George had come around once he'd landed at the atoll and saw the Night Star on the launch pad; only then did Blake share the full details of the trip with him. From that point on, George had been like a kid in a candy shop.

"Cmdr. Thompson, I can't thank you enough for …"

"Doc, wait a minute, we need to get one thing straight. Lose the titles, remember? I'm Blake, you're George. Can you work with that?" Blake chuckled.

"Sure, Commander … I mean, Blake." George smiled meekly. "Sorry, I was raised to respect the military. My dad was a medic in the Gulf War and many of my uncles were retired military as well."

"And you? You never thought about joining the military?"

"Not really, sir … I mean, Blake. Not that I had anything against it; I was just super focused on becoming a specialist on infectious diseases. Although I didn't join, that doesn't mean I can't still help the military out."

"How so?"

"My dad talked a lot about Saddam Hussein and the fears over weapons of mass destruction, some of which were believed to be chemical weapons and some of which were believed to be infectious disease weapons. He sent pictures home showing him and his buddies in full battle gear with gas masks on while it was 120 degrees Fahrenheit outside, and I guess that left quite a mark on me. I knew I would never be the tough military guy, so I figured I could carry on the family tradition by fighting in my own way–in the lab."

"I guess that's good for us, because the White House claims you're the best we have," Blake responded.

"Well, I don't know if I would say that, but I feel I can hold my own with the best. I spent 10 years at the Centers for Disease Control and Prevention in Atlanta and there are a lot of world-class scientists there–it's the best facility in the world. It has the best labs and the best doctors, but just as importantly, the best budgets as well. It really is an impressive place."

"So why did you leave it to come to Houston?"

"I didn't really leave it as I can go back anytime I want to conduct research or to support an investigation. I came to Houston so that I could help start up a new center and teach there, something I've always wanted to do. It also helped that Chancellor VanDeusen made me an outstanding offer that allows me to do both."

"That sounds like a win-win, George, and we're glad to have you with us. We couldn't take Atlanta, or Houston, with us, but I think you will be impressed with the lab facilities that Uncle Sam has waiting for you on the space dock."

"I'm looking forward to seeing it, but … how much could you really get to the dock in just a few days? The equipment I'll need to investigate *their* anatomical structure with and to assess the risk of their diseases on us and ours on them, requires some pretty complex labs, sophisticated equipment and very specialized technicians."

"You're correct, George, that's exactly what we thought. too, as we've remained hopeful that we would meet the Cjarians again. Since the day they departed, the U.S. began to construct a facility on the dock that would provide us with the ability to conduct the necessary research to ensure the safety of both species without ever needing to have the Cjarians land on Earth. This effort began long before the White House finalized their selection search for you, so we've had months to design, construct, equip and populate the lab specifically for you, or someone else like you. We've made no fewer than eight Night Star flights over the last four months that were solely for the purpose of delivering equipment to the lab on the space dock. As for technicians, there are six highly trained military scientists already there–all of whom will be working under your direction. I think you'll find everything you need once you get there."

"Blake, you were right; this really is the biggest thing that has ever happened to me. Thanks for staying with me. I know I didn't sell myself well when we first met, but I didn't know who you were or what you were trying to sign me up for."

"To be 100 percent honest with you, George, thank President Callahan, not me. I was pretty gun shy over your hesitancy, but President Callahan told me that both he and Harry thought you were our guy."

"Speaking of Harry, I know I only met him yesterday, and even then, just briefly, but I've heard some crazy things about him. What's his story?"

"Too much to describe right now, but the short version is that he's the smartest person I've ever met, as well as the finest human being I've ever worked with. You will never find better."

"I hope I get to work with him while we're up there."

"Trust me; you will." Blake smiled. "But first, how about we suit up and get you ready for your first spaceflight?"

*****

Three hours later, seven men and two women entered the Night Star and were strapped into their seats in preparation for liftoff. Blake picked the lone seat behind the rest of the crew. The additional seat had been added after Patty agreed to join the group. The team's newest member, George, was sitting directly in front of Blake in the middle of the second row of crewmembers, with Patty on his right and Vladimir on his left. Jimmy was directly in front of George, in the middle of the first row of crewmembers, with Diego on his right and Harry on his left. The two pilot seats for Rachel and Sean were more isolated in the very front of the ship, side by side, and further separated from the rest of the crew by a number of control panels that the crew would utilize once they were in orbit. Viewing windows were in front of the pilots, as well as on both sides of the ship in line with the crewmember rows.

"George, are you still with us?" Blake queried their newest member.

"Yes, but I'm … wow … I'm really excited, but … holy cow, to say I'm not really nervous would be a total, unmitigated lie … I think I could use some of Maj. Popov's vodka that you guys have been talking about."

"I don't think so, George. You see, in Russia, vodka is for celebration, not for numbing one's senses," Vladimir countered.

"Oh, really, is that true, Vladimir?" Harry responded quizzically. "It seems to me that I have seen a lot of very numb people drinking vodka in Russia.

"As a matter of fact, many of them were so numb, I believe they would have been medically categorized as unconscious," Harry added dryly.

"Harry, you may be correct on their condition, but how do you know that was not at the end of their celebration, da?" Vladimir smiled confidently at his monitor for all to see. "But let us focus on our new friend for now. George, I would sincerely abhor letting you miss out on any of the exhilaration you're about to experience. There is nothing in life that even comes close to a space launch. Furthermore, I was saving the vodka for our meeting with the Cjarians, but let me think … perhaps I can propose an exception for you, Professor George. Let's call it a celebration of your first flight, da? If you can survive the trip to the space dock, I will give you a small shot to celebrate once we have docked. Does that suffice?"

"Assuming I'm still conscious, absolutely. Thank you, Vladimir."

"Do we all get to celebrate his first flight?" Sean feigned innocence.

"No, no, no, Sean. Nice try, my Irish friend. Blake, I think I may need your assistance to keep the Irish wolfhounds away from my liquor cabinet! The rest will be kept in storage for the real celebration with the Cjarians!"

Before anyone could reply, Mission Control interrupted.

"Gentlemen, I don't recall vodka being on the preflight checklist. How about we move on to the more important topics associated with getting this flight under way?"

"Roger that, Mission Control," Rachel replied for the group as a slight murmur of multiple people chuckling under their breaths could be heard. "The crew is ready to commence operations."

A continual stream of questions, answers and validations continued as each of the crewmembers sat listening. Only Rachel and Sean answered the questions directed at the ship.

"Oxygen Purge, check."

"Payload Test Conductor, check."

"Launch Processing System, check."

"This is Houston, FLT, we are taking over."

"Merritt Island Launch is ready."

"Safety Console Coordinator is a go."

"Crew is ready; we have a go," Rachel confirmed.

The unending stream of checks and confirmations continued from NASA flight directors and from the horde of contractors connected to flight operations and vehicle subsystems.

"Weather is a go."

"We are confirmed to proceed to launch."

"Nine minutes and counting to launch."

The nine minutes were both agonizingly slow and yet frighteningly fast; it was the most extreme dichotomy of emotions one could experience. Finally, the anticipated time arrived.

"Commencing countdown. Ten … Nine … Eight … Seven … Six …"

Their world began to rattle and shake as the main engines ignited—a physical attack on their bodies more aggressive than any earthquake or turbulent jet ride could even begin to achieve. "Five … Four … Three … Two … One …."

The solid boosters kicked in with close to three million pounds of ammonium perchlorate generating over seven million pounds of force. The Night Star slowly separated from the launch pad.

"We have liftoff, ladies and gentlemen. We'll check back in 70 seconds after the solid rocket engines are jettisoned. Until then, Godspeed and enjoy the ride."

There was little sense in saying anything else as everyone in the Control Room knew there would be little response from the crew while they fought the extreme violence of liftoff, but it didn't stop the Night Star crew from thinking about it.

As the 1954 hit by Bill Haley and the Comets, "Shake, Rattle and Roll," played over the Night Star speakers, Blake made a mental note to track down the individual who selected that song for takeoff ... maybe he would play Guns and Roses' "Welcome to the Jungle" for him when he returned and walked into their office cubicle... a small, tight smile found its way to Blake's face.

*****

Less than 90 minutes had passed since the launch and the Night Star had exited Earth's upper atmosphere, completed one full orbit and was already approaching the space dock. Unlike the early Apollo and Space Shuttle days, the Night Star's docking operation was fully automated, as well as capable of being fully controlled from the Space Dock. Both the on-board and on-dock computer systems regulated flight path, speed and ship rotation to approach the dock and complete the docking process–without human intervention.

"This is like driving a Tesla!" Sean said with noted distaste. "What fun is it to have a sports car and not be in control of it? I never did understand the attraction."

"In the case of the Tesla and sports cars," Blake responded, "I agree with you 100 percent. However, in this case, with our lives, billions of dollars of Night Star investment and likely a trillion dollars of space dock investment all at risk, let alone the lives of personnel already on the dock, I think I'll go with the computer. But if it makes you feel better, Sean, I'm OK with you keeping your hands on the stick just in case the computer decides to reboot itself in mid-flight."

"Gee, thanks for the vote of confidence, Blake, but it isn't quite working. I expected so much more as a pilot. To be honest, I'm beginning to feel like some sort of an extinct dinosaur. Don't pilots actually *pilot* anymore?"

"Dinosaur?" Harry echoed, "Hmmm, I'll have to research it further when we return to Earth, Sean, but perhaps your hereditary phylum was known as *pilotnomoreasaurus*, categorized as a foul-smelling, extremely small-brained, obnoxious and noisy vertebrate, distantly related to the airborne reptiles of the Mesozoic era. I believe they were later determined to be flightless and were one of the first dinosaur species to become extinct. End of story."

The entire crew broke into laughter, all at Sean's expense.

"Sean, I think that may be Harry's way of telling you that he wants to enjoy the docking process peacefully," Patty volunteered, hoping to make peace.

"Thanks for the translation, Patty … please tell me that Houston wasn't on line for that exchange," Sean replied sheepishly.

"Too late, Sean," Houston responded, "Our staff artist is already rendering a caricature of the beast and … Wow! … It looks amazingly similar to you! We'll make sure we get it on the space dock computer screen savers to celebrate your arrival."

"Man, just feel the love. All right, I get it, but remember … payback is a bitch and revenge is sweeter. Just when you least expect it …"

"Shut up, Sean!" everyone yelled in unison.

"I love ya buddy, but Patty was right. I want a chance to enjoy the docking process uninterrupted," Harry replied understandingly.

"Space Dock, this is Cmdr. Rachel Joslin on board the Night Star requesting permission to dock and come aboard."

"Cmdr. Joslin, Cmdr. Joe Garrity here. Permission granted. Please connect with the computer at docking bay two for auto docking."

"Roger, see you shortly."

For the next 10 minutes, everyone craned their necks to take in the view. The space dock had looked so small when they first approached it, but as they got closer, the enormity of the structure became more apparent—it was huge … gigantic. It looked like a 360-degree monstrous drive-in restaurant on steroids, with its flat, circular shape, radial arms and six docking stations along its outer ring. The dock was slowly spinning about its center axis in order to create a small level of simulated gravity on the outer ring of the dock. The dock also had a vast array of panels and antennas sticking out all around the ship.

"I can understand all of the antennae, but what are all those panels for?" George asked, momentarily breaking the silence. "They're not the ship's structure, because I can clearly see below the panels and they don't look like solar panels, either."

"Correct, George," Jimmy responded. "Those panels are the last line of defense against space debris. They're part of a multi-layer defensive strategy focused on reducing the risk of damage to the ship's interior. Given advanced warnings, they can steer the dock away from large debris, but the dock is so big and so slow, there's no way to avoid all the debris that encircles the planet from previous space missions and satellites, let alone the constant bombardment of dust and rocks present in space. They also have a number of small robotic space tugs patrolling the area. The tugs' primary responsibility is to track, collect, deflect and/or destroy debris heading toward the space dock. Although that may sound easy, you have to remember that space junk can be traveling at over 27,000 kilometers per hour, so it doesn't provide one with a lot of time to react. The dock also has four gallant guns to target incoming debris that gets past the tugs. The panels then provide a last line of defense to absorb as much of the energy as they can from whatever slips by the tugs and gallant guns before it can hit the main structure of the dock. Even with this, there are still occasional hull punctures that drive emergency protocols for safety and repair."

"Hull punctures?" Sean shrieked.

"Living in space sounds pretty cool in books," Jimmy continued, "but there are many dangers that can arise unexpectedly, 24 hours a day, 365 days a year. Once again, it proves how we routinely take for granted all of the work the atmosphere does for all us on a daily basis."

"Thanks, Jimmy, that actually makes a lot of sense, but it's still a bit mind-boggling. On the funny side, it actually looks like a giant shell-covered bug," George responded.

"It does," Rachel chimed in. "They keep the shields closed most of the time to maximize their ability to provide protection, but each one of them can be independently, or in unison, angled to allow maximum visibility from view ports, or to change impact angles with incoming debris, thereby deflecting some of the energy. I watched a 48-hour video of their operation that was sped up to save time and it was incredible! It was as if the surface of the dock was alive as individual panels, or zones of panels, moved here and there across the surface of the dock. Here, give me a minute and keep watching."

"Cmdr. Garrity, can you do a little show-and-tell for us on the panels?"

"Absolutely!" Joe responded a couple seconds later. "Watch this."

To everyone's amazement, a ripple of movement rolled across the dock's surface.

"That's awesome!" Jimmy exclaimed, grinning like a kid seeing his first sports car.

"Put your visors on now and watch this," Joe commanded as everyone pulled their sun visors down over their helmets.

"Oh, my God, that's stunning!" Patty exclaimed 20 seconds later as a wave of light traveled across the top of the dock. "How did you do that?"

"It's all preprogrammed to react to known space debris, but also to the position of the sun so that we don't accidentally blind an incoming ship when the angle with the sun is just right, or should I say, just wrong?" Cmdr. Garrity laughed. "Obviously, we can also take advantage of that same programming to make some pretty good show 'n tell movements as well. OK, back to work ladies and gents. We need to focus on docking this ship."

At the end of their 10-minute-long, final approach to the dock, a mild jolt was felt throughout the ship, followed seconds later by Rachel's announcement that they had successfully docked.

"Can I talk now?" Sean asked innocently.

"No!" was simultaneously shouted by everyone on board, followed by another roll of laughter.

"So when do we meet the Cjarians, Blake?" Patty was excited to finally get a chance to see them.

"I don't really know. I promised them I would signal them once we were safely aboard the dock and then it would be up to them to decide when to approach. They are extremely hesitant about this, so it may be days before we see them."

"Why, Blake?" Vladimir queried.

Blake explained how the Cjarians were concerned that they had been entrusted with the single greatest invention in the history of their world and they felt they were betraying Cjar by sharing the technology with an alien race they knew basically nothing about. They were not only putting themselves at risk, but because of the military potential of the technology, they were putting Cjar at risk as well.

"I've discussed this concern with President Callahan and he agreed that we would approach this meeting very slowly with our number one objective to maintain trust with the Cjarians. If at any time, we find that we need to slow down, or even back away to maintain their trust, we will do so."

"George, I recommend that we get you to your new lab and get acquainted with your new team as well–you have a lot to catch up on."

"Vladimir, I suggest we keep your vodka unopened and celebrate George's momentous occasion with a round of shots at the dock bar later tonight after he has met with his team."

"We have a bar up here?" Diego asked incredulously.

"All in the pursuit of maintaining some resemblance of normalcy," Harry replied matter-of-factly.

"OK, I need to make contact with our Cjarian friends. George, you need to get to the lab. Everyone else, go find your rooms, get unpacked and take some time to familiarize yourself with the dock. We have a meeting in the Apollo 13 conference room at 6 p.m. to review dock safety requirements and critical operational procedures–don't be late because until you receive that training, you are not allowed to freely tour the dock."

"One other note." Rachel jumped in. "Although you will frequently see personnel in the dock wearing their space suits, it is not required, so don't get anxious if you see someone suited up."

"Great point, thanks Rachel," Blake replied. "After the training, let's plan on meeting at the bar at 8 p.m. so we can catch up on the day's events and celebrate George's space baptism."

*****

Blake sat down in his small room, hooked up his personal communication device, officially referred to as a Man Portable Communication device, or MPoC, but now more commonly called LB for short. He chuckled at how quickly the acronym had caught on. The crew of the Armstrong I had been the first to dub the device Little Brother, or LB for short. It had been a reference to George Orwell's fictional character Big Brother that knew all and controlled all. The funniest aspect of the new name was that many were already using the new moniker without any understanding of its meaning or origin. Blake sent a short, encrypted message to the White House through the ship's communication equipment, sat back and waited. He knew the message would be meaningless to anyone not in the know so that it could be forwarded through multiple channels until it reached the right person in the White House situation room, President Callahan himself. Fifteen long minutes later, Blake's LB vibrated.

"Cmdr. Blake Thompson here."

"Hang on, sir, I will connect you with the president." Two clicks and then the unmistakable voice of President Callahan.

"Blake, are you there?"

"Mr. President, good to hear from you. Yes, I am, and ready to talk." Blake smiled.

"OK, hold on. We'll make the next call and then conference all three parties in."

The line clicked and went silent. Ten seconds went by and a series of clicks were then rewarded by a voice that could only belong to one being.

"Hello, Juulys here."

"Juulys! It's great to hear you. This is Blake 'Roger' Thompson and President Callahan."

"Hello, Juulys, it's my pleasure," the president added.

"Thank you, Mr. President, it is our pleasure as well. Blake, you knew I would ask about our code word Roger and you beat me to it." Juulys smiled. "I will never forget the surprise we had when you said 'Roger' and I thought you were talking to someone else that you had not told us about. For a second back then, I was afraid you were trying to sneak someone else onto our ship."

"Yes, it was my slipup, but you and Thjars recovered quite excellently," Blake responded. "Speaking of Thjars, where is he? I hope all is well."

"Yes, he is fine. He should be here shortly. When we received the call, he was taking a short power nap, or siesta, as I believe Diego called it."

"Ahh, yes, one of the great traditions of the male human species, but not always as well understood by our female companions." Blake laughed.

"Blake, is that you?"

"Thjars! It's great to hear your voice again. Juulys just informed us that you have picked up some of our bad habits."

"How so?"

"We heard you were enjoying a siesta!"

"Ahh, yes, thank you, but I can't blame that on you. Back home we called those *spiritssyls*, for recharging your energy and spirits. Unfortunately, the female component of our species referred to those as our 'lazy moments,' which were not viewed as positively as we males rated them."

"Thjars, this is President Callahan. I'm beginning to think our two races have more in common than we may have originally realized!" Everyone except Thjars started chuckling.

"Did I miss something?" Thjars asked as he looked over at Juulys. Juulys was still laughing, but shook her head to signal no.

"OK …" Thjars turned back to the screen. "Hello, Mr. President. Thank you for agreeing to help us out."

"It is my honor, Thjars. I just wanted to give you a quick welcome to Earth as I need to go to another pressing matter, but over the next few days, I will be back in touch to see how you are progressing. My office is monitoring all of the communications and will alert me to anything that might arise. If you need anything, please call or have Blake contact me."

"Thank you, sir."

"You are most welcome. I need to disconnect now. Goodbye, all," President Callahan said as he disconnected from the call.

"Thjars." Blake jumped in. "Not to cut the friendly chatter off, but we have arrived at the space dock. We are excited to meet with you when you are ready."

"Blake, we were watching and saw your ship dock. You didn't waste any time calling."

"Like I said, we are very excited to see you again. I've brought members of my previous SEAL team including Harry, Diego, Sean and Patty. I've also brought Maj. Vladimir Popov from the Armstrong I crew, Jimmy Decker from the Reagan I crew and one new individual, Dr. George McDearmon. Dr. McDearmon is a world-renowned expert on infectious diseases. We've built a lab on the dock for him and his technicians to be able to support any signs of issues between our two species."

"I'm impressed," Thjars responded. "How do you recommend we proceed?"

"Is Qulys available to join us?"

"He is not in the room with us, but he is connected by phone. My apologies that I did not mention that first."

"No problem, Thjars, I assumed he would be involved as he is responsible for your ship's security. Qulys, I'm looking forward to working with you again and I have some ideas on how to keep stress levels down on both sides."

"Somehow I assumed you would, Blake. Let's hear them."

As Thjars and Juulys listened, Blake and Qulys exchanged thoughts and finalized a game plan. After fewer than 30 minutes, they had reached an agreement. Surprisingly, they both had similar ideas before the discussion ever started–another sign that the two sides could continue trusting each other. As it turned out, the safety of the ship was no longer the biggest concern. The single largest risk was now focused on the danger of infectious disease and the fear that something as simple as the common cold could possibly wipe out the Cjarians, or vice versa. They ended up agreeing that Qulys would meet Patty, Harry and Blake in the airlock once they docked, but all four would be fully suited. Everyone else would stay within their respective vehicles for the first visit.

Once the four were in the lock, all air would be vented to space and their suits would be exposed to the cold, harsh, depressurized vacuum of space for five minutes. Then they would re-pressurize the lock with air from the dock and Patty, Harry and Blake would shed their suits long enough for Qulys to inspect the suits–and their owners–to ensure no weapons were brought aboard. The trio would then suit up again and the lock would be depressurized again to be re-exposed to the full vacuum of space for another five minutes. Finally, the lock would be re-pressurized with air from the Jarisst I. The four space travelers would proceed into the Jarisst I docking bay and then beyond to the interior of the Cjarian ship for the first time–a truly historic event.

The single biggest trust factor was now limited to the agreement that Blake, Patty and Harry would not open their spacesuits and risk contamination to the interior of the Jarisst I. This would greatly limit their ability to inspect the Q-PAMS system, but there was simply no better way to ensure the safety of the two species. As Harry pointed out, it could be just as deadly a risk for the earthlings as the Cjarians, so there was a high level of mutual benefit to maintaining the plan.

"There is only one question left," Blake interjected.

"And what is that, Blake?" Thjars responded.

"When do we start?"

"Good question," Thjars acknowledged. "There's really no reason to wait any further as we'd already concluded this was our only option before we contacted you. The only reason to delay would be if you or the space dock required more time."

"Well, then I guess that's settled. We were afraid you'd keep us waiting." Blake chuckled. "How far out are you? Then again, with your ship's capabilities, that's really a moot point, isn't it?"

"Yes, sorry, Blake, but that may be the first moot point I've ever heard you utter before," Patty replied before Thjars could answer, but they all joined in on the laughter.

"All right, touché, Patty." Blake laughed at himself as well. "Then how about we start first thing in the morning, after everyone has finished their morning meal. At say … 8 a.m. Eastern Standard Time. Thjars, that would be 15 Earth hours from now. I checked earlier and we will plan to meet at docking station number four. Is everyone good with that?"

"Sounds like a plan," Thjars responded. "We will see you all in the morning."

*****

CHAPTER 8

Space Dock
Sept. 30, 2029

Word spread quickly through the space dock that night and by 7 a.m., almost every person was positioned at a viewing window where they could watch the approach of the alien ship at docking station number four. For those unable to leave their post, Cmdr. Garrity requested that the event be broadcast over the dock's viewing screens throughout the ship. Everyone on the dock had previously been cleared for secret activities as part of their agreement to work as a dock employee, but this event required further classification and commitment to secrecy. With the exception of the official dock photographer, everyone was notified that no photographs, or even the knowledge of the existence of the ship could be shared with anyone back home. The ship's auto-video system would maintain continuous operations per standard protocol, but access to that content was protected by the ship's computer and the space dock's commander, Joe Garrity.

At 7:40 a.m., the Jarisst I notified the space dock they were 10 minutes out. At exactly 7:48 a.m., the first sighting by naked eye was made. The ship grew in size as it approached the space dock. Blake had already seen and boarded the spacecraft during his first encounter with the Jarisst I near Pluto, but it was still a sight to behold. The ship was 115 meters long and 12 meters wide, with a bulbous nose section approximately 20 meters in diameter. A second, flatter, but also similarly wide bulbous area was located about two-thirds down the axis of the ship where they knew the super-secret Q-PAMS drive was located. The smooth, sleek esthetics of the ship were unlike anything that Earth had produced; it was truly a beautiful craft.

Blake, Patty and Harry were already suited up and watching through the viewing window at dock number four.

"Amazing," was all that the mesmerized Harry could muster to say.

"It sure is, Harry," Blake acknowledged.

"Who would have thought that we would ever get to see something like this?" Patty added. "It's hard to believe what our eyes are actually seeing, let alone what we are about to do. I just can't find the words to explain what I'm feeling right now."

"There is no single word or phrase in the English language that can describe this moment," Harry added unemotionally.

After the Cjarians had left earlier in the year, dock number four had been modified to better accept the Jarisst I–hoping that this day would come. Blake had provided rough dimensions to the NASA engineers, based on what he had seen when he boarded their spacecraft near Pluto. But as the exact dimensions were not available, the engineers designed what they termed a unique, self-adjusting interface that could ensure a vacuum-proof seal on almost any surface or shape with an adjustable mating diameter that could absorb as much as a 30-centimeter diameter error from Blake's estimate. It was actually a quite ingenious design and the engineers proudly referred to it as the International & Universal Docking design–it could also interface with any ship from countries around the world. Unfortunately, it didn't take long for the more mischievous crewmembers to nickname it the Interspace IUD–and the jokes went from there. Patty had sarcastically responded that there were some things about the human race that would never change, especially among the male side of the species.

The Jarisst I continued its approach, now agonizingly slow as the two ships were separated by less than three meters. The view was spectacular. The excitement building by the second. Everyone held their breath, waiting for that final moment–even Sean was speechless.

A slight bump and rebound was noticeable as the ships locked together, followed by one short message over the intercom.

"Docking is complete. We have a successful connection."

The announcement was immediately followed by a bedlam of cheers throughout the ship. Blake and his team were about to be in the midst of another once-in-a-lifetime, history-making moment.

Blake tapped a button on his LB.

"Control, this is Cmdr. Blake Thompson. I'll take it from here."

"Roger that. Good luck, Commander."

Blake tapped a couple more buttons on his LB and connected directly with the Jarisst I.

"Thjars, Blake here. Is everything good on your end?"

"Yes, Blake, everything is good here, except possibly my nerves."

"Well, that makes two of us," Blake countered. "Are we ready to start?"

"Yes, we just started pressurizing the dock and Qulys is in position, ready to enter."

"OK, we'll wait for Qulys to direct us from his side to reduce the risk that we both jump at the same time."

Five minutes ensued before Blake heard Qulys's distinctive voice.

"Cmdr. Blake Thompson, it will be good to see you face to face again. I'm in the dock; you may enter when ready."

Blake had already locked himself, Patty and Harry in the dock port section. He pushed a series of buttons on the wall next to the docking bay entrance to exhaust the air and then shut the exhaust vents, leaving the trio in a controlled vacuum. Blake then opened the outer door that interfaced with the Cjarian docking port and air rushed back in–Cjarian air. Blake made the first push and floated in, followed by Patty and then Harry. Even though the engineers had purposely oversized the docking bay section for just this possibility, it was still going to be a tight fit for all four individuals.

"Sergeant-at-Arms Qulys Plyenysst, it is my distinct pleasure to welcome you to Earth, even if it is only on board this space dock. I hope and pray that our two species are taking one more giant step into the future that will benefit everyone involved, but most importantly, will lead us to a solution that provides your ship the full freedom to operate as you so choose to do and without dependence on planet Earth. And, may I add personally, it sure is great to see you again, Qulys. I still owe you a debt of gratitude for helping us out during our darkest moments near Pluto. I will never forget it."

Blake stuck out his gloved hand and was met halfway by Qulys' extended and gloved hand. A firm, unmistakable handshake between two brothers of the military cemented the welcome.

"Qulys, this is Patty Myers and Harry Lundrum. Harry, Patty, this is Qulys. My experience with him would suggest that the best way to summarize him is to say he could have been one of our SEAL teammates."

The trio quietly exchanged handshakes, leaving the initial conversation totally up to Blake and Qulys.

"As we've already agreed to, our initial visit will be limited to just the three of us for only one hour. Patty is a linguist who is excited to continue working with Juulys and Harry … well, I think you already know a lot about Harry from our events earlier this year. To say that Harry is excited about this opportunity would be one of the greatest understatements in the known universe!" Blake laughed and patted his friend on the shoulder.

"Welcome aboard, to both of you. Any friend of Blake's is a friend of ours," Qulys responded.

"Qulys, should we prepare to remove our suits now?"

"Blake, this is Thjars. I was about to tell Qulys to skip this and simply invite you straight into the ship, but knowing you as I do, somehow I doubt you would accept my offer."

"You are correct," Blake laughed. "A deal is a deal, no shortcuts now, but just the same, thank you for trusting us. I know how concerned you are with what you are about to share."

"Yes, we will commence de-pressurization now from the Jarisst I." The air quickly left as the group was again exposed to a hard vacuum.

Five minutes later, as agreed, the dock was re-pressurized with human air from the space dock.

"Comm?" Blake asked.

"All systems are green, Blake."

The three began disrobing their spacesuits. Unlike on previous space missions, these suits were specially designed to be significantly less clumsy and bulky than typical earthly space suits. The new suits were the slimmest spacesuit model ever made on Earth, designed solely for this trip and its unique purpose. Unlike the normal NASA space suits, manufactured by a spinoff subsidiary of ILC Dover that weighed approximately 23 kilograms, these specially designed suits only weighed 10 kilograms. They were designed for shorter exposures to vacuum where a secondary shell of protection is available, such as the space dock or within another ship–such as the Jarisst I. These suits were much easier to remove and also provide a significantly higher level of flexibility and dexterity while they were working on the Q-PAMS drive on board the Jarisst I. The suits also utilized a smaller air tank for shorter operational windows. Once the occupants of the space dock had seen the new lightweight suits, everyone wanted one.

During their first meeting with the Cjarians, out near Pluto, Blake had been excited to learn that the Cjarians' atmosphere was similar to Earth's. However, that still didn't allow them to utilize Cjarian air as none of them possessed any knowledge of the impact that naturally occurring toxins, bacteria or viruses that might be present in the air could have on the earthlings–or vice versa for that matter. Blake had discussed an idea he had with Jimmy, Harry and George to design a device that could filter and disinfect air from the atmosphere in either ship, as well as from the exhaust from their suits. If successful, it would be relatively simple to integrate it into their suits, thereby eliminating the cumbersome air tanks they were now required to carry. Harry and Jimmy were pretty confident that the electro-mechanical design could be developed, but George's lab techs were still working on techniques that would ensure that any toxins and contaminants, including bacteria and viruses, could be properly dealt with. If they could turn the idea into reality, then they would be able to stay within the Cjarian ship for unlimited time frames without creating undue risk for either species.

Until the decontamination design could be verified and completed, Jimmy and Harry had devised a small cart that carried spare air tanks to extend their visit times. The cart also included a battery-operated device that allowed them to drain and rebottle the air from their suits, rather than dispense potentially hazardous residue air streams into the confines of the Cjarian ship. The system couldn't eliminate risks, as any leaks or misconnections could release unintended human-contaminated air streams into the Cjarian ship, thereby putting their new friends at risk, but it would clearly decrease that possibility.

To better understand the risk of a deadly infection, Blake and Thjars had also agreed to exchange vials of blood from both species so that they could begin dual research relative to antibodies and potentially life-threatening diseases that could impact either species. It would take time, but George was confident that it was possible to develop vaccines that would protect the Cjarians from many human ailments, as well as vice versa, but it would take considerable testing and evaluation before either side would risk trials on live subjects.

With their suits removed, the three SEALs-turned-astronauts were now dressed in skin-tight, sky-blue tights from head to toe. It was easily determined that nothing could be hidden on their bodies. As planned, Qulys inspected their empty suits and requested each of them to rotate 360 degrees for him to visually inspect and verify that nothing was hidden on any of them. He found only one item to question, a small, box-like object that was located on the wrist section of each suit.

"What are these devices, Blake?"

"Those are communication devices; they also double as a computer connection to all the systems on the space dock. We refer to them as our LBs–the name requires a long story that I will have to share with you some other time, but I think you may find it as humorous as we did."

"OK, Thjars, everything looks as promised–and as expected," Qulys relayed.

"Suit back up, Blake; we are one step closer," Thjars directed.

The earthly trio suited back up and the docking bay was de-pressurized for five more minutes before re-pressurizing with air from the Jarisst I.

"Blake, do you remember those special straps we gave you when you entered our bay the first time?"

"Remember? I sure do, how could I ever forget! Qulys, I was hoping you still had them, but I was afraid to ask for fear that you would not have enough for Harry or Patty."

"You can thank Jarns for that. As you might imagine, he's had plenty of free time since we last saw you, so he made a few extra sets to be better prepared for a potential visit from you and your team. They're inside the ship and we'll help each of you put them on once we're inside."

"Thank you, Qulys–and Jarns. Harry, Patty … you're going to love this."

"Knarls, are you in position in the Weapons Bay?" Qulys asked.

"Yes, sir, as we agreed."

"Thank you, Knarls. Thjars, open the bay door, please."

The door at the Jarisst I side of the bay opened and exposed the Cjarian docking bay that Blake had climbed into many months ago. Qulys motioned for the trio to enter and Blake moved aside so that Harry could be first.

"Wow … Blake, it's the first day of school …"

"'Close Encounters of the Third Kind' … very appropriate, Harry," Blake acknowledged, laughed and then explained what it meant to the Cjarians.

The quartet gathered in the Jarisst I docking bay and closed the door behind them. Qulys helped all three strap on the gravity-simulation straps allowing them to magnetically interact with the ship's structure and simulate gravity-induced movement.

"This is unbelievable!" Patty declared.

"I was pretty excited when I first tried it, too, totally amazing," Blake responded.

"What do you think, Harry?"

"I'm actually walking as if there was a gravitational force pulling me down to the ship's floor. You explained how the straps are designed to provide various magnetic forces on different parts of the body, but seeing, or should I say *feeling it* is … absolutely amazing." Harry paused as he moved his arms around and took a couple of steps. "I must have died and gone to heaven … or I'm still in bed, dreaming. In the latter case, don't anyone dare wake me up. Eat your heart out, Tony Stark." Harry smiled, as everyone else laughed.

Qulys opened the final door to the interior of the ship. Juulys and Thjars were front and center, waiting for them. Blake turned to look for Harry, but Harry had stopped moving, or talking.

"Harry, are you still with us?" Blake asked his close friend. "I wanted you to be the first to set foot inside the interior of the ship

"... Harry? ... Harry, are you OK? You're a bit on the quiet side, my good friend." Blake smiled.

"Unbelievable ..." was all Harry could muster to say as he started to move forward again. Harry entered first and stood looking straight ahead at Juulys and Thjars.

"Harry?" Thjars asked.

"Yes, I'm ... I'm Harry ... thank you. Thank you."

Harry stepped aside, allowing Patty and Blake to enter. Qulys followed and then shut the bay door behind them.

"Comm, we're on board and the door has been closed," Blake relayed.

"Wish we were there with you–be safe and enjoy. Over and out."

"Juulys, Thjars, it's good to see you again," Blake said as he shook Thjars's hand firmly and then held Juulys's a second longer than normal before returning his gaze to Thjars. "But we have very little time, so I recommend we catch up on general information another time," Blake added.

By Cjarian standards, Juulys Lystnyng was a beauty. She was a full 1.95 meters in height (6 feet, 5 inches), with long, flowing reddish-gold hair. Patty, an attractive brunette in her own right, was quite tall by Earth standards at 1.75 meters in height (5 feet, 9 inches), but she seemed much shorter the closer she got to Juulys. Thjars was even taller than Blake at 2.01 meters (6 feet, 7 inches).

"Juulys, you are Cjar's top linguist and it is now my distinct pleasure to introduce you to our top linguist, Ms. Patty Myers. I am quite confident you two will hit it off well, and fill any remaining language gaps that exist between our two races."

"Can I see it?" Harry asked.

"See what, Harry?" Thjars asked.

"The Q-PAMS ... I ... I have to see it," he added meekly.

"OK ...?" Thjars looked perplexed.

"Thjars, let me step in for Harry. Harry is the closest semblance to a human sponge I've ever encountered when it comes to his desire to learn anything new. So as you can imagine, the day you left us was the single biggest disappointment in his life because he never even got to see the ship, let alone the secrets it held. Deep down, he was distraught–but he never complained, not even once. But that's Harry; he's one of the most sincere, non-selfish individuals you will ever meet. Today, his journey has gone full circle and this day will now go down as the single most exciting day of his life. So, please pardon his temporary loss of words."

"Well then, let us not make him wait any longer!" Thjars proclaimed. "Follow me, Harry; the next stop is the Q-PAMS."

*****

USSTRATCOM

"Gen. Whittler?"

"Yes."

"The latest Chinese moon mission appears to be returning."

"What is this, their sixth this year?"

"Seventh, sir."

"Good Lord. At a half billion a mission, they are spending some serious money. Anything noteworthy on this mission?"

"Only the lack of a return module, which means they've left another module somewhere on the moon."

"I wonder what the hell they're up to."

"I don't know, General, but whatever it is, it isn't small."

"Have we located where they're leaving these modules?"

"One or two may have gone to the Russian base, but we have no idea where the rest of them are."

"Hell of a hiding spot. Makes one wonder what they're really up to. Thanks, Lieutenant, I'll relay to Gen. Beckman at NMCC. Hopefully, they know more than they're sharing with us."

*****

Jarisst I

The agreed to one-hour duration for the initial visit came and went way too quickly for all involved, especially for Harry. While Blake spent his time reviewing the overall ship layout with Thjars, Patty spent her time with Juulys and Harry dedicated the entire time at the Q-PAMS drive with Jarns and Allympht. Harry was astounded at both the level of technological innovation and the manufacturing skill required. Both Jarns and Allympht had described the system highlights associated with the antimatter sequences, the quantum mechanics and the particle colliders that were the foundational design aspects of the engine system. It was way beyond anything ever seen on Earth. Harry was further astounded to find out that the Q-PAMS drive could actually propel the Jarisst I through space at more than 200 times the speed of light, which finally validated that it was possible to visit distant star systems and planets, something Harry had always dreamed about.

Although smaller and less complex than its earthly cousins, the super collider's mass of wires and piping that surrounded the Q-PAMS was still impressive, but the size difference was the most obvious difference. Earthbound colliders were typically measured in kilometers, but the ship's Q-PAMS colliders were measured in single-digit meters. The now deceased Capt. Blissiart had led the research that created the miniature molecular collider, and designed it such that it could bombard multiple atoms of a number of specially selected elements together to create rare, high-energy isotopes. Blissiart achieved the design within an astounding four-meter diameter envelope–small enough that it could be packaged within a spaceship. Part of the breakthrough had benefited from the use of the extreme cold of the vacuum of space, at only three degrees Kelvin, to provide the cooling capabilities that earthbound colliders required massive systems to achieve.

Similar to earthen particle accelerators, the Q-PAMS collider design included three primary subsystems: beam pipes, accelerating structures and a magnet system. Inside the beryllium beam pipes, beams of accelerated particles traveled in opposite directions under intense vacuum levels. However, where earthen colliders typically operated at 10-12 torr pressure, and required large, reinforced structures to achieve those operating conditions, the Q-PAMS was designed for use in space where a perfect vacuum was already naturally available. By designing the ship in such a manner to keep the Q-PAMS open to the vacuum of space, the Cjarians were able to eliminate the massive containment and cooling systems required back on Earth.

The intense magnetic fields required for collider operation presented another major challenge for the Cjarians. To overcome it, the Cjarians created a new material for their magnets that had required decades of development, a material that far exceeded any naturally occurring elements found on Cjar. Jarns explained that a material called Magnessyst had been developed with 50 times more magnetism than a similar material on Earth called neodymium. Not only was its magnetism stronger than any known magnetic material, but it had surprised Cjarian scientists when they accidentally discovered they could further increase its magnetic strength 100-fold when the material was embedded within an electric field. The result was that the Q-PAMS design, when fully activated in an electric field of 1400 volts per meter and at a frequency of 2.2 megahertz could achieve a staggering five Tesla, or 50,000 gauss.

Another breakthrough was the ability to continually generate rare isotope materials, and their corresponding antimatter isotopes, without allowing them to break down or commingle until the desired moment of collision. To accomplish this, the Q-PAMS design included the placement of four of the four-meter diameter colliders immediately next to each other in a double figure-eight fashion. One set of colliders manufactured the targeted isotopes and the other set of colliders manufactured its required antimatter equivalent. The process required timing accuracies on the order of a hundredth of a millionth of a second to ensure that the creation of the highly unstable isotopes occurred simultaneously, and at the exact time and position necessary for the controlled collision and resultant explosion. The subsequent energy releases were then funneled through a specialized exhaust system down the primary axis of the spacecraft, resulting in the creation of thrust for the ship. The amount of thrust created was dependent on the type of fuel annihilated, the amount of fuel and the frequency of the annihilation process.

Research had identified that different materials created different levels of energy. The energy level record was achieved from two synthetic materials known as Leo-1253 and its antimatter form, as Leo-3521. Both were highly unstable isotopes created by the famous Cjarian scientist Leo Tjassist.

The more Harry heard, the more his appetite to understand demanded yet more information.

"Blake, this is decades, if not centuries, beyond where our technology is. We would require multiple new breakthroughs to just stand at the precipice of this technology. The super colliders they built are beyond anything we've ever achieved. The closest we've come may be from the scientists at the National Accelerator Laboratory in Menlo Park, Calif. They were able to build a small, tube-like chamber filled with super-heated plasma of hydrogen gas. It used a laser to pass energy through a cloud of electrons. Their's does have tremendous potential, but they still haven't been able to turn it into a viable system that can operate for more than a few seconds. The Cjarian Q-PAMS design does it repeatedly on sub-atomic particles, thousands of times per minute, non-stop–and all in just a four-meter diameter! Could you have ever envisioned that, Blake?"

"To be honest, Harry ... not really, but I'm not sure my personal awareness is the measurement bar you want to rate Earth by." Blake laughed. "What else did you find?"

"And then there's the antimatter side of it. Blake, ever since the late 1920s, when the British physicist, Paul Dirac, first wrote down an equation that combined quantum theory and relativity, we've been trying to simply understand and analyze antimatter, let alone figure out how to harness its energy. We know that a collision of matter and antimatter will annihilate both constituents, but we could never generate adequate antimatter particles to sustain a continual annihilation process, typically losing the earlier particles before completing the final particles due to their highly unstable nature. The scientists at CERN would do anything to see this technology."

"Remind me, Harry ... CERN, that's the French nuclear research center, correct?"

"Close, it's actually the European Organization for Nuclear Research, and although a portion of it is in France, its main headquarters is actually in Switzerland. People get confused, like you just did, because the abbreviation is in French and stands for Conseil Europeen pour la Recherche Nucleaire."

"OK, perhaps before you further highlight my technical ignorance in front of our new friends, we should get back to the space dock," Blake hinted with a smile.

"Is there any way we can stay longer?"

"I'm sorry, Harry, but we have an agreement. We need to return to the space dock and all stand down for the next four hours. I'll contact Thjars and we'll review next steps and protocols. We should have plenty of time available to us over the next few days–enough to temper even your insatiable desire to learn more. We really need to go, Harry–we surely don't want to risk contaminating their air, do we?"

Harry immediately turned to face Thjars, pumped his hand profusely while thanking him, then turned and headed for the door.

"Well, we finally have Harry moving, so I guess I'd better move fast before he changes his mind and attempts to return to the Q-PAMS." Blake laughed.

The trio entered the lock and repeated the necessary steps to safely re-enter the space dock. It was going to be a long four hours, Blake thought.

*****

NSA Headquarters, Fort Meade, Md.
Oct. 4, 2029

NSA director, Brad Martinez, was looking over the latest intelligence report on Russia. The report detailed an upcoming military parade, scheduled for Oct. 8, called the Bulavin Revolution Parade. It was a new parade launched by Prime Minister Anton Titov and it looked like this would become another mammoth display of Russian military might. Russian military parades were well known for their pomp and bravado, the most famous of which was their annual Victory Day parade on May 9, commemorating the anniversary of Nazi Germany's surrender in 1945. These parades employed massive numbers of tanks, APCs, missile launchers and soldiers–a showcase of Russian power to emphasize they would never again be caught unprepared, as they had been in WWII.

Director Martinez had never heard of the Bulavin Revolution, so he requested a history dossier on it. The subsequently produced dossier detailed an uprising in 1707 when the Don Cossacks revolted against Imperial Russia, then under the leadership of

Peter I. The catalyst to the nine-month-long revolt occurred on Oct. 8, 1707, when a small band of local Cossack and Haidamak leaders, led by Kondraty Bulavin, ambushed and murdered Yuri Dolgoruki, who was leading a group of bounty hunters in support of Peter I.

How Anton saw this as a Russian success was not fully understood, as Imperial Russia eventually overcame the rebellion. Yet, no fewer than 11 of the 28 pages of the report were dedicated to the theories, opinions and outright guesses at trying to explain it–unfortunately with very few facts. The prevailing NSA opinion was that in some obtuse manner, this was Anton's way of telling the world that he was supporting a more democratic reform of Russia and not the heavy-handed dictatorship Russians had lived under for so much of Russia's history. Brad noted that President Putin, although greatly adored by many Russians for his return to strength, had truly been a dictator, but one more like a wolf in sheepskin. Putin's secret was that he showed well on television, displaying worldly presidential tendencies at times, rather than the blatant and brutal practices of some of his more infamous predecessors like Vladimir Lenin or Joseph Stalin. The last page of the report detailed a growing dispute between Prime Minister Anton Titov and Igor Yakovlev, the Russian military chief of general staff.

Director Martinez looked at his computer and began to type a reply to the analyst who sent the report.

"Good report, Justin, but I guess we'll just have to wait until the parade is over to know what it really represents. Based on the photographs showing the growing parade elements, it should at least be quite the show."

*****

Jarisst I
Oct. 5, 2029

Five days later, after multiple ship visits per day, as well as a number of video conference calls with a highly select group of earthbound experts, Blake's team and the Cjarians still remained at a loss to determine what was wrong with the Q-PAMS drive system. Furthermore, no one had yet to figure out how to even navigate all the complexities they'd identified within the system to a level that would allow them to fully understand how it was actually supposed to work. Sadly, the required expertise had been lost hundreds of years ago when the Jarisst I made its emergency light-speed jump, killing Capt. Zyles Blissiart, Jarns's brother and the inventor of the Q-PAMS drive system. Only two other personnel on the Jarisst I had been granted full access to the highly secret Q-PAMS design and they also died during the ship's emergency jump.

Diego and Sean came over a couple of times to see the ship, but quickly realized the daunting task was well outside their realm of expertise. Both returned to the dock and took turns re-enforcing the space dock's security forces that had been stationed 24/7 where the Jarisst I was docked in order to block unauthorized access. They maintained frequent communication with both Blake and Qulys, as well as greatly reduced Thjars's concern that someone might attempt to board the ship with nefarious intent.

George McDearmon also boarded the ship to get a quick look at the Cjarian Gravity-Cells, better known as G-Cells. George was as impressed with the G-Cells as Harry had been with the Q-PAMS. The G-Cells were a life pod in which the occupant laid in horizontally during lengthy high-G maneuvers. The pod was oriented axially in the direction of the planned acceleration with extreme precision to directional angles based on direct feedback from the flight computer. The occupant was placed in semi-hibernation for the duration of the trip, or as long as the ship was accelerating above 20 Gs. Once the ship slowed below a preset acceleration level or met the time duration of the mission segment, the occupant could be automatically revived through a series of small steps that required a minimum of a few hours, or as long as two days, dependent on the length of the hibernation they had been under.

Once in the G-Cell, the occupant was harnessed and immersed in an electro rheological fluid that changed viscosity with changes in an applied electric field. As acceleration levels were increased, the viscosity was also increased to better absorb the forces on the body. During extreme periods of acceleration, the liquid became gel-like and a circulation system was activated that allowed the gelatin-like material to be liquefied and extracted from the fore section of the G-Cell and then re-injected into the aft section of the G-Cell at very high rates to resist the force driving the occupant backwards during acceleration. The opposite process occurred during times of rapid deceleration and the pod was swung 180 degrees in the opposite direction to ensure blood flow was not diminished from the occupant's head. The combination of zero gravity and the G-Cell was adequate to protect the enclosed traveler for sustained acceleration or deceleration levels in open space.

To maintain bone and muscular system health during extended G-Cell occupation, a well-known deterioration risk for space travelers, the G-Cell suit was further designed to provide a membrane that wrapped around the occupant's entire body. The membrane consisted of thousands of electrical sensors that induced nerve and muscle activity every 60 minutes by twitching muscles to avoid muscular atrophy. In addition, the occupant's temperature was maintained at very low levels to minimize aging effects. That, in combination with a series of chemicals introduced into the occupant's blood flow, allowed the body to be maintained in a mode very similar to hibernation. Studies at the Cjar University for Physical Sciences and Biomedical Engineering demonstrated that the occupant's aging process could be reduced to 1/300th of normal, allowing an individual in a G-Cell to age fewer than five minutes for each day inside the G-Cell.

A hermetically sealed facemask provided oxygen for the G-Cell occupant. In addition, during extended hibernation periods, food and resultant bodily wastes were collected, reprocessed, salts removed, and the remaining water and nutrients then fed back into the body's circulatory system through an IV located on the forearm. Due to the reduced bodily function rates, very little nutrition was required and an individual could survive in the G-Cell indefinitely.

The other big highlight of the week was how well Patty and Juulys hit it off. The two had become inseparable, like sisters, and Patty already was speaking Cjarian as easily as Juulys was speaking English. Patty brought a modified Babylon Pro Package translation software package with her that Rakesh Deshpande had developed on Blake's flight to Pluto where he first met the

Cjarians. Rakesh, a computer expert from India, had joined the Armstrong I crew and first used the basic software package for translation purposes. However, after returning to Earth, he'd further modified the software and began teaching it by using the recorded Cjarian discussions they had obtained. He'd also been successful in modifying the subroutines to accept Cjarian speech by integrating IBM's Watson 2027 AI, self-learning subroutines with the Babylon software. The resulting system allowed Patty and Juulys to hold conversations in alternating Cjarian and English, using the same sentences, and simply watch as the computer created the backbone to a Cjarian-English translation package in days instead of years.

*****

"Harry, it doesn't feel like we're getting anywhere. What's next?" Blake asked.

"I don't know, Blake," Harry said. "As much as I'd like to think that Jimmy, Vladimir and I should be able to brainstorm our way through this, the truth is that we just don't have the expertise, or the tools."

Jimmy and Vladimir nodded in agreement.

"I think Jarns and Allympht can handle the chemistry of the materials, as well as the release timing of those highly unstable isotopes, but we need experts who know how to actually construct super colliders. That gets us back to our discussion from a few days ago; we need CERN–they're the best in the world."

"OK, then are you suggesting we fly some of their experts up here?" Blake replied.

"No."

"Then what, Harry?"

Harry looked at Jarns and Allympht, then at Jimmy and Vladimir. All four were nodding, and Jarns gave a thumbs up sign to Harry.

"Harry, what are you thinking?"

"We need to take the ship to the experts."

A heavy silence ensued, but it was quickly shattered as Thjars and Juulys began an intense emotional debate with Jarns in Cjarian.

"Harry, do you actually intend to land the Jarisst I on the planet … on Earth?" Blake expressed in total shock.

*****

Russian Ministry of Defense, Moscow
Oct. 6, 2029

It was 8 a.m. in Moscow, GMT+3, and an emergency session had just been called by Anton Titov, the prime minister of Russia. Anton had taken office after President Vladimir Putin left in failing health a few years earlier. One of the first things he changed was the scope and title of the top office in Russia, changing it from one of a dictatorial president to a more western-like prime minister. He'd made it his primary goal to soften relations with the West after the Cold War II, as the final years of President Putin's reign had been nicknamed.

Anton and four other high-ranking officials were sequestered in a small room on the second floor, just off the massive, three-story war room in Russia's Ministry of Defense complex. The other four individuals were part of his Executive Office: chief of staff of the Prime Minister Executive Office, Sergei Tolstoy; the director of Foreign Intelligence Service of the Russian Federation, Mikhail Yeltsin; the military chief of general staff, Igor Yakovlev, and his top adviser, Andrei Grigorov.

"Mikhail, show Anton and the group what you've uncovered during the past few days," Igor directed.

Mikhail pulled up a video feed and hit the play button.

"This is the American space dock. Watch as the Cjarian ship approaches from the right and then docks."

"How long ago did this occur?"

"Six days ago, sir, and they've not left since."

"I think I know the answer, Igor, but I will ask just the same … Has the American president, Callahan, made any attempt to contact us on this topic?"

"None, sir."

"Have they communicated with any other countries or have they allowed any other ships to dock there?"

"No, sir, but their Night Star docked there just before the alien ship arrived and it hasn't left. It appears the Americans are secretly meeting with the Cjarians."

"Seems like others must know about this as their satellites could pick it up as easily as ours did, correct?"

"Only if one is looking, Prime Minister," Igor replied flatly.

"So, as far as we know, no one else has any clue that the Cjarians have returned?" Anton asked.

"I didn't say that …"

"That does not make sense, Mikhail." Anton cut Mikhail off in mid-sentence. "Who then?"

"Sir," Igor stepped in, "Vladimir Popov has gone missing. He left over a week ago from his fishing vacation on the Kola Peninsula. His last known location was in Houston, Texas, just days before their Night Star launched for the space dock. He has not been seen or heard from since, and his phone went offline shortly after he arrived in Houston."

"What are you recommending, Igor?" the Prime Minister queried.

"We can launch from China within the next 72 hours. We should attack and disable the dock, and at the same time, give a warning salvo to the aliens, perhaps even damage their ship to prevent it from departing."

"Igor, don't you think you're jumping the gun a bit? Do you really want to start a war, and especially before we can prove the Americans have actually done something wrong?" Anton blurted out in disbelief at his military chief of general staff. "What if the Cjarians take your attack on the Americans as an attack on them? We have no idea what magnitude of weaponry their ship possesses."

"That is correct, Prime Minister, but it is a risk we must take. What if they've already started transferring technology—once that door is open, there's no going back. We cannot sit by idly and let the Americans pull off a coup of this magnitude. If they unilaterally obtain the alien technology, Russia, as it stands today, will be over. We will become a colony to the capitalist regime in America and will have to obey their every demand. Is that what you want?"

"No, Igor, no one wants that, but I think you're assuming way too much, way too early. If you are wrong, then what? It would become a humiliating embarrassment for Russia, and the aliens and their technology could be lost forever. Let us wait a little longer and see where this goes; perhaps they are simply refueling. I do not want to start a war with the Americans, or with the Cjarians for that matter. I will make contact with President Callahan and see what he is willing to acknowledge before we do anything. Is that understood?"

"Yes, Prime Minister," Igor growled, "But I am afraid that rather than being simply embarrassed, you are risking going down in history as the man who killed Russia. By doing nothing and letting the Americans checkmate you, you will cause so much damage to our country that it will make Mikhail Gorbachev's Berlin Wall debacle a simple footnote in Russian history. You seem to be more concerned about your upcoming military parade than you are in protecting Mother Russia. Let it be noted that I strongly object to your vote of non-action."

"Your dissent is noted, Igor, and you may leave–now."

Igor got up and walked out of the meeting, with the others fully expecting that the Prime Minister would attempt to have him arrested ... yet Igor was smiling as he left the office.

*****

Jarisst I

"Thjars! Thjars! Get Platsys down here!" Allympht yelled into the mic from the Comm room.

"Allympht, are you OK?" Thjars responded.

"We did it! We broke the code!"

"Slow down Allympht, what are you talking about?"

"The ship's log, I have access!"

"How is that possible, Allympht?"

"Remember how we attempted to use the code-breaker that Blake's team came up with when we were near Pluto?"

"Yes, but that was months ago; it didn't work on the ship's log, correct?"

"Correct, but Blake and Harry told us how to set one up like the one they had and told us we should just keep it running, so we did, mathematically going through all the possible combinations. It must have gone through millions and millions of options by now, if not even billions, but it finally worked!"

"Allympht, that's great news! We need to tell everyone! ... But, why Platsys first?"

"Cjar! The ship's log will show the flight path we took while we were in the G-Cells–and tell us where Cjar is! Platsys has the astronomy background to figure it out."

Thjars was speechless. He had forgotten about the code-breaker and although he had not shared his thoughts with anyone, the truth was that he'd given up hope of ever contacting Cjar again.

*****

The 11 surviving Jarisst I crewmembers all assembled in the control room. Platsys was at the console, where he had been feverishly working for the past three hours. Everyone whispered and waited as Platsys continued working until he finally broke the near silence.

"I know exactly where Cjar is ... and how we got here," Platsys stated quietly.

Everyone began to talk at the same time, clamoring to ask the same question.

"Whoa, settle down, everyone!" Qulys ordered to regain control, and then signaled to Thjars.

"Thanks, Qulys. The floor is yours, Platsys. Tell us what you found."

"There's good news and bad news, Thjars."

"We all need to hear it, Platsys. Just tell us what you found."

"The Jarisst 1 had just arrived in the Klaxx system and ..."

"The Klaxx system? That's not possible! We weren't heading there," Jarns exploded. "We would have all known that!"

"Sit tight, Jarns," Thjars directed. "I agree we didn't know anything about a trip to Klaxx, but until now, we had zero data on how we got here. So let Platsys tell us what he found and we can debate what we think afterward."

"Yes, sir, sorry."

"As I was saying, we had just arrived in the Klaxx system. The log states that Capt. Blissiart and other members of the crew had been violently re-awakened due to an emergency condition. Apparently, just as they were slowing down within the Klaxx system, and some of the crew were being revived, they fell right into the lap of two Klaxxstinian battle cruisers. The cruisers were not trying to destroy them, as they have done with every other Cjarian ship they ever encountered, but instead appeared to be trying to stun or damage the ship so that they could possibly capture it. It was that realization that caused Capt. Blissiart to order Lt. Pfssiast to re-initiate the Q-PAMS before they could return to their G-Cells–the captain fully knew that he signed the death warrants for everyone who was out of their G-Cells– including both Lt. Pfssiast and himself." Platsys stopped and looked directly at Jarns, the raw pain evident on both of their faces. "I'm sorry, Jarns."

"It's OK," Thjars interjected. "Jarns, Platsys, we both already knew Zyles was dead; now we know that he died a hero in order to save the ship as well as all of us alive today. Your brother saved us, Jarns." Thjars patted Jarns on the back. "Please continue, Platsys."

"The ship was relaunched in emergency mode, which means we accelerated at the extreme capability of the ship until we reached a maximum speed of 200 times the speed of light–a speed that the ship was theoretically capable of, but never validated– until now … I mean, then. The subsequent flight lasted three months, so the Jarisst 1 traveled 50 light years before it exhausted the Q-PAMS fuel reserves and powered to a stop."

"Does that mean we are 50 light years from Cjar?" Juulys asked.

"No, but we are a long distance away. It appears we didn't travel in a straight line the entire way due to a combination of automated, random course changes conducted to avoid detection as well as a number of course changes to avoid known celestial bodies. It also appears that at some point in time, the ship automatically conducted a wide-sweeping maneuver in order to start heading back toward Cjar. It was likely part of the auto-programming code."

"So how far away are we?" Thjars asked.

"I'm not positive yet, but I think the true straight line distance from Cjar to Earth is on the order of 25 to 35 light years."

"Why did the system not wake us up automatically? Why did it take over 500 years to revive us?" Juulys asked, almost crying.

"It will take us a lot longer to figure that out, Juulys, but that's something Allympht is most suited to unravel once he has time to work on it. I expect it'll still take him a lot of digging and research to validate, but our best guess at this point is that it was something built into the software's default logic. It's possible they never foresaw a situation like this and we're just an unlucky outcome from a standard software routine."

"Platsys," Thjars interjected, "so how did we consume all of our fuel?"

"The preprogrammed course changes were aggressive maneuvers, I assume to throw off any potential Klaxx pursuers. There also appears to have been a number of times where the ship slowed down below light speed and then accelerated again, perhaps just to evaluate the possibility of other ships being near, either friend or foe, or possibly to check nearby star systems. We clearly conducted quite a few maneuvers before the fuel system reserves hit critical and its internal programming then used the last remaining fuel to stop the ship where we ended near Pluto. Until proven otherwise, I'm sticking with my assumption that it was an unfortunate programming inadequacy–after all, this was, and still is a prototype ship."

"That's a good summary and a great reminder, Platsys. Thank you," Thjars responded, "but are you telling us that we would have been better off if the ship had just glided through space without any course corrections? We would still have fuel left if that was the case."

"You are correct, Thjars. We would still have fuel left, but unless we impacted something, we would still be gliding through space today, still in hibernation. At the speed we were travelling, we would have departed from our galaxy and entered interstellar space between the galaxies–we would have been lost forever. To be honest, the fact that we did run out of fuel and somehow ended up in this specific solar system, saved our lives–thank Glysst."

"Maybe we should launch a C-Pod and send it to Cjar with a distress call," Knarls interjected. "It could reach Cjar in a couple of months."

The crew was quiet. It was a lot to get one's head around. No one said a word until Juulys brought the group back to the moment at hand.

"Thjars, should we tell Blake about the C-Pod?"

"That's a good question, Juulys. Part of me says yes, and part of me says no. This is not a simple issue because there is so much at risk. Qulys, what do you think?"

"You're correct about the risk, Thjars, so I think we should hold off for now. We can always tell Blake later if we change our mind. This is simply too critical to jump too quickly."

"Thanks, Qulys, I agree with you, at least for now," Thjars responded and then looked at the rest of the crew, knowing that the same debate was likely going on in each of their minds as well.

"I know Blake has become the closest thing we have to a friend, so this will be hard on everyone. It will feel like we are not being truthful with him, but let's look at it as more of a timing issue, rather than a trust issue. We *will* tell him at some point, we just need to be sure of the *when*. Does that work for everyone?"

Juulys nodded.

"But before we decide to launch anything," Platsys interjected, "There is something else you need to know."

"What is that, Platsys?"

"The Klaxx system resides directly between us and Cjar."

*****

U.S. Strategic Command
Offutt Air Force Base

"Sir, we have verified three separate launches from the Xichang Space Center–all three occurred in the past three hours and at this point, all three vessels appear to be on a trajectory to rendezvous with the Russian space station."

"OK, keep tracking and update me immediately if anything changes. I'll alert Washington."

*****

White House
Oct. 7, 2029

A full day of intense debate at the highest levels of the United States government had followed. It was now Sunday, Oct. 7, and President Callahan, Vice President Annie Murphy, NSC Secretary Ben Tellinino, Chief of Staff Frank Pelino and Chairman of the Joint Chiefs of Staff Gen. Landon McMullen were in the White House Situation Room. Cmdr. Blake Thompson, Dr. George McDearmon, Harry Lundrum and the rest of Blake's team had called in from a conference room on the space dock with a video conference phone.

"Blake ... I understand what you're asking for, and more importantly, I understand why. However, it's one thing to visit their ship where isolation and the safety of the hard vacuum of space provides an unbreakable barrier of safety for humanity, but you are suggesting we take the biggest risk this planet may have ever encountered since a meteor wiped out the dinosaurs. Think about it ... if anything on that ship turns out to be deadly to mankind, the animal kingdom or plant life, it would be utterly disastrous. This is not a video game that we can simply hit the reset button, nor is it a battle that we can simply send more soldiers into when the first wave of soldiers is wiped out. This could become the endgame for the world as we know it today. We don't know anything about them."

"Dr. McDearmon."

"Yes, Blake."

"Share what we know so far."

"OK, Blake," George replied and then turned toward the camera.

"Mr. President, it's actually quite astonishing, sir. I don't even know where or how to begin to explain it, but we are amazingly similar."

"You're going to tell me that after just one week of assessment? Really? Let me remind you about history ... do you recall the smallpox epidemic that nearly wiped out American

Indian populations in the 1800s … were they not nearly identical as well? And COVID … COVID was only one decade ago and it spread across the entire globe, killing millions while also decimating the global economy. It took the world years to fully recover."

"Yes, I do, sir, and both are great points. These examples are routinely referenced as examples of what can happen to indigenous populations, as well as global populations, but like I said, this situation is truly quite astonishing. I've analyzed their blood samples and their genealogy is the same as ours–and no, I did not mix the samples up, they were marked in triplicate and monitored by no fewer than two technicians at all times. They are so exact that I believe we can literally transfuse blood between the two species. The ABO antigens are the same, as are the Rhesus antigens–it's almost as if we are somehow related, sir." George paused. "Furthermore, they have macrophages, B-lymphocytes and T-lymphocytes for fighting diseases just like we do. From what I can tell, they already have immunity to our known diseases, almost as if they had evolved in a very similar manner to us, but hundreds, if not thousands of years earlier."

"Do you really believe that, Dr. McDearmon?" the president asked, with growing impatience.

"With all due respect, sir, it's really not what I believe, it's what the data actually show."

"Let's assume for one second that you're right, even if I don't agree with you. What you are saying will protect them, but what about us? Couldn't they have evolved new diseases that could still wipe us out, something we haven't evolved defenses to yet?"

"That is theoretically possible, sir, but I see nothing in their blood nor from their air samples that support that. It's almost as if they're devoid of infectious diseases. I've talked extensively to Jenysys Thalysst, the Jarisst I medical officer, and it seems their medical technology is even further ahead of us then their spaceship technology is."

"George, I know you are one of the top experts in the world, but …"

The president was interrupted by the intense sound of battle stations on the space dock. Lights were flashing and the video from the dock was shaking violently.

"Blake! What's going on? ... Blake?" President Callahan shouted at the phone, but there was no response–the video link had disconnected.

*****

Space Dock

Blake transitioned into emergency mission mode. They were already dressed in their lightweight space suits and their helmets were arranged in a perfect circle on the conference room table.

"Until we know what's going on, helmets on, everyone–now!" Blake thundered above the emergency claxons. Lights were flashing and people were picking themselves up off the floor.

"Sean, Vladimir, get to the control room and locate Cmdr. Garrity. Find out what the hell just happened. Jimmy, Patty, take George and make sure his labs are intact. Diego, Harry, get to dock number two and see if Rachel and the Night Star are OK. I'm heading to dock number four; I need to see if the Jarisst I is safe. Everyone, check in as soon as you have updates."

*****

National Military Command Center (NMCC)
Pentagon

"What the hell?"

"Lieutenant?"

"Gen. Beckman, I think you need to see this."

The lieutenant rewound the satellite video and hit play.

"That's the space dock, correct?"

"Yes, sir. Watch what comes in from the upper left ... right about .... now."

"Was that a meteor hit?"

"I don't know, sir ..."

"Gen. Beckman ... call on line two."

"Let me borrow your phone, Lieutenant."

"NMCC, Gen. Beckman."

"Mark, Gen. Whittler, USSTRATCOM. Glad you're on. We have a potential red alert issue. We just validated a satellite-based missile attack on the space dock."

"A missile attack? Jesus, Louis, are you sure?"

"Yes, and a spacecraft that had been docked at the Russian space station is now heading directly toward the space dock. We need to alert the White House, ASAP!"

*****

White House Situation Room

"Get Russian Prime Minister Titov on the phone now!" President Callahan ordered.

The room was still filling up, but Annie Murphy, Ben Tellinino and Gen. McMullen were already seated.

"What status do we have on the space dock?" President Callahan continued.

"We don't know much yet, Mr. President," Gen. McMullen responded.

"Do we have USSTRATCOM on the line?"

"We're trying to get them on the line now."

"Have we heard from Cmdr. Thompson or Cmdr. Garrity on the dock since the alleged attack?"

"No, sir. Communications are down."

The table phone crackled to life.

"Gen. Whittler, USSTRATCOM here."

"Gen. Whittler, this is President Callahan. What the hell just happened up there?"

"Mr. President, based on the data we have, as well as what we've received from the U.S. Space Force, we believe the Russians have attacked the space dock."

A string of expletives interrupted the general.

"Do you have Titov yet?"

"No, Mr. President, we're still trying."

"Call the hotline then." The president's face was red with rage as he turned back to face the conference phone. "Continue, General."

"The first wave of the attack was carried out with hunter-killer, or HK satellites. No warning of any kind. From what we can assess, the initial salvos were focused on the communications hub as well as the station's defensive systems with most of the focus on the gallant guns. We immediately sent our tugs and our own nearby HK satellites into action to attack the Russian HKs. In so doing we lost two of our tugs. From the results of this skirmish, it appears that the Russian HKs may be superior to ours. We were able to kill two of theirs and perhaps damage two more, but all five of ours were lost. The Russians still have two fully functional HKs stationed near the dock, as well as the two damaged HKs. Of even greater concern, a manned Russian craft has since moved alongside the dock. Initial data suggests that it's the same craft that recently launched from China, the one that surveillance suggested might be a troop carrier."

"What personnel losses have we incurred on the dock and has the dock been compromised operationally?"

"As was stated earlier, we've not been able to re-establish communications with the dock, so we don't know for sure, but there is damage and it looks like docking bay number three is gone. That would suggest that the hull has been compromised."

"Sir," Ben Tellinino interrupted the conversation. "We have Russia on the line."

"Anton. What the hell are you doing? Why have you attacked the space dock?"

"Anton is no longer available. The more important question is what are *you* trying to do, Mr. President? Were you not secretly meeting with the aliens?"

"Who is this?" the president demanded.

"This is President Igor Yakovlev. I am now in charge of Russia–as well as its military. You have threatened the sovereign integrity of Russia and I will continue to defend my country at all costs!"

*****

CHAPTER 9

Space Dock
Oct. 7, 2029

Blake counted at least six major concussions on the space dock. Alarm claxons were still banging out emergency warnings. Automated messages were being repeated every three minutes that alerted crew members to don their space suits as well as to inform everyone that docking bay three had been compromised. Everyone was ordered to avoid the area except for emergency rescue personnel. All others were told to help the injured and to regroup in the mess hall.

Blake was working his way toward the Jarisst I at docking bay number four. He'd passed a number of personnel heading the opposite direction, but for the most part, it was eerily vacant. Blake floated by the final corner and was relieved to see two sentries still guarding the entrance to the Jarisst 1, both now suited up in full space suit attire.

"Is the Jarisst I safe?"

"I don't know, sir," one replied. "It departed shortly after the first detonation, and so did the Night Star."

"Detonation? From what?" Blake responded.

"Not sure yet, but we are under attack from someone."

"Attack?" Blake said as he eyed the man. "Who could possibly attack us out here?"

"The last contact we had with Cmdr. Garrity, he was saying something about hunter-killer satellites and then he broke off. We haven't been able to raise him since."

"OK, I understand. So what are you two doing?"

"Guarding the dock like we were directed to do."

"Well, that's good, I guess, but if the Jarisst I isn't here anymore, I expect you're no longer needed on sentry duty … make sense?"

"Yes, sir, sure does. What should we do?"

Just then, the automated message stopped …

"This is Cmdr. Garrity: we are at risk of being boarded. I repeat, the space dock is at risk of being boarded at docking bay number one. Break out the guns and ammunition and make sure everyone is armed. All guards and military personnel head for bay number one immediately."

"Time to move gents, follow me. By the way, I'm Cmdr. Blake Thompson," Blake said while looking over his shoulder as he started departing. Who are you two?"

"Chris Jones and Paul Belvedere, both privates, first class. Where are we going?"

"Where else? Docking bay number one. Show me the quickest path, but first get me something I can shoot with."

"Nothing here, so we'll need to head to the armory first."

The newly minted trio headed to the armory where they found Master Sgt. Joe Penske, USMC, handing out weapons.

"Master Sergeant, Cmdr. Blake Thompson," Blake said firmly as he stuck out his hand to the master sergeant. "I need a pistol, submachine gun and something that will shoot in a vacuum, and I need it quickly."

"I know who you are, Commander; follow me. The first thing you need to know is that all guns will fire in a vacuum because all ammo contains its own oxidizer. You just won't hear anything and you'd better be well-grounded or tied off because in space, every action has an equal, but opposite reaction, so you don't want to fly off into space and miss the fight after just one shot."

"Thanks, Master Sergeant, I'll try to keep that in mind," Blake answered as he approached close enough to talk in a quieter voice. "I need an honest assessment, Master Sergeant: how strong are your security forces?"

"They weren't put up here to fight, Commander. In your world and my world, most of them are here just to create the perception of security. To be fair, most have some kind of military background, but there are only a few you can truly count on that have experienced battle firsthand. In all reality, I don't think anyone ever planned on them needing to fight a battle. The biggest threat they expected was to keep order between the academics when they had too much to drink from the bar."

"That's good insight, Master Sergeant. Thank you."

While Master Sgt. Penske gathered the weapons, Blake called Diego and Harry, and updated them about the Night Star and Jarisst I departures. Blake directed them to meet at docking bay number one and added that he would bring additional weapons with him in case they couldn't find any.

Master Sgt. Penske armed Blake with a fully loaded SIG Sauer P320 and a belt with five additional, preloaded, 21-round extended magazines. He also handed Blake a fully loaded and very familiar Heckler & Koch MP5, along with a second belt holding five more 30-round magazines.

"Three hundred rounds. I might need more, Joe. Get me a gunnysack and pack it as full as you can. Any chance you have some hand grenades, too?" Blake asked.

"As you might gather, Commander, hand grenades are not part of standard issue on the space dock."

"But you are a Master Sergeant, and that clearly means you know how to make do when some 90-day office wonder doesn't give you what you think you might need. Am I correct, Master Sergeant, that you may have some contraband onboard?"

"Sounds like you've been around the block, Commander, and that would be a safe assumption because I lived on that block. Hang on."

The master sergeant floated to his small office, unlocked and opened a cabinet drawer and pulled out a metal box. He put it into a bag with a belt clip on it, returned to Blake and handed it to him.

"A special favor I called in, just in case. A box of 12 M67 hand grenades. One never knows, right?"

"Bravo Zulu, Master Sergeant, oorah!" Blake then turned to face Chris and Paul.

"All right, gents, let's get moving."

"You're sure as hell not leaving without me, Commander. Hang on; I'll be back in 30 seconds with my own gear."

"I was hoping you'd say that," Blake returned. "Do me one more favor and take an extra 30 seconds. Pack a rucksack with more weapons and ammo. I'm meeting a couple more from my team and I don't know if they've found any weapons."

"Now you're talking, Commander; no bastard ever won a war by dying for his country. He won it by making the other poor bastard die for *his* country, Gen. George Patton."

"Penske, I think we're going to get along just fine."

Two minutes later, the quartet was floating through the hallways, heading for docking bay number one.

*****

Sean and Vladimir had just reached the control room when another concussion rocked the space dock.

"Where's Cmdr. Garrity?" Sean asked the lone person in the control room.

"He left for docking bay number one; the Russians are trying to board us."

"Sons of bitches, let 'em try," Sean responded. "What else do you know?"

"We lost contact with Houston when they shot out our antennae cluster, so we're going on limited data. We can still communicate on board and your LBs will work within our immediate area of space, but until we can get a secondary mast up, we're cut off from Earth."

"Well, it is what it is right now. We've been on our own before, so it's up to us to figure things out. What's happened so far?" Sean asked.

"It appears that they initially attacked us with hunter-killer satellites. They shot out all four of our gallant guns, destroyed docking station number three and our primary communications mast, so we're pretty much unprotected right now. We have at least 10 MIA from docking bay number three, all presumed KIA, and many other personnel remain unaccounted for. In addition, a manned ship arrived at docking bay number one and it looks like it has a troop carrier section on it. We've tallied at least 10 enemy forces that left their ship on safety lines with backpack boosters and are now gathering at the entrance to docking bay number one. That's where our boarding assumption came from, even though there has been no contact yet. Based on what we can see from our external cameras, it looks like they're trying to jump the circuitry to open the door, but we're assuming that they'll blow the door if that doesn't work–and I doubt they'll wait very long before going to option two."

"You have to be friggin' kidding me," Sean replied. "Vladimir, what the hell is going on?"

"I don't know, Sean, honestly. This is highly unusual and not what I would expect from Prime Minister Anton Titov. I am truly upset to hear this. I will help fight them off, unless of course you are concerned about my allegiances."

"I'm pissed as hell right now, Vladimir, but I am not looking at you as part of their attack. If I thought otherwise, I'd have already taken you out. I think it's safe to say that we need your help more than ever."

Sean picked up his radio and called Blake. The two exchanged a few sentences updating each other. When the call ended, Sean looked at the control room lead, a lieutenant, and demanded to know where he could get a weapon.

"There isn't anything left here as Cmdr. Garrity took everyone from the control room and all the weaponry we had with him. The only gun I have left is this Glock 19 pistol and I need it to stand my ground here, Commander's orders."

"OK, Blake has a couple of extra guns with him, as well as three other guys he found. We'll rendezvous with him and join forces. Good luck, Lieutenant. Hold down the fort and don't think twice about pulling the trigger if someone shows up who shouldn't be here."

*****

George, Jimmy and Patty reached the medical lab where George's techs were supposed to be, but the labs were empty. Patty called and updated Blake.

No one had any idea where the lab techs were, but Blake knew they didn't have time to launch a search party now; all they could do was hope they had headed to the mess hall per the recorded messages. Blake directed Patty and her trio to the mess hall and suggested they sit this one out and protect anyone else who was there. He said he would catch up with them later.

Until then, Blake had a fight to engage.

*****

Jarisst I

"Jarns, I need to know if we incurred any damage."

"As far as I can tell, the ship is intact from an operational and a hull integrity perspective, but the fuel tanks might have taken some shrapnel from the explosions at the dock next to us. We're losing fuel quickly from the left tank and I expect it will be exhausted in less than an hour at its current rate."

"Can we patch it?"

"The leak is very aggressive and we can see it venting into space. By the time we could suit up and get outside, the tanks would already be empty. Thank Glysst we didn't have an explosion."

"Qulys, is anyone following us?"

"Their satellites could not keep up with us and have returned to the space dock."

"Who was it?"

"We're not sure yet, Thjars, but from the radio chatter we are picking up, we believe it's the Russians."

"Have you heard anything from Blake, or the ship they came in?"

"The Night Star left, just like we did, likely waiting for orders. It left so quickly I expect Blake and his team are still on the dock. From what we can see from here, it looks like the attacking ship is now trying to board the space dock, so I expect Blake has his hands full and doesn't have time to take calls."

Thjars was pensive. This had been his worst nightmare, that someone would attack, but he didn't expect it quite this way. Yet, he still felt like he had to help Blake, but how?

"Qulys, we need to help Blake. What can we do?"

"Glad to hear you say that, sir," Qulys acknowledged. "The satellites are unmanned. The ship is manned. Jarns has the satellites in his target scope right now."

"You were going to fire?"

"No, just following defensive safety protocol. Their satellites initiated the attack so we need to be prepared in case they attack us too, but … it also works the same for what you just asked about." Qulys smiled. "Just say the word and Jarns will make them disappear."

"Are you sure we won't risk further damage to the space dock?"

"There is some risk of additional shrapnel impact, but in all fairness, that's way less than what those two satellites did with their missiles so far, and they appear to be planning more."

"What about the attacking ship?"

"I recommend we wait and see what it does after we eliminate their satellite support. They may break and run," Qulys suggested.

"What if they turn and attack us?" Thjars responded.

"They will lose. Their choice."

"Thanks, Qulys, somehow I expect I would get a similar response from Blake as well."

"I expect you would," Qulys replied. "What are your orders, sir?"

"One more question, where is the Night Star, the ship that Blake came in?"

"It is well out of range; there will be no danger to their ship."

"Thank you."

"Your orders, then?"

Thjars didn't hesitate.

"Take the satellites out."

Qulys walked over to the nearest console, picked up the mic and called Jarns.

"Jarns?"

"Yes, sir."

"Do you still have the two satellites in range and targeted?"

"Yes, sir, as well as two more that appear damaged, but operational."

"What are you targeting with?"

"The photon beam whip. It should minimize the shrapnel risks by simply cutting the satellites in two."

Qulys looked over at Thjars.

"One last question, sir." Qulys walked directly in front of Thjars and the seasoned sergeant-at-arms looked as serious as ever. "I will support your decision 100 percent; you know that, sir. But I also need to make sure you are aware of the potential consequences before we continue. We will be helping Blake and the personnel on the space dock, and I believe that is the righteous thing to do. However, we will be, for the first time, initiating battle with a new, intelligent species of life located in an unknown star system."

"What are you suggesting will happen, Qulys?"

"That's my point, Thjars: none of us know. This could be a quick skirmish, or it could pull us deep into another war–one which we had no previous involvement, and there will be no assistance coming from Cjar. I think you have to assume the worst case, that case being that we will have committed this ship and its occupants to a new war–one where we have chosen to stand with Blake and his president. Is that your decision, sir?"

Thjars looked at his trusted friend. He surveyed the others in the control room and then paused. He looked over at Juulys, his back straightened and his eyes looked determined.

"Juulys, please record this for the flight log … Under my orders, and my orders alone, I am authorizing and directing this ship to engage in military action against unknown hostiles attacking what we believe to be a friendly space outpost." Then he returned his gaze to Qulys.

"Qulys, you are authorized to attack."

"Aye, aye, sir." Qulys picked up the mic and in a clear and authoritative voice, sent Thjars' command to the weapons center.

"Jarns, the attack is approved. I'm moving the Jarisst I closer and into position. Initiate on my order."

Qulys then turned to face Juulys.

"Juulys, please enter the fact that I support the captain's decision, 100 percent." Qulys then turned and saluted Thjars.

"It is the correct call, sir, and if they attempt to retaliate, we'll be ready. We're scanning all activity in this area; if anything else approaches, we'll know it and respond accordingly." He then held the mic to his mouth.

"Jarns, commence firing."

The ship began to hum. It was a sound none had heard since they exited their deep hibernation so many months ago. Yet it was a sound they all recognized from previous training missions–even though they had never used the weapon in a true attack yet. To the best of their knowledge, the photon beam whip had never been used in open warfare before today. The ship shook four times. As everyone watched, four long beams of brilliant white light reached out from the Jarisst I, separated from the ship and traversed the distance between the Jarisst I and the four remaining satellites, moving almost as if they were alive and seeking prey. Within seconds, the first curving line sliced its way through one of the hunter-killer satellites. That action was followed by three more curving lines slicing through the remaining satellites, literally cutting all the satellites in half. The bright lines vaporized at least a full meter of each of the vehicle's mid-sections, igniting flashes of light on three of the satellites as their fuel supplies were ignited, then continued out into space where the beams dissipated.

"Targets destroyed. That should get their attention," Jarns replied.

"Jarns, how good is your targeting … could you remove their ship's communications antenna mast without damaging their ship?" Qulys asked.

"Yes, that would be relatively easy as they aren't moving, and I could turn the energy level down significantly to reduce the risk to their ship. It shouldn't take anywhere near as much power to simply cut the mast."

"Thjars, permission to further level the playing field by removing their communications capabilities?"

"Permission granted." Thjars nodded.

"OK, Jarns, work your magic."

A fifth, but much thinner, shorter and less brilliant light snaked its way from the Jarisst I and separated the communications mast from the enemy ship.

"Nice work, Jarns." Thjars complimented his young scientist-turned-weapons officer. "Let's wait and see what they attempt next. Is their ship moving?"

"Nothing yet, sir."

"How is our fuel supply holding out, Zalmyt?"

"The left tank is basically empty, as we feared. The right tank is approximately 60 percent full, but also falling. We'll be severely limited on flight options if we're attacked and require extensive maneuvering."

"I understand, Zalmyt," Thjars replied, "but we can easily put a large distance between us and any hostile forces, if and when we need to, without using too much fuel. However, we need to start thinking about repairs and how to bring on additional fuel, especially if the space dock is overrun or damaged beyond repair." Thjars grimaced. "Why has their ship not departed or attempted to counterattack us?"

"It is critical to their mission to continue supporting their landing crew, rather than abandoning them," Qulys responded. "Although I also expect that after seeing how easily we dispatched their satellites, they feel safer closer to the space dock–hoping that we won't shoot because of the greater risk of collateral damage."

"I guess that makes sense, Qulys, especially if we hit their fuel tanks, but that leaves us in a standoff position where no one has the upper hand, doesn't it?"

"Actually, no. They have the upper hand to freely attack the space dock and if they can overpower the security forces there, they may be able to take control of the dock and attack us with the dock's own weaponry."

"Good Glysst! Qulys, we need to do something. Should we attempt a boarding party to support Blake?"

"I like the idea, sir, but I don't recommend we attempt any in-person support until we've made contact with Blake–there's simply too much risk for friendly fire casualties on either side, and let me remind you that there are only 11 of us. I advise that we wait it out, move closer to their Night Star to provide it with additional protection, and pray to Glysst that Blake can handle things on his end, especially now that we've evened the battlefield a bit more for him."

No sooner did Qulys finish his statement, than Juulys called.

"Thjars! Qulys! It's Blake! He told me to pass on his thanks for taking out the satellites. He wants to know if we've sustained any damage. He advises us not to approach the dock and said he'll call once they have things under control again. In the case he can't protect the dock, he is telling me to leave and contact President Callahan. Should I tell him about our fuel situation?"

"No!" Qulys answered. "He has enough to worry about right now. Just tell him we're safe and that we're ready if he needs our help."

*****

Moon Base, Pink Floyd

"Send the message, Boris."

"OK, it's sending now, Dimitri."

"I.Y., the additional personnel have arrived and moved into the new wing. Food and support resources were more than we ever expected. Caviar will be saved for celebration. Thank you. When is equipment scheduled to arrive?"

Stop.

*****

White House Situation Room

President Callahan assembled his key cabinet members in the Situation Room for an emergency session–those who were not in town were connected by secure conference lines. The numerous video screens around the room were cycling through various views of the space dock.

"Mr. President, this was a totally unprovoked attack. Innocent people have been killed, the attack remains underway and the space dock is at risk–the Russians are actually trying to board the dock as we speak. We need to counterattack now before we lose our ability to protect the dock," Gen. McMullen said as he pounded the table.

"What are we to attack, General, the dock itself?" Ben Tellinino asked.

"When was the last time we heard anything from the dock?" President Callahan asked, ignoring the debate between his National Security Council secretary and the Joint Chiefs of Staff.

"Not since the Russians shot out the communications tower on the dock 90 minutes ago," his chief of staff, Frank Pelino, replied.

"Frank, do we have an update on Anton, or Russia?"

"Yes. There are multiple reports you can read later, but here's the elevator version. We're assuming Prime Minister Anton Titov is dead," NSA Director Brad Martinez responded, "or, at best, locked away under guard somewhere. As far as our sources can assess, Igor Yakovlev, the former Russian military chief of general staff used Anton's new Bulavin Revolution Parade as a Trojan horse to secretly post forces loyal to him at strategic locations in the parade route and at key entrances to the Kremlin. His goal was to take over the Kremlin, by force if necessary, during the high point of the parade once Anton came forward to salute the troops. Although he had many key generals under his control already, the troops were not, and it appears it got ugly for a while as many troops were killed during the coup. Unfortunately, Igor had ensured that troops not loyal to him had empty rifles or rifles loaded with fake ammunition, while his own troops were carrying live rounds. The troops loyal to Titov never had a chance. At least 500 have been confirmed dead so far. A number of Russian generals have been executed and many more imprisoned.

The president swore under his breath.

"What is the status of the Jarisst I and our Night Star?"

"Both the Night Star and Jarisst I left as soon as hostilities were initiated. Cmdr. Rachel Joslin is well out of harm's way and awaiting our orders. We've not heard anything from the Jarisst I or Thjars since their departure, but it appears that the Jarisst I has attacked the Russian HKs, destroying them all, and has now moved closer to the Night Star."

"Have we attempted to raise them?"

"Yes, sir, no answer."

"Do we think they consider the Night Star as a potential threat?"

"We have no idea, sir."

"Ladies and gentlemen, I need options." The president surveyed the room, then settled on the head of U.S. Space Force, Gen. Ryan Cobb. Ryan had taken over for Gen. Keith McGraw just two months ago. "Ryan, what is the status of our space forces?"

"Not good, sir. The Night Star was not loaded for military action; its entire payload was dedicated to Cmdr. Thompson's crew and supplies. If we were to send Cmdr. Joslin into battle, she and the ship would likely be lost. We have two other shuttles: the Coral Sea is currently in the middle of a six-month-long D check at the Cape Canaveral MRO facility. The Vega is available, but wouldn't be ready to launch for at least three days, even assuming emergency orders. We also have a number of commercial options we could utilize, including SpaceX and ULA, among others, but they're not currently capable of military options."

"I am not ready to militarize the commercial space companies– so that's out for now. What else do we have, Ryan? What about our hunter-killer satellites?"

"Sir, they really caught us with our guard down–globally. Of our 33 HK satellites around the globe, only five remain. They hit us pretty hard right out of the gate."

"Did we get any of theirs?"

"Only 10, sir. They have another 20 in orbit, not counting the ones the Cjarians just took out."

"What about communications satellites? Why haven't they attacked those yet?"

"That's a good question, sir, but we think they're smart enough not to attack commercial systems due to the satellite-based infrastructure of our internet and telecommunications systems–they would be hurt as bad as us. So, short of a full-out war, we think they're hoping that you will stand down and take the loss of the space dock as collateral damage worth the trade to maintain peace and further destruction. That would also ensure that Mother Russia is better positioned to demand that they share in the gains associated with the alien technology."

"First off," President Callahan interjected, "the aliens have a name, and they refer to themselves as Cjarians. Let's start using that properly."

"Sorry, sir. I stand corrected."

"Mr. President," Ben jumped back into the discussion. "This is the nightmare scenario the experts warned us about. Our telecommunications systems have become so dependent on satellite systems that the loss of those satellites would throw us back more than a century."

"There are times, like right now, where living back in the 1920s almost sounds like it would be refreshing," the president responded.

"Yes, and, no–just not in this case, sir. A hundred years ago we possessed other systems that managed the world–those systems no longer exist as backups. Over the past two decades, we have become increasingly dependent on satellite-based systems for way more than what the average person realizes. Hospital emergency systems would fail, police and fire systems, including radios, would be compromised, commercial agricultural GPS and weather projections would become nonexistent, military GPS capabilities would be severely impacted, telecommunications, including television, cell phones and the internet would be gone overnight, commercial transportation systems would come to a halt, aviation would be grounded, and that's only the beginning. Mass rioting would start. Worse yet, the world only had a population of approximately two billion people in the 1920s. Today, we are closing in on nine billion people across this planet. Grocery runs would deplete supplies within days. Food distribution centers would be unable to deliver food and what was still in distribution centers would rot in place. Mass starvation would occur and we would be thrown into a global disaster like we've never seen. The world would simply be incapable of supporting the billions of people that now take daily services and food for granted–millions and millions of people, if not billions would be at risk in less than 30 days. It would become total anarchy."

"An unjustifiable position," the president responded. "And Russia knows we won't risk that. It's really no different than the assumptions and decisions our leaders had to make during the late 1900s under the Mutual Assured Destruction theories of nuclear destruction."

The president swore again.

"What about our anti-satellite missiles?"

"That is a possibility, sir. Our ASAT inventory is at least 10 times that of the combined total of Russia, China and India. The U.S. secretly spent considerable monies on new ground-based and aircraft-based ASAT systems over the past 20 years, and the bulk of those production budgets were spent on air-launched missiles. That investment stopped after 2026, following the accidental shooting down of a Chinese satellite by the Israelis. After that, the world agreed to a treaty that banned further development and production of all ASATs, primarily due to the risks we discussed earlier. A number of older missiles were also destroyed as part of the agreement, but the U.S. maintained secret supplies of all of its more modern airborne inventories."

"OK, tell me then, what do we have?"

"We have more than 10,000 airborne ASAT missiles remaining in our arsenal, most made by Raytheon, Boeing and Lockheed. That inventory includes over 2,000 of the top line AIM-329 ASAT missiles. This missile has a p93 kill probability with a single launch, even on Russia's newest satellites. It's a real ball buster. It can be launched by both the F-22 and F-35 fighter fleets, as well as the aging F-18 aircraft fleets. It can also be launched from the Northrop Grumman RQ-6 Global Hawk and Triton drone platforms, in addition to the X-49 UCAV."

Gen. McMullen looked over at President Callahan.

"What are you thinking, sir?"

"You tell me, General. I assembled this group to get your ideas."

The conference phone beeped and Vice President Annie Murphy jumped into the discussion.

"Mr. President, this is a legitimate act of war by Igor and the Russians. The entire world will see it that way. We need to level the battle field quickly, as well as send a definitive message to Igor that the United States will not tolerate any further aggression like this."

"What do you suggest, Annie?"

"Take out all their military satellites in one massive attack. Send a message no one can misunderstand and send it quickly."

The room broke into multiple debates, some for and some against. The hyped chatter continued for three minutes, until President Callahan demanded attention.

"As I stated at the beginning of the meeting, I want options. I'm pretty sure Annie initiated one and many versions of that followed, so let's get them up on the board. I want to see option description, pros, cons, probability of success and most likely Russian response as the primary review characteristics. Ben, I just nominated you to be our scribe and facilitator. We have one hour, get it done."

The next 60 minutes went quickly with spirited and at times heated debate. There were three primary options, with at least six additional, modified versions of those three also listed on the board.

Gen. McMullen was opting for a full destruction of all Russian space activities, including their role in the new space station jointly funded by China and the Russian state corporation, Roscosmos. The inclusion of the Russian-Chinese space station in the attack plans was too much for most in the room to consider, but Gen. McMullen was tightly focused on eliminating Russian's military space options and fought off all debate by repeatedly reminding the others in the meeting that Russia initiated the attack on our space dock.

Regardless of how passionate Gen. McMullen had been for the attack on their space station, President Callahan was convinced he did not want to bring the Chinese into the battle. He also struggled over the simple principle of attacking the space station when only a few years ago the Russians had been allied with the Americans on the International Space Station (ISS).

Most world leaders had long been aware that the ISS would fail to gain additional funding after 2024, so efforts to replace the aging station had begun in earnest in 2020, with the Chinese planning to have their station, the Tianhe-1, partially operational by 2022. In 2022, after the European Space Agency (ESA) elected to join the U.S. space dock team, the Russians decided to ink a pact with the Chinese National Space Administration (CNSA). Soon after signing, they finalized plans to transfer two existing Russian modules from the dying ISS over to the Chinese station by the end of 2024. By 2028, the continuingly expanding Chinese-Russian space station was second only to the joint U.S.-E.S.A. space dock.

"If I boil all of this down, I see three primary options," the president stated. "First, stand down on any aggression and try to get Igor to the negotiating table. For what it's worth, I'm with the vice president and Gen. McMullen on this one. The Russian attack is so grievous and unexpected, one could propose it rivals the 1941 Japanese attack on Pearl Harbor for its infamy, boldness and pure audacity–it must be answered with force. Option two is to attack everything the Russians have in space, including the Tianhe-1 space station. I'm not ready to go to war with both Russia and China over this issue, so the space station is out of bounds at this point in the game. That leaves option three: take out their military satellites. What do we have to do, how quickly can we do it and what counter moves should we expect from the Russians? Gen. McMullen, the floor is yours."

"Mr. President, as I mentioned earlier, they have 20 known hunter-killer satellites remaining. There are a minimum of 200 more we believe are also military in nature. Keep in mind that space has gotten very busy in the past decade, so targeting errors are highly likely. For example, in 2017, there were almost 5,000 known satellites circling the globe. Then came SpaceX, Viasat, Amazon, Google and the explosion of commercial satellites for phone and internet services. SpaceX alone launched over 12,000 Starlink satellites. Today, no fewer than 35,000 satellites compete for attention in space. Granted, that's a big area, and many are small, but it is getting crowded up there, so we need to plan on some collateral damage. Give me 48 hours to prepare and we could launch an initial wave of 200 AIM-329 missiles. We could be prepared for a second wave as soon as we have battle results from the first. I also recommend we escalate to DEFCON 2 immediately. Our forces around the world need to be at battle stations."

"I am not looking to risk an all-out satellite war, so the target field is those 20 HKs," President Callahan responded. "I want those 20 satellites eliminated in less than 12 hours, not 48 hours. Can you do that, General?"

"Yes, sir."

"And make damn sure none survive; use additional missiles if you need them. I concur with DEFCON 2, but only in tandem with our attack, not sooner. I want to reduce their reaction time. Until then, light up the commercial networks with the attack, get Russia on the defensive on the world stage. One more thing, in a scenario where Russia decides to escalate satellite attacks and go after our military communication satellites, what do we have to protect them with?"

"We have a fleet of 20 SR-72 Mach 6 Son of Blackbird aircraft that can launch the AIM-300 anti-missile missile, but that will not be enough to shoot down what the Russians could throw into the battlefield. We estimate they have at least 1,000 modern ASATs at their disposal. They have many more aged systems that we believe can be defeated by countermeasures that exist on our military satellites. The SR-72s will only be able to get 50 to 60 of their estimated initial launch. We could use the THAAD Gen II system to eliminate a significant amount of their missiles, assuming they made a full launch of 1,000, but that would reduce our defensive position relative to attacks they might initiate on Earth, including the continental U.S."

"This is going to get ugly quick. How many of our satellites will we lose?"

"We have to assume at least a 50 percent loss to be safe without the THAADs. We might be able to keep the loss below 15 percent with the THAADs. Our military communication capabilities will be impacted, but we can spread the surviving satellites out and still maintain global GPS support of military operations."

"And then what, we attack their military communication satellites in reciprocation? This will escalate very quickly." The president finished, stood up and began pacing the floor. "How can we stop the escalation? Annie, what are you thinking?"

"Mr. President, I don't think there is any way to guarantee that we can stop the escalation, but we can manage the risk to some degree. As soon as the attack is completed, get on the news networks and announce what has been done and why. Further explain that the U.S. is not looking to start a war, only to level the playing field the Russians initiated. Then highlight that the Russians killed Americans on the space dock with a cowardly attack–and underline the fact that the U.S. response did not put any lives at risk. However, this does create one new problem we are not prepared for."

"And what is that, Annie," the president asked.

"In order to save face, Russia will tell the world we were secretly meeting with the Cjarians to keep their technological secrets for ourselves, and that Russia had no choice but to attack in order to protect themselves from future American aggression supported by superior alien technology."

"Damn it!" was all President Callahan could muster.

*****

Johnson Space Center, Houston

"Rich, are you still tracking Chinese space activity?"

"Off and on."

"I can't believe how many moon launches the Chinese have been making. Seven so far this year, and what ... 22 since early 2025?"

"At least that, based on what we know."

"Gotta wonder what the hell they're doing with all those flights. They don't appear to be landing and they aren't publicizing any successes, so why doesn't anyone seem to care?"

"Good question, Matt. Guess we've been so busy with the space dock and the terrorist crap earlier this year that it's fallen to a lower priority in D.C."

"Are you still sending your updates?"

"Sure am, every three months."

"Anyone ever ask you any questions?"

"Nope, not a single question."

"That's crazy. What do you think they're up to?"

"I think they're dropping modules off. They have to be building something."

"On the moon? What would they be building on the moon?"

"I don't know, maybe a base to launch operations from?"

"Wow. And no one cares. All systems normal, man. Makes you wonder why we even bother sometimes, doesn't it?"

"Yep, sure does."

*****

Jarisst I

"Thjars," Qulys whispered, "come with me, we need to talk."

Thjars followed Qulys into his room, where Juulys was already waiting, and closed the door behind them.

"This is rather unusual, Qulys. What's on your mind?"

"We don't know how this is going to turn out. Even if Blake somehow wins, it seems it's only a matter of time until we are in danger again. This world seems to be forever at war."

"I don't disagree with that, but what are you suggesting, Qulys?" Thjars responded.

"I think we should send one of our C-Pods to Cjar with a distress signal."

"Without telling the crew, or Blake?"

"Correct on Blake, sir, but once you have decided, I definitely recommend telling the crew."

"What if somehow we end up bringing Earth into a bigger war; one that they don't currently even know about?"

"Yes, it's a possible risk, but that's why we're discussing it. In the end, it will have to be your call, but we will both support your decision."

"Why not tell Blake?" Thjars countered.

"Thjars, I can support telling Blake, but what if Blake doesn't survive this battle, then what?"

"Good Glysst, Qulys, please don't say that again," Juulys inhaled deeply as she replied.

"We have to be honest with ourselves, Juulys; this is an ugly picture right now and we really don't know who will triumph."

"We could use this ship to make sure he wins," Juulys responded.

"Yes, we could, but for now I want to keep our involvement limited to protecting this nearby sector of space, especially as we are still leaking fuel. I do not want to engage in any hostile activities on any other fronts as we can't risk further loss of crewmembers." Thjars continued. "Qulys, let's wait until we know the outcome of this immediate battle. If Blake survives, we'll share our plan with him. If we lose our good friend, then we'll retreat to a safe location where we can launch the C-Pod, fix our fuel leaks and wait out a response without threat of any ongoing conflicts from Earth. Does that work?"

"Yes, that works," Qulys replied. "Thank you, sir."

*****

CHAPTER 10

Space Dock

Blake arrived at docking bay number one with Chris Jones, Paul Belvedere and Joe Penske. Six members of the space dock security team were already there, led by Lt. Jane Peters.

"Who's in charge?" Blake asked as he floated down the hallway to the docking bay.

"I am, Lt. Jane Peters, and who are you?"

"Cmdr. Blake Thompson. Where's Cmdr. Garrity?"

"He's taking a team outside to flank the intruders before they can override the electrical controls to the dock."

"You need to stop him. How long ago did he leave?"

"He literally just left; he was heading over to the adjacent docking bay, bay number two. Why should I stop him?"

"They won't stand a chance. The Russian ship is parked outside of bay number one and they will pick Garrity and his security detail off one by one before they ever get a shot off. Get on the radio and tell him to stand down. Tell him I have an idea to raise a ruse for him first."

"Roger that, Commander, but we don't have a lot of time here. These locks weren't built with the expectation they would be at risk of break-ins like your house back home might be. I don't expect it will take long to conquer our security protocols."

"Fair point, thanks." Blake faced Master Sgt. Joe Penske.

"Joe, can you access the space tugs?"

"Absolutely, they're part of the security team's responsibility as our primary function was to protect the space dock against space debris. I think we still have two operational."

"That's what I was hoping you would say; come with me. Paul and Chris, stay here and provide backup for Lt. Peters. If any one of my team shows up looking for me, tell them to head to docking bay number six, but keep that info only to those that need it." Blake turned and propelled himself back down the hallway, Joe right behind him.

"Joe, I need a favor. Get on the ship's intercom and turn off that blasted boarding threat that keeps repeating. Everyone knows about it by now. Replace it with a single message that runs only twice, 30 seconds apart."

"Sure, Blake, what's the message?"

"Blake says it's nine o'clock. Where is Crispin Glover? Don't destroy it. They're trapped. They're inside."

"That's it? You're serious?"

"Deathly."

"OK, Blake. This sounds totally crazy, but here goes." Joe stopped his forward momentum, hung on to a wall railing, accessed the main Comm center via the LB on his wrist and turned on his mic; his words echoed throughout the ship.

"Blake says it's nine o'clock. Where is Crispin Glover? Don't destroy it. They're trapped. They're inside."

Joe turned off his connection to the Comm center. "The Comm center uses radio frequencies to broadcast, so you know the Russians likely picked that up as well, correct?"

"Yes. Trust me: timing is everything–it will work."

"If you say so."

*****

"Dang it," Sean whispered. "Turn around, Vladimir; we're going the wrong way."

"What? How do you know?

"The message. That was Blake."

"That did not sound like Mr. Blake."

"It wasn't his voice, but it was his message."

"You are not making sense, Comrade Sean. Where are we going then?"

"Docking bay six. I'll explain later; we have to catch up."

*****

"What the hell does that mean?" Diego asked Harry.

"That was good timing; we're right on top of it. Take a left: we're heading to docking bay number six."

"OK, Harry, how the hell did you decipher that one?"

"You were making a beer run, so you missed it. I'll explain it when we get there, that is, assuming I'm right."

*****

"Oh, my God, does that mean what I think it means?" Jimmy looked over at Patty in total surprise.

"Sure seems like it," Patty replied. "And knowing Blake, sounds like there's going to be action at bay number six, but we already have our orders: we're to find the mess hall and wait it out. If George's lab techs are there, we'll need to make sure they remain protected."

*****

"Jane, how are things holding up?" Joe checked in with the security team at docking bay number one.

"They are through the outer door and inside the inner bay. I'm guessing we have maybe 15 to 20 minutes before they figure out the inner dock lock. They have four soldiers in the inner bay and they've already pressurized the inner bay. They're armed and look like they came to stay."

"Stay strong and hold the bastards at bay … wait a minute; Blake is saying something … oh … that's a great idea!"

"What is?" Jane responded.

"Blake said open both the inner and outer doors simultaneously. It will probably only work once, and then they'll be on to it, but it will buy you some additional time. Reclose the doors once they're outside."

"I like it! Hold on …" Thirty seconds passed until Jane replied again.

"Wow! That was spectacular! Sucked those sons of bitches right out of there like an old mail bag on a freight train pole!"

As Blake predicted, the invaders were violently sucked out of the docking bay and collided with their comrades outside. Suited men quickly became a tangle of lines and attackers. It would take them a few minutes to untangle themselves and restart their attack.

"Wait a minute ... darn it ... there's still one hanging on. He's the one who was working on the lock and he tethered himself to the door. Looks like he was the smart one and he's pulling himself back into the lock now."

"Close the door, quick! Maybe you can still keep him outside."

"No, it's too late; he's pulled himself into the bay."

"Well, Blake says you may be able to do it one more time."

"How so?"

"From where you are, can you close the bulkhead and prepare to vent the hallway as soon as they regroup and get the inner door open?"

"Yes, I can send one of my squad back to the door. What are you thinking?"

"Even if they learned their lesson and tether themselves before they enter the hallway, it will cause them to have one hell of a bumpy ride on those tether lines for a few seconds. If you lock your guys down good and hard, you may be able to take a couple of them out before they can recover."

"Sounds like a plan, Joe. I'm on it–tell Blake thanks."

*****

White House Oval Office

"Frank, get Ben and come to my office ASAP. Have someone get Gen. McMullen, Gen. Whittler and Gen. Cobb on the line with us. Annie is already here."

Five minutes later, the core members of President Callahan's Russian response team were either in his office or online.

"I agree that Igor may leak the news about the Cjarians to the world, but we can't sit by and not retaliate, or worse yet, not defend the people on the space dock–those are our people. And that Russian bastard can still leak the news even if we don't do anything."

"What are you thinking, sir?" Gen. McMullen asked.

"I'm done thinking. I want planes in the air 30 minutes ago and I want every one of those Russian HK satellites off the grid in an hour. Can we do that, Gen. McMullen?"

"Yes, sir. I already took the liberty to load and fuel aircraft. Pilots are on standby at no fewer than 12 bases around the world, all classified top secret, presidential orders."

"Thank you. How can we ensure that we cover all the targets and not overstrike some and allow others to survive?"

"Computers and the software boys. The programming already exists, sir. We input the coordinates of each target, identify the attack platforms, in this case planes, and their various locations around the world and then the software auto-assigns each target to a plane or group of planes based on the highest probability of success. I have a second wave, half the first wave's size, on deck in case we miss any. We can have initial hits within 45 minutes and the second wave 30 minutes later, if needed."

"OK, you have your orders–launch as soon as possible. Update me after the launches and after the first wave has been assessed."

"Frank, I need you to get me on air in 90 minutes. I want the speech we planned on in Switzerland about the Cjarians."

"Yes, sir. What about the Russian attack and our ASATs … do you want me to draft something for you?"

"No, but thank you, Frank. I already know what I want to say to that son of a bitch, as well as what I will say to the world. The gloves are off. I want him on the line five minutes before I go live on the networks."

"What if we can't locate President Yakovlev? Do we delay the broadcast?"

"Hell, no. You tell his staff it will be their problem if he's not. He started this war and I'm not waiting for him–and you can quote me on that, every word! Any word from the dock yet?"

"None, sir. We're still trying," Frank replied.

*****

Space Dock

Blake and Joe arrived at docking bay number six about 90 seconds after Harry and Diego.

"Bingo! That was a great message, Blake. Thank God for movie nights at the atoll," Harry replied just as Sean and Vladimir arrived.

"Could someone please explain how the hell everyone knew to come to bay number six?" Diego asked.

"First things first, Diego. Joe, do you have one of those tugs within range?"

"Ready and raring, Blake, just tell me what to do."

"Hold it ready. Patch me through to Garrity."

"Done."

"Garrity here, is that you, Jane?"

"No, it's Blake. Are you on your security channel?"

"Yes."

"Good, so am I. I'm looking at their ship from bay number six. You're at number two, correct?"

"Yes."

"How many gun ports do you see?"

"They could always have more internalized, but the only one I can see is on the nose, pointing directly at bay number one."

"Same here," Blake responded. "OK, here's the game plan, and Master Sgt. Penske saved the day for us."

"I did?"

"Yes, you did. It appears that being the good ole jarhead he is, he managed to squirrel away a whole box of M67s."

"What? Those weren't approved ..."

"Sweet deal!" Diego jumped in, "I think I know where you're heading."

"Correct. Garrity, you hold for my signal. Joe is going to pilot the tug in from over top of the space dock, directly toward the nose of their rocket and make one quick firing run from his debris gun. That will focus all of their attention on what's coming at them. If he gets lucky, he may be able to pop some holes in that puppy, but Vegas odds suggest it won't take long for them to take out the tug. Regardless, it's only one firing string, Joe, because shortly after that, I'll be heading directly toward the tug's target, got it?"

"Got it, Blake."

"While Joe diverts their attention, I'm going to deliver his special package to that gun port, and yes, I'll have a long pull line tied to the grenade pins. Once out of range, I'll detonate the package and create a new viewing port on their ship, but everyone needs to get down because shrapnel will go everywhere. Hopefully, not only will it destroy their gun and cause havoc inside the ship, but the escaping gas should rotate the ship upwards and start a tumbling action away from the dock. As soon as that happens, we empty out of both bays and start cleaning up the stragglers before they can recover. That initial blast will be your cue to move. Got it?"

"I like it. Let's go," Garrity responded.

"Hang on. I need to make one more call," Blake replied.

Blake tapped his LB and five seconds later, Thjars' voice came on line.

"Thjars, this is Blake. Are you still able and willing to help?"

"Yes, Blake, good to hear you are OK. We are committed now, there's no turning back, but I prefer to keep everyone on board."

"That works, and for what it's worth, I'm both regretful and thankful at the same time."

Blake explained his plan, how they would sacrifice one tug, attack the gallant gun, and if successful, there was a chance the ship would rotate up and tumble away from the dock.

"If we are successful, I'm not asking you to kill anyone, nor destroy their ship for fear of still killing the remaining crew. I'm only asking you to further disable their ship. Can that white lasso of yours slice the rear nozzles off their ship?"

"Hang on, Blake, I need to ask Qulys." The mic went quiet for 45 seconds before Thjars returned.

"Blake, we do not know the design of their ship, so we cannot guarantee that we won't cause an explosion, but we are willing to take the chance in order to protect you and your friends. Qulys himself will take the shot."

"Thank you, Thjars, and please thank Qulys for me as well. You will know if this works or not. If it doesn't work, please stay at distance and wait until I can find another path of attack. I have to go, but I will contact you after our attack."

"What if …"

"Thjars, I don't plan for that kind of failure, but if you don't hear back from me, then I recommend you depart farther out into the solar system until you know more–and don't hesitate to defend yourself against anything that doesn't act friendly." Blake ended the connection.

Blake and Sean floated into the bay along with Joe and Diego. Harry closed the inner bay door behind them. It took him a few minutes to arrange four grenades in such a manner that the tie lines would be aligned on the rings for easy extraction. Once those were removed, the spring arm, or spoon, would release and the grenades would detonate within four to five seconds. Blake removed the safety pins and signaled Harry to open the outer door, but the four men stayed inside, out of sight of the Russian ship.

"All yours, Joe. Happy hunting with that tug."

Joe accelerated tug number two toward the nose of the Russian ship. As soon as the tug began firing, the Russian ship angled slightly up and began firing back at it. It was a crude system, on both sides, but still effective."

"Garrity, did you catch that? They had to angle the ship up to fire. I think that increases the odds that the nose gun is their only shipboard weapon."

"I hope you're right, Blake."

"Joe, cease firing, but keep approaching," Blake ordered.

With the diversion in play, Blake exited the bay, attached to a long tie line at his midsection, and propelled himself toward the Russian ship, while Joe, Diego and Sean moved out of the docking bay and got into position. As expected, the occupants of the ship, as well as the soldiers trying to enter the bay door, were all acutely focused on the tug.

Blake floated noiselessly across the void toward the Russian ship. It was an incredible and indescribable feeling as he traversed open space with Earth below him. His eyes wrestled to absorb it all while instantaneously trying to translate and make sense of what they were seeing. Simultaneously, Blake's body grappled against what seemed like a total loss of physical control to manage his path once he had released himself from the docking bay. Blake had to fight his mind's primeval tendencies intent on driving his body and adrenaline levels into a fight-or-flight panic mode.

Just then, Blake caught the silent explosion of Joe's tug. As expected, the tug hadn't lasted long against the ship's gallant gun, but it further challenged Blake's concentration on the task at hand. His mind was locked on the carnage above the space dock and kept waiting to hear and feel the explosion that never came. Keeping his focus on his mission's target was becoming a major mental melee in itself.

Even in his current adrenaline-induced state, it became clear Blake had misjudged his target due to the opposing movements of the ship and the dock; it was like playing 3D chess while the table was spinning. Blake was going to fly by just underneath the attacking ship and end up in open space–easy prey for the soldiers once they realized the vanquished space tug was not the only threat.

"Sean, quick, tug the line back and down; that should cause me to move upwards as a reaction–do it now!"

As instructed, Sean reached out, grabbed Blake's tie line and gave a strong downward pull on it just as Blake was passing directly under the ship. The requested action jolted Blake into a new path, transposing his linear motion into that of a rapidly moving arc, heading directly toward the bottom of the ship's nose.

"Perfect, Sean," Blake whispered under labored breaths. "Release about two more meters of line."

Sean watched as Blake arced gracefully upwards, but at the same time, concerned with how fast he was moving ...

"Dang it! Sorry, Blake–you're going to hit hard. Hang on!"

Blake grabbed his tie line and twisted his body to avoid face planting against the ship or impaling himself on the gallant gun structure. He extended his right hand just in time to grab the gallant gun support structure, causing his accelerating body to rotate hard into the side of the ship in a rather undignified manner.

"Phew! That was close–thanks, Sean. Hopefully, I didn't wake anyone up inside the ship with my graceful landing."

"Sorry about that, Blake, maybe I pulled too hard. So, how about you set those 'nades and get the hell out of there!"

"I need to tie these off in proper position first; it's going to take a minute or two."

"OK, but you better hurry; now that the tug threat has passed, those guys at the dock are starting to look around their surroundings more, likely looking for where the next attack will come from. Four of them are enclosed in the outer dock bay and 12 more are outside waiting their turn once they break the code."

"I need more time: tell Jane to go ahead and open the inner bay door for them, but first make sure everyone is tied down hard and hidden. As soon as the first four are inside the hallway, she can commence the hallway evacuation and start cleaning up while they're still bouncing off the walls and tethered to their tie lines. That will get the attention of the other 12 focused back on the docking bay and reduce the risk of them seeing me. The next four will enter the hallway better prepared, but by then we should be ready to take the attack to them from out here."

Joe relayed Blake's message to Jane and within seconds, they could hear Jane's voice providing play-by-play updates. Jane had already overridden the security software built into the bay doors as they were designed to prevent the simultaneous opening of both doors—for obvious reasons. The four invaders hit the end of their tie lines like a whip and collided hard with the dock structure, clearly disorienting them.

"Fire!"

Jane's crew, still protected by the structures they had hidden behind, moved into firing positions and started the counterattack. Blake's plan had been established to cheat the odds in their favor and it worked even better than he had hoped. The four invaders were fully exposed, outnumbered and lacked the time to recover. All four were taken out within 30 seconds. One of Jane's squad was also injured by a ricocheting bullet that pierced his suit and arm. Jane and her medic released their lines and propelled over to the stricken soldier to seal his suit.

"I'm restoring pressure so we can bandage up our casualty. Anyone else injured? Belvedere, double check those enemy KIAs and then get a headcount of the friendlies."

"On it."

"Sean, retract me, but start slowly so I don't accidently pull those rings prematurely."

"Got it, boss-man."

Three long, antagonizing minutes later, Blake was back alongside Sean.

"Garrity, is your team in protected positions?"

"Yes."

"Good. Once we blow that gallant gun, make sure your team is set up in pairs: one to fire at their troops and one who is well locked onto the ship and can hold their designated shooter in place. None of us have done this in space yet, but we all know Newton's third law–every action has an equal and opposite reaction. The last thing we want are men flying off into space or bouncing off of the end of their tie-lines. Tell me when your men are paired up and understand their roles."

Ninety seconds later, Garrity was back.

"Ready to go, Blake."

"So are we. Hang on to your seats." Blake and Sean teamed up; Sean would be the sharpshooter and Blake the immovable force holding him in place. The same held for Joe and Diego. Diego was holding and Joe was the shooter.

"Pulling the rings. Four seconds until detonation."

The grenades detonated four seconds later. It was another eerie scene … one quick flash … no noise or impact wave of any kind … fighting in space definitely required an entirely new paradigm of expectations and reactions. The gallant gun separated into pieces and began traveling away from the ship. A quickly dissipating white spray exited the ship where the gun had been, validating that the hull had been breached as well–an unplanned but welcome added victory. The ship's nose began to rise, slowly at first, gaining speed with each passing second. The ship began to tumble. Steering rockets were firing in an attempt to regain stability, but the magnitude of the jetting air from the hull puncture was more than the ship's pilot could overcome with the small maneuvering rockets. The ship spun through three complete rotations, each rotation taking it farther away from the space dock.

Without warning, a blazing white arc blew by the ship and harmlessly disappeared into space.

"What, they missed?" Sean said disappointedly.

"Give them a chance, Sean. Think about when you line up from two miles out and the wind is blowing, and the target is in a crowd. Your first shot is a safe shot to get the line on the target without risking friendly casualties."

No sooner did Blake finish his statement than a second white arc caught the ship on its fourth rotation and separated the aft three meters of nozzles and structure from the ship. As the slice acted in the direction of the spin the ship was already moving in, but was still at a slightly different angle, the attack increased the rotation frequency of the ship and added a gyro-like roll to it as it continued to drift farther into space, spinning wildly.

"OK, you win; I should have figured that out on my own," Sean said meekly. "Good shooting, Qulys. Those boys will be green in the gills by the time they get that spin back under control."

"Garrity, we're ready to attack; get your team in position and let me know when you're ready."

"Moving now, Blake."

A full two minutes passed before Garrity responded. Unfortunately, that was also enough time for the attackers to see what the defenders were up to and they immediately began firing at the emerging defenders. One of Garrity's security team took a shot directly in the chest and was out of action. The attackers, however, had not taken the time to anchor themselves and the shooter became a spinning projectile, impacting three of his nearby comrades.

"We can't wait any longer. Shoot when ready, Sean." Blake locked down on Sean and tensed every muscle he had in an attempt to make both of them one with the structure of the ship.

Sean's body jerked with each successive shot, but Blake kept him locked in place, absorbing each recoil so that Sean could continue rapid shooting. As with the tug and grenade blast, the shots lacked sound–an absence of sensation hard to get used to. Sean was not just a sharpshooter; he was the best of the best, having proven himself in the field and in military shooting competitions. It really wasn't a fair fight, but they'd chosen to start it and Blake was set on finishing it. The attackers were falling rapidly. Sean took out four of the attackers by himself before Garrity's team had taken their first shot. Joe took out two more. Caught in the crossfire with nowhere to hide, and no ship to protect them, the attackers never had a chance. All 12 were taken out in fewer than five minutes.

"Garrity, what's the status of your team?"

"One dead and two injured. We have to get them into the ship before they exhaust their suit air. Blake, you saved our team by telling us to wait. I can't thank you enough for that. And your strategy to pair the guys off was brilliant–that gave us the extra edge we needed. I'll see you inside."

"Thank Joe. He was the one who reminded me about the equal and opposite reaction."

*****

The White House

"Mr. President, I have Gen. McMullen online."

"OK, send his call in."

"Callahan here. What do you have for me, Landon?"

"It's a long story as you may imagine, sir, but the short version is that the objective was a success. All Russian hunter-killer satellites have been destroyed."

"Thank you, Landon. Any losses or issues that I should be aware of?"

"Unfortunately, yes, there were. We lost two F-18s and one F-22."

"How?" The president clenched his lips.

"One F-18 crashed shortly after takeoff, some type of malfunction. We're still looking for the pilot. He launched off the George H.W. Bush Aircraft Carrier, just west of Christmas Island. The other F-18 and the F-22 were shot down; both were part of the second wave. As I relayed earlier, the first wave was very successful. We got 16 of their HKs with definite kills on the first wave of the attack, but four more remained operational, so I launched the second wave. Unfortunately, by that time, the Russians were fully aware of what we were up to and they launched everything they could. Three Sukhoi 57 fighter jets scrambled from the Russian base Klyuchi in Kamchatka Krai and dropped one of the F-18s that launched from Osan Air Base in Korea. The Sukhois never made it back to their base; three F-35 Lightning IIs made sure of that. The F-22 Raptors launched from Elmendorf Air Base in Anchorage, Alaska. We are still investigating that kill, but it appears the Russians launched a volley of new hypersonic missiles at it. The pilot was able to evade the first two, but not the third. We believe both pilots have been lost. Four other U.S aircraft were damaged during the subsequent air battles and at least four more Russian jets were downed. At the moment, battle groups on both sides are positioning, but the fighting has stopped."

President Callahan looked up at the ceiling and shook his head.

"Landon, I hope I'm doing the right thing."

"You are, sir. We are at war, declared or otherwise. They were brave men and they knew what they signed up for–they were committed to protecting this country and acted without hesitation. They are warriors and heroes."

"Yes, they are. Get me their family names and phone numbers; I'll make the calls myself once we have verified their loss."

"Yes, sir, their families will appreciate it."

"What else, Landon? Any collateral damage?"

"Yes, one U.K. satellite, one Chinese satellite and two Russian commercial satellites were lost or damaged. We also took out a few of SpaceX's internet satellites. With the exception of the Russian satellites, we are making contact with the other satellite owners to explain the loss."

"Thank you, Landon. I'll be back in touch. Maintain everything at DEFCON 2 readiness levels until you hear otherwise from me. Let me know immediately if there are any retaliatory strikes."

"Yes, sir."

President Callahan hung up just as the Oval Office door opened and Frank Pelino walked in.

"Mr. President, we have President Igor Yakovlev on the line."

"Thank you, Frank. Put him through."

Frank reached over to the conference phone and clicked on the flashing line.

"This is President Igor Yakovlev of Russia; with whom am I speaking?"

"You can cut the bull crap right now Mr. President, you know damn well who you are talking to. This is President Andrew Callahan." President Callahan looked directly at the videoconference screen, ignoring both the prompter and his notes.

"This conversation will be short, as I have exactly five minutes before I go on the air to explain the tragedy that just occurred on my country's space dock. I will also inform the country and the world that many innocent American lives have already been lost and that the battle to maintain control of the space station remains under way.

"I don't know what the hell you were thinking, Mr. Secretary, but your initial decisions and actions have already set the stage for your legacy to be one of a deranged, misguided, power-hungry despot hell-bent on isolating his country from the world–not leading it. I pray that Prime Minister Anton Titov is still alive; he was a good man who loved and defended his country, and a man that the world, including myself, was beginning to trust.

"To be clear, Mr. Secretary, I acknowledge that I have no responsibility or control over what goes on in your country, but I clearly own the responsibility of what happens on the space dock. Let me also remind you that the space dock is the sovereign property of the United States of America and it houses U.S. and European citizens on it, which means I have a constitutional right to defend it. I've seen the video recordings of your hunter-killer satellites initiating the attack and the damage they caused. I've also seen the video recordings of your spacecraft departing the Chinese-Russian space station, arriving at the space dock and then disgorging soldiers attempting to board the space dock–and it's very clear that those soldiers are armed. I intend to share those videos with the American public and with the world.

"As for attacking the space dock, let me make my next statement absolutely crystal clear: The United States of America and this president view your attack on the space dock and the killing of innocent people on board the dock as a grievous act of war. As I'm sure you're already aware, I've just moved our military to DEFCON 2–something this country has not had to do with Russia since the Cuban Missile Crisis in 1962. I also gave the order to eliminate your hunter-killer satellites in retaliation for their attack on our space dock, but note this Mr. Secretary, unlike your actions, I intentionally did not target any non-military installations or targets, nor did I risk a single Russian life.

"Before you decide to escalate matters further, be forewarned that any further aggression from your country will be met with even greater U.S. resolve and intensity. Do not deceive yourself to think that I can't, or I won't. I will do whatever it takes to protect this country, its people and its interests from external attacks on our sovereignty and safety. I will also protect the Jarisst I and its occupants in the same manner as I would any other U.S. citizen.

"So I suggest you reconsider your next move long and carefully, and perhaps you can even rethink your way through explaining how this was all one big mistake so that both our countries can find a path to standing down without losing face to the world. I will help you establish that path if you decide you want to back away from war. If it helps, the reason the Cjarians were at the dock was because they contacted us for assistance and requested we keep it secret–you can ask them yourself if you desire verification.

"Mr. Secretary, until you convince me otherwise, the United States of America is treating this attack as a hostile act of war and I will tell the world exactly that when I go live on national television in 60 seconds." President Callahan paused. "Peace now depends on you, Secretary Yakovlev. Please choose wisely. Goodbye."

President Callahan hung up the phone and looked directly at his chief of staff, Frank Pelino.

"President Callahan, that speech was a clear and inspiring message, as strong and damning as I've ever heard. You delivered it with credibility, determination and resolve–and eliminated any doubt you would take the country to war over this issue. You put him on notice for his actions, yet you still found a way to keep the door cracked open to discussion that could end this conflict before it gets any uglier. It's his move now. Sir, it was masterful, your best yet–you actually frightened me just listening to it."

"This wasn't about speeches, Frank; it was about getting a lunatic to realize he just made a historic mistake and the United States of America will not tolerate it."

President Callahan thanked his chief of staff, asked him to invite the camera crews in for the nationwide broadcast. He then turned his chair to look out the Oval Office window while the crews feverishly set up their cameras. The *incident* had now become a *war* in Gen. McMullen's and apparently Frank Pelino's eyes as well. Hell, he'd even used the word himself, from his own mouth. Three brave pilots dead. An unknown number of personnel on the space dock also likely dead. The status of the space dock was unknown. The country was now at DEFCON 2 for the first time since the opening phase of Operation Desert Storm during the 1991 Gulf War and the 1962 Cuban Missile Crisis. Russia had apparently suffered a coup and his ally, Prime Minister Anton Titov, was no longer in charge, possibly no longer alive. He didn't even have time to think about contacting the Cjarians. The joy of success and peace that the country felt just a few short months ago, now seemed like ancient history as his presidency and the country were once again standing at the brink of yet another major conflict.

"Mr. President, you are on in 15 seconds; the prompter is keyed," Frank Pelino called President Callahan back to the moment at hand. "As you requested, with the exception of Russia and China, all of the other world leaders that shared in the Armstrong I mission have been notified and agree with your plan–all wished you good luck and repeated their willingness to support the U.S., as needed."

"Thank you, Frank."

It was time to address the nation, and the world.

President Callahan's emergency broadcast interrupted all television and internet stations. It started with the "Breaking News" headline and a picture of the White House. The coverage opened with President Callahan in the Oval Office. The broadcast lasted 20 minutes; it did not provide any opportunity for questions at the end. President Callahan briefed the world on the stunning news of the Cjarian arrival with the same speech the White House speechwriters had previously prepared in defense of Sen. Harley–a now distant priority. He went on to narrate how and why the Cjarians had come to the dock and then the unexpected attack by the Russians from the Chinese-Russian space station. President Callahan outlined why he elevated the nation's current defense readiness condition to DEFCON 2 and promised he and their government were doing everything possible to protect the U.S. and to bring Russia to the negotiating table. However, he also made it clear that if Russia were to pursue additional acts of war, the full power of the U.S. military would be brought to bear. Then he provided additional insight on the Cjarians and the monumental milestone that the discovery represented, reinforcing that the Cjarians were a friendly species that he and our allies looked forward to working with. He further informed the world that there would be additional Cjarian information made public from his administration over the next few days, but at this time, he and the White House needed to focus on the attacks from Russia. President Callahan again asked the nation for prayer, just as he had done earlier in the year during the terrorist attacks, and ended his speech with a solemn "God bless America."

*****

CHAPTER 11

Space Dock

Once everyone was back inside the dock, Blake headed for the Control Room and contacted Thjars, but only after first checking with his other team members to make sure all were accounted for and safe.

"Thjars, we've regained control of the dock with your assistance–thank you, and that was great shooting by Qulys."

"I will tell him for you. Did you lose anyone?"

"We've lost a number of personnel down here and there's a lot of damage to deal with. It will take us some time to get a headcount, repair leaks in the dock structure and get communications re-established with Earth. What's your ship's status and have you picked up any signals from Earth?"

"We've lost a lot of fuel, Blake," Thjars responded. "One tank is empty and the other is slowly draining. We haven't conducted external assessments yet, but we're assuming we must have taken shrapnel from the initial attack when they blew up the docking bay next to ours. To your second question, it does appear that someone tried to contact us, but we were busy monitoring your situation and missed the call. Do you think it was President Callahan?"

"Very likely, Thjars. Hang on for a second; I'll be right back."

Blake looked around for Cmdr. Garrity and located him at the main Comm center desk.

"Garrity."

"Yes?"

"You've got a lot to deal with here, but there's a lot more going on. Can you handle it without my group?"

"Until that ship is out of the picture, I'd really prefer to keep you around, but if you need to go, we'll make do."

"You're down to only one space tug, correct?"

"Correct."

"Maybe I can help on both accounts–hold that thought."

"Thjars, can you hook me up with the White House through your communications systems? I'll send the connection information over."

"Let's give it a try," Thjars responded.

A minute later, Blake was listening to the sound of a phone ringing.

"President Callahan's office."

"This is Cmdr. Blake Thompson. I'm on the space dock and I need to talk to President Callahan. It's critical."

"President Callahan is not available. He is currently addressing the nation."

"I understand. Is Gen. McMullen available?"

"No, he is with President Callahan. There is a national crisis ongoing."

"Tell me about it. OK, please tell him as soon as possible that we have secured the space dock and repelled the Russian attackers–it's critical that he get that news before he talks with Russia again. Also, please have him call Thjars. All of this is related to the crisis you are referring to."

"I will slip him a note, thank you, but Thjars? Who is Thjars?"

"He will know, just tell him T-h-j-a-r-s."

"OK, will do, Commander. Goodbye."

"Wait! Don't hang up yet. Can you reach Gen. Keith McGraw?"

"Hold, I'll try."

While Blake held the line, Diego finally spoke up.

"OK, could someone please explain how the hell you all knew to go to docking bay six? I'm beginning to feel like I'm in Sean's shoes, always one step behind."

"Hey, watch that!" Sean acted insulted.

"Like I told you earlier," Harry interjected, "You left movie night to make a beer run. Remember we were watching 'Nine'? The Tim Burton movie with those weird-looking puppets in a post-apocalyptic world of good versus evil?"

"Yeah …?"

"You left just before the scene where number six grabs number nine's shoulders and tells him not to destroy the contraption that was attacking them because the others were inside. We actually had an interesting debate about the scene so it was fresh in everyone's minds, except yours, of course, because you weren't there. Blake took advantage of the timely discussion and used it to give us directions, knowing there was no way anyone else could ever decipher his hint. Obviously it worked; it was that simple."

"Everything is simple for you, Harry, but I get it now, thanks. Once again, movie night has proven its worth." Diego chuckled.

"Cmdr. Thompson?" Blake looked back at the phone. He had forgotten he was on hold while he tuned in on the group's discussion.

"Yes, Gen. McGraw?"

"Yes."

"Good to hear you, General. I need some help."

Blake spent the next five minutes updating the general.

"So, what can I do for you?"

"It sounds like the President and Gen. McMullen are not available, but I need to get this Russian ship moved well away from the dock, especially if the Cjarians are going to return. I understand we have maintenance tugs that work on the satellites. Is there any chance we can redeploy one to move the Russian ship out of this area of space?"

"Actually, we can, and I can do one better as well. I'll get a message to President Callahan and Gen. McMullen, and for that matter, my replacement Gen. Cobb as well, to make sure they know what we're doing and can also relay a message to the Russians. I'll let the Russians know the maintenance tug will stay alongside their craft until further notice, and if any attempt is made to return to the dock or to damage the maintenance tug, we will auto-detonate it. That should provide for some improvement in the local area of détente, don't you think?"

"Gen. McGraw, I like it. Great idea and thank you."

"Give me about 30 minutes and we should have that maintenance tug on site."

The call disconnected and Blake called Thjars back.

"Blake, I need to update you on something as well. We've debated this quite a bit and to be honest with you, I've even struggled with myself trying to determine if I should tell you or not." Thjars paused.

"This sounds serious, Thjars," Blake said to entice Thjars to speak further.

"It is, Blake. Very serious."

"Like I've told you before, Thjars, the best way to deal with tough discussions is to just get it out on the table and then work it out."

"Yes, you've consistently stated that, but this is still hard," Thjars replied and then continued. "We've finally been able to crack the code to the ship's log, which also contains all of the ship's actions and Capt. Blissart's orders." Thjars went on to share what they'd found, including the knowledge of Cjar's location.

"That's sad to hear about Capt. Blissiart, but it just makes me wish even more that I could have met him. It sounds like he was a great and honorable leader. But all in all, this is great news, Thjars, so why the concern?"

Thjars reviewed their desire to send a C-Pod with a distress signal to Cjar–and the fact that the Klaxx system was between Earth and Cjar. He also reminded Blake that they had no idea of what state Cjar was in, or if it even existed anymore. They discussed the issue for a few more minutes before Blake made a final recommendation.

"Thjars, if I was in your shoes, I would launch the C-Pod. I'm not even sure I can honestly say that I would have shared what you just did if our positions were reversed–I thank you for that. Having said that, had your Q-PAMS not failed, you would have already attempted to find Cjar after you left us, and we wouldn't have known anything, correct?"

"That's correct, Blake. Do you think you need to inform President Callahan?"

"Not urgently. I recommend you make preparations for the launch. I will inform President Callahan of the plan, but that shouldn't change anything."

"Thank you for your understanding, Blake. We'll start preparations."

*****

President Callahan finally managed to free himself up from the cacophony of people trying to get his attention, as well as the issues that had demanded his attention over the past two days. He closed himself in the Oval Office, requested he not be disturbed for the next 60 minutes, and requested a connection to Blake.

Blake took President Callahan's incoming call in Cmdr. Joe Garrity's personal quarters on the space dock. As the space dock communication tower was still out of commission, the call was routed to Blake's personal LB through Cmdr. Rachel Joslin on the Night Star.

The president had already been briefed, but he wanted to hear the unbiased details firsthand from Blake and Joe. It was clear the president was still upset over the Russian attack, but his initial questions focused only on the casualties on the dock and the current safety of the remaining crew. Fourteen crewmembers had died and another 24 were injured, seven of whom were in critical condition and could not make the challenging flight to Earth until they recovered. Five remained unaccounted for and were presumed lost; all had been from docking bay number three. After answering every question the president had regarding space dock personnel, Blake and Joe spent the next 30 minutes answering questions about the attack and subsequent defense of the space dock, including the help provided by the Cjarians. The short summary was that the space dock remained operational but had sustained significant damage that would require months and many Night Star launches to repair.

"How bad is the damage to the Jarisst I?"

"We aren't sure yet, Mr. President," Blake volunteered. "They continue to leak fuel from their remaining tank and if we can't get that repaired soon, the ship and crew will be in peril."

"How long do you estimate they have?"

"Without repairs, less than two weeks at best–and that assumes they remain stationary. High-speed flight operations will obviously exhaust the fuel quicker. So until we know more about what the Russians are really up to, I recommend we keep that fact ultra-secret, sir."

"That makes sense, Blake. I'm in full agreement." The president paused. "Although it will take time and money, I am confident that we can make the necessary repairs to get the space dock back to full operational status—foremost of which is to get the communication gear and debris protection systems back online. What I'm not confident about is the Jarisst I and our Cjarian friends, so what do you recommend we do now, Blake?"

"This is the second time the Cjarians have placed themselves at risk to come to our aid; and in this case, the outcome would have been much different without their attack on the Russian HKs. Based on that alone, we owe them our support and I've decided to delay my return to Earth until we can help them better assess the damage. To start, we're setting up a spacewalk to inspect the fuel tanks and I plan on joining them on the excursion."

"Thank you, Blake. I think that makes sense, especially given everything else that's going on right now, but please be careful," the president said. "Blake, I know Harry still wants to bring the Jarisst I to Earth for repairs of their primary engine drives ... the Q-something?"

"Q-PAMS, sir."

"Yes, the Q-PAMS, thank you. I'm sure that the fuel issue will only increase his, and your interest in such a proposal, am I correct?"

"One hundred percent, sir."

"Blake, I'm still struggling with this for the reasons you already know about. The risks are incalculable, but knowing Harry, he isn't going to stop. Has he made a proposal that would reduce or better control the risks?"

"Actually, he has, and as usual, Harry researched it from every angle he could come up with and I think he has a proposal that may help you reconsider."

President Callahan let out a heavy breath.

"Somehow I expect I'm going to hear it whether I want to or not."

"Sir, if it's OK with you, I'd like to invite Harry in so he can share it with you directly–he's waiting outside the door."

"I should've known that as well." The President laughed. "And I expect you were planning this all along, so go ahead."

"In all fairness, sir, it's not like we have any spare time and I needed to make sure I could cover all critical issues with this call. Fortunately, you initiated the discussion without me needing to bring it up." Blake smiled, opened the door and invited Harry in.

"Hello, President Callahan."

"Hello, Harry. I understand you want to twist my arm again to let the Cjarians land on Earth, so let's get at it: what have you got for me?"

"White Sands, New Mexico."

"The test facility?"

"Yes, sir, they actually have great facilities to support repair and test activities and we can invite CERN scientists to join us there to assess their collider systems."

"Why is this safer?"

"White Sands specializes in hazardous materials research, so they're used to dealing with highly dangerous environments, and they're far away from major population centers in case something did go wrong. El Paso is the closest major city with a population of 700,000, but there are 100 miles of near wasteland landscape in between. If we needed to, we could literally scorch 20,000 square miles of desert and rock to ensure nothing escaped. In addition, Dr. McDearmon can arrange for personnel and equipment to be set up from both the Atlanta and Houston Centers for Disease Control and Prevention. Lastly, Holloman Air Force Base and the 56th Fighter Group are less than 20 miles to the northeast and can provide air cover support. We could easily add another wing, as well as station army patrol groups at strategic highway points and at various locations across the nearby terrain. To be honest with you, sir, based on the technical needs of this operation and the desired security and seclusion aspects required, I believe this is the single best location on the planet."

"OK, gentlemen. Given the circumstances, it's a good proposal, but that doesn't mean you get a *yes*. You're still asking me to put the entire planet at risk–not a small consequence to consider. Let me review it with my staff and we can regroup after your spacewalk, then decide the best next steps. Until then, thank you for the update, but I need to attend to other pressing matters back here on planet Earth. Goodbye, gentlemen."

*****

NASA Headquarters, Washington, D.C.

The conference room door was labeled Classified Meetings Only, and a handful of leading NASA scientists and administrators were inside, huddled around a computer screen.

"Have you double-checked these calculations?" NASA Administrator John McCallistor asked.

"Yes. Upside, downside, frontwards, backwards and crosswise. They are correct. The 39 percent and 17 percent values are based on the final Monte Carlo simulation. We ran it one million times. We compared our results with the German scientist, Klaus Schneider. He concurs. But there is one major variable that could impact the analysis."

"What's that?"

We don't know the density or weight of the body and how it will be impacted by the sun's gravitational field–that could significantly affect its trajectory."

"As I recall, President Callahan requested that Harry Lundrum be consulted as well … does he agree with the numbers?"

"Mr. Lundrum is not available. He was on the space dock during the Russian attack. I understand he survived the attack and is OK, but I expect he has a lot on his plate right now. Regardless, Klaus Schneider is continuing to try to make contact with him."

"A 39 percent probability of impacting either the Earth or the Moon, and a 17 percent probability of impacting Earth," John McCallister muttered under his breath.

"How long do we have?"

"It's still on the other side of the sun, so estimates range from eight to nine weeks."

"What options have we looked at?"

"We're working on it, sir."

"We're working on it? That means nothing, correct?"

"Pretty close to that. The only options currently on the table are nukes and the Cjarians. The Cjarian option is a total unknown that few people are even aware of. In addition, Pentagon rumors are already circulating that their ship took on damage during the Russian attack, so we doubt they will be a viable option. The nukes aren't much better, regardless of what Bruce Willis demonstrated in 'Armageddon.'"

"All right, ladies and gentlemen, this just became NASA's number one priority, but let me remind you, it remains top secret. I don't want a word of this leaked until President Callahan announces it himself. I need a formal report summary on my desk in 60 minutes so we can brief the president."

*****

Russian Ministry of Defense
Oct. 9, 2029

"We expected the Americans to counter our hunter-killer satellites elsewhere around the globe, but could someone explain to me how we lost our rocket and troops at the dock?" President Igor Yakovlev pounded the table in front of him. "We had an entire squad of Spetsnaz backed up by their ship and four hunter-killer satellites. We had the dock schematics and actually trained for this event—and we lost them all? What the hell happened?"

Everyone looked at Sergei Tolstoy, President Yakovlev's chief of staff of the Presidential Executive Office.

"Mr. President, the aliens threw their support in with the Americans. We didn't plan on that, and even if we had, it wouldn't have changed the outcome. The aliens quickly eliminated the hunter-killers we had stationed at the space dock with a weapon we have never seen before, and then they targeted our ship's communication array, thereby eliminating our ability to communicate with our own ship," Sergei explained.

Sergei had been the Russian chief of staff of the Presidential Executive Office for Prime Minister Titov, but he also secretly joined Igor's inner circle prior to the coup. He now continued in the same role for President Yakovlev.

"So? Did we not do the same to their space dock? You are making excuses, Sergei! The Americans evened the playing field, but we still had the element of surprise and 16 fully armed Spetsnaz at the dock. We doubled the original plan for eight soldiers and that still wasn't enough?" President Yakovlev's steely eyes bore into his staff. "Sixteen highly trained Spetsnaz soldiers–the best in the world! How?" he yelled at his staff.

"We are not sure, Mr. President, but we do know that they had a SEAL team on the space dock. Although we are confident their defensive guns had been knocked out by the hunter-killers, our ship was still disabled with some type of explosive device that caused it to tumble out into space. We have yet to make contact with it. Without that support, the Spetsnaz were unable to gain control of the docking bay. They were caught out in the open by the American forces, unable to defend themselves, all sadly, all were slaughtered."

No one said a word for a full minute.

"There's more, Mr. President," Sergei added as he looked over at President Igor Yakovlev's new Military chief of general staff, Gen. Boris Vasiliev.

"Mr. President, Cmdr. Thompson and his team are on board the American space dock. He was there to meet with the Cjarians. He is the same commander that met the Cjarians near Pluto, and … he is also the one who destroyed the Domashev."

President Yakovlev threw his coffee cup across the room, shattering it into a thousand pieces, and simultaneously launched into a volley of expletives.

"Cmdr. Thompson? Are you sure?"

"Yes, Mr. President. We also believe that Maj. Vladimir Popov may be with him."

"Why was I not informed of this?"

The room went silent again. Everyone was well aware of the close relationship between President Yakovlev and Gen. Domashev. They had been schoolmates, enlisted in the military together, and during the original coup plan, Yakovlev would have been the number two man in the new Russia, second only to Domashev. That all changed after Domashev was killed. It had been the same Cmdr. Thompson who had outwitted and destroyed his ship during the race to the Cjarians' ship near Pluto earlier in the year. President Yakovlev had sworn vengeance on him then, and now that he knew that Cmdr. Thompson had struck out at him again, it only increased his craving for revenge.

Gen. Vasiliev finally spoke.

"We should destroy the dock and eliminate the commander and his SEAL team all in the same attack, and if Vladimir is on the dock, he is a traitor to Mother Russia and should die as well."

President Yakovlev looked up from the table at Gen. Vasiliev with a face that reflected pure anger.

"No, Gen. Vasiliev. It turns out you had that chance, but you wasted it–we *were* in a position where we could attack and maintain the ability to tell the world that we were defending ourselves because of the cheating Americans. But not any longer … we lost that opportunity because the alien ship has since departed from their space dock. If we were to attack the American space dock now, we would not be able to justify our actions to the world. Knowing what they already know, a new attack would empower the United Nations to view it as a formal act of war against the Americans–and the world would take their side. They would be justified in any attack they dared to initiate, but worse yet, their President Callahan would get approval to reinstate the sanctions and oil bans that previously took their toll on our country. The Russian economy would have to reach out to the Chinese, or collapse. To make it clear, I am not ready to forfeit our country's financial wellbeing to the Chinese, any more than I am willing to bow to the demands of the damned Americans.

"Gen. Vasiliev, find a better way to stop the Americans from working with the aliens, and find it quick. In the meanwhile, I have other plans in the works for Cmdr. Thompson."

*****

Space Dock
Oct. 10, 2029

Per Blake's request, Cmdr. Rachel Joslin returned to the space dock earlier in the morning after confidence had been re-established that the Russians were no longer capable of mounting a counterattack. Blake told her it was critical she transport him to the Jarisst I so he could help inspect the fuel tanks. To provide additional support, Sean volunteered to co-pilot again.

Blake also requested Jimmy and Harry join him on the spacewalk for the inspection, so all three men loaded their gear and supplies and headed to the docking bay. But this time, unlike their previous trips on the Night Star, or their first visit with the Cjarians, every person on the Night Star would be fully armed for battle–just in case the Russians did show up again.

As the Night Star moved away from the space dock, everyone craned their necks to get a good look at the space dock. Technicians were already working on building a replacement communications tower, but the damage to the rest of the dock was more than anyone expected to see.

"That will take years to repair," Rachel volunteered. "It wouldn't surprise me if they never replace docking bay number three … The entire structure is gone."

"Those sons of bitches need to pay for this," Sean added.

"Remember how all of those debris panels were positioned?" Rachel asked. "At least 30 percent of them are damaged and another 20 percent are gone."

"Their HKs were very effective," Blake acknowledged. "All right, folks, there's nothing more we can do here, so it's time to get back to the mission at hand. How quickly can we get to the Jarisst I, Rachel?"

"They've moved pretty far out for safety reasons, and they're also in a different orbit than we are, attempting to stay in the same location relative to Earth, not the space dock. We should be able to reach them within two hours."

*****

NSA Headquarters

"Sir, we've just received the translation on that Chinese transmission we picked up earlier."

"Yeah, what about it, Lieutenant?"

"I'm not sure, but it sounds like they are building something, but … "

"But what? Where is it coming from, Lieutenant?"

"The translator says it's from the moon."

"What the hell? Did you say, the moon?"

"Yes, sir."

"And they're building something?"

"Yes, it stated that the sixth and final segment is complete. The system is now ready for its first test."

"It must be from the base we heard they're building. Is it from open communication, perhaps trying to drive some misinformation, Lieutenant?"

"No, sir. It was highly encrypted. It took the code crew a lot of work to decipher it. To be honest, the cryptographer who called said that if it wasn't for that new Hacktivist 2030 group, he doubts they would've ever figured it out, so he's pretty sure the Chinese thought it was safe and he thinks this is the real McCoy."

"The NSA has always had the best supercomputers in the world for breaking codes … who the hell is this hack-a-whatever?"

"Hacktivist 2030, its part of the NSA. It's a super-secret group of hackers the NSA put together five years ago with the goal of ensuring the U.S. remained capable of breaking the encryption codes that the Russians, North Koreans and Chinese had been developing. Half of the group were teenagers, almost like these kids were born connected to a computer, and they just look at the world differently. Guessing they all took the red pill from Morpheus," he said as both men laughed.

"The historical approach of just throwing more money at super computers wasn't going to be enough, so they scoured the planet to find the best group of non-conforming hackers, geeks, puzzle-solvers, math geniuses, computer scientists and software programmers in the world, then gave them the best computer toys in the world and said *have fun*."

"Sounds like herding feral cats, count me out. So, if it's supposed to be so super-secret, how the hell do you know about all of this? Was it that prick Snowden again?"

"No, sir, he was long gone before any of these decisions were made, but it did get leaked in a similar manner by another Snowden copycat two or three years ago. At first the U.S. government denied it all, but late last year, Sen. Jeff Dryden from Illinois accidentally leaked it to the press and the White House finally acknowledged the group's existence. The general belief is that the White House released it to increase confidence with the public that the billions of dollars they were spending every year was actually paying off. I'm sure there is a lot more to it, but that's what I know."

"How the bloody heck do you know even that, Lieutenant?"

"Night school, sir. I'm trying to join their team." He smiled back.

"Great, well stay the hell away from my checking account; that's an order."

"Too late, sir," the lieutenant answered with a laugh.

"So, what do you think they're building?"

"No clue, sir, that's all they told me."

"Wonderful."

*****

Jarisst I

By late evening, Blake, Qulys, Jarns, Zalmyt, Jimmy and Harry had undertaken two separate space walks together to assess the fuel tanks. The first walk lasted slightly over two hours and was conducted just to establish an overall assessment of the damage.

One tank had a gaping 3-meter-long slice down the right side, clearly explaining why the tank had emptied so quickly. It was also evident that the gap was so excessive, ragged and distorted, that the crew of the Jarisst I would not be capable of repairing it without a top-tier maintenance, repair and overhaul facility. Why the tank had not exploded was a miracle.

The other tank showed more promise. They identified five small holes that were likely created by small fragments of shrapnel. The holes were still leaking small streams of fuel, but all looked repairable with the onboard repair kits Qulys confirmed the Jarisst I carried. The biggest concern was associated with a long crease across the top of the second tank. Something large and flat had careened off the tank and made a 15-centimeter-deep crease in the top of the tank that was at least two meters long. There were no visible signs of fuel leakage from the crease, but the loss of strength in and around the crease and the increased stress concentrations due to the sharp angle at the bottom of the crease would significantly reduce the fatigue life of the fuel tank shell. As with the first tank, only a major MRO facility would be capable of repairing the crease.

At the end of the two-hour spacewalk, the team returned to their respective ships. Blake then contacted the Jarisst I to discuss the damage with Thjars and his crew. What ensued was an hour-long brief that included pictures, videos and lengthy discussions, but it was clear to everyone on board both ships that the Jarisst I's ability to sustain long-term operations was definitely in jeopardy. In addition, had the Jarisst I been inspected at a Cjarian base, Qulys was quite confident the ship would have been grounded until appropriate repairs could be completed. Blake was convinced that the Cjarian ship would need assistance from the space dock or facilities on Earth. However, until more significant repairs could be planned for, the small leaks still needed to be stopped in order to save fuel, as well as to reduce the risk of fire if they were to attempt to enter Earth's atmosphere.

The second spacewalk lasted a full six hours and the six-man crew was successfully able to stop the fuel leakage from all five holes. Qulys was confident they were no longer at risk of running out of fuel any time soon, but critical repairs were still needed, and needed soon. Blake, Jimmy and Harry returned to the Night Star, removed their bulky suits and devoured a quick meal of tube food before calling Thjars to discuss next steps.

"Thjars, I'll talk to President Callahan as soon as he has time to call back. With the current state of the space dock and the continuing risk of Russian attacks, I see no other option than to have you land the Jarisst I on Earth. I'm planning on heading back to Earth tomorrow to prepare for your arrival. If I don't hear from him before we depart, I'll head to the White House to make my case in person."

"Blake, I'll be honest … I haven't felt this nervous or concerned since we first regained consciousness near the planet you call Pluto. As you recall, I was also deeply concerned about docking at your space dock for fear of someone attempting to take over our ship. Although what occurred was different than I expected, it unfortunately turned out to be a real risk. Now we're contemplating actually landing on your planet, where the risks will be magnified a thousand-fold. I don't like it at all. The countries of your world never stop fighting, do they?"

"I wish I could say otherwise, Thjars, but even if I did, I doubt I could convince you."

"No, I doubt you could either, Blake, but seeing the magnitude of damage that the fuel tanks incurred, I really don't see any other options. I cannot risk the safety of my crew, or the loss of this ship. For those reasons, I hope you can convince your President Callahan, but Blake, you need to be honest with him. He needs to know that I will not land on your planet without all of our weapon systems manned, fully armed and ready to defend ourselves at all times."

*****

No sooner had Blake disconnected from Thjars, Rachel called him on his LB.

"Blake, I have a call for you."

"Who is it?"

"Klaus something or other, he's got a pretty heavy accent. Said he wanted to talk to both you and Harry. The call came through Houston, so it's legit."

"Klaus Schneider? I wonder what he's up to. Put him through, Rachel, thank you."

"Harry, come on over. Klaus Schneider wants to talk to us."

Fifteen minutes later, after Klaus updated them about the incoming comet, Blake disconnected the call and looked at Harry in disbelief.

"There's no way we can get the Jarisst I to check it out, not without repairs anyway. How long do you think it will take to fix the fuel tanks, Harry?"

"That's a hard question, Blake, because we have no idea what the tanks are made from, how to repair them or how to even assess the true damage levels. I'm sure Cryells or Allympht could give us a better estimate, but if President Callahan clears the priority highway for us, I would expect we could have them airborne in less than two weeks–tanks only, that has nothing to do with the Q-PAMS drive."

"Fair point, Harry. I can only imagine what Thjars' reaction will be when I tell them we want them to land on Earth *twice*–once to fix the fuel tanks just so they can help us go comet-chasing and then a second time to begin efforts on the Q-PAMS repair."

"Lucky you, Blake, well nobody's perfect."

"Say again?"

"Well, nobody's perfect."

"OK, Harry, you win one. It sounds familiar, but you got me … what movie?"

"'Some Like it Hot.' It was when Osgood responded to Jerry in response to Jerry taking off his wig and saying 'I'm a man!'"

"There's just no beating you, Harry. I've got the first round of beers when we get back to the dock."

* * * * *

Oct. 11, 2029

"I just validated that our objective will be in the target zone soon. Are you ready?"

"Yes, I can be on the road tonight. Any change in plans?"

"We need more than just a scare. Are you up to it?"

"Are you sure you want to take it to the next level?"

"Yes."

"Your voice sounds different."

"I've got a slight cold."

"How do I know this isn't a trap? What's the code?"

"Three-seven-five-two-seven-nine."

"And?"

"The band, Journey."

"Does the color light red mean anything to you?"

"Don't ever say that again!"

"OK, it's you. Sorry."

"For what?"

"For not trusting who you were and for the fact that my fee just went up another 500,000 due to the higher level of the operation."

"Get it done and you'll get paid–all of it."

"No deal. This needs to be upfront. If all hell breaks loose, I may need to disappear for a while. I need the money deposited tonight."

"It will be there by midnight."

"Deal."

The caller hung up.

*****

Rybachiy Nuclear Submarine Base
Vilyuchinsk, Kamchatka Krai, Russia

"Was that Moscow, Adm. Sokolov?"

"Yes, Capt. Petrov, our orders are confirmed. We launch three Yasens tonight: the Kazan, Novosibirsk and the Ulyanovsk. You and I will lead the hunt from the Kazan."

"Who are we hunting, sir?"

"The Americans. Their John F. Kennedy Carrier Strike Group is near the Marshall Islands."

"Are we targeting their aircraft carrier?"

"President Yakovlev is going to show the Americans they cannot dictate their terms to the world, and he has honored our submarine fleet with the first naval attack."

"The men will be proud, sir."

"Yes, and so will we–more than the young sailors can comprehend," the admiral stated.

"Why this carrier?"

"Captain, do you not see the righteousness of this target?"

"No, sir, I'm sorry, but I don't."

"The ship bears the name of the U.S. president that tricked our government and embarrassed Khrushchev during the Cuban Missile Crisis in 1962–we backed down in front of the entire world." The admiral looked out the window into the dark night and sea.

"Now it is the Americans' turn to back down."

*****

CHAPTER 12

Space Dock
Oct. 12, 2029

Blake's team had reassembled in the dock's cafeteria with Cmdr. Garrity and Master Sgt. Joe Penske. Military facilities historically called cafeterias mess halls, and Blake continued to call it such, but Cmdr. Garrity had insisted on maintaining a more informal environment in an attempt to placate the academics on board the dock who strenuously abhorred the militarization of space. That was all before the Russian attack, which now clearly justified the need for a stronger military presence. Ironically, but not totally unexpected, those same academics were now upset that the military hadn't maintained a strong enough presence to adequately protect them.

"There are a lot of upset PhDs on board right now–the same ones who argued *against* having a strong military presence when the dock was started. Now they want to know why they weren't protected," Cmdr. Garrity said, shaking his head.

"Don't lose any sleep over it, Commander. The ones who matter understand. The other ones aren't worth worrying about until things stabilize further. Right now, the only thing you have to focus on is saving this space dock and the lives aboard.

"Thanks, Blake, but for what it's worth, I'd sure appreciate it if you guys would stay until reinforcements arrive."

"I hear you, Commander, and under any other conditions, we would. Unfortunately, we need to get the Jarisst I out of harm's way and get it repaired, which means we need to depart ASAP. I'm pretty confident you'll be fine. Between Penske and Peters, you have two dependable veterans who can lead your security personnel. Furthermore, I can't imagine the Russians have much left in space to start a manned attack with. I'm betting they're too busy licking their wounds right now."

"Likely so, Blake, but couldn't that drive them to launch unmanned missiles at us instead?"

"That would start World War Three if they did, so let's hope they still have some common sense left. Regardless, if they were to launch missiles, it wouldn't make a difference if we were here or not, would it?"

"Fair point, Blake."

"Master Sgt., help Blake and his crew load up and transfer to the Night Star. I'm heading back to the Control Center." Cmdr. Garrity shook hands with each of them, wished them well and turned to depart.

"For what it's worth, I don't blame him, Blake," Diego volunteered. "It's a pretty sucky situation to be in."

"It is, but so is the situation the Jarisst I is in."

"So, is the doc coming with us, or staying with his techs?" Sean asked.

"George will be coming, but not on this flight–there's too many people for one flight. George will wait for the next flight and come back with some of his techs. The rest of his lab support will stay here to continue working."

"I'll bet that was an interesting down-select process," Sean laughed. "Competition for the one flight out must have been pretty high for a bunch of scared geeks."

"Actually," Joe intervened, "all the techs are military personnel. They're pretty riled up about the attack and want to stay to defend their turf."

"Oorah," Sean responded.

"OK people, let's get moving," Blake ordered.

Blake knew time was short so he was ready to leave.

Blake, Harry, Diego, Sean, Patty, Jimmy and Vladimir, with Master Sgt. Joe Penske in tow, headed toward docking station number five where Cmdr. Rachel Joslin was docked and waiting. It was time to head home to planet Earth.

*****

Three hours later the Night Star and its eight occupants prepared for re-entry. Contrary to the short, but highly physical assault of the launch, re-entry was much longer and significantly less turbulent, yet equally exciting, albeit for very different reasons. The excitement associated with a space launch is drawn almost exclusively from the raw, unmitigated power required for liftoff. During liftoff, there are very few visual effects as the occupants can only look straight into the sky as the colors change from blue to black as the ship departs the atmosphere. But as the crew prepared to re-enter the atmosphere, they were first treated to a long tour of the planet beneath them as the Night Star flew parallel to the edge of the atmosphere, preparing to reenter at an angle between one to two degrees below a horizontal plane perpendicular to the Earth's radius. When the ship finally reentered the atmosphere, at nearly 30,000 kilometers per hour, friction with the air molecules created a glow from the burning atmosphere and the red-hot exterior of the ship.

The view from the windows transitioned from a clear picture of Earth to a kaleidoscope of brilliant and mesmerizing flows of vivid red, orange, purple and white colors streaking by the windows. The ride was bumpy and turbulent, but nowhere near the level of forces that were encountered during lift off. After a few exhilarating minutes, the glowing colors transitioned to a scenic and spacious view of the landscape below, sporting blue skies, rivers, lakes and oceans, as well as the emerald expanses of green, tree-covered mountains. A few minutes later, the ship was buffeted as it transgressed through the sound barrier in preparation for landing. Not long after, Blake and his team were rewarded with a slight bump as the Night Star touched down on the runway at Edwards Air Force Base in California, 150 kilometers north of Los Angeles.

*****

"Sen. Celeste, this is Sen. James Harley. I'm sending you some information I think you may find of high interest. You'll want to jump on this as I believe we can use it to our advantage."

"That sounds interesting, Sen. Harley. I can handle the news release, but who is it and where might we find this individual?"

"I'll send the information by encrypted email. It will include who it is, photos and where the individual is at. The rest is up to you. I need to keep out of this, if you get my drift."

"Perfect, I understand. I'll get this moving immediately and I'll call you back as soon as I've connected. I'll make sure all the major networks are on hand as well."

"Well done, Senator, talk to you soon."

*****

Pearl Harbor
Commander, Submarine Force, U.S.
Pacific Fleet (COMSUBPAC)

"Rear Adm. Bill Pendleton?"

"Yes, this is he."

"Is your line secure?"

"Yes, this line is secure."

"This is Cmdr. Jake Ridder. The USS South Dakota has identified three new launches from the Russian sub base in Vilyuchinsk."

"What types of boats, Commander?"

"Yasen class, sir. Cruise missile submarines. Based on their signatures, we believe they are the Kazan, Novosibirsk and the Ulyanovsk."

"Where are they heading?"

"South, sir. No other information is available yet."

"Who is on the Dakota?"

"Capt. Ricky Perez."

"He's one of our best. Good to hear. Tell him to stay silent and provide updates as he can. Who else can we back him up with?"

"The Virginia Class Utah and Colorado boats, under captains Ted Lambert and Tony Chaparral can launch from Pearl Harbor. At 60 kilometers per hour, and assuming the Russians continue in a southerly direction, they can join up with the South Dakota in two days."

"All three have the new Guardian II tracking systems, correct?"

"Yes, sir."

"OK, relay my orders to send the Utah and the Colorado. I want updates on anything that changes, understood?"

"Yes, sir."

*****

White House Oval Office

"All right, Harry, enough," President Callahan said, holding his hands in the air.

President Callahan was in the Oval Office with Vice President Annie Murphy, Ben Tellinino, Brad Martinez, Gen. Landon McMullen and Frank Pelino. Harry and Blake were on the video feed emanating from a secure conference room at Edwards Air Force Base.

"Annie, gentlemen, we've been discussing this for a full hour now and I think Harry has had ample time to make his case. I agree that the Cjarians need our help, they need it now, and our best option for assistance is to let them land at White Sands, but you all also know the potential risks associated with a visit from an alien species. Harry has laid out a fairly extensive plan to minimize the possibility of a potential health disaster, but he can't eliminate the risks. This will be my decision, but before I finalize, I want to know each of your positions on the topic, Annie first."

"Mr. President, I could give you a long speech, but there would be nothing new in it, just regurgitation of everything already stated. The Cjarians need our help and we would not be who we claim to be if we didn't open our homes to them. My vote is *yes*."

"Ben?"

"Ditto, sir."

"Brad?"

"I'm on board as well, sir."

"Frank?"

"That's four for four, sir."

"OK, Landon, your turn. Same question, plus, my second biggest concern for you is: Are we sure we can protect *them*?"

"Short of a full-on war with missile attacks, that's two more yeses, sir. I've already called in both ground and air reinforcements. Let's get them down here."

"OK, it's done. Blake, get your crew to White Sands. Landon, how long do you need to complete preparations?"

"Counting today, one week."

"Blake, tell the Cjarians we will have White Sands prepared for their landing in six days. I believe that is Thursday, Oct. 18, correct?"

"Correct, sir," Frank verified while looking at his phone.

"Thank you, Mr. President," Harry and Blake replied simultaneously.

"God protect us," President Callahan said and disconnected the call.

*****

"Diego, got a second?"

"On it, what do you need?"

"We just received approval from President Callahan to allow the Jarisst I to land at White Sands."

"That's great news, Blake. Congrats."

"Thanks. Harry was correct, and I really didn't see any alternatives, but there is still a lot of risk associated with the decision from a potential health perspective, as well as from a security perspective–and the latter is where we come in. We need to get a list of critical gear together, as well as work with Gen. McMullen to make sure we have all the angles covered."

Blake and Diego spent the next four hours analyzing maps, laying out plans and discussing options and equipment needs. Blake knew that Gen. McMullen already had staffs full of personnel doing the same thing, but his planning instincts were kicking into high gear; Blake wanted to make sure nothing was missed. He and Diego would submit their own planning input to Gen. McMullen to compare notes.

When they completed their assessment and plans, Blake arranged for a call to the Jarisst I. Juulys answered.

"Juulys, I hope you're doing well," Blake smiled. "I have good news."

"I am, thank you. Should I get Thjars?"

"Normally, yes, but I only have a couple of minutes before I have to head out, so you can relay my message to him, if that's OK."

"Yes, I can do that."

"President Callahan agreed to our plan to allow you to land the Jarisst I at the White Sands facility in what we call New Mexico. We'll need a few days to prepare, and I expect you will as well."

"I don't know if I should be scared or excited, or both," Juulys replied.

"Likely both," Blake smiled. "I'll send you additional information over the next few days, but tell Thjars that we're looking at six days out. Based on your latest fuel reports, you should be fine until then–but obviously, tell us otherwise. For what it's worth, Juulys, I'm really excited to show you, Thjars and Qulys our home world. Granted, you'll only get to see a small piece of it, but I'm hoping we can take some hikes in the nearby mountains while you're there. More importantly though, I think Harry has assembled an impressive team of technical and manufacturing experts that should improve our chances of fixing both your fuel tanks and maybe even the Q-PAMS."

"That's great news, Blake, and although I am scared, I'm honestly looking forward to seeing your world, and of course getting our ship repaired. I hope that someday I may get a chance to show you our home world as well."

"That would be a dream come true, Juulys. I'll talk to you soon." Blake hung up the phone and looked at Diego.

"What are you grinning at?"

"She sure doesn't fit the scary image of a sci-fi alien movie, does she?" Diego asked.

"No, that she doesn't," Blake responded. "But how about we save that for another time, Diego; we need to get going."

"Dang, Blake! Do you ever let anyone know what's going on inside that emotional lockbox of yours? You never share anything about how you're feeling … no emotions, no likes, no dislikes … no nothing! One hundred percent business, one hundred percent of the time. For cripes sake, Blake, you do realize that you're allowed to say she's attractive without breaking any laws, aren't you?"

"Yes, Diego. Are you done yet?"

"Heck, no! Come on, Blake, we've been working together for years and I don't even know if you ever dated someone. How are we supposed to be best buds with that?" Diego paused, waiting for an answer that didn't come. "Well?"

"Diego, there really isn't anything to talk about, and we need to keep focus right now. The Cjarians are coming and it's up to us to make sure they stay safe while they're here. There's a V-22 Osprey crewed and fueled, waiting on the tarmac for us. It's time to get to White Sands. The rest of the team will come out tomorrow."

"I love you like a brother, Blake, but Sean's right, you can be a real butthead sometimes," Diego said, giving up. "Where are we landing?"

"The crew is killing two birds with one flight. They need to get to El Paso, so we'll hitch a ride to El Paso and then drive up to Holloman, and then over to White Sands."

"OK, then El Paso it is."

Thirty minutes later, the duo was on board the V-22 tilt rotor aircraft, ready to depart. The aircraft lifted vertically off the tarmac then tilted forward as the rotors moved into horizontal flight mode.

"Check that out, Blake," Diego pointed out the window as they left the confines of Edwards Air Force Base. "There must be at least 10 cop cars heading into the base. Wonder what that's all about."

"Good question. Looks like television crews, too. Must be some big time dignitary looking to make a splash before the November elections."

"Could be, but they look like they're in a hurry. I sure am happy that we don't need to deal with all that pomp-*ass*," Diego added with heavy emphasis on the last three letters.

*****

White House Situation Room

President Callahan called the emergency session to get an update on the status of the growing Russian threat. The Situation Room was completely full.

"Gen. McMullen, the floor is yours–go ahead and update us, Landon," President Callahan said as he turned the meeting over to his chairman of the Joint Chiefs of Staff.

"Well, sir, the last few days have seen a lot of activity on both sides of the conflict, but it still all appears to be positioning. There have been no new attacks since the battle on the space dock. In the last 24 hours, the Russians have put the majority of their fleets to sea, including many of their first strike submarines, and their air bases are on full alert around the world. We've also registered no fewer than six intrusions into our airspace in just the past 24 hours. It's as if they are goading us to reach out." Over the next 15 minutes, Gen. McMullen moved through a number of photos and videos, providing background and risk assessments associated with each location or element of the Russian military.

"How serious do you believe it is? Are we at war?"

"Yes, and no, sir. In some manner, we have been at war with the Russians ever since the end of World War II. It hasn't been with guns or bombs, but that doesn't mean it hasn't been a war. Right now, all signs point to the Russian military being at full combat readiness. We've never seen them at this level before, not even during the Cuban Missile Crisis, so it feels like we're moving closer to an actual physical confrontation. Not only are they goading us, but it feels like they're testing us."

"How so?"

"They want to see what our strength and resolve levels are. It could be that they're trying to make that decision–to initiate a full-out war, or not."

President Callahan sat back in his chair, "What do you recommend, General?"

"I don't think we have a choice, sir: we need to initiate DEFCON 1."

"Since the initial DEFCON system was first deployed in 1959, some 70 years ago, the U.S. has never been at DEFCON 1. I, for one, am not ready to become the first U.S. president to enact it." President Callahan paused, surveying the faces of everyone in the room.

"Yet, I agree with you, Gen. McMullen. The Russian actions are unprecedented and highly concerning." President Callahan paused.

"Have we heard anything from the Russian government?"

"Nothing, sir."

"Frank."

"Yes, sir?"

"Get President Igor Yakovlev on the phone. Do not take 'no' for an answer. Tell him I am highly concerned that we are on the brink of taking the world into another catastrophic war. Let him know that I still hold him responsible for our space dock, but that I want to talk. The world may depend on us finding a way to walk back from the precipice. Give me two hours if you can."

"Yes, sir."

"Gen. McMullen."

"Yes?"

"I want you to prepare the military as if we were on DEFCON 1, but do not make any official decrees or statements—is that clear?"

"Yes, sir. I'll take care of it."

"That message does not leave this room—by anyone."

The president dismissed the room, except for Annie and his key staff members. He waited for the door to close again before speaking.

"Have you heard from your contact in the Kremlin?" Ben Tellinino asked.

"No, Ben," President Callahan replied. "He is off the grid right now. I don't even know if he is still alive, but we need him now, more than ever before. Brad, what more do we know about Igor?" the president asked.

"Not much that we didn't already know about him, but we do know more about what he has been up to."

"Continue."

"He's cleansing the Kremlin and the military of anyone he doesn't believe supports him. We were able to help extract a few people who provided considerable intelligence before the borders totally shut down, but it is clear he is imposing a Stalin-like environment. Many have been executed and many are in jail. This is a purge the likes of which the world has not seen in decades. Igor *was* a dangerous man, now he is a dangerous *country*."

"Maybe the Cjarians were right," the president mumbled under his breath.

"What was that, sir?" Annie asked.

"The Cjarians said they were concerned about entrusting our world with their technology because we always seemed to be at war, that we were too immature of a race to be trusted. Based on what has occurred over the past 12 months, maybe they're right."

The room remained silent. They could tell by his face that he wasn't done talking, so they waited.

"Annie, we can't allow this war to start. We have to find a way to stop it, yet we must protect the country, and the Cjarians. I don't know what the answer is, but we need to find a way. I told everyone to keep the DEFCON comments within this room, but I'm going to make one exception …."

"Let me guess," Frank interrupted with a knowing look.

"Correct, let Harry and Blake in on our status. They helped pull us back from the horrors of hell earlier this year; maybe they can find a way to help again."

"Will do, sir," Annie responded, "but right now it's time for our next meeting."

"Wonderful. I need to talk to that idiot like I need a hole in my head," President Callahan replied. "With everything else going on, the last thing I need is to waste an hour with that arrogant son of a bitch."

*****

White House Cabinet Room

The Presidential SETI Commission had been in session for 15 minutes, but had yet to establish any common ground. It had started raucously with an outburst from Sen. Harley claiming that Sen. Dempsey and President Callahan had unilaterally announced the news about the Cjarians to intentionally keep him from being heard, and it continued with that same tone for the next 15 minutes.

"The American public will hear about your dishonesty. Now that you've broadcasted the news to the world, this commission no longer needs to be held in secret."

"Sen. Harley, you want honesty, I'll give you honesty. Am I concerned about the possibility of World War Three? Yes. Am I concerned about our Cjarian visitors? Yes. Am I concerned about how the world and especially the American citizens will react to the news I gave them? Yes. Do I give a rat's ass about your personal ego and your need to be present when I broke the news to the nation? Not only no, but *hell no!*"

Sen. Harley began to object and President Callahan cut him off immediately.

"Don't go there, Senator. Don't even get started with me. Yes, we originally agreed to a joint news release, but in case you haven't noticed, the world has changed dramatically since that time–unless of course you really *have* noticed and you were simply hoping to take advantage of it for your own personal gain. Regardless, the short answer is that we are in the midst of another major crisis and I didn't have time to consult with you–nor did I need to." President Callahan let his last statement sink in before he continued.

"So here's my offer, Senator. If you want some television time, I'll agree to make an announcement this afternoon during my press conference that you and Sen. Dempsey have been the primary congressional leads on a previously secret Presidential Commission to address the Cjarian topic. And that up until my recent press announcement, all Cjarian-related issues had been discussed within this commission, including the previous agreement for a joint release. I will then tell the American public I'm declassifying all commission documentation and that the press is free to talk to either of you. Does that work, Senator?"

Sen. Harley grappled with the president's proposal for a few seconds before answering.

"Yes, but with one condition."

"And what would that be, Senator?"

"I'm at the podium with you when you make the announcement."

President Callahan smiled and shook his head.

"No, Senator. This is not a negotiation and we are out of time as I have other more pressing matters to attend to. If I may make a recommendation, it might be a good time to propose some personal leave for your fellow SETI senators to get some family time. I expect that after we make this announcement, everyone associated with this committee will likely be in high demand by the press."

The president got up, acknowledging Sen. Harley and Sen. Dempsey and quickly left the room with Annie in tow. They walked through the halls until they reached the Oval Office, where President Callahan spoke to his administrator who was sitting at the desk near the entrance to his office.

"Please get Harry Lundrum on the phone and don't let anyone disturb me until Annie departs."

"Yes, sir."

President Callahan closed the door after Annie entered and was rewarded with a ringing phone.

"Harry?"

"Yes, sir."

"What do you think?"

"Perfect, just the way Blake predicted it would go. Harley let his own ego and narcissism outwit himself, just like we hoped. He was so set on getting stage time he just agreed to let you publicly announce the entire discussion, as well as acknowledge that he was part of all of the discussions up until your recent declaration—which means he equally owns it. And with your announcement that all of the commission's documentation, which includes recorded meetings, are being declassified, if he tries to suggest otherwise, the recordings will prove him to be the rat he really is. He pretty much just cornered himself. That was brilliant."

"Thanks, Harry, and please pass on my thanks to Blake as well. I was hesitant, but you were both pretty sure Harley wouldn't be able to resist—and you were right."

"Now just follow through with the press conference as we discussed and you should be good to go," Harry added. "Good luck, sir. I've got lots to do on this end, as I'm sure you do as well, but call me back if anything comes up."

The line went silent and President Callahan looked up at Annie.

"I've met a lot of people in my life, but the good Lord definitely used a special mold when he made those two."

"I'll give that a big *amen*," Annie responded with a smile. "But I'm even happier that they're on our team."

*****

"Sen. Harley, this is Sen. Celeste. We missed them."

"Damn it!" Sen. Harley barked. "Now they know we're after them!"

"No they don't. I made sure not to tip our hand. I also found out where they are heading."

"OK, maybe I jumped too quickly, Can you cover the new location, or do you need me to call someone?"

"One of my office aides has been dating an officer there for the past two years. She already called. They'll be waiting for your friends."

*****

Moon Orbit

"Maj. Zhang Wei, we've completed our maneuvers and have reached the targeted stationary orbit about the moon. All systems are ready."

"Good, then we have completed on schedule."

"It's a pretty slick design, sir."

"I must admit, Lt. Wu, I didn't believe the engineers when they first drafted the plans for this weapon system eight years ago, but the modularity of the design and the built-in tugs worked just like they promised–we didn't even need a single spacewalk to integrate the sections. It was like kid's building blocks, simply docking each section to the next, all controlled by the computer."

"Do the Americans know we have it?"

"We can never know for sure, but Beijing claims that the MSS has not identified anything in Washington that would suggest they know yet. Beijing went through extraordinary efforts to ensure secrecy. Each payload section was released from its carrier ship only after it reached the back side of the moon and was then propelled further out from the moon orbit by its own built-in tug. The biggest challenge was keeping track of the various sections in total darkness, especially without any running lights, while ensuring the individual sections all stayed perfectly in line with the moon and Earth to avoid detection."

"But what about the various noon launches the Russians, Americans, Indians and others have launched? Why didn't they see anything when their orbits took them behind the moon?"

"Genius and luck. In the dark vastness of space, and as small as these sections would appear at that distance, they were simply able to hide in plain sight. It also helped that all of the American launches that orbited the moon were fixated on the surface of the moon, not what was beyond it."

"How could we know that, sir?"

"We knew the Americans would be watching, so it was a pretty safe assumption that the Americans would see our returning ships and realize we had jettisoned payloads behind the moon. So last year we intentionally allowed them to break into one of our communication channels while we sent a number of fake messages claiming we were building a new base on the moon. The Americans took it hook, line and sinker, so we are fairly confident that anything they would send to the moon would be hyper focused on the moon's surface. We also made a deal with the Russians to provide help to their personnel that are marooned on their moon base–the one they call the 'dark side of the moon.' We provided them mainly survival supplies, but we also sent some small, portable, ground-to-space missiles in case the Americans attempted to land anything near their site."

"What did we get in exchange?"

"You are now asking classified questions, Lt. Wu."

"Sorry, sir."

"That's OK, Lieutenant; at this point there's no turning back and no ability for anyone to impact this mission. You now need to know."

"Thank you, sir."

"In exchange for our help, the Russians have helped deceive the Americans."

"Do the Russians know about our system?"

"No, they simply think we're working together against the Americans."

"They're marooned; how could they help?"

"We also provided them with a number of erectable modules that, when deployed, appear to be metal modules that have enlarged their base. They're simple fabric-covered structures, but they also emit infrared signatures to create the perception that they are real and active. There was no reason for the Americans to look elsewhere. Furthermore, the only other space-borne systems looking beyond the moon are all in Earth orbit–we easily shielded those views by hiding this system behind the moon."

"Ingenious, sir."

"Yes, it was. As I said, there was a great deal of planning for this mission, but now we are ready for the next phase. We've moved the system to a location barely visible from Earth, so it should still be easy to keep hiding while we take our first shot. Is the target locked in?"

"Yes, sir. It's our own satellite, the one we lost communication with after the U.S. attack on the Russian hunter-killer satellites. That stroke of misfortune turned out to be good fortune as it allows us to test the system without impacting American equipment until we have validated the system and are ready to move on to the next phase."

"The rail gun rounds are so small that they will be invisible to even the best systems the Americans have. If they do get lucky enough to detect our trial shot, it will look like a small hunk of rock hurtling through space–not a weapon. That should help keep it a secret until we're ready to use it against them."

"But how will we really use it against them? Once they know we have it, the projectiles are not maneuverable and it takes many hours to reach their target from such a distance. Couldn't they easily move out of the way?"

"Relative to targets near the Earth, that is correct, but we will still be able to hit their satellites from time to time, as needed. They can't watch all of space, all the time. But the real reason is to protect the moon. China will own the moon. Once this system is fully deployed, anything that approaches the moon will be unable to react quickly enough to overcome the speed of these projectiles and will be destroyed. With our ability to see them coming and the maneuverability of this weapon system, we can mount a surprise attack from any direction they choose to approach from. That will give us time to continue to build up our defenses and to establish a true moon base that we can control space with."

"But what about the Russians?"

"What about them? They are meaningless. They have no way to defend themselves from this system and there is no way the Russians can help that base unless we allow it. At some point, their base will become our base."

"This all makes even more sense now. Thank you, sir."

"You are welcome, Lt. Wu, but now it is time to act. I've just received final authorization from Beijing–you may initiate the system and conduct our first test."

The firing sequence was initiated. Five minutes later, the craft shook as a small, 50-kilogram mass exploded out of the end of the space-borne rail gun, heading straight toward Earth. As there was no atmosphere to slow it down, it would maintain the same velocity until it impacted the target–at more than 20,000 kilometers per hour.

"Major, the projectile has been successfully launched. It will be approximately 14 hours before we can assess the result.

"This will begin an entirely new era for the Chinese people. With this system, we will be able to launch surprise attacks on anything in Earth-orbit, and especially against anything that approaches the moon. China now owns the moon."

*****

El Paso, Texas
Oct. 13, 2029

The V-22 approached El Paso International Airport and touched down on the tarmac near the FedEx shipping terminal. It was immediately surrounded by Texas law officers.

"Any idea what's up?" Blake asked the pilot.

"We're not sure, Commander, but they radioed us about five minutes ago and ordered us to land here. Sorry, but we were told not to forewarn you until we landed. It appears they want to talk to Petty Officer Velasquez."

*****

Two hours had passed while Blake debated Diego's status and all it resulted in was lost time and added frustration. He knew there wasn't anything else he could do tonight, and he was also upset because he had planned to be at White Sands tonight in order to start preparations for the arrival of the Cjarians. Yet leaving Diego felt like he was breaking the "no man left behind" rule. He and Diego had talked at length in private, and Blake assured

Diego that he or Harry would be back tomorrow to check in on him. He also sent a message to both President Callahan and Gen. McMullen asking for their assistance and explained how Diego had been arrested for the murder of the gang members he killed last year while at a family dinner with his brother. As Diego had been cleared at the time by the police, that made Blake concerned that someone was up to no good–and Blake was going to find out who. Blake shook hands with Diego, whispered into his ear and then watched the officers walk him away in handcuffs, photographers snapping pictures left and right.

Blake pulled the Company E lead Texas Ranger aside.

"Make sure he's kept in a safe area, separate from the regular populace. There's something corrupt going down, but it's not Diego–I can guarantee that."

"I understand he's a killer and wanted in California."

"He did kill five gang-bangers, but it was after they attacked him and his brother–total self-defense. I'm telling you straight."

"I hear ya, dude, but I don't know you from Adam and Eve. Get my drift?"

"Yeah, and here's mine. Anything bad happens to Diego and I'll chase the responsible parties to hell and back. Get *my* drift?"

"Are you threatening me, Commander?"

"Just setting expectations," Blake said as he eyed the man with an almost lethal fire in his steely cold eyes. "Keep him isolated and keep him safe. Trust me, he'll be released in less than 48 hours and that release will be accompanied by a few shiny black Cadillac SUVs that will be asking all kinds of questions about why you were involved with locking him up. You can take that to the bank."

Blake turned and left. He'd pre-rented a 2029 Land Rover Defender from the airport Avis car rental agency for the two of them and he still needed to pick up supplies prior to heading to White Sands. But now it was just him. He departed the airport and drove to the Walmart Supercenter at the southeast corner of the intersection of State Route 54 and State Route 375. Blake had paid a hefty extra fee to get the specially requested Defender, but it would be worth it, given what he knew was ahead. The Defender was somewhat luxurious, yet rugged; it was a dependable vehicle that could seat seven occupants–big enough to take some new friends on an excursion.

*****

Unknown location

"He's on the move and he's alone. This is your best chance to get the job done so don't screw it up."

"Relax, I've got it covered as long as he takes the route you gave me."

"There are no guarantees in life, but the tracking data I'm giving you is pretty solid. The sensor has already been planted under the hood, so you'll know it's his vehicle. Let me know when it's done."

*****

Blake completed his shopping, exited Walmart and loaded up the Land Rover after spending a small fortune on food, medical supplies, outdoor gear for the Cjarians, a desktop globe of the planet, some books on Earth and the solar system and some specialty items that might serve as gifts for the Cjarians. Blake knew he could have waited to get government-issued clothes from the base, but he wanted to make sure he had some civilian attire just in case they were able to take the Cjarians on a hike in the nearby mountains–a public area where he wanted to blend in as well as was possible, especially given the challenge of the average height of the Cjarians. Somehow, however, all of that seemed far less important right now, knowing that Diego would be spending the night in jail. Blake knew he had to get his focus back on the task at hand, so he reminded himself that Diego was one hell of a tough Marine, and a SEAL–and he was in a U.S. jail, not a prison in the Middle East–Diego would be safe for the night.

Blake left the parking lot and headed for the State Route 54 north on-ramp. Four miles later, the highway turned to the right and took a distinctive northeast path. As Blake settled into the drive, he thought back to Harry's recommendation. Harry had been right; the White Sands Missile Range was perfect. It was the largest military installation in the United States, encompassing over 3,200 square miles of nothingness–bigger than the combined states of Delaware and Rhode Island–easy to hide within.

At Gen. McMullen's request, Blake's credentials had been upgraded to allow him access to the entire facility in order to prepare and respond to any event that might arise while the Cjarians were there. The result was that Blake could approach or depart from any direction he chose and at any time he desired, so there was no need to make it there by a given time.

It was past dinnertime. Blake was still too pissed off to feel hungry, but he knew he needed to eat, so he started looking. He pulled over near the intersection of Business Route 54 to find a restaurant he'd seen advertised a few miles earlier called The Edge of Texas Steakhouse and Saloon–after all, anything with steak or barbecue in the same sentence with Texas had to be good. Once inside and seated, Blake ordered the ribeye steak, a double order of steamed broccoli, a massive loaded, baked potato and a large Lagartos red ale.

Forty-five minutes later, Blake was on his way again. The sun had set and darkness enveloped the countryside. Blake pulled back on to State Route 54 and continued toward Alamogordo, N.M., where he planned to take State Route 70 to Holloman Air Force Base and meet up with an old acquaintance, Maj. Pat Sullivan. Sullivan had been the F-18 pilot who'd flown him from the USS Washington in the Indian Ocean to Ramstein Airbase in Germany over a year ago, just before he'd found out about the object near Pluto–the object that ended up changing his life forever. The two had hit it off well and they'd reconnected a couple of times since then. Blake wanted as many people as he could find, who he personally knew, involved with the base defense while the Cjarians were at White Sands, and had asked Gen. McMullen to pull some strings for him.

Pat had been notified that Blake initiated the request for him to transfer to New Mexico, but he wasn't told why. As it was far from the front lines he was used to, he was definitely looking forward to hearing what Blake had to say.

Blake shook his head. He'd hoped to introduce Diego and Pat to each other tonight, an introduction that would now have to wait for another time.

The road was empty, quiet and dark, but Blake could make out a faint glow on the horizon in front of him, suggesting another small town perhaps. A few miles later, the lights turned out to be the Otero County Prison facility, which he passed on his left. It quickly disappeared into the darkness behind him. A couple miles later, one lone car waited for him to pass at a quiet intersection, then pulled onto the highway going the opposite direction. Other than the two cars, no signs of life anywhere.

Blake was still chewing on Diego's arrest. It had been a clear case of self-protection after they had attacked Diego and his brother. So why would someone come after him now? It didn't make sense. Who would benefit from this? Blake needed some time to think, and he had a 30-minute ride in front of him. He turned his phone off, the radio on, and searched until he found 92.3 FM, the Fox All Classics radio station and was rewarded by Boston's "More Than a Feeling." It was still a cool, but refreshing, 65 degrees Fahrenheit outside, so Blake opened the driver's window, turned up the radio and got into his thinking zone.

*****

Moon Orbit

"Maj. Wei, we missed."

"By how much?"

"We estimate a good 20 meters."

"Actually, that's better than I expected when you consider we took the shot from over 380,000 kilometers away. Matter of fact, I'd say that was excellent. What next?"

"We've already been discussing the trajectory with Beijing and they believe it has to do with the assumptions we made associated with the moon's gravitational pull twisting the shot a minute amount before the projectile departed the moon's gravitational field. We expect to have a software upgrade loaded in a couple of hours and then we can attempt our second shot."

"Thank you. Let me know if anything changes."

"Yes, sir."

*****

A lone vehicle was approaching as the man laid prone, high on a ledge, about 50 yards off the highway, surrounded by some scrub pine trees. Five minutes earlier, he'd received confirmation his target vehicle was on the way, so he had plenty of time to prepare. His phone vibrated. The special app claimed this was the vehicle. Better yet, no one else was in view. He steeled himself on the ground and wrapped himself about the rifle.

A muffled shot suddenly shattered the quiet of the night, echoing across the darkened landscape. The vehicle had been moving at 60 miles per hour when the bullet ripped through the front right tire causing an instantaneous blow-out that in turn caused the vehicle to pull hard to the right, toward the edge of the highway. The shooter watched as the driver attempted to regain control of his vehicle, nearly rolling over in the middle of the road. The driver fought hard against the pull of the vehicle, almost regaining control before the car caught the edge of the pavement and the softer dirt on the edge of the road. The car slid sideways and flipped into the air, coming down hard on the roof and then rolling three more times down an embankment, crashing hard into the side of a large boulder at the bottom of a gully. The shooter watched through his infrared glasses as dust filled the air around the crash scene. His view was suddenly obliterated by an explosion of green light in the night glasses as the vehicle's fuel tank exploded.

The shooter remained rigid for 60 seconds, watching his surroundings. Still no other vehicles in sight, nor did he detect any movement from the nearby terrain. He had intentionally picked this point to avoid any risk of residential or business witnesses or video security systems–he'd seen more than a few people fall prey to the damned, ever-present, ever-watching, video security systems. The intel he received had been frighteningly accurate–the rest was luck that there were no other vehicles in sight; otherwise, he would have had to wait for another opportunity. He was relieved to get the job over and done with, not just for the money, but so it could be behind him and he could move on. That was another proven saying–the longer one stayed at the site of a planned hit, the greater the chances that someone would recognize you or something could, and would go wrong.

The shooter bagged the spent shell, his Tikka T3X hunting rifle and disappeared into the night, heading away from the crash scene, confident that even if they did find the bullet, the chance of ever tying it to a specific hunting rifle, especially given all the hunting rifles in Texas, was pretty remote. To be safe, he would still melt the gun down once he arrived back at his safe house. There would be no tracing the hit to him or the gun–that was one thing he was very confident of.

Thirty minutes later, and well away from the accident scene, the shooter hopped into his beat-up 2021 Ford Ranger pickup and traded his hunting cap for a Dallas Cowboys baseball cap. He opened a shielded case on the floor of the passenger seat, pulled out a burner phone, turned it on and sent one text message to an unregistered phone number he'd memorized.

"Objective confirmed. Didn't expect the bonfire, but that turned out to be an extra benefit for the evening–pretty spectacular."

The shooter erased the call, turned the burner phone off, dropped it back into the shielded case to ensure it couldn't be traced to the accident scene and drove off into the night. The phone would also get melted down.

*****

Moon Base, Pink Floyd

"Dimitri, the equipment has been recovered. One case was damaged on landing and it will be quite some time before we can determine what is still good, repairable, or pure scrap. The other five are intact. We have plenty of supplies, and formidable firepower now, both for surface battles and ground-to-air defense."

"That's good news, Boris. Let I.Y. know our current status and when we think we will have our final assessment of the delivery. Thank you."

*****

CHAPTER 13

White House Situation Room
Oct. 13, 2029

"Gen. McMullen, what's the latest on the Soviet military buildup?" President Callahan asked as he sat down in his chair.

"It's pretty massive, sir. Every base appears to be on high alert. They are either preparing to defend against an attack from us, or they are preparing to attack."

"Is there any chance this is a major exercise just to get our attention, like a chess game?"

"We discussed that too, but we don't believe that is an option. There is simply too much cost and risk associated with the magnitude of what they are undertaking around the globe."

"You're sure of that?"

"One hundred percent, sir. I'll stake my reputation and career on it–the Russians have mobilized their entire military. They've even called in their reserves."

"For what it's worth, Gen. McMullen, I do value your career and reputation, but in this case, I'm more concerned about what the hell the Russians are truly preparing to do."

"Understood, sir."

"Brad, what does the NSA have on this?"

"Not much, sir. Igor wiped out most of our moles in the recent purges and anyone still left is likely too scared to attempt to communicate. Relative to electronic eavesdropping, everything we've picked up supports Gen. McMullen's position. The Russians are readying for war."

"Have there been any further attacks?"

"No," Gen. McMullen responded.

"Have we achieved DEFCON 1 status, General?"

"No, but we are close, sir. I estimate we're better than 85 percent. We should be at 100 percent readiness within 48 hours."

"Frank, any word from Harry or Blake?"

"Yes and no, sir. We heard from Harry, but not from Blake. Harry wanted to talk through the issues with Blake, but his phone keeps going straight to voicemail. Harry knows that Blake already landed in El Paso because Blake told him about Diego's arrest, but Blake hasn't answered since."

"Is that the same message Blake sent to us?"

"Yes, sir."

"I want this straightened out, and straightened out fast. Get Gov. Townsend on the phone. I'll talk to him myself. If I didn't know better, this smells like something Sen. Harley would do."

President Callahan remained private with his thoughts for a few seconds before Gen. McMullen spoke out.

"If I may ask, what did Igor say when you talked to him last?"

"You may always ask, Landon," President Callahan responded, a little softer. "We're in this together and I have no desire to limit the data you have at your disposal. The more you are all aware of," he added while looking at his staff, "the more you can all help me make better decisions that will benefit this country and the 355 million citizens that pay us to protect them."

President Callahan surveyed everyone's faces before continuing.

"Igor was pretty cold. He clearly did not want to talk–at all. I told him that I did not want to see my country at war with Russia and that I hoped he felt the same way for his people. I also told him that a war between the U.S. and Russia would, without a doubt, engulf the entire world. And furthermore, with the quantity and lethality of today's weapon systems, it would lead to more death and destruction than the world had ever seen before. I implored him to back away from the precipice."

"What did he say, sir?" Annie asked.

"He stated that the only way Russia would back down was if I handed over the Cjarian ship to him, or agreed that it be destroyed."

"How did you respond?" Annie asked, clearly the question everyone wanted to ask.

"I said that I would never bow to a foreign country's blackmail, nor could I ever justify becoming a traitor to our Cjarian friends."

"How did the call end, sir?"

"I told him that I have no intention of stealing the Cjarian technology, nor do they have any intention of giving it to us. But I again clarified that if it was war he wanted, then it was war he would have. Furthermore, if he started it, he would go down in history with the likes of Hitler and Stalin–both of whom lost and are now counted among the most despicable and hated people in history, as well as the country leaders who caused the most death and destruction inside the same countries they claimed allegiance to. Before hanging up, I repeated my offer of peace to talk further, that he could call any time of the night or day and I would take his call, but until then, I would exert the full power of my position and military to protect both the American people and the Cjarians. That's when the call ended." The president paused, then looked at Gen. McMullen.

"Gen. McMullen, don't miss your 48 hour deadline–the United States, and the world may depend on it."

*****

Jarisst I
Oct. 14, 2029

For three days, Thjars kept the Jarisst I in a stationary orbit 400,000 kilometers from Earth. He and Qulys agreed that the position was far enough away from the action to remain safe, yet close enough to keep watch while they waited for Blake to give them the green light to approach Earth. The ship's movements were kept to a minimum in order to conserve fuel, but their previous repairs had at least stopped the fuel loss for now.

Qulys, Cryells, Jarns and Allympht had spent the better part of two days conducting lengthy spacewalks to better assess the operational risk and repair options associated with the large crease on the remaining fuel tank. Jarns remained concerned there was simply no way to repair it without removing the fuel from the tank and providing a permanent patch to the outside of the tank– something only possible to attempt on the ground with proper fueling and repair facilities. They also inspected the five patch repairs and were relieved to report that the temporary patches were holding, but Jarns was quick to point out those would require permanent repairs as well.

In between the space walks, Qulys and Knarls conducted various weapon training and proficiency checks with the entire crew for both hand-held guns and ship-based weapon systems.

"Qulys, what's our status on weapons training?" Thjars asked as he entered the small onboard shooting range. Thjars had looked around the range before he spoke to make sure no one else was present.

"Not as good as I would like," Qulys responded as he looked up from a file of electronic shooting files he was reviewing, "but to be fair, most of our remaining crew are not soldiers; they are scientists and technicians. If they had been soldiers, I'd have chewed their collective heads off. But, they are trying to catch up and trying hard–they've had precious little time. Thjars, they all realize this is a life and death setting, so they know it's up to them, but they also need rest–an untested, but rested warrior can frequently best a trained, but exhausted warrior."

"That's a great point, Qulys. How about we give the crew a 24-hour vacation, other than standard watch shifts, and during that time, you and Knarls take turns putting me to the test down here."

"Sounds like a plan, sir. How about we get started now?" Qulys smiled.

"I'm game, but first let me know who our primary fighting force will be–just in case it comes to that. Obviously, I know you're our lead."

"Jarns, Knarls, Nylsst, and Cryells passed the military marksmanship test; I'm pretty confident with them. Allympht, Platsys and Zalmyt are not quite there, but can hold their own if we are faced with a full-on battle. Juulys and Jenysys … well …"

"Just tell me straight, Qulys."

"They would be better off providing medical backup. After all, Jenysys is our medical officer."

"What about Juulys?"

"Juulys can shoot, to be honest, she's as good a shot as anyone, but …"

"She can't stomach shooting someone."

"Correct, sir. Unfortunately, that is a big part of becoming a soldier; you must be able to pull the trigger, fully expecting to take an enemy's life–the same expectation holds for you, sir."

"Understood, let's get started then. What all do I have to do?"

Qulys spent the next 30 minutes conducting basic, pre-shooting training. Thjars had been through it before, but he knew Qulys would not cut anyone any slack, including himself, so he readied himself for the full training regime, as if he were a new grunt in the military. Qulys explained the function of each handgun and how the electronic shooting range was set up with fake ammunition that simulated the explosive force of a shot, but utilized electronics to determine where on the electronic board the shot would have impacted, leaving a shaded circle to register the virtual impact of the electronic bullet. He then walked Thjars through the various ship weapons systems, each of which had its own console and viewing screen to simulate battle external to the ship. An hour later, Qulys and Thjars were both ready to start the real testing, but were interrupted by the com.

"Thjars, this is Jarns. Our sensors registered a radio burst near the moon. We're not sure what it was, but it was fairly intense, like an explosion of some sort. We replayed the stored data from multiple sensors and whatever it was, it appears to have come from something orbiting the moon, possibly at the very edge of what can be seen from Earth."

"How can you tell, Jarns?" Thjars replied.

"We replayed the thermal imagery to locate it and then looked at it through our long-range cameras. Between the darkness of the moon's shadow and the distance, it's hard to tell what it is, but it's definitely non-natural."

"Is it a weapon system, Jarns?" Qulys asked.

"It's possible, sir. To be fair, though, it also could have been a major explosion on board the vessel, but I really can't tell for sure."

"If it was an explosion, couldn't you detect debris?" Qulys responded.

"I would have thought so too, and we haven't seen any ... that may suggest it is some type of new weapon system that might be entering the playing field."

"OK, thanks, Jarns," Thjars replied. "Please make sure we add that target to the critical watch list." Thjars signed off and then turned to his trusted friend.

"Get me ready, Qulys."

*****

Edwards Air Force Base

Harry called Brad Martinez and asked if the NSA could trace Blake's cell phone, but the NSA technicians had been unable to locate it by satellite or get in touch with him. Brad said that his last ping had been from State Route 54 between El Paso and Alamogordo.

Blake was simply off the grid. Brad called the Texas and New Mexico State Police and neither had reported an accident with victims that fit Blake's description. He also relayed that Diego remained under lock and key in the El Paso jail, waiting for extraction and return to California where he was to be put on trial. Brad further relayed that Diego was still in El Paso only because President Callahan had called and requested a 48-hour hold on the transfer orders even though the people behind Diego's arrest had tried to move him as quickly as they could.

"How could they possibly charge him with murder?" Harry asked.

"They're making their case on the fact that Diego is a trained assassin and is therefore deemed a weapon. Furthermore, with his extensive level of combat training, he should have been able to disable the men without killing them."

"That's a crock," Harry responded. "Who's behind this?"

"We're not sure yet," Brad replied. "But Sen. Harley's name keeps coming up."

"If it was, why would he try to transport him to California so quickly, almost like someone is trying to slow us down or impact our ability to get prepared for the Cjarians."

"That is possible, Harry, but the list wouldn't have many names on it."

"Hmmm … maybe Sean was right."

"How's that, Harry?"

"Just something Sean wanted to do relative to Sen. Harley. Seemed like a reasonable idea back then, sounds even better now, but I think I'll pass on that discussion. What's next?"

"Gen. McMullen needs you and your team to get to El Paso today. We have a C-130 waiting for you at Edwards."

Harry agreed to gather the team together and get them to El Paso. They would retrace Blake's steps as best they knew them, talk to local police, review available video recordings and then head toward White Sands via the same path that Blake was last known to be on–hopefully, with Diego as well.

*****

Moon Orbit

"Maj. Wei, the new software is loaded and ready for the second test firing."

"Is the path to the target still clear, Lt. Wu?"

"Yes, sir."

"Take the shot."

It took another five minutes to prep the system and then the command was given. Five seconds later, the entire craft shook again as a second 50-kilogram round exploded out of the end of the space-borne weapon system and headed toward Earth.

*****

Jarisst I

"Thjars!"

"Yes, Jarns?"

"We've captured a second radio pulse and this time we know it came from the craft near the moon. We also know it did fire something–must be a new weapon system. The infrared sensors clearly tracked a bright signature departing the craft. The sensors were able to track it for a short distance before the heat dissipated from the object and we lost track of it, but it was long enough to know that it's clearly heading toward Earth. Whatever it is, it's very small and appears to be just a dead projectile."

"How can you tell, Jarns?"

"It has no signature at all, whereas the craft it departed from still has thermal and electromagnetic signatures that we can easily detect, now that we know it's there. If it wasn't a dead projectile, we would see signs of electromagnetic activity and/or thermal signatures from its various systems."

"That makes sense, I guess. Did it hit anything?"

"No, not yet, and there's nothing between the moon and Earth that we can detect other than the vast array of satellites orbiting the Earth. At the speed it's traveling, it's at least 12 hours away from hitting anything–that is assuming it has a target."

"If it really is a weapon, are we at risk?"

"Good question," Jarns replied. "Any weapon has risk, so, yes, it could put us at risk. But now that we know its signature, and as long as we keep monitoring it, we'll always know when and in what direction it's shooting. If they did target us, we'd have plenty of time to relocate the ship out of danger. Furthermore, I really doubt they have any clue where we are."

"Thanks, Jarns. Let me know immediately if it strikes anything, or if you uncover something new."

"Yes, sir."

*****

"This is Capt. Trent Moore. I have a 10-55 for a vehicle accident. Deceased appears to be male. Vehicle and body are badly burned. Looks like death occurred at least 24 hours ago."

"What is your location?"

"I've seen many accident scenes over the years, but something just doesn't feel right here. Tell the chief I want a forensics team sent out–quietly. If my instincts are correct, I'd rather not have a bunch of reporters messing up the scene. I'll get online when I'm in the squad car and send the location and additional details."

*****

Pacific Ocean

A small, lightless, buoy-like device broke through the surface of the Pacific Ocean, 200 miles northeast of Midway and released a short, encrypted message.

"In position. 200 kilometers northeast of MA. Trio is broadside. Target is at ten point five kilometers with multiple bogies in vicinity. Request orders."

*****

Thirty minutes later, the device slipped below the surface of the ocean, inverted, filled its small ballast tank with seawater and began a slow, powered, and very quiet descent. The device had collected underwater current speeds and current layer thicknesses as it rose and was therefore able to back-calculate and retrace its path almost exactly to its point of release based on time passed and the velocity and thickness of each underwater current layer. As long as the launch vehicle remained motionless, there was greater than a 95 percent probability of return. Fifteen minutes later, the device detected the metallic hull of the nearby submarine and stopped its descent. It was within five meters of the launch port of the Russian submarine, K-561 Kazan. At this close distance, the seawater was no longer a hindrance to underwater electronic communication. After sending a short arrival message, the device received an encrypted response telling the device to disgorge its message, flood its electronics bay with sea water, and sink to the ocean floor, never to be seen or heard from again.

Capt. Nikolaev smiled.

"It is time. Send this message to our sister boats. We attack in 10 minutes."

"Torpedoes and cruise missiles. Four each from each boat. Today we finally avenge the Cuban missile embarrassment."

*****

"It's a positive ID. He was reported missing a day ago," Inspector Clauson stated.

"Accident?" Chief Baker asked.

"That's what we first thought, Chief, but Capt. Moore felt something was wrong. He said that it just didn't feel right–and he was correct."

"How so?"

"The skid marks on the road clearly show that the driver lost control after the front right tire blew. It looks like the driver attempted to regain control, but the front right wheel caught the edge of the road and the vehicle flipped over a couple of times, rolled down a hill and hit a boulder at the bottom of the gully where it then burst into flames. No one saw the blaze and once it burned out, you could easily drive by and never see the wreck."

"So what's unusual about that?"

"As we started taking pictures, we saw … wait …. Here, it's easier to just see it yourself. Follow me down to the wreck."

The two men walked down the hill to the burned-out vehicle and Inspector Clauson pulled back the tarp on the vehicle.

"Look at this wheel."

"OK, so the tire is melted."

"Look closer, Chief."

"What's that gouge?"

"Now you're looking. Look at the hood. See the hole?"

"Yes … bullet?"

"Bingo, Chief. High-powered hunting rifle. We haven't found the round yet, but I'll bet my career on it."

"Jesus, Clauson, are you trying to tell me that someone intentionally killed him?"

"Sure looks that way. The media is going to be all over this."

"We need to call the White House and the FBI before this gets out. Cordon off the crash site. I'll call Madras and get some additional troopers out here. Nothing moves and no else touches this site until the FBI gets here."

"What about the body?"

"Cover it."

"The family?"

"Nothing. It stays quiet until the FBI gets here, then it's their decision. This is absolutely unbelievable … Sen. James Colburn … murdered. Who the hell would off a sitting U.S. senator?"

*****

El Paso

Harry turned on his cell phone as soon as he and the rest of the team touched down at El Paso International Airport and was rewarded by a series of vibrations, signaling multiple voice messages. Harry looked at his call log and saw numbers that he recognized from Li, Robert and the White House, but there were two numbers he didn't recognize. Although one of the two did look familiar–the other did not at all.

"Likely a scam call," he muttered.

"What did you say?" Patty interjected.

"Looking at my missed calls, looks like one is a scam call."

"Yeah, you and the rest of the world," Sean quipped.

The group collected their luggage, left the plane and gathered in the gate area as Harry checked his voice mails, quietly summarizing them for the group as he listened. Jimmy and Li were making great progress on the hacking software they still hoped to use on Sen. Harley. The White House called about a status update on the Cjarians. Robert called to update Harry that Jimmy and Li had enlisted him to help with the software development effort, but that he wasn't supposed to let either of them know he told him because Blake would get upset for pulling him away from his studies. Another call turned out to be from his dry cleaners and the remaining "likely scam" call left a message.

"Twenty bucks says they tell you your social security number has been compromised, but they can help if you just call this number, right? Maybe we should have Li, Jimmy and Robert hack those guys so we can pay them an unofficial visit … anyone game? Now that would be some fun." Sean laughed wickedly.

Harry didn't respond as he listened to the last voice mail.

"Well?" Sean asked when Harry put his phone back in his pocket. "Did you win the lottery, or do we get to visit some scammers?"

"It was Blake."

"That's it? Really, Harry? He was missing, remember? What happened? You can't leave us hanging like that, Harry. Is he OK?" Sean stammered intensely. "Spill it, Harry!"

"He didn't say much. Just said that he had turned his phone off for a short drive and when he attempted to turn it back on again, it may have auto-updated and that now it wasn't working at all."

"I-phone, right?" Sean replied. "He should've gotten an Android."

Harry ignored him. "He drove on to Holloman Air Force Base to meet with a pilot that he knows. The pilot, some guy named Sullivan, volunteered to take Blake on a flying tour over White Sands this morning to get a better lay of the land before the Cjarians arrived. So last night, they went out to the base pub to discuss plans and have a few beers. Blake must have decided he would call later. They took the tour as planned, and only after they returned did Blake borrow the pilot's cell phone to call me–that was the number I thought was a scam."

"Harry, so Blake is OK, yes?" Patty asked gently.

"Yes, he's fine and waiting for us, but he wants us to check in with Diego first."

"Well, what are we standing here for? Let's go see our favorite Mexican and see if we can break him out of jail and hand-deliver him to Blake," Sean picked up his bag and began walking toward the rental car counters.

*****

"President Callahan, this is President Igor Yakovlev. You have continued to ignore my demands and have now put me in a position where I have no choice. Turn over the alien ship or I will be forced to take additional measures. I need to know now."

"President Yakovlev, as I told you before, if it is war you want, it is war you will have. If you so much as initiate a single attack, I will reciprocate and destroy the attacking force." President Callahan paused.

"You are quite arrogant, President Callahan. You think you are invincible. You can't stop what you don't know about and you can't destroy what you can't see."

"In case you need verification of my intent, do the names Kazan, Novosibirsk and Ulyanovsk mean anything to you?"

Yakovlev immediately terminated the connection.

"Gen. McMullen, get word to Capt. Perez on the South Dakota immediately. If any of those subs so much as squeak, take them out."

*****

White House Oval Office

President Callahan was in the Oval Office reviewing Russian status with Annie Murphy when Frank Pelino knocked and walked in.

"What happened?" Annie asked. "The look on your face … what is it, Frank?"

"Sen. James Colburn of Oregon has been murdered."

"What?" Annie shouted in dismay. "How? When?"

"What do we know, Frank?" President Callahan added.

"He was heading home to Sisters, Ore., to spend a few days with his family, but never made it home. His family called the sheriff after a day passed without any calls. The sheriff was able to review airport video recordings to validate that the senator had indeed landed and then departed the Redmond airport, so they concluded he must have disappeared somewhere between Redmond and Sisters on State Route 126. Troopers fanned out and finally found his car. At first glance, it looked like he lost control and rolled the car before hitting a large boulder where the car burst into fire. But a keen-eyed trooper just didn't like the feel of it and decided to call in the forensics team–as it turns out, his intuition was correct. Someone shot out the front tire and caused the accident. To be honest, we don't know if they truly intended to kill the senator, or just cause an accident. Regardless, it's now a murder investigation. The FBI has joined in to ensure every possible lead is tracked down."

"That's horrible, Frank. Do they have any suspects?"

"No. So far, it's as if the shooter simply vanished. They found tracks behind some pine trees on a knoll nearby where they believe the shot was taken, but no other evidence or leads. It looks like the work of a real professional."

"Is there any chance we have a random killer? Why are they convinced that the senator was targeted?" President Callahan asked.

"It's possible, but Sen. Colburn has been receiving phone threats about his support of the aliens and forwarding them to the Secret Service. Based on some of the more recent threats and the fact that the Cjarians are planning on landing at White Sands, as well as the criticality of the risks that something like this would represent for all of our government officials, everyone is focused on the 'hit' option being the most critical task to resolve."

"That makes sense, although it is highly disturbing," President Callahan replied. "Frank, make sure the Secret Service remains involved. Anything you need, you get it. We need to find whoever did this, and fast. Annie and I will call his wife; her name is Wendy, correct?"

"Yes, sir, and he has three sons."

"When will this hit the news?"

"The family already knows, so I expect it will be sometime today, if it hasn't already hit the local Oregon shows."

"Thanks, Frank. Let me know as soon as you hear anything else."

*****

Pacific Ocean

The United States submarine fleet had been the best in the world for more than 80 years, ever since the defeat of the infamous German U-Boats during World War II. Since that time, the U.S. budget for underwater surveillance technology had been unrivaled and maintained with full intent of keeping that strategic and tactical edge, albeit everyone knew that the Chinese, and especially the Russians, were doing everything they could do to catch up to the United States.

In the late 20-teens, the U.S. finally had to admit defeat in the technology race, but it was not to the Russians or even the Chinese– it was Google. Google had first announced its breakthrough in quantum supremacy in late 2019 when it announced the ability to solve complex problems in minutes, compared to what the best supercomputers of the time could do. The-best-of-the-best computers of that era were estimated to require 10,000 years to conquer the same problem. With the speed and capacity of a computer with this capability, its potential uses would be almost limitless. One of the biggest anticipated breakthroughs was in the field of cryptography, where it was envisioned that a quantum computer would be able to crack any encryption code ever created, literally in seconds, thereby eliminating the power of encryption overnight. At the time, Google's initial breakthrough had been limited to R&D lab work, but Google was intent on pumping millions of dollars into the effort to create the first true quantum mechanics computer. By 2023, Google had its first prototype. Word got out and the U.S. government nationalized the lab and immediately clamped "Top Secret" on everything associated with the results, equipment and personnel. Even though the technology had endless potential for commercial uses, it was simply too dangerous to allow the world access to it. Engineers and technicians were ushered into the highest ranks of security clearances and required to sign extensive secrecy agreements with Uncle Sam. Five years later, the initial militarized systems were secretly released to the U.S. Navy and the NSA. The NSA installed one in a limited-access facility deep within the walls of their ultra-secret Utah Data Center where it was used to decode highly classified communications they were monitoring around the world.

The U.S. Navy's first quantum computer implementation was launched on the submarine forces as an underwater signal detection and analysis system, referred to as the Q-USDAS. The power of Q-USDAS was beyond anyone's expectations. Due to the sheer volume of calculations the computer could undertake and the massive library of sounds it constantly collected via its AI systems, it allowed submariners to detect, assess and track noises that previously could never be pulled out of the background staccato of noise the ocean continually generates. It was being called an once-in-a-lifetime breakthrough, even bigger than the Enigma machine was in World War II. One Naval officer humorously claimed it provided the ability to hear a starfish fart from three kilometers away.

The majority of the sailors using the system had no idea how the Q-USDAS worked, nor did they have access to any of its maintenance procedures or componentry; rather they were only required to respond to what the system told them. The USS South Dakota was the first submarine to receive the system.

"Sir, you have an 'eyes only' message."

"Thank you, send it through," Capt. Perez replied without emotion. He had been trailing the Russian submarines for three days, joined by the Utah and Colorado boats a full day ago. The South Dakota had just slowed down to troll a small communications pod known as a Sea Turtle that floated at a depth of three feet below the ocean surface. The Sea Turtle was only used during stationary operations or at very slow speeds so as not to break the communication line between the boat and the Sea Turtle. The thin fiber optic line provided a continual communications pipeline with the submarine, while the Sea Turtle itself provided the ability to communicate directly with space-borne satellite systems and airborne communications platforms.

Capt. Perez turned to his private monitor, swiped his badge and entered his password. The screen lit up.

"***Top Secret, Eyes Only***

Surveillance from your identified zone has captured electronic communication between the Kazan and Vilyuchinsk. The Russians have been given the green light to attack the USS Kennedy with torpedoes and cruise missiles. Our fleet has been notified. The Russians have been notified by the White House. Your orders are to track and possibly attack the Russian submarines: the Kazan, Novosibirsk and the Ulyanovsk. Wait for the Q-USDAS to identify sounds of water entering the tubes. As soon as that has been identified, you are authorized to attack. Repeat, in that case, orders are to sink the three submarines. Acknowledge."

"Phew ..." Capt. Perez uttered as he acknowledged the message.

"What, sir?"

"Get this off to the Utah and Colorado ASAP. As soon as the Q-USDAS detects water surging into their torpedo bays, we are to attack and destroy. We have the Kazan, Utah has the Ulyanovsk and the Colorado has the Novosibirsk."

"Yes, sir."

The Q-USDAS software also significantly improved the ability to detect and translate underwater electronic messages, even in seawater. However, the messages still had to be highly directed and less than 1,000 meters away–a requirement easy to achieve within a tight pack of hunters such as the three Virginia-class subs.

"Messages received and acknowledged, sir."

"Retract the turtle and prepare to initiate battle stations. Close ranks. Prepare torpedoes and firing solutions. Load four for firing and prep four more in reserve for the second round if needed. Hold for my command."

"Yes, sir."

The sonar operator looked over at Capt. Perez with a questioning look.

"Yes, Ensign Johnson?"

"Are we really going to shoot *first*?"

"They came here to sink the Kennedy, under orders from Moscow. The White House is giving the Kremlin a warning that their boats have been compromised and that they are to retreat immediately or be destroyed. If they open their torpedo doors, then they would have made the first move. Let us hope they turn away."

The minutes passed like hours. Three ... 10 ... 15 ... 25 minutes ...

"Capt. Perez! Q-USDAS detects door openings and water movement on all three Russian subs!"

"Launch immediately!"

*****

The sound of multiple torpedo bays opening within just a few short seconds of each other and from three close, but distinctly different, locations left little to the imagination. The three Russian submarine captains were instantaneously and painfully aware that not only were they no longer alone, but they were caught in the open with their backs to the attackers.

"Admiral, the Americans have somehow gotten into our baffles," Capt. Petrov stated with helplessness in his eyes. "We have counted at least eleven torpedo doors ... Sir! Fish are in the water!"

Adm. Sokolov was stunned, his mind racing as he tried to understand how they could have been trailed without knowing, but worse yet, how was it possible that the Americans were firing first ... almost as if they knew what his plans were ... but that couldn't be possible he thought, or could it? He wanted to keep digging, but he knew he only had seconds to implement his orders and attempt an escape.

"Launch countermeasures! Fire torpedoes and cruise missiles! Initiate evasive maneuvers as soon as possible! How far out are the torpedoes?"

"Based on the sound patterns, they are using supercavitating torpedoes like our VA-111s and VA-148s, and their boats were less than one kilometer away when they launched ... Admiral, we have only seconds until impact ..."

The Kazan shook as four torpedoes launched horizontally from their launch tubes and eight Zircon supersonic cruise missiles launched vertically toward the ocean surface. Adm. Sokolov knew that he and his crew were all dead men walking, but at least they would take the USS Kennedy down with them.

"Launch the distress beacon, Captain. It has been an honor."

Fifteen seconds later, the Kazan vaporized as four Mark 72 supercavitating torpedoes impacted and detonated–but not before four of her torpedoes and four of her cruise missiles began tracking toward the USS Kennedy, 10 nautical miles away.

The Novosibirsk was also able to launch four torpedoes and four cruise missiles before it, too, was destroyed. The Ulyanovsk was the first to be hit and was destroyed without launching a single torpedo or cruise missile.

Three hundred and 75 Russian sailors perished in fewer than 60 seconds.

*****

"Capt. Perez, all three targets have been destroyed, but it looks like at least eight torpedoes and an unknown number of cruise missiles were successfully launched, likely programmed to head toward the USS Kennedy Carrier Strike Group."

"Slow and launch the Sea Turtle, get a message out ASAP. Alert COMSUBPAC and the Kennedy. Remain rigged for ultra-quiet operations. Sweep the baffles and make sure no one is trying to beat us at our own game. Tell the Utah and Colorado to fan out around the west side of the fleet and keep an eye out for the Massachusetts and the Rickover; they are with the carrier group and will cover the east side. Stay sharp, people, we're now at war."

*****

Traverse City, Mich.

"Sen. Dempsey?"

"Yes, who is this?"

"I've been warning you, but you wouldn't listen. Now the blood of Sen. Colburn is on your hands. The aliens must leave." The voice was so heavily modulated that Sen. Dempsey couldn't even tell if it was male or female.

"You will not get away with this; you're a sick individual and this country does not give in to barbaric blackmail. You will be caught and held accountable, and I will do everything in my power to pursue the death penalty for you."

"Sen. Dempsey. You're still not listening. How many children do you have?"

The line went dead.

Sen. Dempsey dialed the White House. It was time to ask for help.

*****

Midway

Rear Adm. Matt Browning stood in the combat information center, or CIC as it was more commonly called, in the USS Kennedy's island structure. Following the attack on the space dock, many military groups, including the Kennedy's Carrier Strike Group (CSG), were significantly reinforced. The CVN-79 CSG now consisted of the USS Kennedy; one overhauled Ticonderoga-class cruiser, the USS Lake Erie; two stealth destroyers, the USS Zumwalt and the USS Michael Monsoor; eight Arleigh Burke-class destroyers; a highly classified new destroyer from the Large Surface Combatant class, or LSC, named the USS Galinis and two escort submarines, the USS Massachusetts and the USS Rickover.

Rear Adm. Browning had been forewarned about the planned attack by the Pentagon and immediately placed all the ships at battle stations. He stationed two stealth destroyers, two of the Burkes, the USS Lake Erie and the USS Galinis between the Kennedy and where they believed the underwater threat was expected to come from. The remaining four destroyers and two submarines established a rear guard for the CSG. The Pentagon also informed him that three U.S. submarines, led by Capt. Perez on the USS South Dakota, were in the area shadowing the Russian subs.

The alert message from Capt. Perez arrived exactly seven seconds before the fleet detected the initial torpedo launches themselves, and a full 30 seconds before the first cruise missile launches broke the surface of the sea–definitely not an eternity in a battlefield, but every second counted.

Rear Adm. Browning ordered two Arleigh Burke destroyers, the USS Patrick Gallagher and the USS Jeremiah Denton, to close in at maximum speed. The GE LM 2500 gas turbines screamed as they drove the two destroyers forward at 35 knots–all gun batteries primed and ready. War preparation was not meant for the faint-hearted; training, skill, overwhelming force and, if available, a little luck were the best equation for survival.

As the cruise missiles broke the surface of the sea, the Gallagher and Denton each released a volley of RIM-162 Evolved Sea Sparrow Block II missiles at the incoming threat. The rear admiral was well versed on the Yasen-class submarines and their armory of Zircon supersonic cruise missiles that were believed to be capable of exceeding Mach 8–it was critical that they destroy as many as possible before they hit supersonic speeds. The fleet would only get one chance to take them down at this relatively close proximity, as there would be precious little time to react against a low-altitude missile traveling at almost three kilometers per second.

The USS Lake Erie and the destroyers took up a defensive position in between the USS Kennedy and the incoming threat. The big U.S.S. Kennedy turned bow first in the direction of the threat in an attempt to at least minimize its underwater profile to torpedo attack. The destroyers zigzagged in front of the Kennedy hoping to attract the torpedoes with their intentionally enlarged profiles, while the USS Lake Erie and its extensive defensive systems sailed parallel and slightly ahead of the Kennedy on its port side. Every Phalanx CIWS on every ship in the CSG was primed and pointed at the direction of the incoming threat.

The U.S. had long attempted to develop an anti-torpedo torpedo, but had yet to achieve that goal. In 2025, concerned with the growing Russian threat, the U.S. had contracted with Atlas Elektronik and Thyrssenkupp to outfit their SeaSpider torpedo interceptor system into all of its deployed CSGs. The system had never been used in combat, but had successfully destroyed incoming torpedoes during testing. However, its success against cavitating torpedoes was known to be less than that against standard torpedoes.

"Deploy SeaSpiders," Cmdr. Ryan Phillips ordered.

Two waves of 10 SeaSpiders each were launched, hungrily reaching out to find their intended targets.

The Patrick Gallagher was the first ship to report in with a sighting.

"We have eight breaches. I repeat, eight breaches. Sea Sparrows are airborne." The tension in the Gallagher's captain's voice was heavy. Ten seconds passed until he spoke again.

"Four bogies destroyed, the other four remain incoming, on the deck and supersonic. We are turning broadside and unleashing the Phalanxes."

Cmdr. Phillips looked at Rear Adm. Browning. No words were needed as both men realized that the two destroyer captains had just committed their ships and crews to the gallant act of taking hits in order to protect the USS Kennedy.

"Get all rescue helicopters in the air yesterday!" Phillips barked. "Tell the CAP to refuel in the air. No landings allowed until this is over."

The first wave of SeaSpiders eliminated two of the incoming torpedoes; six more continued on toward the USS Kennedy. Time stood still while everything around them was changing in microseconds.

The sky around the USS Patrick Gallagher and the USS Jeremiah Denton filled with smoke and metal as their Phalanx systems unloaded everything they had in hopes that the missiles would fly haplessly into their curtain of death. One missile detonated, hit by the barrage of metal thrown forward by the combined Phalanx power of the two destroyers. Simultaneously, the USS Jeremiah Denton took one Zircon broadside as the remaining two flew past, only seconds from engaging the USS Kennedy.

The second wave of SeaSpiders was slightly more successful, destroying four of the Russian torpedoes. Two torpedoes and two cruise missiles continued, heading directly toward the USS Kennedy.

"Incoming!" Phillips yelled. "Fire the Phalanxes!"

The human senses are quickly and easily overwhelmed during battle when the action, noise, thundering concussions, visual effects and adrenalin combine to create total dissonance.

The umbrella of metal being thrown into the air was indescribable. Life or death within the CSG would be determined in the next few seconds.

The USS Lake Erie abruptly cut across the bow of the USS Kennedy, intentionally exposing its port side to the incoming threats in hopes of protecting the massive aircraft carrier. As it was with Secret Service agents protecting the president, so it was for the ships of a CSG–all were willing to take a lethal round to protect their leader.

The devastating tonnage of metal that continued to be thrown into the path of the remaining two cruise missiles was mind numbing, but successfully destroyed one of the two remaining Zircons, in large part due to the more highly accurate firing systems of the USS Galinis. The incoming cruise missile was sliced and pulverized into multiple segments of debris that continued on in a slightly elevated trajectory due to the impact of the Phalanx projectiles–still moving at more than 1,500 meters per second. The remaining Zircon hit the USS Lake Erie mid-ship and detonated while the lethal segments of the destroyed Zircon flew over the Lake Erie and impacted the USS Kennedy in the bow, flight deck and island structure. The concussions of the detonations, impact of flying debris at more than five times the speed of sound, and the subsequent secondary explosions shook the entire ship just as the trailing sound barrier of the missiles ripped across the flight deck. The destroyer USS Jack H. Lucas took the first of the two remaining torpedoes on the starboard side of its bow as it zigged left to cover the USS Kennedy. The remaining torpedo drove deep into the already crippled USS Lake Erie and detonated.

"Full astern! Rudder full starboard!"

The USS Kennedy swayed to the port side and the bow elevated slightly as the massive ship attempted to execute a hard turn to the starboard side in an effort to avoid the crippled USS Lake Erie.

"CAP is authorized to shoot to kill any unidentified aircraft or ship that approaches the CSG!" Cmdr. Phillips had released the circling planes of the Combat Aircraft Patrol to engage at their discretion so that he could focus on saving the fleet. "All ships initiate recovery operations. Notify Pearl Harbor we have been attacked and taken damage."

Smoke and flames were billowing out of four ships: the USS Jack Denton, the USS Jack H. Lucas, the USS Lake Erie and the USS Kennedy. The USS Lake Erie was clearly in the worst condition and at the greatest risk of being lost. Firefighting teams leapt into action on all four ships.

The USS Kennedy, although still dealing with damage and fires of its own, knew that time was critical for the sailors on the USS Lake Erie, so the massive ship continued in a large circular turn that would bring it alongside the USS Lake Erie. Once there, it could train its deck hoses down on the burning ship, as well as assist in recovery operations. Unfortunately, less than half way through the carrier's gigantic turning maneuver, the fires on the USS Lake Erie found the ship's rear magazine bay and the rear of the cruiser disintegrated in a magnificent, but horrific explosion, taking the engine systems with it. The remaining structure began to roll over onto its port side and sink, while fires raged uncontrolled throughout its midsection.

Rear Adm. Matt Browning swore loudly. He knew that casualties on the 330-man crew of the USS Lake Erie were going to be very high. That would be in addition to casualties on the two destroyers and the USS Kennedy. The destroyers each maintained a crew of approximately 150 officers and enlisted sailors, but the damage to those two ships looked significantly less and both ships were still moving under their own power–he prayed the crew loss on those ships would be far less.

The fire brigades on the USS Kennedy were making fast work of the deck fires, recovering dead and wounded sailors from the flight deck where a high-speed missile segment had torn up through the bottom of the deck into two fully loaded F-35C Lightning II aircraft, their flight crews and nearby ancillary equipment.

The cruise missile segment that impacted the island structure did so after careening off the bow of the flight deck and ricocheting into the antennae array 70 feet above the deck. The impact damaged critical communication gear, but fortunately did not injure any seamen or initiate any fires.

The missile segments that impacted further below the deck had also been travelling at Mach 5 and penetrated deep into the ship. The damage in those areas had yet to be assessed and still presented major risk to the survival of the USS Kennedy.

"Admiral, we need to get you off this boat until we know the extent of the damage below decks," Cmdr. Phillips stated flatly to Rear Adm. Matt Browning. "If we were to lose a magazine, like the Lake Erie just did, this ship, and your command, could be at risk. Capt. Lee Spaulding is bringing the Galinis alongside to transfer you and your flag. We need to get you off this ship ASAP."

"Understood. I want constant updates, Ryan—we need to save this ship. Let's get moving."

"Aye, aye, sir."

The battle was over in fewer than 10 minutes, but the toll was staggering—and additional lives remained in the lurch as ships continued burning. On the Russian side, three submarines were destroyed and 375 crewmembers presumed dead. On the U.S. side, one cruiser was sunk, two destroyers heavily damaged, and one aircraft carrier, the USS Kennedy, dealing with serious, but yet-to-be assessed damage. U.S. casualties were in the hundreds, likely more.

This would not be received well in Washington.

*****

CHAPTER 14

White House Situation Room

"Gen. McMullen, give me the short version," President Callahan ordered.

"Mr. President, we're still collecting damage reports from the Kennedy CSG, but it's not good. The cruiser USS Lake Erie and at least 153 of its crew were lost. Two destroyers, the USS Jack Denton and the USS Jack H. Lucas, have been seriously damaged. The Denton is currently under tow. Best estimates are that it has a 50/50 probability of making it back to port. The Denton lost 35 sailors. The Lucas is moving under its own power, but limited to 15 knots; the Lucas lost 19 sailors. The Kennedy is heavily damaged, but in better shape and able to maintain 25 knots. The Kennedy lost 17 men and women and two F-35s. Until their return to Pearl, we've also scrambled two squadrons of F-22 Raptors from Elmendorf with aerial refueling tankers to reinforce the CAP. The Kennedy's flight deck was also damaged, but it's still capable of landing aircraft; the deck should be fully operational within 24 hours. Between the four ships, there are another 221 injured, but there are many walking wounded who have yet to report in and at least 30 MIA. Rear Adm. Matt Browning has transferred his flag from the USS Kennedy to the USS Galinis because of the continuing threat of secondary explosions on the Kennedy. On the Russian side, all three submarines were destroyed by the Utah, Colorado and South Dakota–no survivors. Capt. Perez on the South Dakota led the attack. The CSG is moving slowly, but on its way back to Pearl Harbor. At this time, it looks like the immediate danger is over."

"Any response from Russia?"

"None, sir."

"Gen. McMullen, are we at war, or not?"

"Yes and no, sir."

"More black and white, please."

"These are definitive acts of war and people have died. There is no debating that, but neither side has openly or formally declared war yet. The reality is that we've incurred two separate incidents, with no subsequent continuation once they were over. It's not something we have ever experienced on a major super power level, but if you think about it, this is pretty much how the entire Middle East 'war' was. The enemy would strike out and then run away–maybe the Russians think they learned something from those tactics. Granted, those were small groups of attackers against the much larger U.S. military, whereas today we are talking about similar surprise attacks, but between two of the biggest militaries on the planet. So it's similar, but at the end of the day, very different."

"That may make sense. Why do you think they're doing this?"

"Best guess? They aren't convinced that they're strong enough for a full-out war yet, so they're testing us. Reaching out to see how we respond and if they can find a weak spot to exploit further, or to see if we'll capitulate relative to the Cjarians. So far, the answer has been 'no' on all accounts, but it wouldn't surprise me to see a continuation of such tests."

"Keep me posted if anything changes," President Callahan directed and then got up from the table to leave, but stopped before he opened the door.

"Frank?"

"Yes, Mr. President?"

"Get President Yakovlev on the line for me."

"Yes, sir. What is the agenda, if I may ask?"

"To inform him that all attacks need to stop immediately and that he has 48 hours to stand down or I will announce a declaration of war and take our military to DEFCON 1."

President Callahan turned and left the room.

*****

Moon Orbit
Oct. 15, 2029

"Maj. Wei, we are close to impact time. Is your video feed working?" Lt. Wu asked over the com.

"Yes, Lieutenant, where is the feed coming from?"

"Beijing maneuvered one of our military recon satellites closer to the target to use its high-resolution cameras."

"How much longer until we know if the software update worked?"

"We estimate five minutes, sir."

The two men exchanged comments relative to their anticipation of the test and the potential power that it would help China project against the Americans.

"Major, we are within seconds of the earliest projected impact time."

"I'm watching. This is a great view; the satellite literally fills the screen."

Both men were intently watching their computer screens. Ten intolerable seconds passed.

"Wow! Did you see that?" Maj. Wei exclaimed.

"That was incredible! It literally blew the satellite apart!"

"Play it back in slow motion; I want to see the actual point of impact."

The two men played the video forward and backwards at least 10 times. The sheer brutality and egregiousness of the impact that such a small projectile made on a much larger object was simply hard for the mind to grasp. The old adage, "speed kills," now had more meaning than ever. The magnitude of excitement and exaltation created by this new weapon, the one they now controlled from their own fingertips, was both energizing and intoxicating. This system, and their own direct actions, would help usher in China's role as the new preeminent power on Earth.

*****

Jarisst I

"Thjars, this is Qulys. Juulys and Jarns are with me. Can you come up to the Command Center?"

"I'm in the middle of something; can it wait?"

"It's the new weapon system. I think you need to come see this, Captain."

Thjars caught Qulys' intent; it was rare that they called him *Captain*.

"OK, I'll be right there."

Two minutes later, the four were watching a slightly grainy, but still clear video of the launch and the clear hot trail the projectile created as it left the weapon. The video skipped and the time stamp moved forward 13 hours and five minutes.

"I'm slowing it down so that you can see the impact," Jarns said.

"Based on how small the satellite looks, how am I supposed to see this tiny projectile?"

"Just keep watching, sir," Qulys answered. The four continued watching for the next few seconds, although Jarns, Juulys and Qulys were watching Thjars's face to see his reaction as he watched the screen.

"Good Glysst!" Thjars belted out.

"I never saw the projectile, but the satellite literally blew into pieces! What is it, Qulys?"

"We aren't sure," Qulys replied, "but I think Jarns has the best theory. Jarns, go ahead."

"Thjars, years ago ... well, that's not including the 500 years we slept through ... But years even before that, the Cjarian military developed what we called an electromagnetic gun as a kinetic kill weapon from our space station to destroy small asteroids. They stopped using it when they found it was too small for big asteroids and too big for the multitude of small rocks floating in Cjar's planet system. The military decided that the sweet zone of targets was so small that it wasn't worth it, so they ended the program. As far as we are aware, no one ever attempted to convert it into a weapon system to attack *ships*. Seeing it now, it makes a lot of sense; we just never put two and two together."

"Here, watch the initial video again." Jarns replayed the first segment of the video. "See the sudden surge of electromagnetic energy and heat, and how it moves down the axis of the ship toward the end where the projectile exits?"

"Yes, I see it," Thjars replied without removing his eyes from the screen. "Your theory looks plausible, Jarns. Qulys, what does this mean?"

"In this world, whoever owns that weapon system just took ownership of the moon–no one can approach it from Earth without becoming a target themselves. Furthermore, they can take shots at stationary or predictably moving objects in Earth orbit."

"Except us, Qulys," Juulys spoke for the first time, and everyone turned to look at her.

"Juulys?" Thjars walked over to face her. "What are you saying?"

"Until we figure out how to fix the Q-PAMS, this … this is our home." Tears began to show at the edge of her eyes. "We all need to accept that. We also need to accept the fact that Blake and his team, as well as his President Callahan, are as close to family and friends that we may ever have again. If the owners of that weapon attempt to attack our friends, like the Russians did with the space dock, then the decision has already been made–have we not already chosen sides? If we have to use this ship to protect our friends again, then so be it. It's time to pick a side and fight." Juulys left the room as the trio stood for a few pregnant seconds.

"Well, in Juulys-vernacular, not only do we know where she stands, but I think we just got chewed out!" Qulys said with a smirk.

"Sir, if I can be so bold, I believe she's right," Jarns added.

"She sure can cut straight to the point when she needs to." Thjars chuckled. "I agree that we will continue to help and protect our friends, but keep in mind that until we get our fuel tanks repaired, our options will be limited. We also don't know who the owner is. Although I doubt it belongs to the U.S., for all we know, it could. Furthermore, even if it does belong to another faction, I do not want to get involved in any of their wars or battles if it does not include Blake's country–I only want to get involved from a protection perspective, not an offensive perspective. Let's notify Blake to see if he knows anything about it, and until we know more, just keep monitoring it. Any questions?"

"No, sir," Jarns replied first.

Qulys was standing behind Jarns and smiled at Thjars, simultaneously giving him the thumbs up sign they had all adopted.

*****

White House

President Callahan, Frank Pelino, Ben Tellinino and Annie Murphy had gathered in the Oval Office. The Pro-SETI senators were all home with their families and connected to the meeting by phone. Harry and Blake also called in. Sen. Julie Stiles from Louisiana spoke up first.

"Who would possibly want to assassinate a senator? And of all people, James Colburn was loved by everyone. And based on the call that Sen. Dempsey received, what about our families? Whoever this is, we now have to assume that we *and* our families are all at risk, correct?"

"Not really, Julie," Annie replied as she attempted to prevent group panic from taking over. "Whoever this is, they want us to panic."

"They're definitely succeeding, and after killing James, I think we have to assume they aren't afraid to kill again," John Strong from Maine added, "but this citizen is armed and ready to defend his."

"OK, everyone calm down," President Callahan interjected. "We all need to be extra vigilant right now, because the danger is real. I've sent Secret Service agents to each of your houses to ensure your safety. I'm also sending bulletproof cars to each of your homes. The FBI has moved the identification of this individual to the top position on its top 10 list. They'll find out whoever it is, but it may take some time."

"Mr. President?"

"Yes, Blake."

"It is very possible that he was intentionally murdered, but based on what we know, there is also a very good chance that this was meant to scare Sen. Colburn and the rest of the Pro-SETI team, and that it unexpectedly took a turn for the worse."

"Fair point, Blake. Does that change your thinking?"

"If I'm right, then I expect the group will be safe while the assailant reassesses their position and next steps."

"But what about the message to Sen. Dempsey?"

"It would have the same intent, either way," Harry jumped in.

"How so?" Sen. Strong asked.

"Regardless of the intent of the accident, both options share the same goal: to scare you into distancing yourself from your Pro-SETI position, or even getting you to push for the aliens to leave," Harry responded. "However, if Blake is right, and by the way, I tend to agree with him, whoever ordered this hit is likely staying in hiding for fear of the extensive dragnet they know is now being initiated. Furthermore, I expect they and their hitmen will stay as far away from your houses as possible to avoid suspicion."

"That actually makes a lot of sense," President Callahan responded, "but I also agree that we need to maintain every safety measure we can until whoever is responsible for Sen. Colburn's death is identified and captured. So let's start trying to find the culprit by talking about potential suspects."

"Sen. Harley," Blake volunteered calmly.

"Blake, do you really think he would kill another senator?" Annie asked.

"He may not have been trying to kill him, remember? He may have tried simply to have him scared. I could definitely see Harley hiring someone to do something like this. I think it's also important to remember that these calls started before we publicly announced the presence of the Cjarians." Blake paused. "That can only mean that it had to be from someone inside the government and no person has been more outspoken and negative than Sen. James Harley. That makes him suspect number one in my book."

President Callahan and Vice President Murphy exchanged glances. Everyone else on the call remained quiet.

"That is a huge implication of a sitting senator, Blake," President Callahan finally answered. "For any other suspect, it would be enough to get a judge to approve a search warrant. But add the title 'senator' … and it's just too hard to wrap your head around it."

The group talked for another 10 minutes, but no other names were volunteered.

"Mr. President, do you remember my request to monitor certain activities relating to our government?" Harry asked his question without disclosing any details, as he was confident President Callahan would remember without either of them sharing the specifics with the Pro-SETI group present.

Everyone on the phone could hear a very audible sigh from President Callahan. No one talked. All waited for an answer, but only Harry, Blake, Annie and President Callahan himself would know what that answer would mean or lead to.

"I don't like this at all; I really don't."

"I don't expect you to like it, sir, but that doesn't mean it isn't the right thing to do," Blake replied.

"I know, Blake." The president paused, clearly struggling with his decision process before he spoke again.

"You have my approval. But be extremely careful, gentlemen; this crosses some very dangerous lines."

*****

CHAPTER 15

Houston
Oct. 16, 2029

"Hello. Li here."

"It's Harry."

"Hey, Harry, what's up?"

"I'm going to relay a message, but do not state any more details than I provide. Is that clear?"

"Ahhh, OK. Sure."

"Do you recall the special request we made? The one that you have been prepping for?"

"Absolutely."

"Green light."

"Hot dang! At the proper altitude?"

"Yes, high enough that it's almost close to the Karman line."

"Got it. What's next?"

"You and Jimmy are the only ones approved, but Blake asked if it's safe to assume there may be a third, younger member already in the know?"

"Ahhh, oops …"

"We figured. Just make sure he understands the need to be quiet. Under no circumstance does he go onsite. Understood?"

"Yes."

"Get started."

*****

White House Situation Room

Gen. McMullen stood up at the front of the room, all eyes riveted on the screen behind him.

"We believe the Russians are on the verge of invading Belarus and Ukraine."

"First, why do you think that?" President Callahan asked.

"They have amassed SU-35 Flanker air superiority fighters, SU-25 Grach ground attack aircraft, T-14 Armata tanks and Bumerang APCs on their western front–in addition to the thousands of soldiers relocated there as well. This is without a doubt an invasion-capable force."

"But, why are they doing that?"

"Igor wants to rebuild the USSR."

"This isn't a WWII drama, Gen. McMullen; it's 2029. What in hell would he gain by starting a war with Europe?"

"Technically, some would argue that Belarus and Ukraine are not part of Europe proper, nor are they part of NATO. Given that Russia previously invaded the Crimean Peninsula, but neither Europe nor the United States did anything, he likely sees it as an acceptable risk."

"But what does he expect to gain?"

"Distance. Military separation for a defensive buffer. The border of Belarus is roughly 500 kilometers from Moscow. That is approximately the distance from Buffalo, New York, to Columbus, Ohio–way too close to defend against a ground attack in today's world, let alone an air attack."

"I understand the logic, but that would only make sense if he truly thinks we are going to attack Russia. He knows we aren't going to do that."

"Maybe not today, sir," Gen. McMullen responded, "but if this conflict blows up into a full-fledged war, then it would be a very significant strategic move by Russia."

"So why hasn't he attacked again? If it's a war that he wants, why not attack again before we can regain our footing? This makes no sense," President Callahan muttered.

"There is one other possibility," Annie interjected.

"What's that?" President Callahan turned to look at his VP.

"Maybe he really doesn't want another fight with us and it's a diversionary tactic via our European allies to take our eye off the ball. He lost both rounds with us so far, first on the space dock and secondly in the Pacific. In all fairness, they weren't total lopsided losses, but they were losses. Perhaps he's trying to see if he can find a gap with our allies."

"Continue," President Callahan said.

"We know he still wants that Cjarian ship. It's a safe bet that he saw the magnitude of our western movement in forces we initiated after the attack on the USS Kennedy. Now he's enacting moves on the other side of the world that will pull significant U.S. resources and attention eastward and away from their normal positions in order to respond to this new threat. Our eyes and ears will all be focused outward, away from the U.S. itself–and away from where the Cjarians will be. At the least, he keeps us off balance and following his leads."

"Annie," President Callahan sat back in his chair as he spoke, "that is scary as hell, but a phenomenal observation. If you're right, how could they possibly know we are planning White Sands for the landing?"

"Let's hope he doesn't know that. From his perspective, he likely assumes that *if* we land their craft we would likely land in the U.S.–where else? But, even if we didn't allow them to land, and they stayed in space, he has still achieved his goals of distraction and keeping us jumping around, not knowing when the real hit is coming."

"Gen. McMullen, Brad, Ben, Frank … thoughts?"

Ben Tellinino spoke first. "I hadn't thought about that, Annie, but I can see the logic. It's actually brilliant because it gets both of his objectives accomplished with one move: maximum distraction and staying one step ahead of us. That may explain why he hasn't attacked again, yet; he thinks he has the upper hand right now in this proverbial chess match."

*****

Pentagon

Blake called in from a secure room located in the White Sands U.S. Navy Department building on Dewey Street. FBI agent Joe Foster called in from his Colorado Springs office. They both waited for Gen. Beckman to join.

"Hey, Joe. I think it's just the two of us right now. How are things in Colorado?"

"Pretty good, Blake. Where are you this time, if I'm allowed to ask?"

"You can always ask, Joe, and this time, I can actually tell you." Blake laughed. "I'm in New Mexico."

"New Mexico? That's just down the street a bit in Colorado terms."

"Yes, I suppose it is ..." Blake was interrupted by a third voice.

"Hello. Cmdr. Thompson? Agent Foster? Gen. Mark Beckman, here."

"Yes, sir, we're both on."

"You've both been cleared for what I'm about to share with you. This is not to be shared further. Is that understood?"

"Yes," both men answered.

"The project, as you both know, is called Starburst, and it represents the biggest step in ammunition since the tracer round was developed. You were previously told that it simply detonates once it hits a predetermined location and showers the target with shrapnel. That is only partially correct. The truth is, we've had ammunition like this in various stages of development for years, commonly called smart bullets. Still with me?"

"Yes, please continue," Blake responded.

"Those rounds could only generate small pieces of shrapnel and relied on luck to hit a hidden target. The new rounds are an entirely new generation. Starburst rounds have miniaturized infrared imaging capabilities built into each round that can detect targets before activating. I won't attempt to tell you that I understand it all, but an internal processor tracks the round's speed as it nears the intended target area. Once at the desired location, within a matter of microseconds, it integrates the thermal imaging data, identifies the target or targets, selects the target with the highest probability of engagement and then initiates."

"Initiates?" Blake queried. "You didn't say detonates, you said it activates and initiates."

"That's correct, Commander. The round includes an internal gyroscope that forces the round to go unstable, allowing it to reorient and point at the selected target before the internal round is fired."

"How ..." Blake stuttered, "how does it overcome the projectile's spin rate?"

"It doesn't spin, Commander," Gen. Beckman responded. "The round has small fins that are deployed once it detects the acceleration caused by the initial rifle firing and exits the rifle barrel. The fins provide aerodynamic stability for the round in place of the normal barrel rifling that spin-stabilizes a typical bullet. The fins may not allow the accuracy, distance or speed that a normal rotating bullet has, but since firing accuracy and speed is no longer required at this stage, that responsibility is built into the second, internalized round."

"This is almost unbelievable, Gen. Beckman," Joe interrupted, "and you're telling us that *those* are out in the public's hands now?"

"Unfortunately, we believe they are."

"So why are you telling us this, sir?" Blake asked.

"Let me make sure I clarify the sensitivity of my next statement. This is even more classified than the Starburst discussion. Agent Foster, this will be new to you. It stays only with you." Gen. Beckman paused.

"Blake, as I know you're already aware, President Callahan has authorized your team's surveillance of Sen. Harley's home. That was actually not totally because of *just* you and Harry pushing for it."

"I actually wondered about that, sir. What else was he aware of?"

"President Callahan was already aware of the loss of the ammunition, but he was also aware that Sen. Harley and his fellow Anti-SETI members have informally taken control of the board of directors that runs the business that developed and manufactured the Starburst program ..."

"Pardon my interruption, Gen. Beckman, but ... does the president actually believe that Harley had something to do with it?"

"Does he believe? No. Is he concerned that may be a possibility? Yes."

"This is already way above my pay grade, so why am I involved?" Joe interrupted.

"The two of you were directly involved with the recovery of a portion of the missing ammunition. You were also involved with the search of a certain property near Resolution Mountain in Colorado–which is in your territory, correct?"

"Yes."

"We have reason to believe that Harley, and perhaps other board members, may be tied to that property. I can't share why or how we know it, so you'll have to just hear me out. *If* we can verify the tie between Sen. Harley and that property, then we can get a judge's order to search it to see if the ammunition is being stored on site."

"I'm sure you can search real estate data to find out, can't you?" Joe asked.

"We did, and it's owned by a shell corporation. As is common with these organizations, it's almost impossible to connect a name to it."

"Why can't President Callahan just give the order and send troops in? Send me; I'll get in this time," Blake challenged.

"He could, but he wants to do this by the book, in case he's wrong. Could you imagine how that would be used against him?"

"Yes, and unfortunately, that makes sense, even if I'd rather choose the frontal attack option."

"I'm sure you would, Commander."

"But I may have another way to help."

"What's that, Commander?"

"Let me talk to Harry and I'll get back to you."

*****

White Sands, N.M.

"Blake, any word on Diego yet?" Patty asked.

"Nothing new, but continued thanks to the White House that they are at least keeping him in El Paso."

"This is bullshit, Blake. I know it, you know it, everyone knows it," Sean said and pounded the table. "Why isn't he released yet? If Sen. Harley really is behind this, then why don't they throw *his* butt in jail?"

"I agree with you, Sean," Blake replied, "but you know it doesn't work that way. President Callahan said he would handle it, so let's leave it in his hands for now."

"I hear ya, but I still don't have to like it."

"Harry."

"Yes?"

"I need you to research something for me."

"Sure, what's the topic?"

"This."

"A piece of paper?"

"Yes. Diego, Sean and I found it in a garbage dumpster at that cabin site we told you about near Resolution Mountain. It's a Walmart receipt for a microwave. I need to see if you can trace the specific purchase to someone."

"OK, let me see it …. Wait, let me get a plastic bag first. I doubt we can lift any fingerprints off it by now, other than maybe yours, but we can at least try."

Harry left the room and returned a couple of minutes later with a Hefty Slider storage bag.

"Here, drop it in this. I'll see what I can find out about it."

"Thanks, Harry. By the way, what's the latest on your invite list?"

"I assume you're talking about the scientist list to help out with the Cjarian ship when they arrive. So far, with the help of the White House, I've been able to get everyone I wanted. It's almost as if the scientific community knows something big is up, but they don't know what it is, so of course they all want to be involved to make sure they don't miss out."

"I'm curious, Harry … like who?"

"Well, it's a long list. From memory, I've got the top U.S. scientists from our key national labs. That includes the Jet Propulsion Lab, Oakridge, Sandia, Savannah River National Labs, Princeton Plasma Physics Lab, Fermi National Accelerator Lab, Argonne National Lab, Thomas Jefferson National Accelerator Facility, the Idaho National Lab, the SLAC National Accelerator Lab, Los Alamos and the Brookhaven National Lab."

"Good Lord, Harry. How many scientists do you have coming?"

"That was just a portion of the U.S. list. If I get everyone I want, it will include the top 100 scientists in the world in the energy and materials arena."

"A hundred? How will we keep this secret?"

"Blake, no matter what we try to do, when this ship enters the atmosphere and lands here, there is no way we'll be able to keep it a secret. The cat will be out of the bag."

"I actually wondered about that. Is the White House on board?"

"Yes, they cleared everyone I requested before I was allowed to make contact."

"What other countries will be involved?"

"I've tried to limit foreign exposure, but there will be some. As I mentioned while we were still in space, I've received acceptance from the top five scientists at CERN for both antimatter and accelerator fields of research."

"How about Russia or China?"

"With the exception of Vladimir, Russia is out because of the recent acts of aggression. Relations with China have also been challenging of late, so the White House requested that we leave them out as well. That was unfortunate. From a purely scientific viewpoint, they have some great researchers."

"Who else?"

"We have researchers from a few of India's national labs, including their Physical Research Lab, Harish-Chandra Research Institute and the Tata Institute of Fundamental Research. Germany and Japan are also represented for their manufacturing capabilities. There are a few more handpicked scientists from leading universities around the world as well, but I expect the list to still top out at 100 if everyone makes it here."

"This almost sounds like the Manhattan Project, Harry."

"Actually, Blake, that is the model the White House agreed to duplicate. This will be the greatest gathering of scientists, focused on a single goal, since the Manhattan Project."

*****

Jarisst I

The days had sped by. Preparations for their upcoming Earth landing had consumed the crew, the majority of whom were focused on military preparations as Thjars was adamant that they be prepared to fight their way out, if needed. With that decree, Qulys had transitioned into full drill sergeant mode and had driven the crew hard through individual and group training activities, with both personal arms and the ship's weapon systems. As expected from any seasoned drill sergeant, none of their performance ever measured up to his expectations–as he frequently and harshly reminded them.

Thjars entered the galley to get something to eat and saw his trusted friend sitting alone, eating lunch.

"Qulys, you've been pretty rough on the crew. I get it and I understand, but I need to know what you really think. Are we ready?"

"Your timing is spot on, Thjars."

"How so?"

"I know I've been riding them pretty hard. I had to because they weren't ready for a real battle when we started, but they've come a long way in the past few days. Will they ever be ready to become Cjarian Blast Troopers and storm an enemy ship? No, but for the group they are, I'm quite proud of them; they are ready. If we are attacked, win or lose, live or die, I am confident they will serve Cjar honorably. I intended to pull everyone together and tell them that tomorrow. The teardown and humiliation was necessary; now it's time to rebuild and establish confidence. After all, our planned landing is only a couple of days away."

"That's good to hear, Qulys. Thank you for everything you've done, and I'm sure the crew also understands and appreciates your efforts–they know what's at stake."

"Thank you, sir."

"Have we identified any further activity near the moon?"

"No, Thjars, it's been quiet for the past few days. Nothing appears to be happening near the moon or in Earth orbit, but the ongoing clashes on the planet, between Blake's country and the Russians, appear to be continuing, and we are the primary cause."

"They want our ship, don't they?"

"Yes, they do, but even more, they don't want Blake's country to have it. From what Juulys has picked up, the Russians think the

Americans are trying to get our ship so that they can become the undeniable military leaders of the world. They are convinced that their world will end if they allow the Americans to gain control of our technology."

"If it wasn't for the damage our ship has incurred, I think the best answer would be to leave this system so that we don't further fan the flames of war on their planet," Thjars lamented.

"I agree, Thjars, but the facts are the facts. Right now, we couldn't leave even if we wanted to, so we need to land on their planet and hope they can help us repair the damaged fuel tanks and maybe even the Q-PAMS drive. Then we can decide if we want to stay or depart."

"Qulys, you've always been good at cutting through the fog of indecision and getting straight to the heart of the issue. Yes, we will continue our plans to land on Earth, but once we have our repairs completed, I will feel worlds better about being able to depart this system and return home to Cjar."

"And Blake?"

"You just pulled me back from the fog of indecision; are you going to push me back into it again, Qulys?"

"No," Qulys responded with a smirk, "but I know that both you *and* Juulys will have trouble with that decision, if and when it comes time to make it." Qulys looked up from his plate and smiled at Thjars. "For what it's worth, so will I."

*****

Conway, Ark.
Oct. 17, 2029

"Honey, do you want oatmeal or egg whites this morning?"

"Can I opt for pancakes and bacon?"

"Now Sen. Harley, you know what the doctor said."

"Damn doctors. Give me the oatmeal. Am I allowed to have banana slices in it?" Sen. Harley replied sarcastically, but he knew his wife was correct. He was on a strict diet and if he didn't make some significant changes, he'd likely end up like his father did– dead of a heart attack before the age of 55."

Four hundred and 50 miles to the west, three men huddled around the computer in a nondescript office in the Houston Space Center.

"That's coming through clearer than I expected." Robert Stern piped up. "How did you guys get in so easily? It was only yesterday that we were given the green light, right?"

"Yupper," Li replied. "You helped us write the routines, so we were ready to go. Once approved, all we had to do was find a gap in his home systems to exploit, and we were in–without ever setting foot on his property. Pretty scary isn't it?"

"It sure is. I didn't think it would be that easy … so, what gap did you find?"

"It's his own home management system," Li replied. "It always amazes me how little people think relative to sharing their lives with the world–intentionally or unintentionally. It started with Facebook and Snapchat and then expanded to Amazon's Alexa and Google's Home systems over a decade ago. Systems like Nest and Ring came along after that. Many homes already had built-in, total home sound and video systems, all controllable from your cell phone, but most were independent, so if you found a gap, it only risked that one particular application. Then came the all-in-one, easy-to-control home management systems that integrated everything you had into one easy-to-manage, accessible anywhere, cell phone app. So, all it took was one crack in the barrier and someone could exploit every application and system you had, but everyone simply shrugged their shoulders and just blindly accepted it because *everyone was doing it.*

"Over the past decade, these systems have become exceedingly intelligent, tracking our location while in our own homes, cars and offices. These same systems monitor our office and kitchen supplies, automatically reordering before items run out, recommending books and music based on our most recent selections, automatically scheduling car repairs and standard medical visits, etc., etc.–and recording it all. People are naïve enough to think that info doesn't get shared, but it does. In just a few short years, people went from 'don't invade my privacy' to 'I'm at the grocery store buying lasagna,' and allowing businesses to track and access everything they do in exchange for instant gratification. No way, any of that damn stuff will ever enter my house."

"You didn't answer my question about the gap ..."

"Background, Robert, background. I'm getting there. People think they're safe because of the security systems built into these technologies. To be fair, those security systems are quite impressive and they get better every year. The problem, or the gap as I called it, is the weakest point in the system is the connections people make to them and the passwords people use. Add one poorly designed gadget, toy or video game that interfaces with the system, and that becomes the gap."

"So what did you find?"

"It was a video game, 'Alien Conquerors.' It's one of those multi-player, on-line games, But, this one also allows you to play what they call *neighborhood level*."

"Yeah, I know, I played it, too," Robert interjected. "You wear a helmet with a heads up display that allows you to see where your friends are. The game directs you to imaginary battlefields within your town."

"Righto, Mr. Robert. Well, the security system on that game sucks, to put it bluntly. There are multiple hack paths on it, which exist because of the game's ability to *allow* you to hack others as part of the actual game–and people actually buy this stuff for their kids! If you read the small print, it actually states that as part of the legal acceptance to play the game. I'll bet you didn't read that, did you?"

"Ahhh, nope ..."

"I figured. Well, they claim it's up to the user to maintain password protection to their home system. As long as they do that, then your house is protected. But if you figure out a password, then you're in–and into everything."

"OK, but that doesn't sound so bad. How is that any different than setting the password to the home management system?"

"Because you're dealing with a teenage boy, not a parent and not the home management system. Most people don't think twice about their kids screwing up something."

"And how did you crack, I assume, his teenage son's password?"

"That's the part we kept you out of so that you still had plausible deniability with Blake," Jimmy laughed.

"Well it's done now, so spill the beans," Robert lobbed back.

"The heads up display. Remember how it sees everything?"

"Yes …"

"Well, we could see his entire room. Guess who his favorite movie character was?"

"I don't know, Iron Man?"

"Darth Vader. It only took that assumption, his known birth date and a few lucky guesses–23 to be exact, and we cracked it: DVader714. Once we had that, it allowed access to the home management system where we had the freedom to watch and listen to everything."

"But how did you get access to Sen. Harley's computer?"

"His son again. He walked into his dad's office with his heads up helmet on just as he was typing in his password. Call it luck, but we were in, and yes, faster than any of us planned on. Once in, it didn't take us long to snoop through all his records by filtering it through NSA's computer banks. There's a lot of crap in there, including what looks to be some pretty shady financial deals, but unfortunately, nothing yet that we can nail him to relative to the Cjarian agenda–and that's the only thing we're allowed to officially chase down."

"How about his phone?"

"The home phone is clean …"

"He still has a landline?" Robert expressed in total surprise.

"Yes, he has to because of his governmental responsibilities. That one is clean. But, he also appears to own at least two cell phones that we know of: one personal cell phone and one government-issued cell phone. The government-issued cell phone is totally traceable as it belongs to Uncle Sam. The personal cell phone is the one that we want to crack next."

"Isn't that tied into the home system, too?"

"That's what has us suspicious–it doesn't show up anywhere. We've got his wife's cell phone cracked because she didn't even have a password on it. She has clearly called his government-issued phone many times, daily, but we haven't yet seen a tie to any other phone the senator may have from her calling log. Our best guess is that the second phone is either off the grid, or just one that he hasn't shared knowledge of with the family."

"Or he's told them that it's for classified work only."

"Robert, that's actually a pretty good thought," Li replied, "and it could actually be correct. We'll track that down separately through the White House, but to be safe, we'll continue to assume this phone is off the grid until we learn otherwise from D.C."

"Why are you so positive that he has a second phone if it doesn't show on her call log? ... Oh, never mind, the home video system, correct?"

"Correct, we saw him use two separate phones in the same room, so we know it exists, we just don't have any information on it, yet, and we don't know who he's calling with it either–but we definitely will once we can determine its number."

*****

Moscow

"General Secretary Qiang, this is President Yakovlev. Thank you for taking my call. I believe we share a common objective."

The two men discussed objectives and demands over the next 30 minutes. In general terms, they were in full agreement; it was just a matter of working out some of the extraneous details. They agreed to talk further later in the day after each had an opportunity to review with their inner circles.

*****

White Sands

"Blake, I've got an update for you ... or maybe I should say Jimmy does."

"What's that, Harry?"

"The receipt you gave me yesterday, the one you found at the cabin ... we have some new data on it."

"What did you find?"

"As I just corrected myself, I didn't … Jimmy did, with a little help from the senator himself."

"The senator?"

"Yeah, he bought himself one of the highest resolution security video systems money can buy. It seems he's keeping an eagle eye over his home office. Not only does it have very high quality video, but he stores everything it sees, and I mean everything. From what we can gather, it also alerts him any time the door is opened."

"Interesting, almost like he wants to make sure no one gets in there without him knowing it, doesn't it?"

"Sure does, Blake."

"So how did he help us?"

"He used his credit card from his office desk, typed the numbers into a website to buy, of all things, a burner phone. The last 4 digits match exactly: 2-3-8-9."

"That sure feels like a hit, but it's really not a guarantee, is it?"

"Correct, Blake. To get full validation, we'd need to get a judge to approve a search warrant to open his credit card data to us …"

"How quick can we get one?"

"I can get one by tomorrow, and I will, just to make sure, but there are other ways …"

"Finger prints?"

"Bingo."

"But you'd need to acquire something of his with his prints on it, or get an official copy from the government database–both need someone to approve access, correct?"

"Correct again, Blake," Harry answered and smiled.

"I know that smile, Harry; what are you holding back on, good buddy?"

"Remember that first SETI meeting at the White House I told you about?"

"Yes …"

"I didn't tell you everything."

Harry relayed the story about the paper wad he'd kept after Harley tossed it at Gen. McMullen during a previous White House SETI meeting, and the paper deflected into Harley's lap.

"Well, I kept it. He gave it to me, so technically and legally, I can use it to check his prints."

Now Blake was smiling. "Pompous jackass, isn't he?"

"Sure is."

"And?"

"They match." Harry concluded. "I was surprised I could still lift the prints for as long as it must have been in the dumpster, as well as in your pocket, but there was enough remaining to make a match. And, yes, your prints are there, too. My conclusion? Your man Harley definitely bought the microwave. Whether he delivered the unit to the camp himself, or someone else did, it really doesn't matter. Either option still makes a pretty strong case that he may have a tie to that campsite."

*****

White House

"It's definitely the right thing to do, Mr. President, but you know the media will have a field day with this," Frank Pelino warned.

"I know, but that's the point: it *is* the right thing to do. Let's not forget that we have depositions from two of the police officers that responded, as well as the restaurant manager. We all saw the video from the restaurant. It's way too graphic to release all of it, but we can show the initial confrontation where they clearly demanded money from Mr. Velasquez, threatened him and his brother and then pulled a knife. It's a clear case of self-defense. Call a press conference today and get this material on the network news as an explanation for my decision. Equally important, we must get him out of jail immediately because Blake needs his full team on site before our guests arrive."

"Sen. Harley will likely go after you for abusing your authority anyway."

"Let him." Annie Murphy jumped in for President Callahan. "Article 72 of the United States Constitution gives the president full authority to grant pardons. Every president before him has used it, and the case of Petty Officer First Class Diego Velasquez is far cleaner than many pardons from previous presidents. While you're at it, Frank, I recommend that you also include the fact that

Sen. Celeste fessed up after the Texas trooper verified the source of the arrest orders. She was requested by Sen. Harley to set up the arrest. Turn the tables on him and let the public know that he initiated an unapproved arrest without going through the proper legal channels–he's the one that was abusing his power."

"Sign the paper, Mr. President. We'll notify the Texas Rangers and Gov. Townsend, and then get Cmdr. Thompson on the phone. I expect the commander will quickly make this his number one priority," Annie smiled and sat back in her chair.

"Thanks, Annie … and you, too, Frank. I know you're just watching my back for me, but there's way too much going on right now and on multiple fronts. We need quick resolution on all activities, and I need to know that we have the best people we have on all of our front line risk areas–and that includes Petty Officer First Class Diego Velasquez. Let me know when you reach Cmdr. Thompson so I can talk to him."

Forty-five minutes later, the trio regrouped in the Oval Office to call Blake. Five minutes later, Cmdr. Thompson was on his way to El Paso accompanied by Sean O'Rourke.

*****

The hour and 55 minute drive went quickly. In preparation for their arrival, Diego had been released from the downtown El Paso County Detention Facility and moved to the El Paso County Courthouse next door at 500 E. Overland Ave. Blake and Sean parked in the deck across the street, then walked to the front of the courthouse.

"Pretty nice building," Sean volunteered, "but can you imagine trying to keep all of that shiny glass clean? The entire building is glass and there's at least a dozen floors!"

"Yep, real pretty. If you want the job, I'll see if I can get you a job interview. Otherwise, let's get Diego and get the hell out of Dodge. That work for you, Sean?"

"Sure, bossman, I was just acknowledging the surroundings. Where is he, anyway?"

"They said they would meet us in the lobby once we signed in."

"Good thing they moved him over from the brig next store. That had to suck big time."

The two men walked up the four steps and entered the lobby.

"Well, if it isn't good ole Lady Justice," Sean continued. "Where the heck was she when Diego needed her?"

"Focus, Sean. We need to get through the checkpoint first."

"Good morning, officer. We are both military, we are carrying and we have approved paperwork with us. It's your house; you call the ball."

"Thank you, Commander. Just for protocol, let me call a few more officers over and then I'll let you lay your arms on the belt. We'll hold them until you're ready to leave."

"Good here, Captain."

A few minutes later, Blake and Sean were escorted to a side room where they were told to wait until Diego was brought down to meet them. There was a knock on the door and Diego was escorted in.

"Diego! Ya'll done with yer vacation and ready to git back to work again? We thought maybe you were trying to get back to Mexico to visit family. After all, the border is only one mile south of 'ere."

"Trust me, Blake, after four days in solitary confinement, even that bloody mick's voice sounds good."

The three men laughed and shook hands.

"How about we get out of here before someone changes their mind again?" Blake asked.

"That's an invite I don't need to hear twice; let's go, gents!"

Ten minutes later, the reunited trio was heading north on South Campbell Street, toward U.S. Interstate 10.

"Diego, you OK, buddy?"

"Yeah, thanks, Sean. Sucked like hell, but nothing I can't handle."

"Hungry?" Blake asked.

"Heck yes!" Sean replied.

"You're always hungry, McIrish. I was asking Diego."

"Now that you mention it, I'd love a good burger and fries. The guy in the cell next to me said something about Rosco's Burger Inn, said it was the best in town."

"Well, if you have the *inside* scoop, then it must be good." Blake laughed. "Sean, punch it up on your phone and let's go get some burgers."

*****

CHAPTER 16

White Sands
Oct. 18, 2029

Everyone had stayed up late celebrating Diego's return, but they also knew there was precious little time remaining before the Cjarians would arrive, and they had work to do.

"The Cjarians will be here tomorrow." Blake spoke up. "Li, Robert and Jimmy will arrive this afternoon. Harry, I want you to round up Vladimir."

"I almost forgot about him. What's he been doing?"

"He's still a Russian citizen, so we have to keep him in a base apartment, under confinement, until the Cjarians arrive. Patty has been checking in on him each day to make sure he's doing OK. Harry, I need the two of you to get your gaggle of scientists together and establish their ground rules. We aren't going to allow everyone on the ship. For the first few days, only our team will go on board. There may be an exception or two based on Harry's assessment of what's needed, but those are the rules. The scientists have been assigned to various conference rooms where they will be allowed to work on selected efforts. Harry, it will be up to you to determine what gets shared with whom. Remember that we need to fix their ship, but we also need to protect their technology as well. I want everything compartmentalized so that no one, except you, has the entire picture. Is that clear?"

"Crystal."

"Good."

"When you're done with them, get with the base subs and contractors and go through the same script. They will obviously have to work on the ship itself, but only when and on what we decide. The good news with this group is that they all already work at White Sands and Holloman so they're cleared to work on classified projects–make sure they realize that simply knowing about this project is classified, let alone what they are about to see and work on. You will need to plan morning and evening debriefings with each group."

"Will do, Blake. Are you planning on being in the debriefings?"

"I will by phone, not in person. Sean, Diego and I will be focusing on base security. Sean will be part of the CAP, along with Maj. Pat Sullivan and Cmdr. Rachel Joslin; each of them will lead a separate CAP group and maintain 24/7 air coverage. Diego will be integrated into the ground force groups and I'll be staying at Holloman AFB, which will be Command Central for security operations."

"You're not even going to meet with the Cjarians when they arrive?" Patty asked.

"I will, once they've landed and given us the all-clear sign. I'll copter in just to meet them for a few minutes, but I'll return to and stay at Holloman. I've already talked it through with Thjars, Qulys and Juulys and they're good with it. If they, or any of you see anything of concern, I'll return ASAP; otherwise, I'll be at the airbase. Holloman has significantly greater surveillance and military capabilities that can be used across the entire New Mexico area."

"Speaking of Li." Diego jumped in to change the topic. "Any progress on nailing that SOB Harley?"

"Unfortunately, no," Blake replied. "He and Jimmy were able to access his home phone and his government-issued cell phone, but so far there's nothing to tie him to the ammunition or the attack on Sen. Colburn. He's definitely made a stink over the Cjarians, has potential ties to the cabin site in Colorado and was the driving force behind getting you arrested, but that's not what we're looking for."

"Well, it's enough for me. You weren't the one that had to spend three days in jail, Chief. If it were my vote, you'd put me on a plane tonight and let me find a way to have a private chat with him in the middle of the night. I'll get the proof. He deserves it just because of what he did to me."

"I agree, Diego, for both your own payback and for the likely possibility that he has some ownership in highly illegal and deadly activities, but I need you here right now. Jimmy, Robert and Li will continue tracking him down once they get set up here. Harley has a D.C. office and a vacation home in Colorado that we haven't checked out yet. Trust me, my gut says you'll get your chance."

*****

Klaus Schneider had been consumed by the comet since he first learned of it. Once the potential threat had been validated, Klaus set up office at the European Southern Observatory in Garching, Munich, to monitor new data feeds from the International Asteroid Warning Network, or IAWN. As best they could estimate, the comet was somewhere between 100 and 150 kilometers in diameter–a true monster, travelling at close to 250,000 kilometers per hour. The probability of impact with either Earth or the moon had become a daily debate within the IAWN circle of scientists that had been cleared by their governments to be part of the core monitoring team. The impact projections from the group varied from 28 percent to 42 percent for the Earth and 5 percent to 28 percent for the moon.

Klaus had gotten excited about his projections early on, but he had stopped trading estimates with the other scientists and astronomers as he knew it was a waste of time until it passed the sun. As they had clarified before, without knowing what the true mass and makeup of the comet was, there was no way to predict what the sun's impact on its trajectory would be. Klaus also pointed out that the current trajectory could cause the comet to be pulled into the sun and destroyed, or pulled close enough to slingshot away, impacting both its resulting trajectory and its speed.

The truth was that no one would know for at least another 15 to 20 days, until the comet finally neared and passed the sun. It would then require another 25 days to reach the Earth–assuming it still remained on a collision path.

*****

White Sands
Oct. 19, 2029

The day had finally arrived. In some ways, Blake thought, it seemed like it took forever. Yet, relative to preparing for the visit, it felt like it came way too soon. Blake knew that no matter how much time they had, they would've still wanted more from a preparation perspective.

"Thjars, are we ready?"

"Yes, Blake, to be honest, the sooner we get this over with the better. The flight path you provided us with looks fairly safe and away from any major cities. We'll enter over North Dakota and then fly south, toward the San Isabel National Forest in Colorado, while descending to an altitude of 10,000 meters above the terrain. Then we head straight south to White Sands, N.M., correct?"

"That's correct, Thjars. President Callahan has also ordered a curtailment of all commercial flight operations west of the Mississippi River, which includes more than 50 percent of the country. The only planes flying will be U.S. military aircraft, and of those, the majority will be flying parallel to your route to ensure your protection."

"Thank you, Blake, and please thank President Callahan for me. We do not underestimate the disruption this must be causing your country, and all for our safety. How is he doing that without alerting the country to our arrival?"

"We had Microsoft announce they found a loophole in the Western U.S. Air Traffic Control software that requires an emergency system shutdown and update. That way we were able to provide people with advance notice to minimize disruptions."

"That's pretty impressive," Thjars responded, "but I may think twice about anything else you tell me now!"

They both laughed.

"Are there any space-based weapons that we need to be aware of?"

"Unfortunately, yes, but to our knowledge, none are set up to shoot autonomously, which means if you approach fast and straight, there shouldn't be any time for someone to detect you, communicate the finding and then get an approval to initiate an attack before you enter the atmosphere–and you surely won't have to worry about that from the U.S. Furthermore, if you approach directly from the sun that should greatly minimize the ability for anyone to detect you. Once in our atmosphere, you'll be above the United States and we'll be able to protect you from missile or aircraft attacks."

"Then it's settled. We'll program a wide arc that brings us in from the direction of your star. We should be entering your atmosphere in less than two hours. Glysst be with us all."

The next 45 minutes were filled with a conflicting set of emotions for everyone involved, battling the excitement of the monumental event itself, as well as fears from the inherent dangers that came with the actual visit. The risks covered a wide range of issues, from the typical re-entry risks, to threats from non-friendly countries, to the unknown risks associated with the damaged fuel tanks. No one knew if the tanks would survive re-entry or not. The next hour was going to be euphoric, but at the same time, a gut-wrenching time for both the Cjarians and for those who were "in the know" across the Dakotas, Nebraska, Colorado, New Mexico, Texas and Washington, D.C.

To reduce the risk to the fuel tanks, the Cjarians planned to fly the ship down under controlled speed, rather than the normal fireball-generating EDL (Entry-Descent-Landing) approaches that were representative of nearly all earthly designs like those of the Apollo, Space Shuttle and Night Star eras. The driving reason for this approach was the large amount of fuel required–fuel that added unacceptable expense and weight to the initial launch of the vehicle. It wasn't until 2026 that the first controlled, slow velocity, re-entry flight was successfully attempted by man. The first-of-its-kind flight was made on a small, NASA-built vehicle–an effort made possible only after the space dock became operational and could supply fuel to the returning ship. However, even with the space dock, the costs associated with transporting fuel to the space dock were so excruciatingly high that space flights continued to rely on the controlled, free-flight approach.

In this case, the Jarisst I was already carrying fuel and actually needed to remove fuel from the tanks before the tanks could be repaired, so using fuel up during re-entry made sense to everyone. The only question was if they had adequate fuel for the complete EDL, including the flight from Colorado to White Sands, while still maintaining adequate safety reserves in case something went wrong. Although it would be tight, Thjars was convinced that his crew had analyzed the possibilities and risks from every conceivable perspective and all the assessments still supported the plan.

At a top speed of 40 percent of the speed of light, it required the Jarisst I just 57 minutes to make short work of the planned arc trajectory, including an acceleration and deceleration phase at the start and end of the arc. All of the occupants were in their G-Suits to reduce the impact of the G-forces. Although the forces would be deemed significant from earthly perspectives, they were low enough to not require the G-Cells.

The Jarisst 1 was now at the Earth's so-called Karman line, approximately 100 kilometers above the Earth, ready to enter the edge of the atmosphere at a relatively slow speed of Mach 3. Without the turbulence of a fireball-related re-entry, Thjars was able to maintain constant communication with Blake at the Holloman AFB Control Center. The Jarisst I had entered the atmosphere, as planned, directly over Minot, N.D.–well within the protective boundaries of North America and over a fairly non-populated region.

"Blake, we are over your city called Minot, heading south at three times the speed of sound. We should be over Colorado at an altitude of 30 kilometers in a little less than 15 minutes as we'll begin our deceleration to ninety percent of your speed of sound over the northern border of Colorado to reduce the risk of any sound barrier disturbances. From there, it will be another 50 minutes to White Sands. Where should we expect to see your military jet escorts?"

"Welcome to Earth, Thjars. As we discussed, we have eight F-35 aircraft that will pick you up as you cross the Colorado border. They will all be flying below you until you drop below 30 kilometers. Note that they will be ahead of you so that you can easily see them. Once at the targeted altitude, the aircraft will slow down for you to overtake them and then they will separate into pairs, two above, two below and two on either side of your aircraft to ensure protection from all directions. We also have four flights of six F-22 aircraft each that will patrol your flight path further out to the south, east, west and north to ensure nothing approaches you from any direction."

"Thank you, Blake, we're excited to see your planet. The view so far is amazing. Thank you for all the thought and preparation that went into the escorts. It definitely helps reduce my anxieties for my ship and crew."

"You're welcome, Thjars. Maj. Pat Sullivan will be in charge of the four F-22 patrols; you'll only hear from him if an unexpected issue arises, so hopefully you won't talk to him until you're on the ground." Blake chuckled. "And a more familiar name, Cmdr. Rachel Joslin, will be in charge of the F-35s that will directly escort you. She'll make contact with you over Nebraska."

"Is that the pilot of the Night Star you flew on?"

"Yes, the one and only. She's already seen the Jarisst I, so she knows what to expect. Not only is she a Night Star pilot, but she's one of our best fighter pilots. Just assume Qulys is flying protection for you and you'll understand how good she is."

"That's a pretty high measuring bar, as I know you are well aware, Blake, so that tells me everything I need to know."

"Thjars, I'll stay on line so you can reach me at any time, but I want you free to monitor your flight as well as to take in the views. Enjoy the flight; I'll talk to you when you're ready to land."

Ten minutes passed in total silence until the radio crackled and a new, feminine, but authoritative voice was heard.

"Capt. Thjars Chjssiast, welcome to Earth. This is Cmdr. Rachel Joslin, reporting for escort services. It's good to see that beautiful ship of yours again. On your approval, I will deploy my eight F-35 aircraft around the Jarisst I to escort you to White Sands. Do you have any questions?"

"No, we are good to go. Please deploy. And thank you, Commander, I appreciate having someone who is familiar with our ship."

"Roger that. We are deploying now. I will be flying point, port side. I will waggle my wings when in position so that you know which aircraft is mine."

A short time later, Thjars responded.

"Wings acknowledged, Commander. Lead the way."

"Enjoy the ride Captain, I wish the clouds would clear so you could enjoy the Rocky Mountains, but Colorado is having a rare overcast day. At least that will decrease the probability of anyone seeing us."

The remainder of the flight went quickly. Qulys studied the F-35s while Thjars monitored the skies around them. He could see all 32 fighters on the radar scope. It was also clear that President Callahan was good to his word again. Nothing else was flying–the skies belonged to the Jarisst I and its escorts.

*****

Moscow

"Gen. Boris Vasiliev?"

"Yes, this is he; who is interrupting my meeting, Aleksei?" The general knew his trusted aide would not interrupt him for anything trivial.

"The alien aircraft has entered our atmosphere over the United States. It is now over Colorado heading south and escorted by at least 32 fighter jets."

"So the Americans have lied to us all this time. By surrounding the alien craft with so many fighters, and secretly making a landing within the U.S., they clearly do not want us involved. Yakovlev will see this as an act of war–as he should. Thank you, Aleksei, I will take it from here. Let me know where it lands the second you know. Do not tell anyone else who is not directly involved in this activity."

"Yes, sir."

*****

New Mexico

"Blake, we are ready to land. Our systems have picked up many ground-based radar systems targeting our ship. We are assuming they are all yours; is that correct?"

"I would think so, Thjars, but there is only one way to know. Hang on a second."

Blake put Thjars on hold and called over the commander of the 49th Wing at Holloman AFB, Col. Brian Watts.

"Colonel, can we turn all of the ground-based radar systems off for 30 seconds to verify that only our systems are targeting the Jarisst I?"

"Absolutely."

"Thjars," Blake picked up Thjars' call again, "hang tight. You should shortly see everything turn off for a full 30 seconds. If anything else remains on, we'll investigate it promptly."

A few seconds passed and Thjars spoke up.

"Systems are mostly off. The only remaining systems we see are at what appear to be airports outside of the White Sands facilities."

"OK, good Thjars. As one final check, recall the IFF equipment, software and codes we gave you while you were docked at the space dock?"

"Yes … that was your Identification, Friend or Foe system, correct?

"Correct. We will go ahead and turn all of our systems back on. Access the system now and turn it on; the codes were already activated for your use. If you see anything near White Sands without an identification number, let me know immediately."

"OK … hang on … it's on, and … good news, Blake, everything has a number. Looks like all friendlies."

"That was expected, but still good to hear. So how about we get this bird on the ground?"

"Bird?"

"Sorry, that's another one of our sayings. We frequently refer to aircraft as birds, and many military aircraft have actually been named after birds of prey."

"Roger that," a feminine voice interjected.

"Juulys!" Blake laughed. "You've been way too quiet. Welcome to Earth. I'm looking forward to seeing you."

Five minutes later, with ovation and awe from everyone on the ground, the Jarisst I thundered to a soft, vertical landing on the Northrup Strip of the White Sands complex lakebed.

"We are safely down and shutting down the engines," Thjars notified Blake.

"Thjars, Juulys, as far as we are aware, you and your crew are the first non-earthlings to ever set foot on this planet. Congrats and welcome to Earth. If this had been a Hollywood movie script and we were in a period of peace, we would have had marching bands, flags, banners, TV reporters and President Callahan himself. But given today's environment, it seemed better to keep this quiet and under the radar, so to speak."

"I agree and knowing what we do know, I am quite content to keep it that way," Thjars responded.

"I'm heading out to a waiting helicopter and I'll be there shortly," Blake replied. "No one else should approach your ship until I arrive. For all those listening, just to make sure everyone remembers our agreement and no one mistakes any of the Jarisst's actions, please remember that we agreed that while the Jarisst I is here, it would keep all weapon systems armed and ready as a precautionary measure. In addition, the only people allowed to approach the ship must be pre-approved by Harry or myself, correct, Thjars?"

"Yes, thank you, Blake. Likewise, only Qulys or I can give the orders to initiate the weapon systems, so we have locked our side down as well."

"Thank you, Thjars. See you shortly."

*****

Twenty minutes later, Blake's helicopter settled on the Northrup Strip, just 200 meters away from the Jarisst I. Blake stepped off and headed toward a parked car that Harry emerged from. The helicopter lifted off and departed. No one else was visible within the immediate area, but Blake knew there were soldiers stationed all around the White Sands facility.

Harry waited for Blake to reach him and then both men turned to face the Jarisst I. They were mid-ship, on the port side. The ship was an amazing sight to behold on the ground. At 115 meters in length, it was slightly longer than a full football field, including both end zone sections, and at 12 meters in diameter, it was about one quarter of a football field's width.

"Blake, I never thought about it before, but the Jarisst I is actually almost the same length and diameter as the Saturn V rocket. But that rocket was all fuel and once it jettisoned its spent rockets, it was way smaller than what we're looking at now. This is truly stunning."

"I agree, Harry, it's a beautiful craft, and it's another experience I'll never forget."

"Where are our suits?" Harry asked.

"Let me call in your new dress code." Blake chuckled and then called someone on his radio. "Enjoy the view while we wait to see what the tailor brought you. Let's call Thjars to check his status. Hopefully, he's better prepared than we just appeared to be."

Blake pulled out his radio and called Thjars.

"Blake?"

"Hi, Thjars. Yes, it's Harry and me. We're waiting on our suits. How's the ship's status?"

"Well, I think we can safely say that the fuel tanks survived." He laughed nervously. "We made it with about 10 percent fuel reserve. Everything else looks good. The exterior temperatures are below 120 degrees Fahrenheit, so we're ready for your visit, once you are."

"Here comes our tailor now," Blake replied looking over his shoulder. "The delivery vehicle is what we call a tractor trailer, but it's actually a portable decontamination and testing lab. We'll use it each time we enter and depart your ship, as well as for storage for all of our suits. The driver is none other than Dr. George McDearmon. He's hoping to continue his research while you're here, even though he's convinced that our species will be safe together. But as you well know, that is a highly complex and dangerous decision, and President Callahan isn't quite ready to make it yet. Hopefully, George and Jenysys can help convince us all. I'll call you back as soon as we're ready."

*****

White House

"President Callahan, President Yakovlev is demanding to talk to you," Frank Pelino said as he stuck his head into the Oval Office from the door.

"Put him through, Frank, thank you."

President Callahan looked over at the bust of Abraham Lincoln that sat directly under a portrait of George Washington.

He clearly wasn't the first president that had to deal with what felt like insurmountable odds, nor would he be the last. Even in more recent times, President Franklin Roosevelt dealt with World War II, President George W. Bush dealt with the 9/11 attacks and President Donald Trump dealt with the Pandemic of 2020–and they all obviously succeeded in one form or another. His eyes moved over to the Bronco Buster statue created by Frederic Remington back in 1895 and given to Theodore Roosevelt by the Rough Riders in 1898. The statue had been a mainstay in the Oval Office for many presidents before him. A portion of Remington's quote was kept on the table:

"Only those who have ridden a bronco the first time it was saddled, or have lived through a railroad accident, can form any conception of the solemnity of such experiences."

President Callahan smiled. Both the statue, and the quote were great reminders of what a tumultuous ride it could be when you are the president of the United States. Success requires one to hold on tight and confidently and calmly deal with and overcome the challenges the world threw at you.

The phone on his desk buzzed. President Callahan picked up the phone and answered.

"President Callahan here."

"This is President Yakovlev. You have again lied to the world."

"Good evening to you as well, President Yakovlev. And why is that?"

"Don't play games with me. You secretly landed the alien aircraft at your White Sands facility in New Mexico, did you not?"

"I haven't said it hasn't, have I?"

"You're playing games, Mr. President, and games like this start wars."

"Let me remind you, President Yakovlev, without any provocation or due process, you physically attacked and killed personnel on United States property, twice now. That is how wars are started."

"You know how concerned I and others were about your secretive meetings with the aliens, and our fear that you would use their technology to create an unchallengeable military position to dominate the world with. Yet you continued your meetings, and now you have gone so far as to land their spacecraft within your country for your scientists to analyze. How would you react if our positions were reversed?"

"That's a fair question President Yakovlev, but for starters, I would not have attacked your space station, which means this is a totally hypothetical discussion. So let's get back to the facts. We are where we are because you *did* attack our space station. As I told you previously, their ship was damaged and they asked for our assistance–they initiated the request, not me or anyone else in the United States. Furthermore, you caused additional damage to their ship when you attacked the space dock; the shrapnel from the explosions punctured both of their fuel tanks. One was totally drained of fuel and the other was temporarily repaired in time to save some fuel, but their ability to safely conduct future space travel was eliminated by *your* actions, and your actions alone. So let me turn your question back on you, Mr. President. If you were in their position, would you contact the same country for help that had already attacked you? I think not, Mr. President."

"I will repeat my position. Russia cannot allow you to gain access to their technology without our scientists being directly involved. There are other superpowers on this planet that you have hidden the truth from as well. They, like Russia, realize that something must be done if you do not allow them access. I am giving you 24 hours to meet my demands."

"That is not within my power to decide, President Yakovlev. You need to talk to the owners of that ship yourself, the Cjarians, and you could start by apologizing and asking how you might make amends. Until then, they are on U.S. soil and I will use the entire capability of the U.S. military to protect them and the United States. If the time comes when you decide you are ready for an open and candid discussion, one that is focused on resolving issues in a peaceful way, I will be there to meet you, halfway. Until then, I believe this conversation is over."

President Callahan disconnected the call and sat back in his chair. Who was President Yakovlev referring to? Likely the Chinese, but would they ever agree to play second fiddle to the Russians? They didn't want to play second fiddle to anyone, but then again, neither did the Russians or the Americans.

The Chinese had gotten much bolder over the past decade and a half, and they'd spent considerable time and resources making significant progress with their military capabilities, from both a qualitative and quantitative perspective. President Callahan knew that a combined Russian-Chinese threat would exceed that of what the Axis did in World War II … a very sobering and frightening consideration.

He punched the intercom and requested his staff meet him in the Situation Room in 60 minutes. The bronco that had been delivered for his turn as president was looking less tamable by the day.

*****

White Sands

Blake and Harry exited the trailer five meters from the Jarisst I docking bay. They were both wearing simple, lightweight, plastic chemical suits with a thin, flexible, transparent, plastic envelope around their heads. Each suit came with a double cartridge respirator and latex gloves, similar to what was used at the disease centers where George worked.

"Thjars, we are ready to visit and I even have some house-warming gifts for you!" Blake held up a bag as he chuckled.

"What is a house warming?"

"Ahh, another teachable moment. In our world, when you visit someone's house, especially for the first time, it is customary to bring gifts to show warmth and love among friends and family. Right now, the Jarisst I is your home and we are visiting."

"That makes sense, Blake, but it seems we are visiting you and your planet, so *we* should have brought gifts. On Cjar, we do something similar, but it is always with food."

"Don't tell Sean, Thjars," Harry interjected, "or he'll never leave!"

"I heard that, Harry." Sean was with a ground unit two kilometers out, but obviously listening in on a very limited-access frequency. "You're going to ruin my reputation across the galaxy before I even get a chance to visit!"

Everyone chuckled, and as usual, all at Sean's expense.

"Thjars, the technical data you sent on the fuel and the tank designs were exactly what we needed. The base technicians are prepared to safely evacuate the tanks once you give the green light. As we discussed, Vladimir will oversee the technicians out here. Is Cryells still planning on directing the overall activity?"

"Yes, I'll have Cryells suit up and join Vladimir."

"I expect Vladimir and Cryells can handle the tanks while Harry and Allympht continue their efforts on the Q-PAMS drive; hopefully we can conquer both in parallel."

*****

Washington, D.C.

A white van heading northeast on New Hampshire Avenue NW entered Dupont Circle where it traversed one quarter of the circle and then exited to the right on P Street NW. The van headed east for 100 meters and then turned left on 18th Street NW. Two short blocks later, the van turned right on Church Street NW. Three hundred meters later, the driver eyed an open parking spot on the right and quickly pulled into it, cut the engine and picked up his cell phone. The van had large blue letters on each of its sides, clearly identifying it as an ADT security van.

Five minutes later, two men exited the van and walked across the street and ascended the stairs to the front door of the property identified as 1743 Church Street NW. The driver rang the doorbell and was rewarded with the sounds of footsteps approaching the front door. The door opened and the two men were greeted by what appeared to be a cleaning lady.

"Hello, ma'am, I'm Juan and this is Wade," the man said as he handed her their business cards, politely displayed on the palm of his white-gloved hand. "We're here to do the annual checkup on your security system. The office should have validated our arrival time for you; did they?"

"Yes, they did about 30 minutes ago, thank you. Come on in. It makes me feel a lot safer when I know who is coming and when."

"That's exactly why we do it, ma'am," Juan replied. "Our notes state that the main control is in an office; can you show us?"

"Yes, it's in the senator's office. Please follow me."

The two men followed her through the living room and down a short hallway to a study that clearly belonged to someone who was used to living the good life. The room was covered with wall-to-wall mahogany shelves and included a large, antique Resolute desk in the center of the room. The room had no fewer than four antique lamps on decorative inlaid wooden tables strategically located around the room, in addition to two smaller lamps on the desk itself. Statues and collectibles from a multitude of famous cities and tourist areas the senator had visited around the globe decorated every shelf wherever a gap between the hundreds of books lining the shelves had been freed up. Framed pictures of the senator with other famous people adorned the walls.

"Here's the panel, gentlemen. Do you need help with anything?"

"Thank you, ma'am. Actually, we do," Wade answered. "If you could take Juan to each of the windows and doors, I'll make sure each alarm shows correctly on the main panel. You also have two cameras that are due to be upgraded, so once we've completed the checkout, I'll turn the system off to exchange the cameras and that should take care of it for today. We should be done and out of your hair in less than 45 minutes."

Juan and the cleaning lady completed their window and door sensor validation rounds in fewer than 15 minutes.

"Good news, everything alarmed correctly, ma'am. If you'll let Juan back out the front door, he'll get the two cameras and we'll switch them out. The first camera is right here in the senator's office and the other is at the back door."

As Juan and the cleaning lady headed toward the front door, Wade quickly turned the ADT system off and began disassembling the Google Home unit on the senator's desk. He had practiced the modification many times, so many times that he could almost do it with his eyes closed. Forty-five seconds later, the update was complete. No one would ever notice the small super-secret microphones he added next to the Home's own MEMS microphones. Anything that was discussed in the senator's study or near any other similar device in the apartment could now be captured with his installation. The built-in lithium batteries would power the small units for at least 12 months. He quickly removed the camera in the office and waited for the duo to return.

"Here are the two cameras, Wade."

"I've got the first one down already. I'll install the new unit here and you start removing the second unit in the back. We are way ahead of schedule–at this rate, we may be able to be done within 30 minutes!"

Thirteen minutes later, Wade rebooted the system and updated it for the two new cameras. They cleaned up, wished the cleaning lady a happy afternoon and walked back across the street to their van. Once back inside the van, Wade sent one short text.

"System is updated, everything is working well. Heading back to the office."

The two cameras were not only an upgrade, but the newest in surveillance technology the CIA had. Each included audio eavesdropping capabilities in addition to the high-fidelity video systems. The system also allowed the operator, in this case secretly, to tap into the home control systems, thereby providing full access to the security system and to any computer system tied into it. In the senator's case, that included his home wi-fi, laptop, phones, cloud storage, router and television systems.

*****

Two thousand miles away, in a computer-filled conference room at a heavily protected and highly classified location on the White Sands base, Jimmy, Li and Robert engaged their systems and waited. The walls of the conference room were full of camera feeds and monitors. Video displays of the senator's D.C. office immediately sprang to life.

"OK, gentlemen," Li spoke first, "let's get to work. Time to see what we can find on our not-so-good friend, Sen. Harley. Jimmy, you work his computer. Robert, you check the video recordings out and I'll start working on the phone records. Harley thinks he has a special, non-advertised, executive version of ADT's premium security system–let's make sure he gets his money's worth." Li laughed.

*****

Four hours later, the trio took their first break.

"Robert, find anything yet?" Li asked.

"Yes and no."

"How's that?"

"I didn't see anything or anyone that suggests he's done something wrong, but there are multiple instances where he intentionally turns the system off, but based on his cell phone traces, he still remained in the house. That seems a little odd … like maybe he meets with some people that he doesn't want recorded."

"Hmmm, I agree, it does seem odd," Li replied. "Well, keep digging. Maybe he slipped up somewhere. Jimmy, what did you find?"

"Li, this will take weeks or maybe even months. He has so much material stored that I'm not even sure where to start yet. And that doesn't include the material that I know is password protected. Bottom line, I've got nothing so far." Jimmy frowned before turning the question back to Li. "Did you do any better with the phones?"

"With the exception of a couple of phones that look like burner phones I can't trace, he's pretty clean so far. If this guy really is guilty, he's been amazingly careful with his data trails."

*****

Taipei, Taiwan
Oct. 20, 2029

"President Jin-Lin, I assume you are still in Washington, D.C., yes?"

"Yes."

"Are you somewhere safe?"

"Yes, I'm in my hotel room."

"Good, stay there and make yourself invisible, or better yet, if you are able to get to the White House immediately. Do it as soon as we hang up, before the door closes."

"What's going on, Chia?"

"Turn your TV on. The nightmare scenario we have long feared is upon us," Secretary Gen. Chia Ling spoke quietly into the phone.

"Please explain, Chia."

"Air Force Command Headquarters in Kaohsiung, Zuoying Naval Airfield in Kaohsiung City and Hsinchu Air Base in Hsinchu City all went offline within the past 30 minutes. Their last messages stated that military transports from the People's Republic of China (PRC) were landing at their bases and the sky was full of military fighters escorting them."

"Where is the minister of defense?"

"The minister of defense and chief of the general staff have not answered calls and no one knows where they are, Mr. President. There is more, sir." Chia Ling paused.

"I have their Fox News on ... I'm seeing pictures of PRC ships ... near Taiwan?" President Jin-Lin stammered.

"That's correct, sir. Hundreds of PRC military ships that were staging maneuvers in the Taiwan Strait suddenly converged on Taiwan. The PRC Navy has surrounded Taiwan and cut us off from the world. There also appears to be multiple transport ships disguised as cargo ships now unloading thousands of troops and support vehicles at the Port of Taipei in the Bali District."

"Are you sure this is the PRC?"

"Yes, sir. The general secretary and president of China, Zhou Qiang, called five minutes ago and demanded your surrender. I told him that I didn't know exactly where you were, but I would find you."

"What options do we have?"

"If we try to fight, we will lose and many civilians will be killed. They have overwhelming forces and equipment at their disposal. They have control of the skies and are threatening to shoot down any aircraft that attempts to depart Taiwan, including civilian flights."

"Have you contacted Washington?"

"Yes, but it appears this is not the only issue they are dealing with this morning. They have promised to express their concern to Beijing, to demand an end to all hostilities and to withdraw their troops, but based on the news I'm hearing, I do not believe the U.S. is in a position to back up their demands."

"Then what am I to do, Chia Ling?"

"Sir, I see no choice but to surrender peacefully. We are on our own. Any other option will be met with certain death and destruction. Please get to the White House as quickly as possible, but also as quietly as you can."

*****

Kyiv, Ukraine

"Gen. Dombrowsky, how is this possible? Where are our fighters? Where is NATO? Where is Washington?" President Fedir Chevchenko demanded.

"Mr. President. We need to leave now," Gen. Oleksiy Dombrowsky demanded. "We can continue talking in the car, but we must get you out of Kyiv now, and I mean now, sir! The Russians are within 30 kilometers of Kyiv. If you are not out of the city by noon, I expect you will become a prisoner of war, or worse yet, murdered. Your family is already in transit to Bucharest, so take what you must have from this office, but we need to get you out of here quickly and secretly. Once we're in Bucharest, we can make contact with the U.S. Embassy and Washington, but stealth and swiftness are of the utmost importance right now."

President Chevchenko began picking up a few critical items and stuffing them into his satchel. As he did so, he looked up with an expression of disgust.

"You want me to leave the country and my people, Oleksiy, and run like a scared rabbit?"

"No, sir. I want you to run like an intelligent man and live to fight another day for your people–they will still need a leader. With all due respect, sir, today is not the day to make a stand. The Russians are in total control and have easily overrun the eastern 200 kilometers of Ukrainian soil–we do not know where or when they intend to stop."

"How did they catch us so unaware, Oleksiy?"

"They have been practicing war maneuvers for over a week on our eastern border, but they camouflaged it as bravado against the Americans. No one expected them to truly attack a sovereign nation again."

"What about our military?"

"Sir, we have less than 100 fighter aircraft, most of which are very old …. Mig-29s, Su-24s, Su-25s, and Su-27s. Most never got off the ground. Those that did were destroyed quickly. Our tanks and other defensive measures didn't fare any better. Russia simply has numerical and technical advantages that are orders of magnitude beyond what we have. We are trying to make one final stand to the east of Kyiv, but the truth is, if they want the city, there is nothing we can do to stop them."

"What has Washington said?"

"I do not expect we will get their help any time soon. Apparently, the Russians are also invading Belarus and the Chinese have invaded Taiwan. The Americans have been caught by surprise in multiple areas and are waiting to see what other attacks, if any, are in the works."

"Have we heard from President Nikita Makarevich in Minsk yet?"

"No, sir, nothing."

"What about all of our documents …"

"We have a handful of people who will stay behind and destroy as much as they can, sir. Come now, we do not have time for idle discussion, we must leave now!"

Once again under the shadow of war, a group of grim men and women hastily left the oncoming front as quietly and quickly as they could. It was a six-hour drive to Moldova and another seven hours to Bucharest. Assuming they could successfully escape the Russian attack, they would be driving into the early hours of the following morning. President Chevchenko could only hope that his family was well ahead of him and that they would meet up again in Moldova.

*****

CHAPTER 17

White House Situation Room

"Status," President Callahan stated crisply. Everyone in the room quickly took note of the lack of standard preamble and pleasantries from the president.

"The Russians are already 200 kilometers deep into both Ukraine and Belarus, and a wave of reinforcements is already staged at their far western border with both countries," Gen. McMullen volunteered.

"Have we heard from President Chevchenko or President Makarevich?" President Callahan queried.

"Not directly, sir, but our sources inside their countries claim that both presidents, their families and their key cabinet members are all heading west by car. The Ukrainian members are heading toward Bucharest, Romania, via Moldova, and we believe the Belarusian members are heading west toward Warsaw, Poland, but that has not yet been confirmed. Both contingents have long, dangerous rides ahead of them, regardless of their intended destinations, and they need to maintain as much secrecy as possible to reduce the risk of Russia identifying their location and sending attack aircraft after their convoys."

"Do we have the ability to provide air cover?"

"Yes, sir, it's already under way, but we have to be careful that our efforts to help don't end up giving away their locations, so we are providing general air cover to all of Eastern Europe. I've also given orders to engage any aircraft west of Kyiv or Minsk."

"Notify President Yakovlev immediately of our intention to defend that line, but that line stays east of Kyiv and Minsk, not west of it."

"Yes, sir."

"What else?"

"As you heard, the Chinese have demanded the surrender of Taiwan. They have the island blockaded with their Navy and have landed troops and vehicles at the port of Taiwan. Multiple air bases are now offline as they also landed troop carriers at all major military installations. Fortunately, President Jin-Lin was already in the U.S. per your invitation for tomorrow's economic review; that meeting is obviously tabled now. In addition, he just arrived at the White House where we should be able to ensure his protection. We have him under guard, without knowledge of the White House press corps, and he is hoping to meet with you immediately after this session."

President Callahan looked over at Frank Pelino and nodded his concurrence.

"OK, Gen. McMullen, where is NATO in all of this and what options do you recommend?"

"Mr. President, it should come as no surprise to any of us that NATO simply isn't prepared for a full-on war with Russia. They can and are demanding an end to the Russian aggression, even going as far as to state that they will cut ties with Russia, but everyone, including the Russians, knows they are bluffing. At the end of the day, Europe still depends on Russian energy for their economies. Even after all of their cries to cut demand after Russia annexed the Crimea region of Ukraine in 2014, the truth is that Europe still imports more than 80 percent of its natural gas, crude oil and solid fuels from Russia–and each year has seen that total increase. Winter is almost upon us and every household in Europe depends on Mother Russia to heat their homes, let alone their industrial centers. Europe is simply not in any position to help."

"Then what do you recommend?" President Callahan appealed to his leading general.

"That we either give ground like Chamberlain did before the German military machine in World War II, or we fight. There doesn't seem to be many options, and history proved that Chamberlain's approach only further played into Hitler's plans."

"I agree with your history lesson, Gen. McMullen, but unfortunately, we are not in a position to defend all of Europe right now. If we were to attack, I expect we would lose, correct?"

"Yes, but ..."

"No buts, General. If we lose, it will only sway power more to the Russians and provoke them into attacking further while they have us on our heels. And then there's the Chinese; we don't even know how they tie into this entire fiasco, but I highly doubt it's coincidental."

The room went silent.

The president surveyed his cabinet and the others in the room. There were no volunteers, so President Callahan continued.

"We need to get their attention and we need to do it hard and fast, but in such a manner that it shows we are willing to go to war, and that we can hurt them–but at the same time, not trigger an all-out war."

"What are you suggesting, sir?" Frank Pelino asked.

"I'm not totally sure; that's what we need to figure out. That's what I have all of you here for–to come up with ideas, correct? For example, I'm talking about something as significant as taking out some of their own oil refineries, perhaps hitting Rosneft itself. Rosneft is estimated to own more than 35 percent of the total Russian national output. The same tools work today that worked 90 years ago with the Germans. Break their fuel or food supply lines and the war machine grinds to a halt."

"You want to attack Russia itself?" Annie replied, almost in total shock. "With all respect, Mr. President, that is not like you."

"You are correct, Annie, maybe we don't attack their in-country refineries, but … maybe we do. I need aggressive ideas and I'm trying to prime the engine here. Remember, to Eastern Europe, this is tantamount to the Japanese attack on Pearl Harbor. They still remember the Cold War and Russian tanks on their street corners. The Russians also own oil refineries in Germany, Belarus and India. Let's put some pressure on Germany and India to nationalize those refineries immediately. It's likely too late for Belarus, but perhaps we can still cripple any of their interests there as well. And one more, blow up the damn Russian oil and gas pipelines through Europe. Tell Europe to start hoarding blankets for the winter. As long as those pipelines are running, the Russians will have easy access for their war machine. We simply can't allow that."

"We also need to start cutting off critical export streams to Russia. Russia depends on the world for automobiles, medicines and computers. We need to drive an immediate, worldwide halt to all exports of these items to Russia. Make them hurt, isolate them further. We need to do something hard and fast, so give me a list of your best ideas and the inherent risks each comes with–and I want that list before dinner tonight. Frank, you're in charge."

President Callahan stood up abruptly and left the room.

*****

"Mr. President?"

"Yes, Frank."

"We're ready. Can you join us in the Situation Room?"

"Yes, I'll be there shortly."

Ten minutes passed and President Callahan walked into the Situation Room. No one had left; ties were off and the gathered group of cabinet members and support personnel looked haggard.

"What are your recommendations, Frank?" President Callahan asked as he sat down at the head of the table.

"Well, to be honest, sir, you started us off at a pretty aggressive and gutsy flight level. Had you not, I don't think we would've gotten as far as we did. We also bounced a number of ideas off of some of our key military strategists, including Blake and Harry, so this is partly their plan as well."

President Callahan nodded.

"For starters, we agree with the dismantlement of the Russian gas and oil pipelines, but we think we need to be prepared to step up our own deliveries of gas and oil to Europe as the curtailment of Russian supplies will create significant disruption to both sides. Our only difference on the pipeline objective is that we want to do it on the ground, rather than by air. If we send our aircraft in directly, Russia will know it was us and call it an act of war, regardless of who started the shooting. We recommend using ground forces from the affected countries to conduct simultaneous, covert operations on the various pipelines, even if it's with the help of our own special ops groups. That will demonstrate both the solidarity of Europe and also create some doubt in the Kremlin as to who the real driver is. They may suspect the U.S., but they'll never know for sure. The same holds for any refineries in Belarus or Ukraine the Russians plan on using.

"Relative to bombing Rosneft refineries," Frank continued, "we are recommending you hold off. We agree that it would severely reduce Russian's ability to conduct military operations, but it would also result in the U.S. bombing of Russia itself. We believe that could only lead to a rapid escalation of the war." Frank Pelino stopped and waited.

"For what it's worth, everyone, I agree," President Callahan acknowledged as he surveyed the room. "I was not high on the idea, but I knew I had to light a fire and make sure that the people in this room did not limit their thoughts. We are in a very delicate situation where one wrong action could spark World War III. At the same time, we must react, as well as react with strength and resolve in order to *avoid* World War III. As I said, it's a very delicate situation. Please continue."

"Russia has many military bases outside of Russia, and we see those as legitimate targets, especially those in Europe. If you look at this map on the wall, they have active bases where the red pins are. That includes Armenia, Belarus, Georgia, Kazakhstan, Kyrgyzstan, Moldova, Syria, Tajikistan and Vietnam. We recommend hitting all locations with U.S. and NATO cruise missiles to take out radar, SAM sites and aircraft on the ground– some by plane, but the majority will come from our naval ships and NATO ground sites. We also recommend an immediate follow-up by a combined attack with U.S. and NATO aircraft strikes. The goal will not be to eliminate the bases, rather to significantly impact their ability to maintain operations–as well as to send a clear message to Russia."

"How severe will our losses be, Gen. McMullen?"

"Heavy, sir. The Russians are on high alert around the globe. Obviously, we will consume a large number of cruise missiles to lead the attack and that should help soften their defenses, but we still have to assume we will lose a large number of attacking aircraft."

"How many, Landon?"

"Best estimates, at least 50, sir, maybe more. Ugly, but it would be much worse if they didn't have their forces focused in Eastern Europe. That's where we'll take our worst hits, especially near the war front in Belarus and Moldova. But we don't think they'll be expecting attacks outside of Europe, for example in

Vietnam, Syria, Georgia or the Stans. Net-net, the damage will be much heavier on their side."

"When can you have our forces ready?"

"Immediately, sir. Recall that you directed us to be DEFCON 1 ready, but not actually trigger DEFCON 1 status. We are already prepped for events like this and because of your request, we reinforced Europe and other bases around the world with additional squadrons of fighters from across the U.S."

"What about our NATO allies?"

"Great question, sir. We can initiate pipeline attacks tonight, but the cruise missile and aircraft attacks will need at least 24 hours. Europe is not ready."

"Tell me who, General. I'll call and get it in 12 hours. Be ready."

"Yes, sir."

"What else?"

"We have one more trump card to play, but it's your call, sir," Frank added.

"What's that?"

"Cyber warfare. Everyone is doing it, some quietly, some openly. As you are aware, each time we do something, the target is defeated, but they also learn from it and get stronger. It's the software-internet version of the missile for the missile for the missile–there is always another defense and another offense. We have been holding out on the Calamity virus for years."

"Remind me, what can it do?"

"I'm not the expert," Frank replied, "but in a nutshell, similar to what the neutron bomb was for taking out weapons, but not people, the Calamity virus only attacks military software systems and was designed specifically for Russia. We get one shot with it, so we need to keep it for the most critical opportunity. We can set their attack back at least a week, maybe two weeks once we use it. Simulations project it will be 90 percent lethal to their operations."

"Yes, I remember now. Gen. McMullen, that's the one you referred to as the knockout punch, correct?"

"Yes, Mr. President. It was for the final kill. Apply the virus and then attack with everything we have in the hope of so seriously damaging their military capabilities that they would have to sue for peace, or surrender."

"It's tempting, but it doesn't feel quite right on timing yet. If the Russians attack our mainland, or that of a major allied country, then we may consider it, but not yet; otherwise I could imagine them hitting our utility and non-military security and control systems as revenge. As I recall the Russians are pretty damn good at that game as well, so it's off the table for now—are we clear on that?"

"Yes, sir," Gen. McMullen and Frank Pelino replied in unison.

"Anything else?"

"We have identified our top 10 military targets outside of Russia we could take action on."

"I'm interested in that, but I'd rather have a separate follow up on the details later tonight. Set it up, Gen. McMullen."

"Yes, sir."

"What about Taiwan, Frank?"

It was clear that President Callahan had already moved into war mode, and his cabinet needed to catch up quickly.

"We're not there yet, sir. That one is pretty complicated and we all know the Chinese have Taiwan in their sights ever since the government of the Republic of China moved to Taipei in 1949, and it only strengthened its desire to acquire Taiwan as the PRC rose to world superpower status earlier this century. General Secretary and President Zhou Qiang and the PRC have put themselves in position to fight and win a war for Taiwan. Unless we want to fight Russia and China at the same time, this may be the end of the Republic of China."

"That's unacceptable," President Callahan stammered. "There must be something we can do to get their attention, short of a full-blown war, isn't there?"

"There is, but it requires another allied country to help," Frank replied.

"The Delhi Fulcrum?"

"Correct, Mr. President. Besides the U.S., the only country China fears is India. They both have approximately 1.5 billion people; they are the most populous countries on the planet. India finally surpassed China in population by 100,000 people just two years ago. Their military capabilities have grown significantly in the past decade, their software and cyber warfare capabilities are as good as or better than even our own and their economy is now within the top three in the world, having passed Germany five years ago. They are now third after the U.S. and China. They've had a number of border clashes over the years …"

"But China is still India's top trading partner, which means for the most part, they get along well, correct?"

"Yes, Mr. President. I didn't say they would be excited to contest China, but that is the one card we have that could make China think twice. If we could at least get them to take our side, it might get the Chinese to pause."

"It's a good thought, Frank. I'll contact Prime Minister Riddhi Khatri and see where her head is at. Until then, can we at least reinforce our naval and air presence in the area?"

"We can, sir," Gen. McMullen interrupted, "but we are starting to get spread pretty thin, and I expect the Russians and Chinese are aware of that. It's one thing to project presence and it's another thing to fight an actual war where your resources are constantly attrited. We can project presence, and we're good at that across all the conflict areas of the world, but if a superpower really decided to fight in their own backyard, it would be over quickly–assuming we don't open the nuclear option."

"We are definitely not doing that, General, but your point is well taken. Which Carrier Strike Group is in the western Pacific?"

"Carrier Strike Group Five of the Fifth Fleet, sir, led by the USS Ronald Reagan. The Seventh Fleet's USS Kennedy Carrier Strike Group was also in the area until the Russian attack."

"Have the Chinese declared new maritime borders yet?" President Callahan asked.

"No, they haven't, sir, but it's likely coming soon," Gen. McMullen answered.

"Let's move it as close to Taiwan's eastern side as we can–your call, Gen. McMullen on how close. Send additional squadrons to the Philippines, South Korea and Japan and make our patrols more visible."

"And if they attack us, sir?"

"I realize skirmishes and singular issues may occur; that's a risk I am willing to take, but if they launch full-out assaults, then you have my authority to defend and to attack–without nukes–but I pray to God it doesn't come to that."

The President stood up and prepared to leave. "Get some food and get some rest, people. We're going to need to be at the top of our game. Gen. McMullen, I'll see you later to discuss Russian targets–it's high time they understand that we will deal out accountability, and one target on your list needs to include the number of tanks that are approaching Minsk and Kyiv–those tanks need to stay east of those cities, either by their choice, or ours."

President Callahan left the meeting.

*****

White Sands
Oct. 21, 2029

Blake surveyed the scene. The Jarisst I was surrounded by scaffolding and cranes. Both fuel tanks had been removed and transported to a maintenance facility at Holloman Air Force Base, fewer than 12 hours after their landing at White Sands, and repairs were already under way. The base mechanics quickly purged all remaining fuel, back-filled with argon gas and were welding stainless steel plates on the damaged areas before the first sunrise occurred. Even Thjars had been impressed with the speed of the progress.

A big part of that progress was an unexpected, but welcome surprise when the mechanics discovered that the Cjarian tank metal turned out to be weldable with standard MIG welding techniques and 1/8-inch thick stainless steel plates. In the mechanics world, and on these big surfaces, it was a dream job.

Blake watched as two trucks carrying the two fuel tanks rolled to a stop next to the Jarisst I. Blake walked over to the first truck just as the lead mechanic jumped out of the truck's cab.

"Bravo Zulu Chief, you must have one hell of a team of wrench benders." Blake smiled as he stuck out his big paw to thank him. "That was some damn impressive work you guys did. Have you slept at all in the past 48 hours?"

"Hell no, that's what 'Rip It' is for, right? Oorah! We both know that there will be plenty of time to rack out once we get this bird back in the air; I just wish I could go up on it."

"I hear you, Chief. Unfortunately, not on this flight, but if there is a future possibility, you have my word, I'll sure as hell remember and try."

"Thank you, Commander. I'll hold you to it, but right now, I need to get back to work," the chief said as he turned and walked briskly toward the space ship.

Blake had a smile on his face as Harry and Vladimir caught up with him.

"What was that all about?" Harry asked.

"It's about the guys like that chief–those guys are the real heroes that hold our military together. That guy and his crew are solid gold."

"Sure are. They really kicked butt on this one, Blake. We'll have those tanks removed, cleaned, repaired, re-installed and re-fueled in less than 48 hours. That would make a Formula One pit crew envious."

"Good reminder, Harry ... what are we using for fuel?"

"The same fuel that we topped them off with earlier this year at the space dock. It's a simple pnictogen hydride, hypergolic propellant that ignites when it comes in contact with an oxidizer …"

"Whoa, hold on, Harry, English please, English." Blake chuckled as he held his hands up.

"Sorry, Blake, but I think I now know why Vladimir went into chemical engineering instead of just chemistry. When I studied chemistry in school, it was all about researching every aspect of a substance or molecule or the reactions they were involved with, but chemical engineering takes off where the chemistry ends. Not only do you need to understand the chemistry, but you then get to design and work with the equipment to manufacture the chemical or the equipment that uses the chemical–like the rocket system on the Jarisst I. It's really pretty cool stuff, Blake. I've got a lot of homework to do to catch up with Vladimir."

"Somehow," Vladimir laughed, "I doubt it will take you very long to catch up, Harry."

"Amen to that statement." Blake joined in on the banter. "So, keep going, Harry."

"They use hydrazine, or N2H4, just like we do. It's the oxidizer that's the challenge. The oxidizers are in smaller tanks that were interior to the ship so they weren't damaged and are still relatively full. But our oxidizers are very different from theirs, so Vladimir and I have been trying to understand how they do it. Ours are nasty stuff–very toxic. We use a mixture of hydrofluoric acid, nitric acid, dinitrogen tetroxide and water. Their system is way safer to handle. If we are going to help keep them flying long-term, then we need to figure out how to make it. But for now, we just have to replace the hydrazine. That's what that fleet of tanker trucks on the other side of the runway is carrying.

"But, there's more, Blake. They've figured out how to use the fuel way more efficiently. Because of that, these tanks will last them much longer than any projections we would have had. Once refilled, and in space, they'll be good for a long time, but to make sure, we'll need to arrange to have them stop by the space dock and top off again as planetary launches still consume a great amount of fuel."

"See, nothing to it, Harry." Blake laughed. "Now that my English-based science class is over, how about we see if we can find Thjars?"

The trio headed toward the Jarisst I. It was still an amazing sight to behold. As they neared a door located just forward of amidships, it opened and Thjars waved.

"Hello, Thjars. Are you ready? As we discussed, we think it's safer to have everyone off the ship while we reinstall the fuel tanks. We have a trailer that your crew can stay in while the effort is under way, but I expect that you, Cryells and Allympht will continue to help oversee the effort. Is Qulys still planning on staying on the ship?"

"Yes, Blake, that is still the plan. Qulys refuses to not be in position to protect the ship, if needed."

"I fully understand, Thjars. Tell him 'oorah' for me."

"Oorah, Blake." The radio Thjars was carrying came to life as Qulys's voice was heard.

"Qulys, I should have known you'd be listening," Blake replied as he flashed a thumbs up toward the control room windows, where he knew Qulys would be watching.

"Roger that thumb, Blake," Qulys responded and everyone enjoyed a light laugh.

"Well, let's get the rest of your crew off the ship."

Thjars stepped to the side as Juulys was the first to exit the craft. Blake walked over to the bottom of the portable stairs that led up to the door and extended his hand to help Juulys step off the ladder.

"Great to see you, Juulys. I hope all is well."

"Hello, Blake." Juulys responded with a smile that lit up everyone on the tarmac. "Yes it is. And you?"

"Always good," Blake replied.

"Where's my Patty?"

"She's waiting in the trailer," Blake answered. "Harry, can you escort Juulys and the crew to the trailer?"

"Got it, Blake."

Blake helped each member of the Jarisst crew make the final step down and then watched as they followed the now diminutive-looking Harry as he led what looked like an NBA basketball team to the trailer where Patty waited.

"Ready?"

"Let's do it, Blake," Thjars responded.

"It's all yours, chief," Blake spoke into his mic. "Allympht and Cryells are heading toward you to guide the installation."

"Thjars, there are some other things you need to know. Do you want to wait until after the tank work is completed, or can we discuss now?"

"Cryells and Allympht can easily handle this without me. What's going on, Blake?"

Blake led Thjars further back from the ship, and away from earshot of anyone else, still remaining in clear view of the ship and the ongoing work.

"I know Harry, Vladimir, the scientists that we brought with us, and your crew were able to make great progress relative to understanding the Q-PAMS drive over the past two days, but the truth is, we aren't close to knowing how to fix it yet. In addition, I've talked with President Callahan's chief of staff, Frank Pelino, and I need to share some new information with you–there's a lot going on right now."

"I was wondering. I was actually hoping President Callahan would find a way to visit us while we were here. I assume this is not good news ..."

"Unfortunately, you are correct, Thjars. This planet is once again on the brink of a major war. President Callahan and I both think that we need to complete the repair of your fuel tanks and get you airborne and back into space as soon as we can. Once you are in space, you can control the safety of your ship and crew much better than remaining on Earth."

"Are you expecting your country to be attacked?"

"No, not the continental United States, but our interests elsewhere, yes."

Blake spent the next 15 minutes providing Thjars with insight on the attacks in Europe and in Taiwan, as well as the naval battle that had recently taken place, and the saber rattling from Russia and China, all the while answering questions from Thjars.

"Once again, I thank you for your honesty, Blake, but I continue to remain concerned for you and your friends. Your planet is so hostile. Why can your countries not see the waste and uselessness of these conflicts?"

"That is a question that has been asked millions of times, Thjars, but no one has found the answer yet. I believe the root cause is about power and the desire for more power. As long as a country feels they have an opportunity to take advantage of a situation, and extend their zone of influence and power, most will do it."

"According to our history books, we were once like that as well, Blake, but we grew out of it. And then the war with the Klaxx started and the planet truly became one with a common foe. It's been that way ever since."

"We've had a couple of major world wars where we came close to that level of unification, but there were always at least two major groups of warring factions, and even though we felt the wars were long, the truth was they were relatively short compared to yours–nothing that would have endured through generations of people at a world-wide level that would have forced us to change. And we've never had an existential alien force that drove our own need to unify as one entity against a greater foe, like you experienced. As I've shared with you, before we discovered your ship, we didn't have any proof that life even existed anywhere else in the universe. We assumed and somewhat hoped it did, but as I said, we had zero evidence. From what little you've shared with me about the Klaxx, I hope we will never meet a race like theirs, as our planet, unlike yours, could not even begin to fight a foe like that–the war would be over very quickly."

*****

White House

"I demand to see the president now!" Sen. James Harley yelled at the president's personal secretary just outside the Oval Office.

"He is dealing with some very critical issues right now and can't be interrupted, Senator, but I will let him know that you want to talk with him."

"That's not acceptable. I need to see him now!" Harley demanded.

The door to the Oval Office opened and President Callahan stood in the opening.

"First off, I don't have to give you a second of my time, Senator. Secondly, and more importantly, you owe her an apology before I even begin to consider your request."

Sen. Harley apologized as requested.

"Come in Senator, but you have five minutes, no more. Understood?"

Sen. Harley didn't answer, but walked straight into the Oval Office. President Callahan closed the door behind him, walked back to his desk and sat down.

"You allowed the aliens to land and didn't even tell me or the rest of the committee? You have just put the entire world at risk without a vote from my group or from Congress. You didn't have the right to leave me out of that decision, especially as you knew I would not agree with the decision."

President Callahan sat back in his chair, waiting for the senator to end his tantrum. It lasted at least another full minute.

"Are you done?"

"What?"

"Is that what you came here to discuss?"

"Yes! Are you not going to respond? If not, I'm going straight to a press release and I'll let the world know what you've done. I'll …"

"No you won't, Senator, and please remember that everything in this room is being recorded. Per Executive Order 12356, I've classified their landing, which also includes this discussion and anything related to it, as top secret."

"That's total bullshit, and you know it, Mr. President. That Order is for issues related to national defense and foreign affairs. This had nothing to do with either … If anything, it endangers national defense. Foreign affairs … really?"

"If the aliens do not fit the bill as foreign affairs, then nothing does, correct, Senator? In addition, this could cause further strain on our foreign relations with countries like Russia and China. The leaders of our friends around the world have already been notified and some have even sent their leading scientists to assist. My classification stands, Senator."

"The Russians and Chinese, and even others, will figure it out if they haven't already. They all have satellite coverage of the planet. Are you really that naive? Who's running your secret op, your new best buddy, that Harry guy? What the hell does he really know that allows him to make these kinds of decisions?"

"I realize other countries will learn of it, Senator, and I also don't appreciate your insinuations about me or Harry, especially given that I didn't need to give you any time for discussion today, or any other day for that matter. As I said, other countries will figure it out, just like many other things we've classified in the past. I'm simply buying time for a friend in need."

"I have a room full of media and journalists waiting for me to return from this discussion …."

President Callahan cut him off abruptly. "You will not hold your press discussion or leak any of this information or I will have you arrested. Good day, Senator. You may leave now."

*****

In an office far from Washington, D.C., a phone rang.

"Yes?"

"Harry is key to the aliens."

"Why?"

"President Callahan worships him. He'll do anything Harry recommends."

"So, you think it's actually Harry that sold the alien landing?"

"Positive."

"Hmmm."

"I need ideas. We need to discredit him in some way and break the connection that Callahan has with him. Can I count on you?"

"Always."

"Thank you. Let me know what you come up with."

The call disconnected.

*****

White House Oval Office

President Callahan, Vice President Annie Murphy, Frank Pelino, Ben Tellinino and Gen. Landon McMullen were all gathered in the Oval Office for the call. President Callahan's phone buzzed on his desk.

"Yes, Liz?"

"I have them on the phone, Mr. President."

"Thank you, Liz. Put them through, please."

"This is President Callahan, and I have my key cabinet members here as well."

"This is Zhou Qiang, general secretary and president of China, and Igor Yakovlev, president of Russia. We are demanding access to the alien ship at your White Sands facility in New Mexico."

"That will not happen," President Callahan responded firmly. "You are both guilty of initiating acts of wars and killing innocent people."

"I'll remind you ..." President Yakovlev attempted to interrupt.

"Let me finish, but I will start with you, President Yakovlev. You attacked and killed your own people, including hundreds of soldiers who pledged their life to protect your own country. Then, without any cause or provocation, you attacked our space dock and one of our naval fleets, killing many of our people. You have now attacked the sovereign countries of Belarus and Ukraine. What's next, the rest of Europe?" President Callahan asked, but continued talking without waiting for an answer. "On top of that, your actions damaged the very vessel you demand to have access to, and could have killed the Cjarians. President Yakovlev, your credibility is almost nonexistent with the free world.

"And General Secretary Zhou Qiang, you have attacked and blockaded the sovereign country of Taiwan. You may claim that it always should have belonged to mainland China, but the world disagrees with you. To put it bluntly, neither of you has any right to accuse the United States of wrong doing to your countries, or demanding access to the alien technology. In addition, the world still hasn't forgotten your handling of the COVID-19 pandemic a decade ago. You were untruthful then, and you are once again portraying highly distrustful actions.

"A sane individual could only come to one conclusion, that being it would not be wise or safe to allow you access to that technology. If you want the United States and our allies to even consider your proposal, you must immediately cease all hostile operations against the United States, Ukraine, Belarus and Taiwan–as well as complete a total, unrestricted withdrawal of your troops from the countries you have invaded."

"That is not happening," the general secretary responded. "So, your answer is no?"

"That is correct, General Secretary."

"Then we have no choice but to inform you that the countries of Russia and China are united in their agreement that either the United States immediately turn over the alien ship to us, allow our access to it, or outright destroy it, the latter of which will require our witness and validation. Until that time, neither China, nor Russia, will submit to your requests."

The line disconnected.

"Well, I believe we have a clear understanding of where each side stands." Annie was the first to speak. Her statement was followed by similar comments from all of President Callahan's staff. The group debated potential next steps for 15 minutes, until President Callahan recalled that he still had Blake and Harry on the line as well.

"Blake, are you and Harry still there? What are your thoughts?" President Callahan asked, looking at a second phone on his desk.

"It doesn't sound good, Mr. President," Blake responded. "I'm afraid further escalation and a possible full-fledged war may be unavoidable. I hope we are all wrong, but if not, we may be very close to World War III, and this time, instead of the Germans and the Japanese, now it's Russia and China–and all of the players are coming to the conflict with nuclear weapons already in their portfolio. Scary times, sir."

"I'm afraid it's time."

"Mr. President?" Ben Tellinino responded. "Time for what?"

"We have been formally attacked, twice ... once on the space dock and then in the Pacific Ocean. In both cases, innocent lives were lost and American property was destroyed. It was deliberate, unprovoked, and premeditated. Like it or not, we cannot deny any longer–the United States of America is now in a state of war. Frank, I need to get on television and tell the country–please set it up."

"Yes, sir."

"Gen. McMullen," President Callahan said as he turned to face his Joint Chiefs of Staff. "Implement Project Albatross. We need to go beyond just making a statement."

"Yes, sir."

"Blake, I'm hanging up. President Riddhi Khatr and I have a call to make with Mr. Zhou Qiang, the general secretary and president of China. We are going to suggest that his move into Taiwan may not be in his best long-term interest, and attempt to drive a wedge between the Russians and the Chinese before their relationship progresses further, as well as to convince General Secretary Zhou Qiang to get the Chinese the hell out of Taiwan."

"Good luck, Mr. President."

"Thank you. Stay in touch. I'd like an update on the Cjarians, but not today."

"Yes, sir, goodbye," Blake responded and disconnected the call.

"Albatross?" Harry asked.

"Yes, an interesting choice for a name, Harry, but I'd hazard a guess that it fits well with President Callahan's desire to rid himself of a certain albatross that he has inherited."

"And a damn big one at that," Harry responded, "But you might be onto something, Blake … it was metaphorically used as a psychological burden. I believe it came from an old English poet some 200 years ago. If my memory is correct, I think his name was Coleridge. I'll look it up when we get back to our room tonight."

"Don't sweat it, Harry. That has to be somewhere around number 1,032 on my priority list, even if that high–I'll survive without it." Blake replied.

*****

Europe
Oct. 23, 2029

The American counterattack, code-named Albatross, was under way. Fifty U.S. F-22 Raptor air superiority fighters and ten specially-modified F-35 Lightning II Weasel air-defense/ground-attack and electronic warfare aircraft departed into the night skies from Ramstein Air Base in Germany, heading east at treetop level to avoid long-range radar detection. They were joined shortly thereafter by a flight of 24 U.K. Tempest fighters–the U.K.'s newest fighter, one that wasn't supposed to be available in the battlefield for another four or five years yet. Obviously, the U.K. was still capable of maintaining a few secrets of its own.

A second, identical group of aircraft took off from Incirlik Air Base in Turkey, also at treetop level, heading northeast. All 168 aircraft were heading toward a common area to the east.

An armada of other planes at higher altitudes was about to join them from multiple points on the compass around Russia.

*****

Russian radar alerts began screaming in from the southern and northern perimeters of the country. Two large groups of aircraft were climbing to an altitude of 5,000 meters, albeit at subsonic speeds. One group was heading south from the Baltic Sea between Helsinki and Tallin and a second group was heading north from the coast of Turkmenistan. Both groups were on a direct flight path to Moscow. In each case, a small group appeared to be separating from the main body, accelerating forward at supersonic speeds.

The Americans were doing exactly as President Igor Yakovlev had predicted, and he was ready for them. Fighter planes had been armed for air-to-air battle at all of Russia's western airfields and pilots were ready to take to the air at a moment's notice. President Yakovlev immediately ordered them to the attack. Hundreds of Russian fighters were scrambled, all going supersonic soon after take-off in an attempt to quickly intercept the enemy planes. The Russian aircraft were all equipped with upgraded Vympel NPO R-77X medium range air-to-air missiles and the newest variant of the R-37M long-range air-to-air missiles, both of which were as good, or better, than the American's AMRAAM missile family. The R-37M missiles would take out the lead planes before they were in sight and the Vympel's would then clean up the rest as the fighters closed in. Whatever aircraft were lucky enough to make it to the Russian border would have to deal with the convoys of S-350 Vityaz missile launchers he had strategically located across the western Russian border. To further ensure his victory, Yakovlev ordered the deployment of four new, mobile, directional EMP-generating devices that could target airborne aircraft without damaging nearby ground installations. The systems were so large they could only be transported by rail, but Yakovlev was convinced that the Americans would follow major pipelines and railways into the country.

The Russians clearly had numerical and performance supremacy both on the ground and in the air–they would deal the Americans a serious blow that they could not recover from within Europe. NATO's back would be broken in Europe and the attack on Moscow would be over before it could start. Yakovlev knew he had set up a turkey shoot and he had little concern for the American pilots who were about to die in vain. With his ongoing tank attack to the west, President Yakovlev had created a 200-kilometer wide buffer to allow more reaction time to an American attack from the west, and he had already eliminated the weak NATO Air Forces in both countries. This would allow him the freedom to better protect

Moscow from the north and south with additional resources–and this was exactly where the Americans were now attacking from. He was sure that the northern attack must have come from Finnish air bases at the southern end of the country. He made a mental note to address the Finns at a later time. The southern attack was surprisingly coming from Turkmenistan–how the Americans were able to sneak attack aircraft into that country without his military being aware of it was a failure that infuriated him. He would deal with appropriate retributions of his generals after the attack, but the American fighters needed to be dealt with first.

For the immediate moment, Yakovlev found himself bothered by only one small detail–the fact that the speed of the majority of the attacking planes remained slower than expected, still flying at subsonic speeds, with only the smaller body closing at supersonic speeds. What were the Americans doing? Were they trying to draw his fighters out with the lead aircraft so that they could provide a secondary attack with the main body, or was the main group made up with drones and the smaller, faster group made up with manned fighter aircraft that would attempt to clear their way? Yakovlev was convinced that it was an approach where the American president wanted to limit his pilot losses by limiting the number of manned aircraft. Yakovlev was confident that none of the planes would ever see Moscow. His fighters and ground forces would engage and defeat them all well before they could ever get close to their target, but he couldn't lower his guard until they validated the makeup of the attacking planes.

Never go to a fight unless you go prepared to win, he grimaced. He had clearly learned his lesson regarding that old adage from both the space dock and USS Kennedy attacks, and he was not about to let it happen again. This time he would clearly overwhelm the American forces.

There were two primary groups of Russian Su-35 Flanker-E air-superiority fighters formed from the various airfields that had blasted aircraft into the night sky, one heading north and one heading south. Each group contained no fewer than 150 aircraft, heading straight toward the oncoming attacks from Helsinki and Turkmenistan–an overwhelming and devastating fighting force, and they were closing quickly.

"The American aircraft flying south from Finland have all disappeared! They must have dropped to ground level. Are the satellite systems still tracking them?"

"No, we've lost them … totally. We have nothing from the satellite or ground radar."

"That's not possible," President Yakovlev yelled. "They must be in our river valleys, hidden by hills. Launch the second wave squadrons. Find those fighters!"

"How can that be …"

"What, Lieutenant?"

"Mr. President, there is a new attack force coming from the White Sea … it's … huge … they must have hundreds of aircraft in it. The signatures are small, possibly stealth fighters like the F-35."

"Stealth fighters? They don't have that many. They must be cruise missiles!"

"The initial aircraft might have been a ruse, Mr. President. The main attack now looks to be coming from the White Sea."

"That's impossible! There's no way they could have launched that many aircraft from the White Sea. They don't even have any carriers near there! It must be cruise missiles coming from their submarines."

"It could still be aircraft. If they are, they must have come over the Arctic Ocean from Greenland, perhaps right at sea level altitude. Mr. President, what are your orders, sir?"

"Regardless whether they are cruise missiles or fighters, we will destroy them. How big is the attack?"

"It looks like five separate groups of at least 50 targets each, and whatever they are, they are flying at supersonic speeds–and heading straight toward Moscow."

President Yakovlev released a stream of vulgarities. "Redirect our in-flight fighters and launch everything we have in backup, now!"

"Yes, sir, but many of the in-flight aircraft will require refueling."

"Then refuel them! The American forces cannot be allowed to reach Moscow. Activate all the anti-aircraft batteries on their flight path to engage and destroy."

*****

Fifty-six new, super-secret U.S. Skull-Kracker terrain-following, air-launched cruise missiles launched from each of the USS Montana and the USS Vermont, Virginia-class submarines, just north of the Gulf of Gdansk, while another 56 were launched from each of the USS Utah and the USS Idaho submarines, west of Albania in the Adriatic Sea.

The Skull Kracker cruise missile is a modified, highly stealthy, tactical munitions dispenser; each capable of carrying 36 8.75-pound, BLU-135 top-attack, anti-tank submunitions. Within the tactical munitions dispenser itself, on-board radar, infrared sensors, magnetic sensors and various computer systems identify targets by their thermal, magnetic and dimensional signatures. The Skull Kracker, upon identifying a target, or targets, then ejects a selectable number of submunitions per target and assigns each submunition to a specific target via programming instructions handed off from the dispenser to the submunition just prior to ejection. In that manner, a single tank, a platoon of tanks, or multiple platoons can be attacked with a single Skull Kracker cruise missile dispenser load.

The BLU-135 submunition provides a major upgrade from the older BLU-108 submunition, but similarly deploys a parachute to decelerate over the target, orient itself vertically, reacquire the target with its own internal sensors, as well as the hand-off GPS data from the cruise missile, and then detonate a 4.5-pound internally-contained shape charge, discharging a super-sonic molten slug of metal into the least-protected, top area of the tank. In the case of the Armata Battle Tank, the Russians had installed metal dispersion grids across the top of each tank as a means of breaking up the shape charge slug and reducing its kill potential. To overcome that feature, U.S. simulated tank wars assigned no fewer than three submunitions to each tank as a means to destroy the grid with the first two and open a path for the final submunition to engage and kill the tank with a clear, unobstructed shot.

NATO intelligence had identified no fewer than 700 Russian tanks currently in Ukraine and Belarus, while 8,064 armor-piercing, tank killers were now heading toward them in an attempt to balance the battlefield.

*****

CHAPTER 18

White Sands

"Harry, it's good to see you again. How are you?"

"Doing well, Senator. I'm glad you were able to join us to see the spacecraft. I believe you will be the first senator to see it. By the way, this is Cmdr. Blake Thompson," Harry replied as he shook her hand and pointed to Blake.

"Cmdr. Thompson. I'm Sen. Ronnie Dempsey. I've heard a lot about you from Harry; it's good to finally meet you."

"Likewise," Blake replied while shaking her hand. "Welcome to the wild, wild West. You are in for a big treat." Blake smiled. "Have you been to the West before?"

"Yes, many times, although to be honest, my favorite area is the western half of Colorado, up in the mountains."

"I must agree with you, Senator. I was there last month with two other members of our team, enjoying some great mountain jeeping. It was my first trip to Colorado and I'll never forget it. We finished up the visit at the Air Force Academy in Colorado Springs to watch the Notre Dame football game. I was in seventh heaven–it just doesn't get any better than that." Blake smiled.

"What a coincidence! I was supposed to be at that game, too, but I had to cancel at the last minute because of a family issue. I would have loved to have seen that game."

"You what?" Blake asked in astonishment.

"I said I would have loved to see the game. I was so disappointed I couldn't go, but family comes first, right? Fortunately, I gave my tickets to a friend who was able to take his son to the game and it sounds like it was the best father-son outing he could have asked for, especially as he *is* a Notre Dame fan." Sen. Dempsey laughed, then paused as she watched Blake's expression.

"Blake, are you all right? ... You don't look very well."

"Where were your seats, Senator?" Blake demanded.

"You can call me Ronnie, Commander, but you're beginning to make me feel worried that I'm missing something. The seats were on the 50-yard line, about half way up on the west side–great seats. Why do you ask?"

"How well known was it that you canceled your planned trip?"

"It wasn't intentional, but looking back, I don't think I informed many people beyond my friend and my office staff. We didn't even cancel the flight as I let my friend and his son take my place."

"Blake, does this have to do with ..." Harry began to speak.

"Yes, but not right now. Senator, we need to delay your visit to the ship. Right now, you and I need to get on the phone with the White House and the FBI. How public were your travel plans for this trip?"

"Blake, you *are* worrying me right now. What's going on?" she demanded.

*****

Russia

"Mr. President, our aircraft just launched the first wave of R-37M long-range air-to-air missiles. They should be in visual range shortly."

"What about the two groups of aircraft to the east?"

"They have not returned, sir. It looks like it was a ruse, but we don't think they've left the arena."

"Why is that, Lieutenant?"

"We keep getting quick, but small radar signatures that come and go throughout the western half of Belarus and Ukraine. They are in a different area from where the aircraft were flying, but it could still be their fighters at very low altitudes in between the hills."

"Wouldn't they need refueling by now ..." President Yakovlev asked, but was interrupted as news reports began streaming in.

"We are under attack in Ukraine, sir!"

"What? From where?"

"Now in Belarus, too!"

"What kind of attack? From where?" President Yakovlev demanded.

"Aircraft, sir. The Americans are attacking–their aircraft are hitting our missile batteries hard ... wait ... We're receiving additional reports of cruise missiles now ... They are attacking our tanks!"

"Damn it!" President Yakovlev yelled. "How many of our fighters do we have left in Ukraine and Belarus?"

"Not many, sir. Those that remained are engaging the enemy aircraft and they have shot down a few lead aircraft, but they are badly outnumbered and are taking heavy losses. The Americans will achieve and hold air domination until we can get more aircraft in the arena."

President Yakovlev didn't respond immediately. He kept glaring at the console, waiting for something to give him a clue what to do, but nothing materialized.

"What are our pilots reporting from the White Sea attack?" President Yakovlev finally responded.

"It appears that the Americans have tricked us, sir. Our lead fighters are reporting no aircraft, but they shot down at least five very large cruise missiles and the aircraft then simply disappeared, just like the aircraft we were tracking earlier to the east."

"What?" President Yakovlev responded. "This is not possible; aircraft can't simply disappear. Is Moscow under attack, or not?"

"Based on what we are seeing right now, there is no imminent attack on Moscow, or Russia itself. It appears the Americans' primary objective was to create a diversion that would pull our aircraft away from the western theater so that they could attack our tanks. According to all the reports coming in, they are succeeding."

"How are they hitting our tanks? What are they using?"

"We don't know, sir, other than they are top attack weapons. We are getting multiple reports that submunitions with parachutes were ejected from cruise missiles."

"Our new designs were made to stop their top-attack tank killers; our tanks will survive!" President Yakovlev pumped his fist in the air.

"I'm sorry, sir, but they must have a newer weapon we are not aware of. The reports state that we have lost scores of tanks. Many more are damaged and the attack remains under way."

*****

White House
Oct. 24, 2029

"Mr. President, I have Zhou Qiang, general secretary and president of the People's Republic of China on line two. Were you expecting his call?"

"No, I wasn't … did he say what it is about?"

"No, but he did say it was urgent," his administrator replied.

"Send him though, please." President Callahan could only imagine where this call would go.

"This is President Callahan."

"This is General Secretary and President Zhou Qiang. There is no one else on the phone so that I may ask you a very direct and personal question."

"Go ahead, General Secretary."

"Are you going to allow my country access to the alien spacecraft?"

"No," President Callahan answered calmly.

"Have you asked them to depart Earth?"

Again, the president answered in a calm voice.

"No."

"You are not giving me much room to negotiate for my people, Mr. President."

"I understand, General Secretary, but there really isn't much to negotiate."

"I know what you are planning to do to the Russians, and you are leaving me little choice on my options. Is that your final stand?"

"Yes, it is."

"Good day, Mr. President."

The call disconnected before President Callahan could respond. He pushed line 1 on his phone and requested his staff join him immediately. Thirty minutes later, a solemn and determined group left the Oval Office and President Callahan was left to ponder what the Chinese leader had alluded to.

*****

White Sands

Blake and Sen. Dempsey were alone in a small, nondescript conference room. Blake had just dialed FBI agent, Joe Foster.

"Hello?"

"Hi, Joe, it's Blake Thompson and I want you to meet someone. Sen. Dempsey, FBI Agent Joe Foster. Joe, Sen. Ronnie Dempsey."

"Hello, Senator. Hi, Blake. It's sure good to hear from you, but these sure are troubling times in Europe based on the breaking news reports on my television right now."

"Yes, they are–and I hope you can still say you're happy to hear from me when we're done talking."

"OK … that sounded like a loaded statement, Blake. Just hit me with it; what's up?"

Blake updated Joe on the football discussion he'd had with Sen. Dempsey and then asked Joe to update the senator on what had transpired in Colorado.

"Joe, you're thinking that someone was trying to kill *me*? But why?" the senator asked.

"We think it's because of your support of the aliens," Blake interjected.

"Oh, my God! Was this from the same people that killed Sen. Colburn?"

"It's beginning to look like that, Senator," Joe replied. "We were initially convinced that they were after Blake and his team, but in light of the information you just provided, it appears we were wrong, and that you were likely the primary target, especially given the likelihood that they were not aware of your change of plans.

"I think you need to stay on base until we can provide an FBI security detail for you. I also need to report this ASAP to the White House to alert them that other members of your SETI team may also be at risk. Whoever is behind this is not only well-connected, but they must be very powerful or well supported by someone else who has inside knowledge of the White House at a very high level."

"Any ideas who it could be?" Joe asked.

"Why does the name James Harley keep coming to the forefront?" Blake asked.

"Yeah, especially with his ties to the information pipeline he has within the Armed Services Committee," Joe replied.

*****

Blake searched for Diego and Sean, with Harry in tow. He finally found them with the help of a security detail near the Jarisst I, and gave them a quick update on the surprising news.

"Hard to believe, isn't it?" Diego replied.

"Yes, pretty amazing that someone would literally plan and carry out attacks on U.S. soil against our own senators, but that is what the data suggests," Blake answered and then turned to Harry.

"Harry, I've also received an update on the battle in Europe with the Russians, as well as the fact that the Chinese have launched an attack on Taiwan. Things are getting crazier and it appears the world is again at the gateway to a full-fledged worldwide war, so it's important we get the Cjarians back into space before this gets any worse. I want them off this planet and in free space where they can better protect themselves and remain out of this war. What's their ship's status?"

"The fuel tanks have been repaired and refueled," Harry replied. "Final checkouts were completed this morning and the Cjarians can launch now, if desired, but we have not cracked their Q-PAMS drive issue yet."

"OK, that will have to wait until another time. Sean, start removing people and equipment from around their ship. I'll talk to Thjars, but I want him back in space, for his own safety, as soon as possible."

"Aye, aye, Chief," Sean acknowledged.

"Harry, I have a special mission for you, and take Diego with you, but I need you to pick up a package at Alamogordo for me to give the Cjarians before they leave," Blake paused, clearly thinking of something else.

"Wait, let's change that up. I don't want anyone traveling alone anywhere–including Sen. Dempsey. Diego, you stay here and help guard the senator until her security detail can be arranged. Harry, contact the base military police and request they go with you, but make sure you're armed. You're to meet with Allen Hayes, curator of the New Mexico Museum of Space History. He has a special package for me to give to the Cjarians. He has no idea what it's for, so don't spill the beans. You should be able to get there and back in less than an hour, before the Cjarians are ready to depart."

*****

White House

"President Callahan, the ruse worked as planned; Yakovlev withdrew his fighters from the western front and headed toward our fake forces attacking from the north and south. Their fighters will now all need refueling so that should give us ample time to withdraw our fighters in Belarus and Ukraine and get them safely back to our European bases."

"How many aircraft did we lose, Gen. McMullen?"

"A least 12, sir. A number of pilots are assumed dead, three have been recovered by our friendly ground forces after ejecting and at least five are MIA. Eight of the 12 were the Weasel aircraft; two shot down by Russian ground based missile batteries and at least six from what appears to be a new focused EMP weapon."

"A what?"

"An electromagnetic pulse weapon, or EMP. But rather than bathe an entire area in electronic-destroying EMP waves, like a nuke would do, they seem to have found a way to focus the EMP energy in a directed cone at oncoming targets–and it appears to be extremely deadly if it gets a lock on an aircraft. The only good news about this new weapon is that the aircraft must be in direct line with the weapon to be attacked. Now that we know what it is, it will be easier to avoid at low altitudes, but high-flying aircraft, like reconnaissance aircraft, will remain at high risk to this weapon."

"How portable are these weapons, Gen. McMullen?"

"We were able to get a few seconds of video during flyovers and they're huge. They look like they can only be transported by rail." Gen. McMullen paused. "Mr. President, we think they only have three or four of them and we now know where they are … we could take them out …"

"I agree, Gen. McMullen; take them out, but do it damn quick before their fighters can re-engage. Can we do it with cruise missiles?"

"We could try, but based on what we have in our inventory, and the danger associated with this new weapon, we still think our best chance is by low-flying ground attack aircraft. We believe the weapon can only fire in one direction at a time, so we would use Predator drones and swarm drones to create targets and then attack from their unprotected side."

"It needs to be quick before the Russians recover. General, how long do you need?"

"We already have an attack plan in place and planes are armed and on the runway. The attack includes 12 F-35s, three for each target, with full load outs of 2,000 lb guided Mk 84 bombs."

"That's great planning on your part, General, but why such an old bomb for a highly complex new weapon?"

"We need to minimize electronic signatures and drop something at very low altitudes directly over the target; we can't come in from above. This is the perfect weapon as it doesn't have any electronics. Once it's launched, the new weapon will be powerless to stop it. The pilots will be at risk for a very short time period while directly over the target, but we believe the drone targets will keep the weapon occupied during that period of time. Furthermore, the Mk 84s will deploy air-inflatable Ballutes to slow the bombs down and allow the aircraft time to depart prior to detonation. Delivery will be at supersonic speeds, so the attack will have the additional benefit of disabling and disorienting ground soldiers on or near the units for a few seconds as the aircrafts' sonic booms impact."

"Understood. What else do you need?"

"Mr. President, we just need your approval."

"Approved. Take them out."

President Callahan waited while Gen. McMullen called in the strike approval. The call was short. Gen. McMullen hung up the phone and looked at the president and his advisers.

"The fighters are launching right now," he relayed.

"God help them that they can hit their targets and return safely," President Callahan responded. "OK, General, you've got 15 more minutes of my time. Please debrief me on the effectiveness of the drones, the cruise missiles and the tank attack."

"Yes, sir, first the drones. We sent in two groups of drones, one from the southernmost airbase in Finland and the other from a base in Turkmenistan that we used during the various Mideast wars. These fleets included as many subsonic drones as we could scrape up, mostly older Global Hawks, with the intent of simulating a large attack force. All had been modified to increase their radar signatures once they were airborne. Each group also had six Valkyrie supersonic drones that accelerated toward the target to create the perception of a dual wave attack force. Once the Russians launched their fighters, we turned off the radar modifications and sent the drones to lower altitudes and scattered them in multiple directions. We lost a half dozen or so Global Hawks, but all of the Valkyries returned undamaged. The ruse worked as planned and Yakovlev took the bait, sending his fighters to both target sets. The next stage of the attack worked even better. We sent seven sub-launched, experimental drones in from the White Sea. These are the ones we spoke about during our planning review. We lost two due to reliability issues that will need to be addressed by the engineers, but the five that made it through worked better than we ever dreamed of. Each cruise missile successfully projected 50 radar signatures of F-22s and F-35s, signaling the Russians that we had at least 250 aircraft heading toward Moscow at supersonic speeds. Although the Russians succeeded in shooting the cruise missiles down with long range missiles, our missiles were still able to successfully complete their mission before they were destroyed by pulling the Russian air assault farther away."

"How does it work, General?" President Callahan asked.

"To be honest, Mr. President, I have no clue. The science came out of the Skunk Works and MIT and I doubt there are more than five people who truly understand it, but the important point is, it worked."

"Fair point," President Callahan responded. "How many tanks did we get?"

"The Skull Krackers worked exceptionally well, sir. We launched 224 of them from a total of four submarines and the new submunitions were extremely effective on the Russian tanks, even the most recently modified T-14 Armatas. Of the 700-plus tanks that we were able to identify prior to the attack, our most recent satellite thermal imaging data suggest at least 400, maybe even as many as 500 are burning. How many more are damaged, but not burning, is beyond our ability to determine at this point in time. Of the remaining tanks, some are still holding their positions, but many are openly retreating. The attack cost us a number of pilots, many aircraft and drones, as well as created a significant hit on our cruise missile inventory, especially for Skull Krackers, but all in all, it was a tremendous success, especially as you can clearly tell the world that you did not attack Russian soil. The entire U.S. attack, less of course the drone and cruise missile ruses, was directed at defending Belarus and Ukraine on their own soil. Per your final recommendation, we have not yet attacked the gas and oil pipelines. We'll wait to see what the Russian response is first."

"Thank you, Gen. McMullen, you and your team put together a formidable and impressive plan, but more importantly, you carried it out. I, and the American people, are grateful and thank you. Please get me the names of the downed pilots and keep me posted on the MIA status. It looks like I have some calls to make, starting with President Yakovlev to see if he is willing to negotiate at least a temporary truce."

*****

Alamogordo, N.M.

Harry was traveling to Alamogordo with Capt. Ed Jones of the White Sands Military Police deployment. Just inside of Alamogordo city limits, they stopped at a Shell gas station at the corner of West 8th Street and North White Sands Blvd for Ed to use the restroom while Harry fueled up.

Two minutes later, Ed exited the restroom and looked around for Harry and their vehicle. There was no sign of him in the store or parking lot, and the car was gone. Ed quickly called Harry's cell phone and was immediately rewarded with a ring from the garbage can near the gas pumps.

His next call was to alert Blake and ask for backup, followed by a lengthy call with the local Alamogordo Police Department to report a missing person and possible carjacking. He described the car, license plates and Harry's description, and then sat down to wait for the police to arrive. Hopefully, they would be able to get quick access to the gas station's video surveillance system. Until then, there was nothing else Ed could do but wait for Blake and his fellow military police members to arrive and join in the search.

*****

Tucson, Ariz.

"Mayday, mayday. Air China flight 29 from Changsha, Huanghua International Airport en route to Phoenix, Sky Harbor International Airport, is declaring a flight emergency. We cannot maintain our flight path, and we are drifting south of the U.S.-Mexico border. Requesting emergency reroute to Gen. Roberto Fierro Villalobos International Airport in Chihuahua, Mexico."

"Copy that, flight 29. This is the Tucson International Airport tower; we have you on radar. We are contacting Mexican authorities to clear runways at Villalobos International. Do you need an escort or emergency ground service support?"

"No escort required, but recommend emergency ground service. We cannot turn to port. I repeat: we cannot turn to port, but we can turn to starboard. We will align with the designated runway as we get closer to the airport. Please provide the best east-west runway option as we may only get one chance."

"Flight 29, please be advised that there is no east-west runway option. Advise secondary airport. Do you have adequate fuel to conduct a large-circle maneuver to the starboard and realign with El Paso, Texas?"

"Yes, but it will be close, Tucson."

"Emergency vehicles are deploying. Please maintain radio contact. As you approach the U.S. border, we will hand you off to the El Paso tower. Be advised that military aircraft will be sent to escort."

"Copy that. Thank you, Tucson."

*****

NORAD, Colorado Springs

"Major, Air China flight 29 has just split into four bogies. Repeat, I see four bogies, and three of them have accelerated away from what appears to be the commercial bogey. All are heading toward El Paso, Texas."

"Alert White Sands and Holloman, Lieutenant. Launch cover flight from Peterson. Maintain updates. Calls were quickly initiated.

"Holloman Air Force Base."

"This is Maj. Beaudry at NORAD; we have a priority alert for the base commander."

"Yes, sir, but he's in the AOC and he's pretty busy right now. Is this about the Air China flight?"

"Yes."

"He's aware, but I'll patch you through to Cmdr. Johnson. Hold, please."

"Cmdr. Johnson speaking."

"Sir, this is Maj. Beaudry at NORAD. We have four confirmed bogies heading north toward El Paso, one of which may be a commercial aircraft."

"Acknowledged. We've scrambled six F-16s and have six F-22s loading. NORAD, are you aware of any other potential threats."

"Not at this time ..." The major was cut off in mid-sentence. NORAD could detect excited discussion as the commander was talking to someone else in the room.

"NORAD, we have visual verification on three Chinese J-20 Mighty Dragons. They are accelerating past El Paso. The F-16s are engaging. We need to alert White Sands."

*****

White Sands

Blake departed White Sands with a convoy of five military jeeps loaded with military police, lights flashing and sirens blaring, heading northeast at high speed on State Route 70, toward Alamogordo.

Blake was almost to the edge of Alamogordo when his cell phone rang again. He picked it up, fully expecting to hear Ed's or Harry's voice, but it was Diego.

"We have incoming aircraft at White Sands!" Diego barked

"What? How? From where?" Blake responded.

"I don't know, Blake. The sirens sounded about a minute ago, but we only now just received the message as to why, and I immediately called you ..." Diego attempted to complete his sentence, but was drowned out by the unmistakable sounds of low-flying military jets at max thrust from very near his location.

A few seconds later, Blake could also hear the sounds of aircraft, in the distance behind him, banking at high speed directly over Holloman Air Force Base. He turned in time to see dots in the sky, all heading south at what looked and sounded like an emergency response. Blake was immediately torn between two critical needs: search for his friend and teammate, or return to defend the Cjarians–even though he had no idea what he was defending against.

Blake instantly made the decision.

"Sergeant, call and inform the other vehicles that they are to continue on to support the search for Harry. We have an incident that has triggered an alpha scramble at the base and this Jeep is going straight back with all occupants."

"Yes, sir," the sergeant responded and immediately called one of the other Jeeps as Blake slid the vehicle into a 180-degree slide in the middle of the intersection, tires spinning and white smoke billowing into the air. The Jeep rocketed out of the cloud of smoke and headed straight back toward White Sands.

Blake knew Harry would understand his dilemma, but putting Harry's needs second to the Cjarians was still tearing at his emotions. Blake knew he had to fight the emotional urge, and fast. As the Jeep roared down the road, Blake pushed his mind into military engagement mode–everything else was instantly put on hold.

"Here's my phone, sergeant. Diego was my last call. Call him back and find out what the hell we're up against. I also need to know what the status of the Jarisst I and its crew is–specifically, are they safe and have they taken off yet? And if they haven't, why the hell not, and when will they?"

*****

A melee of technology collided in the skies between El Paso and White Sands. The older F-16s were badly outclassed by the newer J-20s. Four of the F-16s were destroyed before the first J-20 went down, but not before it was able to launch three missiles. It quickly became clear that none of the missiles were intended for the oncoming F-16s as the three missiles sped by the F-16s and continued to the north, unimpeded.

"This is Bravo Leader one. Four F-16s and one J-20 are down. Survivors unknown. Two J-20s and missiles are en route to White Sands. The alien aircraft must be their target. I repeat: the alien aircraft must be the target. Two remaining F-16s are banking to re-engage. We need those F22's now! Where are they?"

"They're taxiing to the main runway and will be airborne shortly."

"Then they're too damn late! Alert White Sands they have incoming," the pilot strained as the high-g turn pulled at his body.

*****

Sean was stationed inside the Holloman Flight Control center and communicating with Diego by phone. The IADS and its portable air defense systems located at tactical positions around White Sands were already on high alert after receiving direct feedback from the integrated battlefield warning systems on the F-16s. Radar warning systems showed at least nine incoming missiles and the two remaining J-20s were turning to the northwest.

Diego forewarned Sean that they would likely lose contact as soon as the electronic jamming units went live, which immediately occurred and Diego's call went silent.

Sean was convinced that the two J-20s were buying time for a final attack on the Jarisst I from the north to ensure its destruction in case the missiles didn't succeed. It was a pretty daring attack. But with the obvious fact the pilots had committed their lives to this mission, with no hope of survival, it was one they would be 100 percent committed to. The only way to stop them was to shoot them down, and quickly.

"Quick, sector the F-22s to the north. The J-20s will be making a wide arc for a return attack from the north," Sean barked.

Prior to the attack, the Jarisst I crew had been out of the spacecraft, sharing thank yous and goodbyes with the men and women who'd helped repair the ship. Diego interrupted the processions and relayed that the short attack notice didn't leave time for them to return to the ship, so he directed the Cjarians and base workers to follow him to a bunker. Diego could only hope they would reach safety in time.

*****

Blake's Jeep was nearing the White Sands entrance on State Route 70 as the sound of six F-22s screaming at max speed blasted away from Holloman. He could also hear the distant sound of jets banking to the west. Trails of smoke showed in the sky to the south. It was hard to comprehend that someone was actually attacking the Jarisst I, let alone within the borders of the United States, but he was sure there were only two countries with the capability to pull it off: Russia and China–both of which were already at or near the brink of war with the U.S.

The sergeant in Blake's Jeep kept trying to reach Diego or Sean, or anyone else for that matter, but had been unsuccessful so far.

"Forget it, Sergeant. Get your rifles ready. We're heading straight to the runways," Blake commanded the Jeep's occupants. They reached the gate to see armed guards taking firing positions, with one lone sentry standing in the middle of the road, his attack rifle pointing directly at their oncoming vehicle and his left hand in the air signaling them to stop. Blake locked up the brakes and skidded to a halt, hands in the air for all to see, and ordered his fellow passengers to do the same as the lone sentry approached.

"I'm Cmdr. Blake Thompson. Reach into my left breast pocket and you'll see my orders. I need to get to the Northrup Strip 10 minutes ago."

The sentry did as ordered as the rest of his squad spread out around the Jeep, guns at the ready. The sentry retrieved Blake's orders, looked at his ID and face, and then waved his squad's guns down, following that motion with a quick salute to Blake and a yell to open the gates.

"Good luck, sir. Stay safe."

Blake floored the Jeep and headed through the gate. Additional sounds could be heard ahead from more incoming aircraft or missiles and then the ground batteries opened up.

*****

The Duke II EWTV electronic jamming MRAP vehicles on the southern side of the base began pounding the incoming missiles with highly concentrated energy beams. All systems were set on barrage jamming in order to overwhelm the incoming missile systems with the assumption that they were operating on phased-array sensor system platforms.

The jamming was working and three missiles dropped from the sky, but there were too many of them and they were coming in too quickly at low altitude–leaving precious little time to acquire, attack and destroy the invading missiles.

The skins of the remaining missiles parted; the missiles then spun up to high RPM and thousands of bomblets were ejected centrifugally, littering the sky with an umbrella of death and destruction–all focused on the Jarisst I.

Simultaneously, the F-22s closed on the two remaining J-20s, dispatching both before they could complete their turns for their final attacking run. But it was too late; the surprise attack was more than White Sands had been prepared to defend against.

Blake was now halfway to the Northrup Strip and could clearly see the unfolding attack plan; it was painfully clear that the attack had a high probability of overwhelming the defenses near the Jarisst I. The enemy pilots would likely achieve their goals–

even if none of the attackers survived. Whoever was behind this had just selfishly changed the future of the world.

Blake knew he was too late, that he had failed the Cjarians, and for that matter, President Callahan as well. But worse, he had failed himself. The great planner had been out-planned.

Blake floored the Jeep toward the Jarisst I's location, praying that somehow he could still help, or at the worst, find survivors. Even though he had steeled himself for the imminent explosions, he was still caught off guard by the magnitude of the explosions as the sky erupted in brilliant light and flame ahead of him, followed by the heat and shock wave of an intense blast that rocked his Jeep and its occupants.

The Jeep sputtered and died and Blake let it glide to a stop on the side of the road, his hands clenched on the steering wheel, his face red with anger. He would make sure that whoever did this would pay dearly.

Blake attempted to call Diego, but his phone appeared to be dead. The electronic magnitude of the detonations must have been significant enough to kill all nearby unprotected electronics–including his Jeep and phone.

The four men began double-timing on foot toward the impact site.

*****

President Callahan was in the Oval Office when the call came in alerting him to the attack. The news that Chinese J-20s had been identified brought him to his feet. He paced the room while he shook his head in disgust.

Not only was America at war with the Russians, but the United States was now at war with the Chinese. But this was the first direct attack on U.S soil by an enemy force since 9/11, and from an independent and sovereign nation since the Pearl Harbor attack in 1941–and it was all occurring under his watch. Worse yet was the attack on the Cjarians. He had promised Thjars that the greatest country, with the greatest military in the world, was more than capable of protecting him–and he alone would make sure of it.

*****

Blake and his companions, sweating and breathing hard, were now close enough to the Northrup Strip to finally see the aftermath of the attack. Blake stopped in his tracks, trying to make sense of the distant scene in front of him.

"Oh, my God ... how ..." was all he could utter.

*****

Fifteen minutes later, Diego handed Blake and the men with him four water bottles, which they quickly emptied.

"Where are they, Diego?" his parched throat spat out.

"Ten of them are in the bunker. I'm keeping them there until we figure out what the hell just happened," Diego replied.

"Ten? Who's missing?"

"Juulys, Blake. We don't know where she is. Thjars thinks she was outside when the blast hit," Diego added with sadness in his face. "Anyone caught outside likely didn't make it. I'm afraid to see what our losses were on the missile trucks located around the base."

"How is the ship still in one piece? We saw the explosions from across the base. It even knocked out our Jeep and phones from as far away as we were."

"Same with everything outside, but our bunker communications are still working. It appears that the bunker was a hardened bunker, so even my phone is working. Holloman didn't share what they did, but Sean is on the way. I expect that copter on the horizon is his," Diego said, pointing to the east. "Nellis is also flying in everything they have right now. They caught us with our guard down, Blake. It's unacceptable, but it won't happen again."

"You're right about one thing, Diego."

"What's that?"

"It was unacceptable. We've lost Harry and we almost lost the Cjarians—we failed to protect them. Worse yet, we failed our word to them." Blake paused, struggling with the inner demon he was battling. "Who did save them?"

"I'm not sure how, Blake, but it had to be the Holloman guys. The ground jammers took out some of the missiles and the F-22s got the remaining Chinese fighters, but we don't know how Holloman took out the bomblets. There must have been hundreds of them, and as best our radar showed until it was taken down, they were on target."

"Leave Thjars with his crew, but get Qulys out here first. I'll talk to Thjars a little later; right now we need to keep him safe. No one else goes near that ship until after Thjars and I talk. Get troops out as far as you think Juulys could have wandered …. and find her. We at least owe them that."

*****

The AH-64 Apache helicopter touched down near the Jarisst I and Sean popped out of the cockpit and jogged toward Blake, just as Diego exited the bunker with Qulys by his side.

As the three groups of men approached each other, Diego was the first to speak.

"What did those Holloman boys do to stop the attack?"

Sean looked at him in total surprise before replying.

"That's what I was going to ask you … we didn't do anything other than attack their aircraft. Cmdr. Rachel Joslin actually got one of those bastards. Are all of the Cjarians safe?" Sean asked.

"All but one, Sean," Blake interjected. "We can't find Juulys."

"Just to be safe, Blake, keep your teams looking … but I think there is one place where they can't look and if my suspicions are correct, she is there."

"And where might that be?" Blake responded for all three men who were now waiting to hear what Qulys would say next.

"The ship."

*****

CHAPTER 19

Alamogordo

"We've found Harry's vehicle," the officer radioed in. "There's no sign of Mr. Lundrum anywhere, but there are some fresh blood smears in the car. Not major blood loss, more like someone was roughed up and laid on the seat. My guess is he was tied up."

"Do you think he is still alive?" the chief asked.

"Well, he was at the time they removed him from the vehicle. They left the car off the main drag, in the middle of the desert, and you can clearly see in the sandy dirt where he was half dragged and half hopped to another vehicle that must have taken him elsewhere."

"Can you tell where they went, or what the escape vehicle was?"

"No clue on direction, but based on the wheel span and tire size, we think it's a van."

"Any nearby video?"

"No, the only video we have so far is from the gas station."

"Have you gotten anything from that yet?"

"Yes, and no. We can see two guys: one clearly hit him on the back of the head and pushed him into the back seat, while the other man jumped into the driver's seat. It was professional, over and gone in less than 30 seconds."

"Damn."

"Yea, someone was definitely ready for him. If it had been a random hit for money, they would have left him there. Someone wanted Mr. Lundrum, specifically."

"Anything from Holloman or White Sands?"

"I guess you haven't heard yet …"

"What?"

"White Sands was attacked at about the same time by Chinese fighter aircraft–those places are closed up tighter than a steel drum."

"Holy shit! Were the two guys Chinese?"

"Couldn't tell; they had masks on. We're rounding up video from other nearby locations to see if they can be identified before they donned their masks."

"Smart thinkin'–who the hell is this Lundrum guy?"

"Supposedly some genius the military uses. Unofficial word is that they have an alien ship at White Sands and this guy knows everything about it."

"Damn! That's unbelievable–Area 51 right in our own back yard! Sounds like the Chinese found out and tried to do something about it. First the Russians, now the Chinese? This is going to get ugly fast."

"You know it. Photograph the area and tow the vehicle back here."

"Oh yeah, I almost forgot. Wait, I'll send you a picture. Remember I told you that I could tell Lundrum was hobbled, but alive because I saw his tracks?"

"Yeah …"

"Well, just as he got into the second vehicle, it looks like he may have left a message. It's messy, but it looks like a number four, followed by two letters, 'C' and 'O' … I have no clue what that means."

"Hmm, I'm looking at it now, and yes, I agree it looks like '4CO' … maybe four Chinese operatives?"

"Good guess, Chief. If this guy, Lundrum, is as smart as his friends claim he is, I'll bet he was trying to tell us something."

*****

White Sands

"Follow me, Blake, I'll show you where Juulys must be," Qulys volunteered.

"How so, Qulys?" Blake replied.

"A subtle difference with the front of the ship. I'll explain when we're on board."

Diego and Sean remained on guard outside while Blake and Qulys entered the ship. Two minutes later they entered the weapons command center and as Qulys suspected, there was Juulys, looking upset and exhausted.

"Juulys, are you OK?" Qulys asked in their native tongue.

Juulys nodded.

"You fired the Blitzcloud, didn't you?" Qulys replied in English, remembering that Blake was with him.

She nodded again.

"What is a Blitzcloud?" Blake asked.

"It's an emergency, single-use weapon used only for close in fighting, and as a means of last resort. It could have blown up the Jarisst I just as easily, especially as close as it was and in an oxygen-rich atmosphere."

"I'm sorry, Qulys," Juulys interjected.

"No, Juulys, don't be. It turns out that you saved all of us, including the ship."

"How?" Blake asked.

"It's a combination of three different weapons, all used in quick succession. First, it uses a devastating electronic barrage to wipe out as much of the attacking forces sensor and control capability as is possible. Nearly simultaneously, it launches thousands of fuel balls, each about the size of your palm, straight toward the oncoming threat."

"That's why you made the comment about the front of the ship," Blake added.

"That's correct, Blake. Those balls travel a programmed distance, based on radar and incoming telemetry readings, to activate at the leading edge of the attack. The activation causes each of them to blow apart and dissipate their contents into a very fine mist ..."

"Like an FAE, a Fuel-Air Explosive," Blake interjected again.

"I am not familiar with your term, but it sounds correct," Qulys replied. "It creates a devastating explosion once ignited–which is the third aspect of the weapon. Remember how we cut the rocket end off of the ship that was attacking your space dock?"

"Yes ..."

"The system automatically discharges that same photon beam whip which ignites the fuel cloud and anything else it can reach that radar has identified. Whatever those bombs were, they likewise detonated. Had they been too close to the ship when Juulys had activated the system, it would have taken the ship with it. Fortunately, with the help of the weapons control center computer, she nailed it perfectly."

"But why were you in the ship by yourself when everyone else was outside?" Blake asked as he looked at Juulys.

"I wasn't. I was at the tail end of the group, actually back quite a bit behind everyone else while they were talking to the technicians and thanking everyone, so I was closer to the ship than anyone else. When the sirens went off and everyone pulled out their guns and started pushing our crew toward that bunker, I panicked. I thought they were capturing the crew, just like Thjars was always concerned about … Wait, where is Thjars?"

"I told him to stay with the crew; he's OK," Qulys answered. "Blake's friends were actually trying to help, and they did, but apparently their base suffered many losses during the attack."

"But who attacked us?" Juulys half screamed out.

"We're not positive, but the planes that were shot down were Chinese," Blake answered.

"I'm so sorry that I distrusted your friends, again, and I'm even sorrier to hear that you lost more people because of us."

"Thank you, but everyone here was here only to protect you, your crew and the ship–they knew that responsibility came with risks. However, at the end of the day, the truth is," Blake started, but his facial expression tightened as he continued, "I am the one that owes you, Thjars and Qulys an apology."

"Why?"

"I let you down. I promised we could protect you, but my failure forced you to have to protect yourself."

"I don't see it that way, Blake," Juulys responded. "Now that we know what happened, how could you have prevented every possible attack path? You can't, so you didn't fail us–those attackers failed your world because of us."

"Thank you, Juulys, but I'm just not ready to let go of that yet. So, explain what happened during the attack," Blake requested, attempting to change the subject.

"After I panicked, I ran back to the ship thinking that I could threaten the base if they didn't release the crew, but then I saw the alerts identifying airborne attackers and I realized it wasn't your friends, that the base was under attack, so I waited for the computer to give me options, and I picked the Blitzcloud. Thank Glysst that Qulys spent days teaching all of us how to use these systems before we landed here. Qulys," Juulys smiled as she turned to face Qulys, "*you* saved us with your training regimen; otherwise, I wouldn't have known what to do."

"Well, the good news is that you both did exactly what well-trained soldiers do, and because of that you're all safe and the Jarisst I appears to be undamaged," Blake replied.

Blake then broke the news about Harry and told them he needed to leave the ship to return to the search. The truth was that he also needed time alone to process what had just happened, and how he could have, or should have, prevented the attack.

Blake requested that Qulys get their crew back on board and tell Thjars to depart as soon as possible. Qulys estimated that they could be in the air in fewer than 30 minutes, once everyone was back on board. Blake shook hands with the two of them, then turned to leave, but then looked over his shoulder to make one last request.

"Qulys, please make sure you contact me once you've left Earth orbit and have achieved safe distance. Now do it quickly, before it gets worse down here," Blake said seriously.

"One more thing ..." Now Blake smiled. "Since Juulys destroyed my phone, you will need to make contact directly with President Callahan's office until I can get a replacement. I'll make sure he knows. Please tell Thjars and the crew I hope to join you soon, but I need to help find Harry, so unfortunately, that doesn't allow me time to say goodbye in person right now."

"Good luck, Blake–please let us know when you find Harry or if we can help," Qulys replied.

"Thank you. Be safe, and I hope we'll see each other soon. I'm still hoping that we can help you fix the Q-PAMS drive."

"That may still be possible, Blake. Allympht told me that Harry had one more idea he wanted to pursue."

"Please be safe, Blake," Juulys added as Blake walked out of the ship and joined Sean and Diego.

"Are your phones working?"

"Yes," Diego replied, "I'm guessing that mine was protected inside the bunker and Sean was far enough away that his wasn't affected at all."

"That's good. Sean, call the White House and provide a brief update to Gen. McMullen to relay to President Callahan. Diego, call the Alamogordo Police station and find out what their latest status is, then round up the three guys that came here with me and see if they can make contact with the other Jeeps that were searching for Harry."

*****

White House
Oct. 25, 2029

"Mr. President," Gen. McMullen stuck his head into the Oval Office.

"Yes, Landon, come in and shut the door."

"I know we have a lot more to deal with, but Diego Velasquez just called in for Cmdr. Thompson. The attack in New Mexico was a direct attempt by the Chinese to destroy the Cjarian ship."

"Good God, on American soil? Are we sure it was the Chinese?"

"Yes, sir, we believe so. They used a distressed Chinese commercial airliner as a ruse and flew three Chinese J-20 Mighty Dragons directly into White Sands, then launched a surprise missile attack on the Jarisst I. Blake said the Cjarians are OK and the ship is intact, but we lost a number of F-16s, crews and soldiers on the ground. In so doing, we destroyed all three Chinese aircraft, but apparently, the Cjarians used their own ship to defend itself by destroying the incoming missiles."

"Thank God. Are the Cjarians staying or departing?"

"Their fuel tanks had already been repaired and refueled, but their light-speed drive is still not operational. Regardless, Blake directed them to depart as soon as possible to get them a safe distance away from Earth until the threat of war has passed."

"That sounds like the right decision given current events. Anything else?"

"Yes … Harry Lundrum is missing and appears to have been kidnapped." Gen. McMullen updated President Callahan.

"Damn!" President Callahan stood up and paced across the room. "Do we think he is still alive? Who do we think is behind it?" President Callahan asked.

"He was alive when they transferred him to another vehicle, so we're assuming they want him that way. We don't know who did it yet, sir, but based on the Chinese attack, it's a fair assumption to target them as the leading suspect."

"If that's the case, where the hell would they take him? They're on American soil; they can't just check into a hotel!"

"Agreed, sir. Blake and the Alamogordo police have put out a statewide dragnet on the ground and by air. Unfortunately, we have nothing so far."

"With everything else going on, it looks like Cmdr. Thompson will have to deal with this without us. Please keep me posted on any new developments–I'll see you in another hour when we talk with General Secretary Zhou Qiang."

Gen. McMullen took the cue, thanked the president and departed the Oval Office.

*****

White Sands

"Li, it's Blake. Are Robert and Jimmy with you?"

"Yes, they're both here, Blake."

"Good. Are you in a location where you can put me on speaker?"

"Yes, but hang on one second … Jimmy, get the door … OK, we're good Blake. What's up?"

"Everyone suspects the Chinese had something to do with Harry's disappearance because of the attack on the Jarisst I, but I'm not convinced the two events are necessarily related. The New Mexico State Police are doing everything they can, but by now Harry could easily have been transported out of state. President Callahan will talk with the Chinese about the bigger issue of a growing war, but I expect their ability to support us in our search for Harry will be very limited for the time being. So, gentlemen, it's up to us."

"Good here, Blake," Li responded, "that's what we've been trained for, but why aren't Sean, Patty and Diego here, too?"

"Good question, Li, I'm breaking the team into three operating groups. Diego, Sean and I will be the field team. Patty, Rachel and Vladimir will remain with the scientists here at White Sands and continue working the Q-PAMS challenge with Patty being our primary contact path with the Cjarians, through Juulys. You three are going to step up your surveillance on our good friend. What's your status on the SH surveillance?"

"Hmmm." Li chewed on Blake's last statement. "You're not thinking it was the Chinese, are you?"

"No." Blake explained the "4CO" that the police found in the sand where Harry was moved into a second vehicle.

"The police thought maybe it was 'four Chinese operatives'."

"That's creative, but sure doesn't sound like Harry."

"Bingo. I think it means 4 abductors and Colorado."

"*That* sounds like Harry," Li replied. "That does point to our good buddy. Unfortunately, as I'm sure you're aware, we've not done too much over the past few days, but if you're ready to pick it back up again, we're ready and raring to go. What are you thinking?"

"He has a vacation home in Breckenridge and at least three cars, albeit two of them are family cars …"

"And let me guess, you want some eyes and ears on those properties, correct?"

"Bingo again. Let me know what you need, but let's get it done. How long do you think it will take?"

"Phew … by the time we get the required gear, transport it and then wait for an opportunity to install our gadgets … it will be a few days, Blake."

"Well, I think I found a quicker path. Remember our good friend, Joe Foster?"

"Yes …?"

"I called him up. Told him that Harry had been abducted, and that we needed his help. He jumped on it. He called up his contact with the Tenth Special Forces Group at Fort Carson last night and got approval from the base commander for a little help. They're classifying it as a training op. They hustled an Airborne Special Forces team to Breckenridge during the middle of the night, killed local power and set up electronic jamming devices to block his surveillance equipment. They were in and out in 15 minutes, and then power was restored, so it looked like a simple power bump. You now have a suite of micro-sized acoustic sensors on his vacation home windows and the underside of his cars. The base commander in turn called up an old friend, a West Point grad, who happens to be the commander of the 20th Special Forces Group, also Airborne, and these guys focus on special reconnaissance missions. They also received approval to conduct a special training op last night, one that just happened to be near a certain Dupont Circle address. Totally coincidental. of course."

"Oorah!" Li responded. "I just love coincidences, but what's the risk they will detect the window sensors?"

"I asked the same question. Turns out their new sensor technology is incredible. They build them into window labels that bear the security company's name and icon, so they look perfectly legit hiding in the open. Tiny little things, yet they even include a self-charging capability."

"Solar?"

"No, actually they're MEMS, Joe said ..."

"Microelectromechanical Systems?"

"Correct, Li," Blake replied. "The devices harvest vibrational energy from the window movement and convert it into electricity. They also use those same vibrations to monitor voices. All that's left to do is filter out undesirable vibration patterns, like walking, washing machines or even wind-induced modulations so that the voice-induced modulations can be more easily extracted and heard."

"That's pretty impressive! What about music, Blake?"

"Give me a break, Li; I didn't take a course on it," Blake replied.

"OK, regardless, that sounds pretty impressive."

"It sure is. Get with Agent Joe Foster and he'll connect you up so you can start listening. At the first hint of anything connected to Harry, call me–and yes, I have a new cell phone, same number. Good hunting, gentlemen."

*****

White House Situation Room

President Callahan, Annie Murphy, Ben Tellinino, Gen. McMullen and Frank Pelino were gathered in the Situation Room in preparation for a call with General Secretary Zhou Qiang.

"Blake, are you on?"

"Yes, Mr. President. I'll be the proverbial fly on the wall."

"Before we call the Chinese, do we have any updates on the Russian front, Gen. McMullen?"

"It's been quiet since our counterattack in Europe, sir. That doesn't mean they aren't planning their next foray, but at this point, we aren't seeing any signs of it. In fairness, they took some pretty heavy tank and troop losses. We estimate no fewer than 472 tanks were destroyed and at least another 150 were damaged, and assuming three or four men per tank, we estimate that they likely had in excess of 1,500 casualties, many of which had to be KIAs."

"I detest the killings, but …"

"Remember, Mr. President, even you acknowledged that they left you with no choice," Annie interjected. "I feel remorse for the soldiers and their families as well, but the blame falls to their Russian leaders, not you. Focus on how many American and European lives you may have just saved–and before you say it, yes, we did lose a few pilots. Those men and women, and their families, I truly mourn for them. They gave the ultimate sacrifice in full awareness of their desire to protect our country and those of our allies–we need to honor the commitment they made and not stop now."

"I know, Annie; it just doesn't sit well, that's all. We may be experiencing here-and-there acts of war, and technically, one could claim we are reacting as if we are at war, but legally, no one has claimed war yet. It's as bizarre a setting as I've ever seen. We have at least two, and maybe even three superpowers, not just making feints and claims against each other, but actually killing each other on a theoretically small enough scale to avoid an escalation to World War III. This is taking insanity to an entirely new level."

"I agree with the insanity statement, Mr. President, but I might disagree or downplay your comments on scale," Gen. McMullen responded. "The magnitude of the attacks on Belarus, Ukraine and our Pacific fleet, let alone our own tank attack, have all been commensurate with the epic battles of World War II, it's just that this has been one-and-out fights, not an unending continuum of battles–so far."

"Just make sure we don't let our guard down, Gen. McMullen, I don't want any more surprises."

"We're doing our best, sir."

"I know, Landon, I trust you." President Callahan put his hand on his general's shoulder.

"OK, it's time: we need to call Qiang. Hook us up, Frank."

A few frustrated minutes went by as Frank worked with the Chinese to get the general secretary on the phone.

"General Secretary Zhou Qiang, this is President Callahan. I think it's safe to assume you know why I'm calling."

"If it's about Taiwan that is none of your business. That is an internal Chinese dispute."

"To be clear, I do not agree with your claim of ownership, and we will be discussing that further, but that is not the source of this immediate call."

"Then what is, Mr. President?"

"Are you suggesting that you are unaware of your fighter jet attack on our White Sands facility–the same facility where the Cjarians have been stationed?"

"I am not familiar with it; are you sure they're ours?"

"J-20 Mighty Dragons. The last I knew, only the Chinese military had those and China was not selling their top-line fighter elsewhere. Is that still a correct assumption, General Secretary?"

A long silence ensued.

"General Secretary? I need to know if you have waged an act of war on my country, or if this was a rogue group of pilots … or if somehow this is just a mistake of monumental stupidity."

"Mr. President, I may need to apologize. I am being informed that we may have had three rogue pilots and their aircraft have gone missing. How many aircraft attacked your base?"

"How coincidental, General Secretary, it was three."

"Where are they now?"

"On the desert floor, and what remains of them will stay there. After we verified that the pilots did not eject, we left them to burn where they were. As I am sure you will understand, we have a lot we are dealing with right now. And just in case you're curious, the Jarisst I survived and has since taken off and departed Earth orbit."

"Yes, I was aware of that."

"That does not surprise me either, General Secretary. So, are you telling me that I can safely assume this was not a sanctioned attack by you or your government, and that I do not have to mobilize my forces further?"

"That would be correct, Mr. President."

"I'll be 100 percent honest with you, General Secretary. Right now, I'm not feeling the sincerity of your response. I will trust that you are being honest with me, but I will not risk standing my forces down. You should also be aware that the three fighters hid themselves from radar by flying underneath a China Airline's passenger-carrying, commercial aircraft. As I recall, that is a state-owned airline, i.e.: yours. For those reasons, I've just shut down all commercial air traffic between our countries, and for that matter, I have received concurrence from the Canadian Prime Minister and the President of Mexico to do likewise. This effectively eliminates any future risk of such a foolish attempt as North America is now off limits to China. Exceptions will be made, but must be approved by my office. In each and every exception, when approved by me, those planes will be escorted by our fighter jets. Those fighters will have authority to act on their own accord and will not have to wait for my approval for action. Furthermore, all Chinese-registered cargo ships will be stopped 22 kilometers from shore at our internationally recognized maritime borders, and searched. Is that understood?"

"I find your response excessive, but it is understood. It would be fair for me to act in equal response against your country as well."

"Agreed." President Callahan responded. "While we are having such open conversation and making such notable progress, I have one more question for you."

"And what would that be?"

"Are you aware of a man named Harry Lundrum, and especially his whereabouts?"

"No, I don't believe I'm familiar with that name. Have I met him before?"

"Never mind, General Secretary. On another topic of high interest, have you heard from Prime Minister Khatri of India?"

"Not recently. Should I expect a call?"

"Yes, I expect you may. She is rather disappointed with recent events in Taiwan and was planning on discussing options with you." President Callahan smiled. "Well, that's enough for this call. Have a good evening, General Secretary."

President Callahan disconnected the call and sat back in his chair.

"Thoughts?"

"What a crock of cow dung," Gen. McMullen responded first.

"That's putting it mildly, General," Annie replied.

"I agree, but that's clearly his line for the time being. Blake, your thoughts?"

"Personally, I think we are better off not believing anything he says right now, which also means that I fully agree with the sanctions you just invoked. Relative to Harry, the general secretary may honestly not know him, but that doesn't mean he isn't behind Harry's disappearance. However, for what it's worth, I don't think it was China."

"Who do you suspect?"

"I don't have the facts to prove it yet, but my gut says it was an internal operation. That leaves one very familiar suspect at the top of the list."

*****

Jarisst I

The Jarisst I was holding near the planet Mars while waiting to hear back from Blake. The crew had maintained reasonably good spirits early on, but that was before the adrenaline surge associated with the attack and subsequent, near-emergency flight to Mars had worn off. Once they were again surrounded by the quiet emptiness of space, and everyone had ample time to reflect on what had almost happened, they'd become shaken over the continued fear of being alone and unable to return home–made worse by the realization that they were no longer safe to land where their only known friends were, on Earth.

Thjars could sense the building risk that the crew would return to a state of hopelessness that had consumed them when they first emerged from their near-eternal sleep one year ago. Just as happened then, he knew he had to keep them busy now as well. He assigned Juulys to monitor Earth-based communications, with special attention on the status of war between the U.S., China and Russia. He then assigned Qulys and Knarls to monitor space around the inner planets so they wouldn't be caught napping by enemy ships, and Platsys to monitor space in the direction of Cjar to see if he could identify any possible sources of friendly contact. The remainder of the engineers and technicians were placed under Jarns's and Allympht's command to continue efforts to repair the Q-PAMS drive. With the recent events, it only increased everyone's desire to fix the Q-PAMS and get back to Cjar–and Thjars was using that to his benefit.

Harry and his scientific team had also been challenged, and defeated, by their inability to resolve the dilemma, but Harry had worked with Allympht to develop a prioritized checklist of issues to further investigate, and that is where Jarns and Allympht decided to start.

Thjars walked into the communications center to check up on Juulys and to see if there were any new developments on Earth.

"Hello, Juulys. Anything new since our departure?"

"No, it's actually been fairly quiet since the attack at White Sands, but Blake did send a message asking you to make contact with him when you had a chance. His message noted that it was not an emergency, so I waited until we ran into each other … now." She smiled.

"Now is as good a time as any. Let's give him a call."

Juulys turned back to her console, pushed a few buttons, hit the speaker and waited. They were quickly rewarded.

"Hello, Cmdr. Thompson here."

"Hello, Blake, it's Juulys and Thjars, returning your call," Juulys replied.

"Ah, it's good to hear from you."

"Did you find Harry yet?" Thjars asked hopefully.

"No, not yet, but the good news is that we believe he's still alive."

"Do you know who is behind his disappearance? Was it the same people who attacked us?"

"No, we don't know yet, but we have some suspicious leads we're chasing down."

Blake, Thjars and Juulys talked for another 10 minutes, exchanging status, objectives and plans. They agreed to continue touching base on a daily basis, before finally disconnecting the call.

*****

Unknown location
Oct. 26, 2029

Harry rolled over onto his left side. His unknown captors had kept him blindfolded and tied up except when it was time to eat or relieve himself. Even then, they remained masked and distant, and said as little as possible. He had no idea why he was kidnapped, who did it or where he was, except that he was in a long, thin rectangular room with padded walls and a metal floor. The door was handle-less and there were no windows.

Harry had been focusing all of his energy on his auditory senses, trying to pick up whatever he could, but had yet to learn anything of real value. Each time a guard left, he could tell that they banged on the door with their rifle butt and shortly thereafter, the door opened and they departed, leaving him in silence until it was time to eat or relieve himself again. Based on the visit frequency and his silent counting, Harry was certain that they had established a two-hour visit frequency during the day and what felt like every four hours during the night. From that, Harry estimated that he had been detained for at least two, maybe two and a half days. During the last visit he was given some poorly prepared scrambled eggs, breakfast, so he was fairly certain that the current time was around 10 in the morning and that someone would be showing up any minute.

Harry was quickly rewarded with the distinct scraping sound of a metal bar sliding against metal. The door opened and footsteps headed toward him.

"I really appreciate you guys allowing me to walk and move my arms every few hours," Harry offered, careful not to give away his time awareness for concern they would start mixing the times up to keep him confused.

No one answered, but he could hear someone breathing.

"Hello?"

No answer, but no boot kick, either, Harry thought, so he ventured further.

"Would it be possible to at least lose the blindfold?" Harry asked. "It's not like I'm going anywhere."

No verbal response was provided, but Harry could clearly make out the fading sound of footsteps as his captor headed back toward the door, followed shortly by the standard exiting protocol.

*****

Two hours passed and the door opened again. This time, the unknown person spoke when he approached Harry. It was a man with a distinctly husky vice.

"Roll onto your stomach," he ordered.

Harry did so, without saying a word. He didn't know if this was the same individual, or someone else. Was it someone coming to talk, or to penalize him for even asking his question two hours earlier? He held his breath and braced himself for a kick or a jab from a rifle butt, but nothing followed. Sixty seconds came and went before the man spoke again.

"If you so much as even attempt to attack or escape, you will be shot instantly. Is that understood?"

"Yes," Harry replied.

"I'm dead serious."

"I can sense that. I believe you."

"I know your history as a SEAL, so was I, so don't think I won't," the man continued.

"Message received, I'm not looking to get shot."

That changed the playing field. The man was from his own SEAL organization. Perhaps it was someone turned rogue, or someone with revenge in his heart for something Harry had no clue of. It really didn't matter as his actions would be the same, Harry thought–except for one thing ... An evil person wouldn't care if someone were uncomfortable or not. This man did. That meant that he was either an expert interrogator, or someone who still had some decency left in his heart. Regardless, the man was a threat that needed to be respected. Stay calm, be good, play the game, Harry thought.

The man untied his hands and told Harry to roll on his back and then untied his feet. Standard protocol to previous visits.

"Same dance. Keep your hands down until I tell you to remove the blindfold."

Harry did as he was commanded, even though he badly wanted to massage his wrists. He heard the man back away and then stop.

"You can remove your blindfold. Do not attempt to turn to see me. Understood?"

"Yes."

Harry reached behind his head and untied the heavy black fabric that had kept him in darkness. He knew the man was behind him, so he took his time, intentionally not turning.

"Thank you," Harry said lightly. "I know you didn't have to do that, so I appreciate it." Harry thought it seemed like the right thing to say, given the circumstances, and the fact that it was simply so good just to be able to see his surroundings.

The man didn't respond.

Harry rubbed his wrists. Then he massaged his ankles. Finally, he began to stretch his arms and his neck.

"Am I allowed to stand up?" Harry questioned his captor.

"In a minute. Let me leave first. There is food on the table, and you know where the pot is. I'll let you have your freedom within this cell, but don't screw with me and don't try to get cute. The truth is, we'll get what we want whether you're alive or dead. The next time I enter, I will have another guard with me. If you do anything, or attempt to set a trap, one of us will shoot you dead. Are we still reading from the same script?"

"Yes."

"I'm placing a red taped X on the floor. Each time I come, you sit on this X and face away from the door. If you miss it one time, we return to the blindfold and ties. Understood?"

"Yes." Harry listened as the man pulled out lengths of tape and placed them on the floor. He then heard the man walk to the door, pound with his rifle butt and then depart after the door opened and quickly closed again. Harry stood up. The red X was immediately behind him. He ate his meager meal, downed a bottle of water and then relieved himself. He scanned the room. He didn't see any obvious cameras, but he expected they must be there somewhere.

"Time to explore my cell," he thought.

*****

White House Rose Garden

The sun stood out brightly in the deep blue Washington, D.C., fall sky as President Callahan and Prime Minister Riddhi Khatri of India held a live press conference from the White House Rose Garden, partially framed a Japanese cherry tree. President Khatri was attired in a traditional saffron-colored Bengal cotton sari, while President Callahan wore a deep blue suit with a bright saffron tie to honor his important ally and guest. It was a stunning picture that would subsequently warrant a very prominent and visible location in both the White House and India's Parliament House, the Sansad Bhavan.

The White House announcement had been equally bold and intentional, with the singular goal to show the world that the United States of America and India stood united. Every news organization in the western world and India were present for the historic occasion. Both President Callahan and Prime Minister Khatri took their turns at the podium, validating the importance of their mutual success, while equally condemning the Chinese invasion of Taiwan.

Following the standard speeches, a ceremonial agreement was signed by both parties, pledging their countries' mutual support, both economically and militarily.

President Callahan smiled as he left the signing table. There would no longer be any doubt in Beijing, or even in Moscow for that matter, that taking on the United States came with taking on the number one military power in the world, but it also now came with taking on the most populous country in the world,

India, which possessed one of the largest active duty armies in the world, second only to China.

*****

CHAPTER 20

Breckenridge, Colo.
Oct. 27, 2029

As planned, Patty, Vladimir, Jimmy and Robert remained in Houston as a backup team in case anything else was needed, as well as to communicate with Juulys relative to any ideas the scientists came up with for the Q-PAMS investigation. Blake, Li, Sean and Diego drove to Breckenridge and arrived just before sunset, driving in a two-vehicle convoy. Li and Sean drove a specially modified, commercial utility van, loaded with the team's gear, while Blake and Sean led the way in a Jeep Wrangler, similar to the one that Blake had enjoyed during their first tour of Colorado.

The foursome pulled over at the top of Hoosier Pass, elevation 3,518 meters, and enjoyed a 15-minute break to soak in the beautiful Colorado view again. The subsequent winding drive down the north side of Hoosier Pass on State Route 9 provided the perfect welcome to what lay ahead in the scenic Breckenridge Valley.

Sixty minutes later, after stopping at the local City Market at 400 North Parkway to load up on supplies, the quartet headed up Ski Hill Road, turned off at Shock Hill Drive and then pulled into Hatari Lodge on Peerless Drive. Joe Foster was there waiting for them and gave them a quick tour of the property they would be staying at, all courtesy of Uncle Sam. Blake thanked him for once again exceeding all expectations as they checked in and unloaded supplies. The lodge, hidden in the trees, was quite ritzy and obviously way above Blake's pay range.

Two hours later, Joe finished briefing the team on the target location where Sen. James Harley's vacation home was located, fewer than 400 meters away at the end of Iron Mask Drive, as well as the equipment they would be using and the additional security tied into their systems. To ensure that Blake's team remained *legally in bounds* at all times, Joe would stay with them and a team of specialists back at Fort Carson would also remain tied in at all times.

Joe showed Li and Blake how to use the surveillance equipment that his team had already set up in their room. They listened in to the chatter from Sen. Harley's vacation home for close to an hour verifying that Harley and his entire family were there. Once everyone was convinced the systems were working to their liking, then Li and Sean agreed to take the 10-hour long, late night shift until 1 in the morning, while Blake and Diego would take the 10-hour long, early morning shift starting at 5. If Harley planned any suspicious calls with his family present, it would likely be late at night, early in the morning, or in one of his vehicles, but they all were comfortable that the 1 a.m. to 5 a.m. window was safe to assume that everyone in the house would be sleeping. The good news was that everything was bugged and everything was being recorded, so nothing would be missed even if it were during the four-hour window in the morning.

It was time to wait.

*****

Philippine Sea
Oct. 30, 2029

The U.S. Pacific Fleet's ability to operate at full battle readiness had been impacted by the Russian submarine attack on the USS Kennedy two weeks earlier. As a means of reinforcement, a significant segment of the U.S. Third Fleet, stationed out of San Diego, had been sent to reinforce the Seventh Fleet, now including CSG Nine, led by the USS Theodore Roosevelt, CSG One, led by the USS Carl Vinson, and CSG Five, led by the USS Ronald Reagan. The formidable power of the combined CSGs was now centered in the Philippine Sea and western Pacific Ocean, and protected by a 24-7 CAP of F-35 Lightning II and F/A-18E/F strike fighters, as well as a flotilla of destroyers, submarines and other support ships. In addition, the U.S. also maintained the USS Abraham Lincoln CSG stationed at Yokosuka, Japan that could also be brought to battle if needed.

The CSGs, each separated by hundreds of kilometers of empty ocean, had assembled over the past 72 hours and were awaiting the arrival of the promised Indian contingency in the next day or two. India was sending its two aircraft carrier groups, the INS Vikrant and the brand new INS Vishal. U.S. Adm. Mack Young would be in charge of the combined U.S. and India fleets, and maintained his flag on the USS Theodore Roosevelt.

These six aircraft carriers and their associated defense and support ships would be contested by China's three aircraft carriers, as well as a significant risk associated with land-based fighters and missiles. It was not President Callahan's desire to go to war; rather his intent was to project a strong message to China that would convince them to exit Taiwan. The U.S. carrier forces were clearly the best in the world; there wasn't even a close second, but with the advent of precision nuclear weapons and highly-accurate, long-range, supersonic anti-ship missiles, President Callahan feared that the day of the aircraft carrier might be passing–just like that of the famous battleships after World War II. If his worst fears were realized, then he was placing more than 40,000 U.S. and Indian sailors at risk.

Gen. McMullen understood President Callahan's concern, but had convinced him that the anti-missile capabilities of no fewer than 20 destroyers and over 400 fighter aircraft from the combined fleet, as well as the multiple squadrons of F-16s, F-18s, F-22s, F-35s and drones that had been flown in to Japan, the Philippines and Guam, would provide a formidable defensive and offensive capability. In addition, the U.S submarine-launched missile capabilities, and the two-fisted stealth bomber punch from the B-2 and newer B-21 rounded out a powerful message for detente. If the Chinese did start a shooting war, there was little doubt that devastating U.S. retaliatory strikes would follow, and those strikes could easily include military target options outside of China, as well as on mainland China itself.

The combined total of nine carrier groups represented the largest collection of aircraft carrier combatants the world had ever seen in a single battle arena, but the bigger questions that remained unanswered were: what would the Russians do and what were they already planning? In today's age of satellite surveillance, there would be no hiding the fact that the U.S. was coming to Taiwan's aid, so President Callahan also knew that both the Chinese, and the Russians, had a choice to make. Would they call the U.S. action a bluff and stand their ground, or would they reconsider the risks and initiate a pullout from Taiwan? Worse yet, if a standoff did occur, then President Callahan was putting the U.S. in a position of backing down and withdrawing in front of the entire world, or initiating an attack–the latter of which he had great hesitation to do.

After the events of last year and the trust he had developed with Blake and Harry, the President, even knowing that Harry had been kidnapped, still requested that at least Blake be pulled into the final debrief. As expected, Blake sided with Gen. McMullen. Blake held firm that this was one of those critical line-in-the-sand moments where the U.S. would need to show the world that they were still the preeminent military power and their allies could continue to trust the U.S. had their backs. If not, Taiwan would be lost and the U.S would have backed down from the neighborhood bullies on the world stage. Additionally, the risks that both the Chinese and Russians would be further emboldened to attack U.S. and allied interests would only escalate. Blake further suggested that it really wasn't worth debating if a potential American attack might start a war, as the first shot had already been fired by the other side. If the President balked on taking the second shot, then he shouldn't have sent his fleet in the first place.

*****

Breckenridge
Oct. 31, 2029

They'd been on stakeout for three days now and other than standard business calls or discussions with friends about upcoming dinner outings, they had nothing. It was Halloween night and the senator had trick-or-treat aged children, so the expectation was set that everyone would be out trick-or-treating and the duo was in for another long, dull night. Sean and Li were debating who had the most boring shift–theirs at night, or Blake and Diego's in the morning–when their one-sided debate was interrupted by a knock at the door.

"Who the heck could that be?" Sean asked.

"I don't know, maybe the landlord?" Li replied.

"Go check it out; I'll keep listening."

Li headed to the front door, peeped through the eyehole and then opened the door.

"Well, if this doesn't seal the deal on you making agent of the year, I don't know what will. Check it out, Sean!"

"Damn, pizza! You da man, Joe. Better yet, I dub you Super Joe from here on out. Where'd you find it?"

"A place called Fatty's Pizzeria on Ridge Street. It's a Sicilian deep dish, New York-style with the works. I figured that would be right up your alley, Sean."

"Sure as heck is, but what about Li? One pizza is only enough for me." Sean laughed.

"I'll bet you 20 you can't finish this puppy in one sitting by yourself, but just to be safe, I got something else for Li as well."

"And what that might be?" Li asked innocently.

"Blake ratted on you and told me you claim to be a connoisseur of sushi, so I picked up a big smorgasbord of various samples from the Wasabi Japanese restaurant on Main Street."

"Joe, you have no idea how much we appreciate this. Come on in and join us."

The three men ate heartily while discussing what had transpired over the past three days. They were disappointed not to have picked anything up yet, but Joe had warned them it was a 50/50 proposition at best and that these types of surveillance assignments could last days or even weeks before picking up anything of interest.

"Joe, I don't know how anyone could ever want an office job; I'd go stark raving mad if I had to sit like this every day I went to work," Sean vented. "The only thing keeping us remotely sane is our afternoon run just before we relieve Blake and Diego. Other than that, we might as well be locked up somewhere."

"Unfortunately, with every good gig, there's always some trash that comes with it," Joe replied.

"On the positive side," Li interjected, "the air is so crisp and clean up here, and the sky so amazingly blue, now I understand why Blake kept calling it God's country."

"Amen to that, but I still haven't seen a moose. All those stories about moose, I'm beginning to think it's all an old wives tale, just like Bigfoot," Sean complained.

"Trust me, Sean," Joe replied, "If you do see one close up, you may wish you hadn't. Not only are they bigger than you would imagine, but they can be downright nasty if you cross their path."

"Well, I'm still waiting." Sean continued griping.

"I'm assuming you can track his car location as well, right?" Li decided to change the discussion back to the topic at hand.

"Sure can, Li," Joe replied, "but they're all home eating dinner right now, correct, Sean?"

"Sounds like it. The missus cooked up lasagna, garlic bread and cheesecake. Like that SOB deserves her, a good lasagna or especially that cheesecake—I'd kill for that right now," Sean chided. "How about we go bust his door down right now and run off with the cheesecake? ... Wait a minute: sounds like dinner is over and they may be heading out."

Sean turned the sound control to speaker mode to let Li and Joe listen in.

"Whoa, so he's skipping out on the kids' trick-or-treating night. Sounds like the neighborhood moms are in charge tonight."

"If you don't mind," Joe volunteered, "I just might stick around for a bit ... let's see: it's 6:45 ... that's 8:45 back east. Maybe he has a conference call planned that we can listen in on."

"Always good to have you around, Super Joe. Beers are in the fridge."

As it turned out, Sen. Harley did have a conference call, but it was standard D.C. bureaucratic red tape—nothing of interest. A full hour later, they were still batting zero.

"Where's the missus at, Joe? Maybe we still have time for him to take another call," Sean asked.

"Looks like they're at the Outlets at Silverthorne. Must be one of those sites where the kids just go from store to store and get candy handouts."

"Well, that suggests we have at least another 45 minutes, if not more before they get back home," Li concluded.

"Hey, I think we got another call coming in," Sean interrupted Li.

"Hello."

"Are we good?"

"Yes, they're all out trick-or-treating."

"This line still clean?"

"Yes, no one even knows I have it."

"That's what you think, asshole," Sean whispered. "It's that untraceable phone you guys identified. I'll bet it's a damn burner phone from Walmart. Wanna bet? Li, can you get a fix on it while he's talking? What's that term you used, some fancy MIT triangle bull crap? I'd love to be able to get a lock on this one."

"On it, Sean. By the way, it's called triangulation."

"Triangles, squares, tetrahedrals, I don't care what you call them; put your hacking hat on and hack that SOB."

"Anything new on Colburn?"

"They're convinced it was an intentional hit and he was murdered, but they have no idea who's behind it," Harley replied.

"The inner circles are talking."

"Yeah, what are they saying?"

"They claim that damn Thompson is throwing your name around."

"Shit. That pain in the ass doesn't know when to stay out of things. Him and that damn android Harry of his are pissing me off. Speaking of Blake, what are they saying about the bust he made at the Air Force game?"

"That's been pretty tight, too, but they know it's our ammunition and they're snooping around the facility in Bend, Ore., and asking lots of questions. Have they called you yet?"

"No, not yet, but thanks for the heads up. Are you still at the cabin?"

"Yes, best vacation I've had in a long time and the hunting is great."

Both men laughed.

"Son of a bitch!" Sean barked.

"What?" Joe replied.

"Could it be the same cabin you guys went to?" Li asked Sean.

"Wake up Blake and Diego. They need to hear this now. Joe and I will keep listening in case anything else comes up."

Two minutes later, the trio expanded to a quintet and the five men huddled around the speaker, soaking in every word. The call didn't last much longer.

"Can you replay it from the beginning, Li?"

"Sure thing, Blake, hang on."

"Did you get the triangle on that phone?" Sean asked.

"Triangulate, you dumb Mick," Li laughed. "Oh yeah, I can definitely pick this phone up again, and with the NSA's help, we should be able to find past recorded discussions as well–this may be the break we've been waiting on."

They listened through the short recording three times and when they were done, everyone looked at Blake.

"I need to call the White House and let them know that Mr. Harley just cemented the top position on the suspect list."

"Then what?" Sean queried, smiling like he already knew the answer.

"Correct, we are going back to Resolution Mountain."

But Blake wasn't smiling. Blake looked more like the Grim Reaper returned in the flesh.

"Load up the Jeep; we're leaving tonight," Blake continued. "Joe, you're staying at the resort to keep an ear on this. Call me if anything comes up."

"I agree that the senator's comments on a secret phone smell and smell badly, but are you sure you want to spring the trap this quickly?" Joe asked. "Regardless, I should notify my superiors."

"Notify who you need to, Joe, but tell them to stay the hell out of the way. I screwed up everything in New Mexico–this is my fault. I lost Harry and I almost lost the group I was in New Mexico to protect. This one is mine to fix and mine alone, and I need to make sure I know who is where on the battlefield without any surprises."

"Who were you protecting, Blake?"

"It's classified," Blake grumbled back.

"Just being careful, Blake. If there's one thing the FBI does well, it's to teach their agents to not jump the gun–especially if there are government entities involved."

"Right now, I could give a crap about Harley. This is about getting Harry back. I'll deal with Harley after that."

"We don't know if Harley is guilty or not," Joe responded, still trying to slow Blake down.

"Joe, I'm sure you've had many times over your career where you had to rely on your gut instincts and your intuition. Well, it's been the same for me, but I've learned that it's better to jump fast and deal with cleanup when I was wrong versus not jumping fast enough and then having to deal with a loss that can't be taken back. This is Harry. This is personal. And my gut is screaming at me that Harry's up there. Remember that microwave receipt? This has Harley written all over it. If it makes you feel better, President Callahan will be aware of all of it."

"OK, there's obviously no stopping you, but before you wake up the president, let me make a quick call."

Ten minutes later, Joe hung up his phone.

"I called NORAD. They've been doing a lot of satellite monitoring on this topic because of the death of one senator and the possible attempt on a second. Anything we bring up, they add to their tracking list–including Resolution Mountain from your first visit."

"And?"

"You can say you told me so, but … there is definite human activity at the Resolution Mountain cabin. I know this is your battle, Blake, but I'll have a Blackhawk chopper loaded and ready just in case you need backup."

*****

"President Callahan here, and by the way, it's almost midnight. This better be good, Blake."

"I need three minutes. I need your approval."

"Go on."

Three and a half minutes later, Blake hung up and turned to his close-knit group.

"Saddle up, gentlemen."

*****

Beijing, China
Nov. 1, 2029

"Prime Minister Riddhi Khatri?"

"Yes, this is she."

"This is Zhou Qiang, general secretary and president of China."

"And what may I ask is the subject of this call?"

"It is rather delicate, but highly critical and time-sensitive in nature. We need to talk openly with each other."

"I'm listening."

"I acknowledge that you've already publicly stated that you do not agree with our country's effort to unite the island of Taiwan with its rightful country, the People's Republic of China, but I am not here to debate that right now. Rather I would like to discuss your two aircraft carriers that appear to be heading toward the Philippines to meet up with the Americans."

"I am not at liberty to share information on classified military maneuvers."

"We do not have much time, Prime Minister."

"Perhaps you need to be clearer, General Secretary."

"Perhaps I do. Let me try this. If your ships join the American effort and the American ships initiate an attack on my country and the people of the Republic of China, we will not be able to distinguish between your ships and those of the Americans in a retaliatory strike."

"I am supporting a request of a key ally of India and you invaded a free and independent country."

"I told you that I do not have much time, Madame Prime Minister; you should be taking my comments seriously."

"Nor do I, General Secretary, and you should be taking mine seriously as well."

"How many astronauts are on your current moon flight, five? Are they not within a day of reaching the moon?"

"What has that got to do with your country invading Taiwan?"

"It would be a shame if your astronauts were to experience an accident so far from home, Madame Prime Minister."

"Are you threatening our astronauts and our mission?"

"I'm just suggesting that these are very tenuous times, Madame Prime Minister. You need to make your decisions accordingly. Good day, Madame Prime Minister."

The call disconnected.

*****

Resolution Mountain, Colo.

A little over two hours later at just after two in the morning, Blake exited at Camp Hale and found Resolution Road #702, where he pulled the Jeep over to the side of the road and killed the lights. All four men donned their night vision goggles and began the slow drive toward the camp near Resolution Mountain.

Once they cleared Ptarmigan Pass, Blake found the same pullover they'd used last time prior to approaching the camp, but this time was different. This time, they knew the camp had occupants based on the satellite imagery Joe had received from NORAD. There could be more in the buildings, but the two that were identified clearly looked like they were posted as sentries at a set distance from the camp.

"We're on foot from here. I'll take the north approach. Diego, you take the south. Li, you have the west, and Sean, that leaves you with the eastern approach. We're about 1,200 meters from the camp, but we need to approach slowly until we know what we're dealing with. Check back in 30 minutes. That should give each of us time to get to our post and survey our zones. If there are two sentries, then that suggests there has to be at least two backups and maybe one or two more leading the group, so I'm estimating a minimum of five potential combatants. Any questions?"

"If they've got Harry, they're in for a mighty rude awakening," Sean volunteered first.

"Let's get moving," Blake replied, and the four men disappeared into the darkness with their night goggles on.

*****

Thirty minutes later, all four men checked in. It was 3 a.m., cold and quiet. From what the four could see, there were, indeed, two sentries. The sentries each covered 180-degree segments of the camp's perimeter, about 50 meters out from the camp, moving in opposite directions to ensure they were never at the same intersection point. One had the east side and one had the west. It was now quite clear that this was not a typical hunting party.

"First blush, they looked guilty as sin," Sean volunteered, "but it's hard to know if they are Harry-guilty, drug-guilty, or something-else guilty."

"Roger that," Blake responded. "We need to interrogate at least one of these guys. Diego, you move in on the eastern sentry and I'll take the western one. Sean and Li will cover for us. Once the guard makes his turn to head back the other direction, that's when we'll take them, simultaneously. Did anyone see any signs of night vision gear?"

"None."

"OK, Diego, let's move into position. Sean, I won't be able to see Diego because the cabin blocks our view. You make the call on timing."

"Oorah."

It took at least another 20 minutes to get into position as there was only a small time window where they could move without being seen by either of the two sentries, but they finally made it. Blake and Diego both gave a wave that could easily be seen by Sean and Li with their night vision goggles.

The guards continued communicating with each other every third turn. Definitely a good move for security purposes, but more than likely just to ensure no one fell asleep. Blake was confident that this turn was the communication turn and whispered into his mic.

"This turn, Diego. Sean, you call it. Li, keep us clean."

As the men approached the opposite ends of their path, each pulled up their radio. As soon as they started talking, Sean gave the signal and both Blake and Diego bolted out of their hiding spots and tackled their targets. Blake cupped his target's mouth with one hand and held a knife to the man's throat with his other hand, letting his momentum carry the two of them to the ground.

"If you want to live to see the sunrise, keep your mouth shut and don't resist," Blake whispered into the man's ear. "Otherwise,

I'll leave you out here for the wildlife to feed on your carcass. Nod if you understand."

The man nodded. Diego found a similar result with his sentry.

"Do you have a captive at this site?" Blake asked his captive.

No response.

Blake rolled onto his back with his captive on top and scissor locked his legs around the man, simultaneously holding the blade of his KA-BAR knife on the man's jugular vein.

"Don't make me ask again. No answer means yes, and you're done."

The man nodded.

"Good answer. What's his name? And you better whisper."

"Some egghead named Harry, that's all I know. I've only seen him once."

"Very good. See how easy this is? Now, is he still OK?"

"Yes."

"You're almost a millionaire. Three more questions. Where?"

"In the shipping container."

"How many guys?"

"Eleven, maybe 12. A couple of guys come and go, or are monitoring at a wider distance from the camp. I really don't know more than that."

"Who is paying you?"

"I don't know."

"Do you think I was born yesterday?"

"Look, man, I really don't know. There's one guy running the show and a big dude that seems to be his right-hand man. There are four of us sentries that take six-hour shifts in pairs. The two main guys don't have names, but they're paying us a thousand bucks a day–good money that's hard to come by. The other four guys are always armed, but haven't done anything yet. That's all I know. I'm telling you the truth."

Blake rolled the man over, tied his hands and feet behind his back and gagged him.

"You hit me as a guy that walked over the wrong line, but can still be salvaged. Stay here and stay quiet, and I'll come back to get you when we're done.

"Diego, what do you have?"

"This guy wouldn't talk, and then the mulehead actually tried to call a warning in."

"And?"

"Well, he's not talking now, and won't be for a while. He's unconscious, hog tied and gagged. How about your guy?"

"Tied and gagged, but he talked. Harry is here and there are eight more guys, four of which sound like possible mercs."

*****

White House

"President Callahan, thank you for taking my call. I apologize for calling so early, but it is urgent. I'm very worried that the Chinese have the ability to attack our lunar spacecraft."

"Why would you think that?" President Callahan responded.

Prime Minister Riddhi Khatri quickly updated the president on what General Secretary Zhou Qiang said to her.

"How could he possibly attack our spacecraft when it is already approaching lunar orbit?"

"I'm afraid he can, Madame Prime Minister," President Callahan replied and then explained what the Cjarians had accidentally discovered in the moon's shadow and relayed to Blake.

"It appears that the Chinese have built and placed into full operation a rail gun that can hurl objects at oncoming ships. If their attack is detected early enough, you may have the ability to shoot down or avoid impact once the object's trajectory has been determined. Based on what we know, they are dumb rounds without the ability to steer and change course, but it won't be long before they graduate to something more lethal. Unfortunately, the closer you get to the moon, the less time your crew will have to react to a nearby attack."

"Then he is basically telling me to withdraw my carriers or he will destroy our lunar spacecraft and the astronauts on board. I can't back out of our support for the United States or Taiwan's right for freedom, but I also can't stand by and watch my astronauts be executed in front of the entire world. What options do I have?"

"I'm not sure. Do you have enough fuel to turn away from the moon and still return to Earth?"

"I will check, but I highly doubt it."

"He expects you to approach the moon from the left side based on your current trajectory. Is there any chance you could change your approach to the right and buy yourself more time?"

"I have no idea, but I will ask that as well."

"Did he give you a deadline?"

"No, but he said that time was of critical essence. This is not making me feel any more confident, Mr. President."

"I understand, Madame Prime Minister. Let me talk with my staff and see if we have any options that could possibly help. I will get back to you later today."

"Thank you, Mr. President."

Prime Minister Riddhi Khatri hung up and immediately called the chairman of the Indian Department of Space.

*****

Resolution Mountain

"Shit, heads up, guys," Sean whispered into his mic.

"What?" Blake asked.

"We've got company. Our luck may have just run out. Looks like the next shift is coming this way."

"Double that, this guy's radio just buzzed. I'll bet they're trying to contact him right now," Diego added.

"What are the ground rules, Blake?" Sean requested.

"The gloves are officially off."

"We started at four-on-10, now it's four-on-eight; Li, how about we make it four on six-on-six real quick like? I'll take the left one, you take the right."

"Ready when you are," Li replied almost instantly.

"Three, two, one," Diego whispered and then yelled ... "Hey, what the hell are you guys doing up here?"

His yell was answered with automatic gunfire.

Two return rifle shots echoed through the trees so simultaneously that it sounded like a single shot, and two men dropped to the ground.

"Eyes sharp, expect a response and assume the next wave has night vision gogg ...," Blake didn't even finish his statement before the night lit up with ground-launched, parachute flares and gunfire erupted from the cabins.

"Hit the deck!" Blake yelled while ripping off his night vision goggles, knowing that they were all momentarily blinded from the flares.

The gunfire was intense. Blake directed everyone to lay low until they reloaded, then to lay down a countering barrage and each head to separate positions with better cover. He wanted to keep all four compass positions manned so that the cabin inhabitants had nowhere safe to hide. When the shooting finally slowed down, Blake yelled out.

"Counter!"

The foursome laid down a withering fire as they headed to the best nearby protection they could find. Blake and Li both found rock outcroppings to hide behind while Sean found a shallow dip behind a bush and Diego found a large pine tree to hide behind the trunk. At least one man cried out in pain near the northernmost cabin. The glow of the two descending flares projected an eerie light across the area.

Blake decided to test the waters and offer the unknown men surrender terms to see how they would respond.

"We have you surrounded. Drop your guns and place your hands on top of your heads!"

Blake had just enough time to lean back behind the rock outcropping as bullets whizzed by and zinged off the rock cover directly in front of him. A rather direct rejection of his proposal, he thought.

"Anyone have a bead on these guys?"

A rifle shot rang out and registered the unmistakable thud that only a direct hit on a body could make.

"I'll take *yes* for 500, Alex," Sean replied matter-of-factly. "Make that four-on-five now. I'm waiting for the guy on the western edge of the northernmost cabin to stick his head out for one more peek and it'll be four-on-four."

Blake could hear the men talking, but couldn't make out what they were saying. It seemed like they were having a conference.

Either these guys were damn lucky or this layout was intentionally made in order to create a small safe area in the center between the buildings, shipping container and their vehicles.

"I can't see any of them, and for all we know, they have guys inside at the windows as well," Diego added.

Just then, a new sound emanated from near the buildings. It started with a deeper thud from a round exiting a rifle, followed by a weird whizzing sound, and then all hell broke loose as shrapnel shredded the bushes and trees around them.

"They're using the Starburst rounds!" Blake yelled. "Keep moving so they can't lock in on your location!"

Unfortunately, Blake found himself pinned down and assumed the others were as well. The flares were too bright to remain hidden, even with the trees.

"Take the flares out!"

All four started firing into the sky and the two flares dropped from the sky as their chutes became riddled with bullet holes.

The battlefield was once again dark, but the enemy now knew their approximate position locations and were homing in. These guys were pros. They were using the Starbursts to, at the least, flush them out, if not injure them, and once in the open, they would use their assault rifles to mow them down.

"Scatter!" Blake yelled.

The firing intensified.

"I'm hit!"

It was Sean. Blake knew they were badly outgunned and it was only a matter of time before they took another hit. He thought about calling in Joe's Blackhawk, but knew he would be putting those troops in harm's way before they even landed.

"Diego, you get to Sean. Li, light the bastards up. I'm going to take out those Starbursts … Now!"

Li let loose with an entire magazine on the area between the buildings as Blake sprinted straight toward the cluster. Starbursts continued to fly over his head as bullets whizzed by. At least one tore through his left sleeve and he felt a quick burning sensation, but Blake kept sprinting toward the camp. As he closed in on the northernmost building, the glass shattered on one window and a rifle barrel rotated into the opening with a dark shape behind it. Blake let loose a quick rip from his Heckler & Koch

HK416 assault rifle and was rewarded with a definite hit inside the window.

Now it was four-on-four, perhaps three-on-four, depending on Sean's condition.

Blake sped past the edge of the northernmost building, exploding into the protected center. Two men were firing what must have been the Starbursts over the top of the cabin. Blake mowed both men down before either could respond.

Two left, but where were they?

Blake ran to the side of the first truck and yelled into the darkness.

"There's only two of you left. This is your last chance to surrender."

A voice answered from near the shipping container.

"What makes you think you have the better negotiation hand?"

"The fact that you just lost eight men."

"Yes, but you came for your man, didn't you?"

Blake chose not to answer.

"What's his name? Harry Lundblad, I believe. So let me make you an offer. You put your guns down and put your hands on top of your head, and then call your other men in one at a time to do the same thing."

"I don't see that version of this engagement happening," Blake replied.

"If you don't, then I blow the shipping container and you can have whatever is left of your friend."

"You're bluffing," Blake replied. "The metal shell will protect him."

"Am I? Will it? I think not. The explosives are on the inside. We know you were here once already, so we wanted an extra insurance policy in case you somehow found your way back."

A chill crept up Blake's spine, but before he could respond, Diego and Sean burst through the trees on the far side of the shipping container, guns blazing. The last two men desperately returned fire, but it was obviously a lost cause. As the last man fell to his knees, he pushed the detonator button in his hand and the charges detonated inside the shipping container with a deafening *vvwhoomp*!

"Harry," was all Blake could muster to whisper.

Blake and Li ran over to Diego and Sean. Both were injured. Diego had taken a round to his left leg, but it appeared to be a clean exit wound without damage to the bone or any major blood vessels. Diego refused assistance and pointed at Sean. Sean was another matter. He had taken shrapnel from the Starburst rounds earlier in the melee, but had still kept fighting. He took at least two rounds during their final attack, one in the midsection, and was bleeding heavily.

"Li, help slow the bleeding. I'll call in the Blackhawk. Sean, hang in there; help is on the way."

Blake picked up his satellite phone and called Agent Foster.

"Joe, we need a medic and we need one quick, Sean's shot up pretty bad. How quick can you get here?"

"The chopper is at the Camp Hale exit. It'll be there in two minutes and I'm on it with eight Army Rangers and one medic."

"Thanks, Joe. I'll drop a ground flare where you can land. We need to get him to a hospital ASAP. Call ahead."

Blake dropped the flare then walked over to the smoking shipping container. Anyone inside was clearly gone. Why Harry, he thought, he was the best of the best.

Diego watched him and called out. "Blake, we didn't know."

"I know."

Blake walked toward the Blackhawk as it descended near the flare.

Once on the ground, the personnel unloaded. Blake pointed the medic toward Sean and directed four of the Rangers to find the two men back in the trees they had tied up. He asked the other four to search the cabins.

"Blake, you're injured." Joe pointed at his arm.

"I'm fine. We need to open this shipping container. Come look at the door."

Li looked over at Diego. "It was Harry! What the hell's wrong with him? He's like a damn robot."

"It's the way he's programmed himself. Ever since he lost his father in the 9/11 attack, he tries not to let anyone get emotionally close, but Harry is family; we are family. He doesn't know how to handle it, so he's trying to push it out of his head. That way he can stay focused on task and not go down that deep dark hole he remembers from 9/11. It's how he rewired himself to survive. But, he's a hell of a soldier and a great friend, so you just have to keep reminding yourself not to take it personally."

"Kind of sad, when you think about it."

"It sure is, Li, it sure is."

*****

CHAPTER 21

White House

"Hello, Thjars, this is President Callahan."

"It's good to hear from you, Mr. President."

"I hope you and your crew are doing well and are safe. Is there anything you need?"

"No, we are doing fine, thank you. Other than repairing our Q-PAMS drive, we have everything we need, especially after you helped repair our fuel tanks for our sub-light speed engines."

"That's good to hear, Thjars. I'd normally have Blake contact you, but he is currently unavailable and I have a serious issue I'd like to discuss with you, and perhaps Qulys as well."

"Qulys is here with me. I hope Blake is OK."

"He is, but he's on a mission. Hello, Qulys."

"Hello Mr. President," Qulys replied

"What is the issue?" Thjars asked.

President Callahan spent the next few minutes updating Thjars and Qulys on what had transpired since they had departed Earth and how a potential global war was on the verge of breaking out.

"To be clear, Thjars, I do not want you to get involved in our war. However, in times of need, especially relative to a spacecraft emergency, I am willing to ask for your help–even though I humbly acknowledge that we have yet to complete our promises we made to you and your crew."

"Mr. President, you have not failed due to lack of effort or intention. Where you have failed, we have failed as well. In contrast, you have done many things to help us that we were unable to achieve by ourselves, so for that reason, I thank you, for myself and my crew."

"You are most generous, Thjars. Thank you."

"So, what is the current problem you would like to discuss?"

"We are concerned that the Chinese are threatening to shoot down an unarmed, manned spacecraft from India in free space on a scientific mission, heading into orbit around the moon."

"Why would they do such a thing?"

"Because India has sided with the United States in our request for China to end hostilities with their neighboring country, Taiwan. We believe they plan on using the rail gun you discovered."

"That would be terrible. What can we do to help?"

"That is the million dollar question. I do not want to put your ship at risk, nor do I want to injure or permanently maroon any of the Chinese occupants on the rail gun, but I want to protect the Indian spacecraft. Do you or Qulys have any ideas?"

The call went silent for a few seconds, and then Qulys spoke up.

"I believe we have an option that can accommodate all of your objectives. How soon do we need to act?"

"I'm afraid I don't know, but I believe we don't have much time."

"We'll get started immediately," Thjars replied. "Is there anything else?"

"Yes." President Callahan paused. "I need to ask … why are you willing to fulfill my request?"

Thjars answered without hesitation. "We've watched you and Blake and how you handle things, as well as how you speak. We have no doubt of your integrity or your intention. For example, you could have asked us to destroy the ship. You didn't. You could have asked us to join your side of the war. Not only did you not, but you requested that we stay out of it for our own safety. Finally, what you did ask for was to stop an aggressor without killing them. That is honorable. We trust our friendship with you and Blake."

"Thank you, Thjars. For what it's worth, that means a lot. I will relay to the prime minister of India that she can expect assistance to ensure the safety of her astronauts. Please be safe."

*****

Resolution Mountain

The medic assessed Sean's wounds and began treatment as they loaded him onto the Blackhawk. Blake asked if he was going to make it and the medic could only answer with a "We'll do all we can," before he boarded the Blackhawk. They were back in the air fewer than 10 minutes after landing and headed toward Porter Adventist Hospital in Parker, Colo., just south of Denver, where a team of surgeons was prepped and waiting.

An hour later, a second chopper arrived with a metal cutting torch to remove the cargo door and an FBI forensics team to collect evidence from the site. During the delay, the Rangers had discovered Harry's wallet on a desk in the main cabin as they conducted a full sweep of the property. They located Blake and handed it to him. Blake slid the wallet into his vest pocket and quietly thanked the Rangers.

As the Colorado sun rose, the Fort Carson techs finally burned through the door hinges and then used a winch to pry the door back. A quick look inside was all they needed to verify that someone had been in it, but it would take a forensic team days to validate it was Harry. Blake didn't need days to know the answer.

Joe informed Blake that after the forensics team was done, a CH-47 would be sent to lift the shipping container and fly it over to the Camp Hale exit where a flatbed truck would be waiting to haul it back to Fort Carson, but that would likely be days from now, if not longer, due to all of the evidence that needed to be collected. Joe offered Blake a ride back on the Blackhawk, but Blake turned it down. He directed Li and Diego to go with Agent Foster, but said he would drive the Jeep. There was no debating his decision and it was clear Blake wanted time by himself. It would be the end of a very long night when he finally returned to Breckenridge.

Agent Foster reached out to shake Blake's hand. "Blake, I'm sorry. I know how much Harry meant to you and this team, but I also have to warn you that you can't approach Sen. Harley. He is strictly out of bounds until we have clear evidence of his involvement. We will have Secret Service agents assigned to him in order to ensure his safety and that of his family. Is that clear?"

Blake nodded.

"Are you sure you don't want company?"

Blake nodded again.

"Drive safely, my friend; we don't need any more losses."

Agent Joe Foster released his grip, turned and headed toward the helicopter.

*****

Moon Orbit

"So, Qulys, what's the plan?" Thjars asked.

"Get Juulys up here; we'll need her assistance."

Ten minutes later, Qulys outlined his plan to Juulys and Thjars.

"I like it, Qulys," Thjars replied, "but Juulys, how well do you think you can speak Chinese?"

"Not great, but I think well enough to pull off what Qulys is asking for, especially if I drive a more one-way dictatorial approach."

"You, dictatorial?" Thjars challenged humorously.

"Normally, not, but I can't tolerate wicked things … it reminds me too much of the Klaxx … and if this planned attack on the Indian astronauts is real, then it is truly wicked and must be stopped. So, yes, I can be dictatorial."

"Good Glysst, Thjars, remind me not to make her angry at me!" Qulys chuckled.

"Let's get started, Qulys. I think we need to move quickly based on President Callahan's timing concerns."

*****

Nov. 2, 2029

Blake kept in constant contact with the hospital as he drove back. Sean was in bad shape and had lost a lot of blood, but the surgeons had been able to stop the bleeding and stabilize him. Fortunately, there hadn't been any major damage to his internal organs. The biggest remaining risks were from hypovolemic shock or infection, both of which the hospital team was well prepared to monitor and treat. The lead doctor informed Blake that Sean would likely remain unconscious for a couple of days, but he promised to call if there were any change in his status, for better or worse.

As Blake drove back to Breckenridge, he reanalyzed the events of the past 24 hours in his head, over and over. In his mind, Harry's loss was one more example of his recent string of failures. He evaluated various options he could've taken, but none of them guaranteed a better outcome. Even if he had allowed the Rangers to join the mission, without the knowledge of the Starburst ammunition, there would have been more injured or dead soldiers. From the perspective of personnel loss, a small force was still the best answer to the surprise enemy stronghold they had encountered. They also couldn't have known about the booby-trapped shipping container. And even if Diego and Sean had overheard the discussion where Blake was directed to drop his gun, Blake still would have attacked exactly as they did. It would have been certain death for all had they surrendered–that fact Blake was convinced of. From every angle Blake approached, they still lost.

Blake made it back to Breckenridge and spent the rest of the day documenting the events of the past 24 hours and collecting his gear to head out. Sen. Harley had departed Breckenridge that morning to head back to Washington, D.C., which is exactly where Blake intended to go. The FBI would continue monitoring Harley's vacation home if and when he returned.

*****

USSTRATCOM

"Gen. Beckman, this is Gen. Whittler. We have just detected an explosion near the moon. It also appears that the Chinese rail gun has broken into pieces. We are trying to get a higher resolution satellite into position, but from what we can see, the rail gun has been destroyed."

"That's good news, General. I'll relay to the White House. Let us know when you have more details."

*****

Jarisst I

"Thjars, President Callahan is on the line."

"OK, picking up now."

"Mr. President, this is Thjars."

"Hello, Thjars, thank you for taking my call. I also have Blake on the line."

"We will always make time to talk to you or Blake, but with both on, that's even better. Hello, Blake."

"Hello, Thjars. It's good to hear you as well. How are Qulys and Juulys doing?" Blake intentionally did not mention Harry.

"They are on as well, and doing fine. I expect I know why President Callahan is calling."

"You are correct, Thjars. I received word that the rail gun has been destroyed. May I ask what happened?"

"Absolutely, but I wouldn't exactly say 'destroyed,' more like it has been dismantled."

"But we recorded an explosion," President Callahan said.

"That is also correct."

"If I didn't know better, I expect Thjars is smiling right now," Blake interjected.

"And that is also correct." Thjars chuckled. "Let me explain."

"Thank Glysst that Juulys is such an accomplished and versatile linguist. She struggles more with the Chinese dialect pronunciation than she does English, but she has been practicing all of the major dialects of Earth for over a year now, so all in all, she did very well. As you may recall, Juulys is steadfast on not killing anyone, but Qulys was firm on sending a definitive and unequivocally clear message."

"Somewhat opposing objectives, given the situation," President Callahan volunteered.

"Yes, they are, but I am happy to say that we found a way to do both. Juulys made the initial contact with the Chinese craft and immediately demanded they cease hostilities toward the Indian spacecraft. Of course, they initially denied any such intent, so we sent them a video of their test firing when they impacted the satellite, as well as the discussion that their general secretary had with the prime minister of India, at least as much as you had shared with us."

"And what was their reply?" President Callahan asked.

"They quickly went from denial to hostile. They threatened to shoot us down, and we confidently informed them that they had no idea where we were. Then Qulys began barking in his native Cjarian language like he was chewing out a new recruit for messing up on a critical training assignment. Trust me, it didn't take a translator to know he was angry. I believe his name was Maj. Zhang Wei, or something like that, but he demanded to know what Qulys was saying. Juulys then directed their attention to the moon below them where we would demonstrate why they might want to comply with our request. Thirty seconds later, a Thjern VI nuclear space-to-ground missile detonated on the surface of the moon. It was actually quite spectacular, but in hindsight, perhaps we should have asked before we added a new crater to your moon. Our sincere apologies."

"You're forgiven, Thjars. At least that will keep our astronomers busy for a time ... perhaps I can get them to call it the Cjarian Basin," President Callahan interjected. "Please continue."

"Needless to say, that did get their attention, but they still continued to resist–that was Qulys' queue to start barking again, like only a good sergeant at arms can do. Juulys again translated and gave them his two options: either they separate the front section of the rail gun from their ship or we would separate it for them–either way, we recommended they not leave any people in that section. They got very quiet, but we assumed they were communicating with Earth, so we waited. Five minutes later, the fore section of the ship separated and I think it's important to note that it appeared the craft is made up of a number of sections, each of which has a built-in, but limited propulsion capability. We think it was there to enable them to line up and mate the sections after they were dropped off from Earth."

"That sounds like the Chinese have been working on this for quite some time," President Callahan reflected.

"That is likely correct. We then asked them to separate the fore section by at least 10 of your kilometers. This request made Maj. Wei very angry, but Qulys told me to relay that we were going to destroy the section in exactly five minutes, regardless of where it was located. Not surprisingly, they complied and Qulys released a Flosset V non-nuclear homing missile at it. Even if it is what you call a conventional explosive, it is still an extremely powerful missile. The fore section was utterly destroyed–that is likely the explosion your people witnessed. At this point, they had no alternative but to comply with our demands. Juulys then directed them to start their return to Earth, and if they had not left the moon's orbit within 60 minutes, we would destroy their ship– all of it. We made it clear that this was their only option to ensure their survival. If you have your people check, I believe they will see that the Chinese craft is clearly on the way back to Earth, but without the moon's use to create a slingshot effect, they are in for a long, slow return to Earth."

"Thjars, I can't thank you and your crew enough, but thank you for saving those astronauts. I will relay your success to Madame Prime Minister Khatri. Juulys, it sounds like we owe you a medal of honor!"

"Thank you, Mr. President, but I almost passed out once we disconnected the call. I am not comfortable yelling at people like that."

"I understand, but as Blake has told me many times, sometimes people leave you no choice, and if you don't do it, then you put yourself, and the people you love at risk. As you may guess, I have a very full plate to attend to right now, so I must go to deal with other issues. Thank you all again, and goodbye for now."

*****

White House
Nov. 2, 2029

Agent Joe Foster and Blake were on the conference call, waiting for President Callahan to join.

"How is Sean doing?" Joe asked.

"He's still unconscious, but in stable condition. The doc says he'll make it as long as they can stave off shock or infection complications."

"That's great news. Are you OK?"

"Yes, thank you. Any word yet on who those men were at the cabin or who they were working for?"

"Not much yet, Blake, but we'll enlist the NSA to see what they can get from their phones, computers and radios. Based on the two that you captured, the four sentries were outsiders that were simply paid, and paid well, to play the role of sentries. The other six appear to be hardcore. Two are ex-military and we think the other four were part of a hire-for-money militia group that appears to be a newcomer to the U.S. militia ranks. They focus on disenchanted ex-police and ex-military personnel. They have the ingredients to become one of the most dangerous, pro-anarchy groups in the country."

"Who are they working for?"

"We don't know yet, but the fact that they have Starburst ammunition and that three of the board members from that Oregon ammunition company are on the Anti-SETI group, a lot of our focus is there right now."

There was a long silence and then Blake spoke again. "Does he know about Harry?"

"Yes, we provided President Callahan an update last night."

"Where's Sen. Harley now?"

"I'm not sure I want to tell you, Blake. I'm concerned that you may pay him an unscheduled visit."

"I would very much like to do so, but you know I don't work that way, Joe. I already knew he went back to D.C., which means he's probably at his Dupont Circle abode. If I wanted to step over the line–which I have never done before–I wouldn't ask the FBI, I would just show up in the middle of the night and take care of business."

"I know, Blake, but imagine if something did happen and you were known to have been in the area, even if you were just 'monitoring' … Given what happened to Sean and Harry, the media and feds would have you labeled as suspect number one."

There was a beep and President Callahan joined the call.

"I'm not sure I want to know exactly what you two were just talking about, but I'll assume that I can continue to maintain 100 percent confidence in both of you. Blake," the president continued, "I share your grief over Harry. I was devastated to hear the news.

He was a great man. God bless him. I've also requested that all flags be flown at half-staff in his honor."

"Thank you, Mr. President."

"I understand Sean has stabilized."

"Yes, still unconscious, but stable. We think he'll pull through. Thank you for asking." Blake was amazed that with everything else going on, the president still asked someone to keep him updated on Blake's team.

"Do you need some time away?"

"No, sir. We are at war, both internal and external to the country. Now is not the time; there will be plenty of time later." Blake continued. "Then you were also debriefed about the Starburst rounds?"

"Yes, that was most concerning, but the good news is that it sounds like almost all of the missing ammunition has been found or assumed used at the site. The remaining missing ammunition was likely used up in training by these guys."

"That makes sense, sir, but that brings me to another point."

"What's that, Blake?"

"We should show those men from the Great Wolf Lodge in Colorado pictures of the dead bodies and see if they will finally talk. At this point, we should assume they were from the same group, even if our previous interrogations didn't uncover that connection. If we watch closely, you may be able to see a response in their eyes or facial muscles."

"Actually," Joe interjected, "that's a great idea. We'll take care of it and make sure it's brought up in a surprise delivery manner so they don't see it coming."

"Mr. President," Blake spoke, "I previously mentioned to you that I thought I knew who was behind Harry's kidnapping, but I didn't tell you who. I still can't prove it, but I'm convinced that Sen. James Harley should be at the top of the suspect list. There are simply too many data points with his name on them, or easily connected to him."

"That is a pretty high claim for a sitting U.S. senator, Blake … kidnapping … murder … theft of secret ammunition … misuse of power … a long list."

"These are pretty extreme times, Mr. President, and his actions have put him in that position."

"Fair enough," President Callahan answered after a pause. "It's not like you didn't already convince me, especially as I previously approved the wire-tapping you requested. He is an individual that I do not trust. I'm just not sure I'm ready to include murder yet."

"As you said, fair enough," Blake responded.

"Joe …"

"Yes, Mr. President."

"What I'm about to share with you is classified. Blake is already cleared. I've also cleared you through the FBI. Please acknowledge you understand the sensitivity."

"Yes, sir, I acknowledge."

The trio talked about the Cjarians, spent a few minutes reviewing the president's request for aid from the Cjarians and then the current U.S.-China-Russia status.

"Joe, I need to go, but as I'm sure you're still trying to get you head around who or what the Cjarians are, I'll let Blake update you further after we hang up."

"I think I'm beginning to piece together some previous events that Blake was unable or unwilling to explain to me." Joe chuckled. "I'm looking forward to that discussion, Blake."

*****

Philippine Sea

Taiwan and the opposing U.S.-China forces had been in a stalemate for 24 hours. China hadn't departed the island as President Callahan and many other world leaders had demanded, but the U.S. had not gone on the offensive either. Both sides of the growing conflict seemed to be waiting to see what the other side would do first. There was also the acknowledgement that both sides realized that they were standing on the brink of a major world conflict, already dubbed the "impending World War III conflict" by the media. Only one lit match would be required for it to become an instant inferno. There had been multiple close calls as fighters buzzed opposing aircraft, but no accidents or intentional hostilities had yet occurred. Although China openly boasted of its ability to defend Taiwan directly from the mainland, it was also clear that a U.S. counterattack would place their largest cities at immediate risk.

In fear of accidental loss of commercial ships and aircraft, world air and sea travel had ground to a sudden halt across the entire region, from Vietnam to the Philippines and as far north as South Korea, everything was on lockdown and under military control.

The world quietly held its breath, waiting for the first punch to land.

Adm. Mack Young was in the CVIC on the USS Theodore Roosevelt when he received the alert.

"Admiral, a convoy of four Chinese cargo ships has departed the Chinese port in Quanzhou and is heading directly for Taichung City. Satellite reconnaissance shows clear evidence of troops, tanks, APC and anti-aircraft missile batteries."

"Get the Pentagon on the phone."

*****

White House Situation Room

"I'm done talking. Send a message to Beijing, to the general secretary at his residence in South Zhongnanhai."

President Callahan was upset. The Chinese had just crossed the proverbial line in the water and were sending significant reinforcements to Taiwan. They were digging in to hold the island with hopes that the western world would tire and abandon Taiwan's defense.

"Attach photos of the ships, their obvious route and whatever cargo you can identify," President Callahan said, "I want those ships turned around in less than one hour–we cannot allow them to dock at the Taichung City harbors." He glanced over at Blake and Gen. McMullen.

"Any recommendations on what I should state is the penalty for not turning back?"

"Sir, we cannot allow those ships to dock and unload their cargo," Gen. McMullen responded "They need to turn back, or be destroyed."

"Blake?"

"You have a major conundrum, Mr. President. They are clearly testing your resolve for all the world to see. The winner of this facedown will be the world leader. If you don't attack, you and the U.S. lose. If you do attack, they will claim you are the aggressor that started World War III."

"Blake, I think we're all aware of that, so how do I get a win out of this?"

"I'm not sure, Mr. President, but I agree with Gen. McMullen that those ships cannot be allowed to dock and unload their cargo. I think we can let them dock as a sign of trust that they are simply trying to show their people and their allies a sign of strength and resolve."

"I'm not sure I follow you, Blake ..." Gen. McMullen said sourly.

"I think I do," President Callahan stated. "Continue, Blake."

"What if you tell them on worldwide media that the U.S. and its allies accuse China of escalating the conflict if they dock and unload their cargo–note that my emphasis was on the word *unload*, not *dock*. That way, their docking provides a means for them to look strong and save face with their own people relative to their age-old goal to unify China, but ... and this is the big *but* ... They can't unload–that's the line they can't cross, regardless of their long-standing goal and their stated position. As the world is clearly supporting the U.S.'s stand and Taiwan's right for independence, China will be perceived as doing the right thing when they turn the ships around, regardless of what has transpired so far. If they do unload the ships, then China will have provided the world with a clear message that they have accepted sole responsibility for initiating what could become World War III."

"Why not just tell them not to dock?" Gen. McMullen interrupted.

"Because, I don't want to leave any doubt to any government, or its people, across the entire globe, that we gave them every possible chance, right down to the final boarding ramp, to back down and choose the correct answer. Everyone needs to be crystal clear on how we translate their actions, what we will do and who will be held responsible–and we will broadcast across worldwide media their minute-by-minute moves. This will allow the Chinese to show strength and resolve by crossing the Taiwan Strait and docking, but still not lose face when they decide to withdraw due to overwhelming worldwide support of President Callahan's decree. They will also realize the tremendous financial impact this will have on China if the entire free world shuts down imports from China. The world isn't as dependent on China as they were in 2020 when the COVID-19 pandemic hit and left countries struggling to get critical medicines and medical supplies. Most, if not all countries took steps to reduce their dependence on China–a wrong move by the Chinese relative to Taiwan would isolate them further and shut them down financially."

"I think I'm liking this, Blake; keep going," President Callahan responded. "What else do we need to do?"

"We need to send a message to the Taiwanese to evacuate the harbor areas and we need to make sure our allies are as vocally supportive as they can be to ensure China receives a worldwide response."

"What do we do if they start unloading their cargo and troops?"

"We take them out with overwhelming power and destruction."

"A nuke?" President Callahan stammered.

"No nukes. This is where Gen. McMullen comes in. We need to determine how to destroy those cargo ships with conventional weapons, assuming they do initiate unloading of their cargo and troops. It needs to be an intensive attack with absolute certainty of success, both in avoiding Chinese defensive capabilities and in destroying the ships. Unfortunately, that level of attack will likely lead to the decimation of the harbor."

Everyone was quiet.

"Does anyone have a better idea?" President Callahan spoke first.

"No, I think it's as best as we can play our cards right now, and still hope for the best," Vice President Annie Murphy replied.

"I agree," echoed Frank Pelino.

"Count me in," added Ben Tellinino.

"General?"

"I think it's masterful. I really do, Blake."

"Well said," President Callahan replied. "I want this typed up, reviewed and approved by me and sent out to the general secretary and the world in less than 60 minutes. I also need your plan, Gen.

McMullen on how to destroy those ships, if it's required–and I need it in that same time period. Get moving people. Meet back here in 45 minutes."

*****

Nov. 3, 2029

The message was sent and the world watched. Western world media broadcast the updates as leader after leader supported the U.S, India, Taiwan and their allies. The Chinese didn't respond, but also never slowed down, continuing their trek toward Taichung City where they eventually docked, but did not unload. The world waited, on the brink of war, with every step magnified in detail and theories espoused by many of the self-proclaimed experts in the media.

*****

Breckenridge

"Blake, it's Joe Foster. I think we found what you were looking for. Li, Robert and Jimmy have worked around the clock on that extra phone we uncovered while you were in Breckenridge. They were not only able to keep track of that phone, but it tied them into other phones–one of which was the treasure trove. The NSA is having a field day. I'm boarding in ten minutes on the first nonstop Denver-to-Dulles flight of the day to meet up with you. I should be in D.C. by early afternoon–I'll call again as soon as I land. We need to meet face-to-face as soon as possible."

*****

Old Ebbitt Grill
675 15th St., Washington, D.C.

Sen. James Harley parked his Lexus LX in the LAZ Parking lot, exited and started walking toward the Old Ebbitt Grill to meet a small group for dinner. As soon as he heard the locking beep from his key fob, he turned and saw him.

"Cmdr. Thompson. Are you following me? I can have you arrested for stalking, or would you like to threaten me so that we can elevate the stakes a little more?"

"You really are an arrogant son of a bitch aren't you? Let's just call this a very fortuitous meeting and I have someone that I want you to meet. Joe, come on over."

Joe Foster walked out from behind a parked van.

"FBI Agent Joe Foster, meet the *honorable* Sen. James Harley."

"FBI? What the hell is going on? I have rights, I'll …"

"You'll shut the F up is what you'll do, and listen." Blake cut him off in mid-sentence. "Joe is here to make sure you walk away in one piece–i.e.: he's your protection, so don't push your luck. I'm here to share some evidence with you and then we can talk options. I'm also here to tell you that I will do everything in my power to legally bring all of the perpetrators to justice. And if that doesn't work, I will deal with the guilty parties myself–justice will be served."

"What the hell are you talking about?"

"The kidnapping and murder of Harry Lundrum, and I have one whale of a load of evidence that points in your direction–and President Callahan has already been notified."

*****

European Southern Observatory
Garching bei München, Germany

The two weeks had finally passed and the comet was now moving by the sun. Klaus Schneider spent every waking moment watching, monitoring and modeling the comet and its path. The next few days would determine the true risk that Earth might be impacted by a killer comet, but as each day went by, the probability that Earth would be in its direct path only seemed to increase. The previously unknown comet was now known as the Klaus-Weber comet, named after the two astronomers who discovered it.

Klaus completed his daily update and hit send. His message went to a very select and limited group of world leaders.

*****

"They may be on to us. Harley relayed that he was stopped by the FBI and that damn Thompson guy today."

"Damn! What should we do?"

"Start destroying any evidence we have and get ready to disappear for a while. I'll be back in touch."

"What about my payment?"

"It will be deposited tonight. I have to go."

The call disconnected.

*****

CHAPTER 22

Jarisst I
Nov. 4, 2029

"Thjars!"

"Yes, Allympht."

"Come down to the Q-PAMS engine bay."

"What happened?"

"We think we fixed the Q-PAMS drive."

"What? How?"

"It was an idea that Harry had, he just didn't get a chance to finish it before we had to depart Earth after the attack."

"Does Harry know?"

"No, we haven't heard from Harry in quite some time."

"Let me come down and see it. I'm almost afraid to get excited or tell anyone ... in case, it really isn't fixed."

"I agree, Thjars. I felt the same way, but I've been running small trials that deflect the thrust equally out of the side ports so that we didn't cause any acceleration to the ship. Come down and see for yourself. It works."

Five minutes later, Thjars entered the Q-PAMS engine bay with Qulys and Juulys, and was greeted by a beaming Allympht.

"Follow me and see for yourself."

Over the next 30 minutes, Allympht conducted a number of small trials until everyone was satisfied that it did appear to be functioning.

"What was Harry's idea?"

"We had re-verified 10 times over that we had the correct fuel flow paths, fuel quantities, fuel mixtures and precise collision points for the matter and antimatter particles. Everything was exactly as designed; that's what had us so confused. But then

Harry became focused on acoustical resonation; he'd said it was something a friend of his named Robert had successfully tried when they activated our C-POD on Mars. Don't ask me to explain the science behind it, because I don't understand *how* it works, just that it *does* work–the science is way over my head. It turns out that the fuel components each have a different resonant frequency that they need to vibrate at prior to the matter and antimatter impact point. The differences are extremely minute, but if not tuned perfectly, the required resonance and harmonics are never achieved."

"I'll take your word for that, Allympht. How about we take it for a trial run? We can move away from the planets and attempt a slow acceleration so that we can avoid the G-Cells and just stay in our standard G-suits. Anyone have any concerns or hesitation?"

No one did.

"Suit up!"

Thirty minutes later, all 11 remaining crewmembers of the Jarisst I were in their G-suits and chairs.

"Allympht, take us out toward the outer edge of their planetary system with the standard sub-light speed drive and then initiate the Q-PAMS, but do not exceed two Gs."

"Roger that!" Allympht smiled as he gave Juulys a thumbs up sign.

"Thank you Allympht. It's too bad Blake and Harry aren't here to enjoy this," Juulys responded sadly.

"Not to ruin a good discussion, but that is an interesting question," Thjars responded.

"What question, Thjars?" Juulys asked.

"Do we let Blake know?"

*****

U.S. Senate Chambers

The Senate had been called to order 15 minutes earlier when the Southern Lobby doors burst open and Blake walked in with Diego at his side, both in military gear. Simultaneously, President Callahan was escorted in through the Senators' Lobby door by seat 18.

"Good afternoon, Vice President Murphy, may I join you?"

"This is quite a surprise, Mr. President, but yes, you may. May I ask to what we owe this honor?"

"My guest of honor, Cmdr. Blake Thompson and his right-hand man, Diego Velasquez, SEAL petty officer first class."

"Are they here to accept an award?"

"Yes … and no … but they have my approval."

President Callahan then turned to Blake.

"Cmdr. Thompson, the floor is yours."

"This is highly irregular, Madame Vice President. This topic is not on the docket," Sen. James Harley yelled, out of turn and obviously upset, from his seat, number 27.

"Well, it is now, Sen. Harley," Blake stated calmly as he strode up the center aisle, "I guess you didn't get the updated agenda, but now you know."

"Why is he here, Madame Vice President? I wish to lodge a formal complaint. I demand that the Office of the Parliamentarian make a ruling on my request immediately!"

"Overruled," President Callahan replied calmly but sternly.

A guard started to walk down the aisle toward Blake, but Diego stopped him.

"With all due respect, I suggest you might just want to sit this one out."

Blake was now standing between seat 12 and 13, looking directly at Sen. Harley.

"I am here as part of the investigation into the murder of one Harry Lundrum, Navy SEAL specialist, but more importantly, one of the best human beings I've ever met in my life."

"Are you suggesting that I had something to do with it?" Harley had calmed down and gotten his feet back under him. "This is my turf and you don't just walk in here and treat this chamber with such disrespect."

"I'm not leaving until Harry's killer goes with me. I've got all day and all night. And by the way, I have all the evidence any court in this land would ever need to convict the killer. Which, by the way, is how I was able to get this visit approved."

"Then let everyone hear it if you're so sure of yourself, but keep in mind, if you're wrong, you'll be in jail before I ever leave these chambers."

"Fair deal," Blake replied and then provided a high-level summary of everything that had transpired up through the explosion of the shipping container that Harry had been held captive in and the killing of the men that had held him, as well as many of the key investigation points.

"Is that it? How does that possibly tie to me? Just because you found a microwave receipt with my fingerprints on it?"

"We were able to use the FBI voice pattern recognition software to match specific phone conversations with voice patterns from public presentations."

"This is bull; I'm not guilty."

"That's correct, Sen. Harley, I didn't say you were, but the real killer of both Harry Lundrum and Sen. James Colburn is here, and we know that his least favorite color is light red, better known as pink, and that the same conversation was traced back to a tidy $500,000 bonus payout—would that be correct Sen. Pinkerton?" Blake stated as he turned right to face seat 25.

Sen. Jerry Pinkerton literally fell backwards out of his chair as he attempted to escape, but Diego had already moved behind his desk.

"You're not going this way, Senator," Diego said as he stood firmly in the way, "but if you'd like to try, you'd really make my day."

"Sergeant at Arms, read him his rights and take him away," Blake commanded.

One hour later, after everyone had been debriefed, Diego, Blake and President Callahan left together. Blake explained that he had been totally convinced it had to be Sen. Harley, but through the FBI, with Joe, Li, Jimmy and Robert's help, they had hacked various systems to identify Sen. Pinkerton as the leader of the rogue group that had killed Harry and Sen. Colburn. Pinkerton had tried, and almost succeeded in setting up Sen. Harley to take the fall. His goal had been to take over the powerful Senate Armed Services Committee and pursue additional control over the Oregon ammunition company that manufactured the Starburst rounds. Pinkerton had leveraged his personal friendship and his working partnership with Sen. Harley as a weapon to use against him by simply taking advantage of Harley's single-focused and self-centered goal to become the next president. Harley was blinded by his own ambition and never saw it coming. As it turned out, Pinkerton never intended for anyone to be killed, but that didn't diminish his guilt.

Joe and Blake had been able to give Sen. Harley a heads up at the Old Ebbitt Grill and plan their staged event to catch Pinkerton as he unsuspiciously but happily watched Harley take the fall for him–or so Pinkerton thought. His facial expression and reaction to Blake's statement of "pink" and "$500,000" was all anyone needed to see, let alone the trove of evidence they'd found once they tied Pinkerton's burner phone to Harley's. The NSA files on all phone recordings were then able to be linked and traced.

*****

Nov. 6, 2029

Yesterday had been a whirlwind day, Blake thought, culminating in the arrest of Sen. Pinkerton in the Senate Chambers. Blake still didn't have much regard for Sen. Harley, and had actually told him so as he thanked him for his Senate Chambers performance, but he once again realized that his own gut instincts had been wrong, again. Blake had been as convinced as ever that Harley was guilty. His personal errors of the past few weeks were beginning to nag at him deeply. The truth was, the loss of Harry hurt–it hurt a lot. Blake couldn't find a way to push that fact into the vault in the back of his head where he locked away everything else that brought emotional pain.

But Diego interrupted before he could pursue his internal frustration further.

"You know what we need, my good friend?"

"I'm all ears, Diego."

"Beer."

"It's lunchtime, isn't it?"

"Yes, but in a sports bar that's not only legal, but expected," Diego smiled. "I miss Harry too; he was more than a one in a million."

"God broke the mold after He made Harry," Blake replied.

"Amen, Blake, that's as good of a toast as I can come up with. How about we go take in an EPL soccer match and toast an honor to Harry? I found a place that plays all of the EPL matches. It's called The Lucky Bar over on 1221 Connecticut Ave. NW and it looks like our style."

"Diego, that may be the best idea you've had all year," Blake smiled. "Let's go."

*****

Two hours later, having watched a thrilling 3-2 Liverpool victory over Crystal Palace while downing a couple of pints of beer, Buffalo chicken wings and a double round of fish and chips, the two friends left a hefty tip in Harry's honor and departed from The Lucky Bar.

"Diego, I owe you one–I needed that," Blake said.

"It's not like you haven't been there for me or any of the others before, Blake. We'll get through this–as a team. If you don't mind some honesty, Sean was right. Sometimes you can be a bit of a butthead when it comes to keeping your emotional distance. I'm just saying …"

Blake's phone began vibrating. "Saved by the buzz," Blake replied and answered the phone.

"Blake here. Yes, but we're not in a good location right now. Give us two minutes to get to our car and call us back. Thank you."

"What was that all about?"

"The White House, something about an urgent call from Thjars."

*****

"Blake, I was calling to share some fantastic news with you, but President Callahan spoke to me briefly and told me about Harry. We are so sorry. Allympht was the closest to him and was devastated to hear the news, but the truth is, we all liked him. That is a horrible loss."

"Thank you, Thjars, we are all struggling with it as well. What was the news you were calling about?" Blake asked.

"Harry helped fix the Q-PAMS."

"How is that possible?"

Thjars relayed what Allympht had learned and accomplished based on a theory that Harry had proposed. He described the test flights they had experimented with that convinced them everything was working properly now.

"I assume you'll be leaving soon to go back, correct?"

"Well, to be honest, yes, but we struggled making that decision. Everyone we ever knew on Cjar is long gone. We don't even know what it's like there and there is some fear that we could be in danger if we do return. The truth is, our closest friends are now you and your team, and we are struggling with leaving you, especially knowing that you may need our help again."

"That means a lot, Thjars, but I think you have to go back, just to see what's left. Otherwise, it will always remain an open question. I expect you will find great relief in going. Obviously, you can always come back." Blake smiled.

"That's how we finally came to the decision we made, but Juulys has a question for you. Hang on while I get her on the call."

A few seconds later, Blake heard her voice.

"Hello, Blake."

"Hi, Juulys," Blake replied. "So what is the big question?"

"We want you to come back with us."

"Whoa, I didn't see that coming!" Blake replied.

"We want to show you our world and where we came from. We also know that there are a lot of unknowns out there and having both you and Qulys with us to guide us through them provides the crew with a lot more confidence. As we don't know how your body would respond to our G-Cells, we already agreed that we wouldn't use them. We would lengthen our acceleration phases to ensure you could handle the travel stresses in a standard G-suit."

"I ... I don't know what to say, Juulys. I'm honored. But ... I don't think now is the time. It's too soon after Harry's death and we are also in the midst of a potential worldwide war again. I can't walk out on President Callahan. But to be clear, I do want to see your world, so I'm hoping you will extend what we call a rain check. Perhaps that will ensure that you do return and if we have finally conquered our current trials and tribulations, then I will gladly join you."

"To be honest, we expected you to say that, Blake, but we ... I ... I had to ask anyway."

"When will you be departing?"

"We are ready to go now."

"Phew, then this is goodbye for now. Thank you for reaching out to us before you departed and for all of the help you gave us. Be safe and I will await your return. Please say goodbye to the crew for me."

"And you do the same with President Callahan and your team. Take care, Blake."

*****

EPILOGUE

Blake, Diego, Li, Jimmy, Patty, Robert and Vladimir were all gathered in Sean's hospital room. Sean was still unconscious and everyone was now missing their favorite obnoxious Irishman. Patty made an analogy to a tired parent wishing their noisy child would just be quiet for a few minutes and how that wish changed when the same child became sick, then wishing that the child would soon be rambunctious again. All agreed that, especially with the gap Harry left, they badly wanted to once again hear Sean's insufferable taunting.

Blake reflected over everything that had occurred these past few months and the momentous loss he was feeling of both Harry and the departed Cjarians. He knew his world would never be the same again. He prayed the Cjarians would get home safely and somehow find a way to maintain contact with him.

And yet, the world he knew was still at risk of significant change that could impact his life and that of many others. Sean was foremost in his mind, but there were still cleanup activities to complete regarding what was now being called the Pinkerton investigation. The U.S. was fundamentally at war with both China and Russia, and Blake also knew there still remained a possible threat from a killer comet that would make all wars a moot point.

Lastly, and most importantly, Blake had an upcoming funeral to prepare for. He needed to follow up with Joe and the FBI forensic team, and then write his eulogy for Harry. He would start first thing in the morning.

*****

A distant solar system

"Maj. Aztgar, we have validated the flight paths. They are correct. The flurry of light recorded from that Cjarian ship hundreds of years ago has now occurred twice. Once heading toward Cjar and once returning the way it came. We have not seen a ship like this since the Great Battle over 500 years ago. The photon meters across our planetary system all validate the same finding: something passed by Klaxx at faster than the speed of light."

"Can we target it?"

"Possibly, but it would have to be on the exact flight path because we would basically be throwing a rock out in front of it for the ship to hit. But it is possible because the two flights traversed the same path and both times the time interval was exactly the same."

"How fast do you estimate it was going?"

"At least 200 times the speed of light. That doesn't leave us time to initiate an attack–assuming it comes back again. We'll need to set our traps on both sides of our star system where their flight path crossed."

"If we can capture that technology we could finally destroy those repulsive Cjarians," Maj. Aztgar responded through clenched teeth. "We could easily blow it up with a series of nuclear missiles, but I want that ship. We need to disable it, not destroy it."

It was Maj. Aztgar's family name that had attempted to capture a rogue ship half a millennium ago when they first learned that faster-than-light travel was actually possible. His distant ancestor, Gen. Atzgar, had been one of the greatest military strategists in the history of Klaxx and the proud lineage of officers that bore his family name had all continued his crusade to find that ship.

Maj. Atzgar now owned the second sighting, and opportunity.

*****

The couple had slipped away from the confines of Denver city life, parked for the night in the CDOT Rest Area Vail Pass and set out to enjoy a quiet evening in the cloudless night that was already well lit by the glowing full moon. Tomorrow, they would drive to the Vail Valley where they had reserved a ritzy rental for a couple of days, but tonight they intended to enjoy the quiet freedom of the outdoors without having to spend a single penny on lodging or food. The couple had prepacked their backpacks in anticipation of the evening and were planning on making the most of it. They loaded up their gear and headed into the trees.

It was early November in the Rockies, and the temperature was close to freezing. More than a fair amount of the ground was covered in snow, but not yet deep enough to require snowshoes, so walking was relatively easy. Thirty minutes later, they found the perfect secluded spot, slightly less than two kilometers southwest of the parking lot. They started a small fire, pitched their tent, and snuggled into a single doublewide sleeping bag. The sound of a popping wine cork and a female giggle was quickly absorbed by the surrounding pine trees. No one knew they were here and they intended to make the most of their peaceful evening.

They hadn't finished their first glass of wine when the couple heard something moving in the nearby trees.

"I hope that's a deer … not a bear," the woman whispered.

"I'm sorry, Miss, but I need to borrow your campfire before I progress further into hypothermia. I won't hurt you, but I do need to borrow your phone–it's a national emergency. Just place it outside the tent and I'll put it back when I'm done."

It was clearly a man's voice, but who could have possibly found them, or maybe followed them to this secluded location– and what did he *really* want?

The cracking sounds of breaking branches were followed by the distinctive *whoooff* of pine needles blossoming into flame.

*****

For More News About Phil Sheehan, Signup For Our Newsletter:

http://wbp.bz/newsletter

Word-of-mouth is critical to an author's long-term success. If you appreciated this book please leave a review on the Amazon sales page:

http://wbp.bz/tribulationsa

AVAILABLE FROM PHIL SHEEHAN
AND WILDBLUE PRESS!

HAPPENSTANCE by PHIL SHEEHAN

http://wbp.bz/happenstancea

**THE FIRST IN THE MONSTERS AND MEN
TRILOGY BY LAWRENCE DAVIS!**

BLUNT FORCE MAGIC by LAWRENCE DAVIS

http://wbp.bz/bfma

Made in the USA
Columbia, SC
20 March 2022